'T
si

'A unique twist on the bad boy meets good girl tale. I could not put it down!'
Aestas Book Blog

By Penelope Douglas

Bully

Until You

Rival

Falling Away

Falling Away

A Fall Away Novel

PENELOPE DOUGLAS

piatkus

PIATKUS

First published in the US in 2015 by New American Library
A division of Penguin Group (USA) LLC,
First published in Great Britain in 2015 by Piatkus

A CIP catalogue record for this book
is available from the British Library.

ISBN 978-0-349-40583-4

Printed and bound by CPI Group (UK) Ltd, Croydon, CR0 4YY

Papers used by Piatkus are from well-managed forests
and other responsible sources.

MIX
Paper from
responsible sources
FSC
www.fsc.org   FSC® C104740

Piatkus
An imprint of
Little, Brown Book Group
100 Victoria Embankment
London EC4Y 0DY

An Hachette UK Company
www.hachette.co.uk

www.piatkus.co.uk

FALLING AWAY PLAYLIST

"Again"	by Alice in Chains
"Battle Born"	by Five Finger Death Punch
"Better Than Me"	by Hinder
"Bones"	by Young Guns
"Cruel Summer"	by Bananarama
"Deal with the Devil"	by Pop Evil
"The Deep End"	by Crossfade
"Down with the Sickness"	by Disturbed
"Dragula"	by Rob Zombie
"Falling Away from Me"	by Korn
"Firework"	by Katy Perry
"Good Man"	by Devour the Day
"Heaven Knows"	by the Pretty Reckless
"Hemorrhage (In My Hands)"	by Fuel
"Here Without You"	by 3 Doors Down
"The High Road"	by Three Days Grace
"I Hate Myself for Loving You"	by Joan Jett & the Blackhearts
"I'm Not Jesus"	by Apocalyptica
"Me So Horny"	by 2 Live Crew
"My Demons"	by Starset
"Never Gonna Stop (The Red, Red Kroovy)"	by Rob Zombie
"Slept So Long"	by Jay Gordon
"Stupify"	by Disturbed

"Take Out the Gunman"	by Chevelle
"Talk Dirty to Me"	by Poison
"Tired by Stone"	by Stone Sour
"Torn to Pieces"	by Pop Evil
"Trenches"	by Pop Evil

To all the good people who had bad parents.
We're going to be okay.

ACKNOWLEDGMENTS

To my parents, two who taught me the right way and one who taught me the wrong way but all who loved me. I learned that honesty and trust are golden and character and integrity are prized. Thank you.

To my husband and daughter, both who sacrificed to see these characters live. I owe my daughter lots of trips to the park, and my husband . . . well, you know what I owe you, honey. And I'll get on that. Soon. Totally soon. I promise.

To my support system at New American Library, all of whom put up with my endless questions and work hard to protect my vision for the Fall Away Series. Thank you, Kerry, Isabel, and Courtney for your trust, advice, and help.

To Jane Dystel at Dystel & Goderich Literary Management, who found me, and thank goodness for that! You're always working, and I always feel important. Thanks to you, Miriam and Mike, for staying on top of everything and taking care of me.

To my street team, the House of PenDragon, who are a wonderful group of women—and one guy—who hold one another up and create a community of friendship and fun times. Needless to say, I laugh my butt off watching your conversations online, and I enjoy seeing how close you all have become. Bananas forever!

To Eden Butler, Lisa Pantano Kane, Ing Cruz, and Marilyn Medina, who are all available at the drop of a hat to look at a scene or provide quick emergency feedback. Thank you for walking with me through this process and being honest.

ACKNOWLEDGMENTS

To Vibeke Courtney. Plain and simple, this is all you. If I had never met you, I might never have tried writing a book. And without you, it would never have been successful. My writing was nearly all narration before you got your hands on it, and you helped create my voice. Thank you, thank you, thank you.

To the readers and reviewers, thank you for keeping my work alive and showing your love and support! Your feedback, thoughts, and ideas have been incredibly important as these stories developed, and I always write with you in mind. I hope I can continue to give you characters you want to reread over and over again!

K.C.

Three whole years.

I'd had a boyfriend for three whole years, and I still had more orgasms when I was by myself.

"Damn, baby, you feel good." His sleepy whisper felt wet on my neck as he dragged his lazy lips over my skin.

Packing. That was what I'd forgotten to add to my to-do list for tomorrow. It wasn't likely I'd forget to pack for college, but everything needed to go on the list so it could be checked off.

"You're so hot." Liam's fish lips tickled my neck in short, slow pecks. It once made me giggle, but now it kind of made me want to bite him.

And a pharmacy run, I remembered. I wanted to stock up on my pill so I wouldn't have to worry about it for a while. *Packing and the pharmacy. Packing and the pharmacy. Packing and the pharmacy. Don't forget, K.C.*

Liam thrust his hips between my legs, and I rolled my eyes.

We were still clothed, but I wasn't sure he realized that.

If I weren't so tired, I'd laugh. He rarely got drunk after all—tonight only because it was an end-of-summer bash. And although I'd never been overwhelmed with a desire for sex, I did love that he tried to jump my bones at every opportunity. It made me feel wanted.

But it just wasn't happening tonight.

"Liam," I grunted, twisting up my lips as I pushed his hand off my breast, "I think we're done for the night, okay? Let's lock up the car and walk to your house."

We'd been in his car for over a half hour—me trying to indulge his fantasy of sex in risky places and him trying to . . . Hell, I didn't even know what he was trying to do.

I felt guilty for not being more into it lately. I felt guilty for not helping him get into it tonight. And I felt guilty for making mental additions to my to-do list while he was trying—keyword, *trying*—to get it on with me.

We hadn't made love in a long time, and I didn't know what my problem was anymore.

His head sank into my shoulder, and I felt the weight of his hundred and eighty pounds collapse on my body.

He didn't move, and I let out a sigh, relaxing into the passenger seat of his Camaro, my muscles burning from trying to support his body weight all this time.

He'd given up. *Thank God.*

But then I groaned, registering that his body had gone a little too still, except for the slow, soft rhythm of his breathing.

Great. Now he was passed out.

"Liam," I whispered, not sure why, since we were completely alone in his car on a dark, quiet street outside my friend Tate Brandt's house.

Arching my head up, I spoke into his ear that was nearly covered by his blond hair. "Liam, wake up!" I wheezed, since his weight was hindering my oxygen intake.

He moaned but didn't budge.

I slammed my head back onto the headrest and ground my teeth together. What the hell was I going to do now?

We'd gone to the Loop tonight for the last race before college started next week and then Tate and her boyfriend, Jared Trent, had thrown a party at his house, which just happened to be right outside, next door to her place. I'd told my mom that I'd be sleeping over at her house when I was really planning on spending the night with my boyfriend.

Who was now passed out.

Tate's house was locked, I didn't know how to drive Liam's car, and the last thing I was ever going to do was call my mother for a ride.

Reaching for the handle, I swung the car door open and pulled my right leg from under Liam. I pushed against his chest, raising him off me only as much as I needed to squirm out from underneath his body and stumble out of the car. He groaned but didn't open his eyes, and I wondered if I should be worried about how much he'd had to drink.

Leaning in, I watched his chest rise and fall in quiet, steady movements. I grabbed the keys he'd dropped on the floor and my wrist purse with my cell phone and slammed the door shut, locking the car.

Liam didn't live too far, and even though I knew it was a lot to ask, I was going to have to wake up Tate. If Jared was even letting her get any sleep at all.

I ran my hands down my strapless white summer dress and powered quietly down the sidewalk in my rhinestone sandals. Pretty dressed up for the race track earlier, but I wanted to look nice at the party. It was the last time I was going to see some of these people. For a while, anyway.

Squeezing my little purse—small enough for my phone and some money—in my hand, I traipsed up the small incline into Jared's yard and up the front steps of his house. No light shone from inside, but I knew there had to be some people still here, since the street was littered with a few unfamiliar cars and I heard the low beat of music still pouring out. Lyrics saying something about "down with the sickness."

I turned the knob, stepped into the house, and peered around the corner into the living room.

And stopped. Dead. *What the . . . ?*

The room was dark, not a single light showing other than the blue glow from the screen on the stereo.

Maybe there were other lights on in the house. Maybe there were other people still here. I couldn't say.

All I could do was fucking stand there as my eyes stung, and a lump stretched my throat, at the sight of Jaxon Trent damn near naked on top of another girl.

I instantly looked away, closing my eyes.

Jax. I shook my head. *No.* I didn't care about this. Why was my heart beating so fast?

Jaxon Trent was Tate's boyfriend's little brother. Nothing more. Just a kid.

A kid who watched me. A kid I rarely ever talked to. A kid who felt like a threat just standing next to me.

A kid who was looking less and less like one every day.

And right now he wasn't coming up for air. I jerked my body toward the door, not wanting him—or her—to see me, but . . .

"Jax," the girl gasped. "More. Please."

And I stopped, unable to move again. *Just leave, K.C. You don't care.*

I squeezed the doorknob, sucking in quick breaths, but I didn't move. Couldn't move.

I didn't know why my hands shook.

Chewing my bottom lip, I inched around the corner again and saw him and the girl.

My heart pounded like a jackhammer in my chest. And it hurt.

The girl—I didn't recognize her from school—was completely naked, lying on her stomach on the couch. Jax was sprawled on top of her from behind, and judging from his jeans pushed down below his ass and his thrusting hips, he was inside her.

He didn't even get fully undressed to make love to a girl. He couldn't even look her in the face. I wasn't surprised. With the arrogance he displayed around school, Jax could do whatever he wanted, and he did.

Holding himself up with one arm, he used the other to wrap around her face and twist her chin toward him before he leaned down and covered her mouth with his.

Liam had never kissed me like that. Or I'd never kissed him like that.

The girl—long blond hair fanning around her face and spilling over her shoulders—kissed him back with full force, their jaws moving in sync as his tongue and teeth worked her.

Jax's smooth, sculpted hips ground into her in slow, savory movements while his hand left her face to run down her back and then slide underneath her body to cup her breast. He didn't do one thing at a time. Every part of his body was in this, and everything he did looked as if it felt good.

And why wouldn't it? Jax was coveted by the girls in this town for a reason after all. He was suave, confident, and good-looking. Not my type, but there was no denying that he was sexy. According to Tate, he was part Native American.

His skin was like toffee—smooth, unblemished, and warm-looking. His hair was a deep brown, almost black, and it hung halfway down his back. He often braided pieces of it before tying it back into a ponytail midskull, which he did *all* the time. I'd never seen his hair hanging loose.

He had to be six feet tall by now and would probably be exceeding his brother in height in no time. I'd seen Jax on the lacrosse field at school and at the gym where we both worked out. The dips in his biceps and triceps flexed as he held himself above the girl and worked his body into hers. With the moonlight coming through the window, I could just make out the V in his torso as it descended to his abs and lower.

He didn't break pace as he whispered in her ear, and as if she were given an order, she dropped her foot to the floor, bent her knee, and arched her back.

Jax let his head fall back and bared his teeth as he sank deeper into her, and I stared, absently tracing the scar on the inside of my wrist.

I wanted it to be like that for me. I wanted to be breathless like her. Gasping and desperate. Passionate and hungry.

Liam had made me happy once, and when he messed up, I took him back, because I thought the relationship was worth it.

But now, seeing this . . . I knew we were missing something.

I didn't know when the tear spilled over, but I felt it drop onto my dress, and I blinked rapidly, wiping my face.

And then my eye caught something, and I blinked again, noticing someone else in the room. Another girl, nearly naked in her bra and panties.

I swallowed a gasp, sucked in air, and then swallowed again.

What the hell?

She walked across the room—she must've been over by the windows, because I hadn't seen her until now—and leaned down, kissing Jax hard.

Acid bile crept up my throat.

"Ugh!" I growled, and stumbled backward, hitting the opposite wall in the entryway. Scrambling, I yanked open the front door and flew outside without looking back.

Jumping the steps, I had hit the grass running when a deep voice commanded behind me, "Stop!"

I didn't.

Screw him. Screw Jaxon Trent. I didn't know why I was mad, and who the hell cared?

Running across the lawn, I bolted for the sidewalk, wishing I'd worn sneakers instead of sandals that flopped around on my feet.

"Stop, or I will take you to the ground, K.C.!" Jax's loud bellow threatened behind me, and I brought myself to a sudden halt.

Shit. My eyes darted from left to right, searching for an escape. He wouldn't really do that, would he?

I inched around slowly, watching as he stepped off the stairs and walked toward me. He was wearing pants, thank God. But I guess that was easy, since he never really took them off. The dark-washed jeans hung off his hips, and I got a damn clear look at the muscles framing his abs. He had a swimmer's body, but I wasn't sure if he was actually a swimmer. From the way the top of his jeans barely hung just above his hairline, I guessed he wasn't wearing boxers . . . or anything under the jeans. I thought of what was just beneath his pants, and heat warmed my belly. I clenched my thighs together.

I shot my eyes down to the ground, wondering how I could stand the sight of him. He was just a kid. Did he do things like that with a lot of girls?

He came up to stand in front of me, hovering down, since he was nearly a half foot taller. "What are you doing here?" he accused.

I locked my mouth shut and scowled at the air around him, still avoiding eye contact.

"You left with your dipshit boyfriend an hour ago," he pointed out.

I kept my hot eyes averted.

"K.C.!" He shoved his hand in my face, snapping his fingers a few times. "Let's process what you just saw in there. You entered my house uninvited in the middle of the night and witnessed me having sex with a girl in the privacy of my own home. Now let's move on. Why are you roaming around in the dark alone?"

I finally looked up and sneered. I always had to do that to cover up the way my face felt on fire at the sight of his blue eyes. For someone so dark and wild, his eyes were completely out of place but never seemed wrong. They were the color of a tropical sea. The color of the sky right before storm clouds rolled in. Tate called them azure. I called them hell.

Crossing my arms over my chest, I took a deep breath. "Liam's too drunk to drive, all right?" I bit out. "He passed out in the car."

He looked down the street to where Liam's car sat and narrowed his eyes before scowling back down at me. "So why can't you drive him home?" he asked.

"I can't drive a clutch."

He closed his eyes and shook his head. Running his hand through his hair, he stopped and fisted it midstroke. "Your boyfriend is a fucking idiot," he snarled, and then dropped his hand, looking exasperated.

I sighed, not wanting to get into it. He and Liam never got along, and while I didn't know why, I did know it was mostly Jax's fault.

I'd known him for almost a year, and even though I knew small details—he was into computers, his real parents weren't around, and he thought of his brother's mother as his own—he was still a mystery to me. All I knew was that he looked at me sometimes, and lately, it was with disdain. As if he was disappointed.

I tipped my chin up and kept my tone flat. "I knew Tate was staying with Jared tonight, and I didn't want to wake up her dad to let me in the house to crash. I need her to help me get Liam home and to let me in her house. Is she up?" I asked.

He shook his head, and I wasn't sure if that meant "no" or "you've got to be kidding me."

Digging in his jeans pocket, he pulled out keys. "I'll drive you home."

"No," I rushed. "My mom thinks I'm staying at Tate's tonight."

His eyes narrowed on me, and I felt judged. Yeah, I was lying to my mother to spend the night with my boyfriend. And, yes, I was eighteen years old and still not allowed the freedom of an adult. *Stop looking at me like that.*

"Don't move," he ordered, and then turned around, walking back to his house.

After less than a minute he walked back out and started across the lawn to Tate's, jerking his chin at me to follow. I assumed he had a key, so I jogged up to his side as he climbed the porch steps.

"What about Liam?" I couldn't leave my boyfriend sleeping in his car all night. What if something happened to him? Or he got sick? And Tate's dad would have a fit if I tried to bring him inside.

He unlocked the front door—I wasn't sure if he had Tate's or Jared's keys—and stepped inside the darkened foyer. Turning to me, he waved his hand in a big show, inviting me in.

"I'll get Jared to follow me in his car while I drive Dick-wad home in his, okay?" He hooded his eyes, looking bored.

"Don't hurt him," I warned, crossing the threshold and walking past him.

"I won't, but he deserves it."

I swung back around to face him, arching an eyebrow. "Oh, you think you're so much better, Jax?" I smiled. "Do you even know those skanks' names in there?"

His mouth instantly tightened. "They're not skanks, K.C. They're friends. And I'd make damn sure any girlfriend of mine knew how to drive a manual, and I wouldn't have gotten so drunk that I couldn't keep her safe."

His quick temper threw me, and I immediately dropped my eyes, hating the rush of guilt that prickled my skin.

Why was I trying to cut him up? Jax definitely got under my skin, but he wasn't a bad guy. His behavior at school was certainly better than his brother's had been in the past. And Jax was respectful to teachers and friendly to everyone.

Almost everyone.

I took a deep breath and straightened my shoulders, ready to swallow a mouthful of pride. "Thank you. Thank you for driving Liam home," I offered, handing him the keys. "But what about your . . ." I gestured with my hand, trying to find the right word. "Your . . . dates?"

"They'll wait." He smirked.

I rolled my eyes. *Oooookay*.

Reaching up, I worked my messy bun loose, pulling my mahogany hair down around my shoulders. But then I shot my eyes back up when I noticed Jax approaching me.

His voice was low and strong, without even a hint of humor. "Unless you want me to send them home, K.C.," he suggested, stepping closer, his chest nearly brushing mine.

Send them home?

I shook my head, blowing off his flirtation. It was the same way I'd reacted last fall the first time I met him, and every time after that when he made a suggestive remark. It was my safe, patented response, because I couldn't allow myself to react any other way.

But this time he wasn't smiling or being cocky. He might've been serious. If I told him to send the girls away, would he?

And as he reached out with a slow, soft finger and grazed my collarbone, I let time stop as I entertained the idea.

Jax's hot breath on my neck, my hair a tangled mess around my body, my clothes ripped apart on the floor as he bit my lips and made me sweat.

Oh, Jesus. I sucked in a breath and looked away, narrowing my eyes to get my damn head under control. *What the hell?*

But then Jax laughed.

Not a sympathetic laugh. Not a laugh that said he was just kidding. No, it was a laugh that told me I was the joke.

"Don't worry, K.C." He smiled, looking down on me as if I was pathetic. "I'm well aware your pussy is too precious for me, okay?"

Excuse me?

I knocked his hand away from my collarbone. "You know what?" I shot out, my fingers fisting. "I can't believe I'm saying this, but you actually make Jared look like a gentleman."

And the little shit grinned. "I love my brother, but get one thing straight." He leaned in. "He and I are nothing alike."

Yeah. My heart didn't pound around Jared. The hair on my arms didn't stand on end around him, either. I wasn't conscious of where he was and what he was doing every second that we were in the same room together. Jax and Jared were very different.

"Tattoos," I muttered.

"What?"

Shit! Did I just say that out loud?

"Um . . . ," I choked out, staring wide-eyed in front of me, which just happened to be at his bare chest. "Tattoos. Jared has them. You don't. How come?" I asked, finally looking up.

His eyebrows inched together, but he didn't look angry. It was more . . . befuddled.

Jared's back, shoulder, arm, and part of his torso were covered with tattoos. Even Jared and Jax's best friend, Madoc Caruthers, had one. You would think with those influences, Jax would've gotten at least one by now. But he hadn't. His long torso and arms were unmarked.

I waited as he stared at me and then licked his lips. "I have tattoos," he whispered, looking lost in thought. "Too many."

I didn't know what I saw in his eyes at that moment, but I knew I'd never seen it before.

Backing away, he wouldn't meet my gaze as he turned and left the house. He closed the door, locked it, and walked down the porch steps quietly.

Moments later, I heard Jared's Boss and Liam's Camaro fire up and speed down the dark street.

And an hour later, I was still lying awake in Tate's bed, running my finger over the spot he'd touched on my collarbone and wondering about the Jaxon Trent I never got to know.

CHAPTER 1

———————————

K.C.

Two years later

Shelburne Falls was an average-size town in northern Illinois. Not too small but barely big enough to have its own mall. To the naked eye, it was picturesque. Sweet in its "no two homes are alike" originality and welcoming in its "can I help you carry your groceries to the car?" kind of way.

Secrets were kept behind closed doors, and there were always too many prying eyes, but the sky was blue, the leaves rustling in the wind sounded like music, and kids still played outside rather than zoned out on video games *all* the time.

I loved it here. But I also hated who I was here.

When I left for college two years ago, I had made a promise to spend every day trying to be better than I was. I was going to be an attentive girlfriend, a trustworthy friend, and a perfect daughter.

I rarely came home, choosing to spend last summer counseling at a summer camp in Oregon and visiting my college roommate, Nik, at her home in San Diego. My mother got to brag about my busy lifestyle, and my old friends really didn't seem to miss me, so it all worked out.

Shelburne Falls wasn't a bad place. It was perfect, actually. But I was less than perfect here, and I didn't want to come home until I could show all of them that I was stronger, tougher, and smarter.

But that shit blew up in my face. Big-time.

Not only did I breeze back into town much sooner than I'd wanted, but my arrival was on the heels of a court order. *Awesome impression, K.C.*

My phone rang, and I blinked as I came out of my thoughts. Adjusting the covers, I sat up in bed and slid the screen on my Galaxy.

"Tate, hi." I smiled, not even bothering to say hello. "You're up early."

"Sorry. Didn't mean to wake you." Her cheerful voice was a relief.

"You didn't." I swung my legs out of bed and stood up, stretching. "I was just getting up."

Tate had been my best friend all through high school. She still was, I guess. During senior year, though, I'd changed our friendship. I wasn't there when she needed me, and now she kept about two feet of personal space when I was around. I didn't blame her. I messed up, and I hadn't manned up to talk about it. Or apologize.

And despite my mother's oft-repeated words of "wisdom," I should have. *"Apologizing is lowering yourself, K.C. Nothing is really a mistake until you admit you're sorry for it. Until then, it's just a difference of opinion. Don't ever apologize. It weakens you in front of others."*

But Tate rolled with it. I guess she figured that I needed her friendship more than she needed me to say I was sorry.

But all in all, I was positive of two things. She loved me, but she didn't trust me.

She was chewing something as she spoke, and I heard a refrigerator door shut in the background. "I just wanted to make sure you got settled in okay and that you're comfortable."

I pulled my white cami back down over my stomach as I walked to the French doors. "Tate, thank you so much to you and your dad for letting me crash here. I feel like a burden."

"Are you kidding?" she burst out, her voice high-pitched in surprise. "You're always welcome, and you'll stay for as long as you need."

After I'd gotten in to Shelburne Falls last night—by plane and then by cab—I'd made quick work of unpacking all my clothes in Tate's old room, showering, and inventorying the cabinets for any food I might need. Turned out I needed nothing. The cabinets and the refrigerator were crammed full of fresh food, which was weird, considering that Tate's dad had been in Japan since May and would be there until fall.

"Thanks," I offered, dropping my head. I felt guilty at her generosity. "My mom may warm up as the summer progresses."

"What's her problem?" Her honest question threw me.

I let out a bitter laugh as I opened up her white French doors to let the fragrant summer breeze in. "My police record doesn't match her lily-white living room. That's her problem, Tate."

My mother only lived a few blocks away, so it was funny that she actually thought she'd escape gossip by not letting me stay at home while I completed my community service. Those Rotary Club bitches were going to be on her case either way.

That wasn't funny. I shouldn't laugh.

"Your 'police record,'" Tate mimicked. "I never thought I'd see the day."

"Don't tease me, please."

"I'm not," she assured me. "I'm proud of you."

Huh?

"Not for breaking the law," she was quick to add. "But for standing up for yourself. Everyone knows I'd probably have a police record if not for Jared and Madoc tossing their weight around. You make mistakes like everyone else, but if you ask me, that asshole Liam got exactly what he deserved. So, yes. I'm proud of you."

I stayed quiet, knowing she was trying to make me feel better about dumping my boyfriend—kind of violently—after a five-year relationship.

But then I shook my head as I inhaled the clean morning air. Everyone may make mistakes, but not everyone gets arrested.

I could do better. A lot better. And I would.

Straightening my back, I held the phone with one hand and inspected the fingernails of the other.

"So, when will you be home?" I asked.

"Not for a couple of weeks. Madoc and Fallon left for a vacation yesterday to Mexico, and Jared's at 'Commando Camp' until late June. I'm going to visit my father soon, but for now, I'm taking the opportunity while Jared is away to pretty up the apartment."

"Ah," I mused, staring absently through the trees to the house next door. "Here come the scented candles and throw pillows," I teased.

"Don't forget the frilly toilet seat covers and accent lamps."

We laughed, but mine was forced. I didn't like hearing about their lives that I hadn't been a part of. Jared and Tate were going to college and living together in Chicago. He was in ROTC or something and was off on a training session in Florida. His best friend, Madoc—a fellow classmate of mine from high school—was married already and going to college in Chicago with Jared, Tate, and his wife, Fallon, whom I barely knew.

They were all some sort of little gang that I wasn't a part of anymore, and suddenly a heavy weight settled on my heart. I missed my friends.

"Anyway," she continued, "everyone will be home soon. We're

thinking of a camping trip for the Fourth of July, so do yourself a favor. Get ready. Be wild. Don't shower today. Wear a mismatched bra and panty set. Go get a hot bikini. Be. Wild. Got it?"

Hot bikini. Camping. Tate, Fallon, Jared, and Madoc and their wild ways. Two couples and me the fifth wheel.

Riiiiight.

I looked across at the darkened house next door, where Tate's boyfriend had once lived. His brother, Jax, used to live there, too, and all of a sudden I wanted to ask Tate about him.

Wild.

I shook my head, tears pooling in my eyes.

Tate. Jared. Fallon. Madoc.

All wild.

Jaxon Trent, and all the chances he gave me that I never took. Wild.

The silent tears dropped, but I stayed silent.

"K.C.?" Tate prompted when I said nothing. "The world has plans for you, baby. Whether you're ready or not. You can be either a driver or a passenger. Now get yourself a hot bikini for the camping trip. Got it?"

I swallowed the Brillo Pad in my throat and nodded. "Got it."

"Now go open the top drawer of my dresser. I left two presents in there when I was home this past weekend."

My eyebrows pinched together as I walked. "You were just home?"

I wished I hadn't missed her. We hadn't seen each other in about a year and a half.

"Well, I wanted to make sure it was clean," she answered as I headed to the opposite wall to her dresser, "and that you had food. I'm sorry I couldn't stay to greet you, though."

Yanking open the drawer, I immediately froze. My breathing halted, and my eyes went round.

"Tate?" My voice squeaked like a mouse's.

"You like?" she taunted, the smirk on her face practically visible through the phone. "It's waterproof."

I reached in with a shaky hand and took out the purple "Jack Rabbit" vibrator still in its clear plastic packaging.

Oh, my God.

"It's huge!" I burst out, dropping both the phone and the vibrator. "Shit!"

Scrambling, I snatched the phone off the rug and hugged myself as I laughed. "You're crazy. You know that?"

The delighted sound of her laughter filled my ears, and I had gone from tears to smiles in no time.

There was a time when I was more experienced than Tate. Who knew she'd be buying me my first vibrator?

"I have one just like it," she said. "It's getting me through Jared's absence. And the iPod has angry rock music," she pointed out.

Oh, that's right. I peered into the drawer again, seeing the iPod Touch already opened with earbuds wrapped around it. She must already have loaded music onto it.

"It *will* help you forget that asshole." She referred to Liam. The reason I was in trouble in the first place.

"Maybe it will help me forget K. C. Carter," I teased.

Bending down, I picked up the vibrator and caught myself wondering what kind of batteries it took. "Thank you, Tate." I hoped she could hear the sincerity in my voice. "If nothing else, I already feel better."

"Use them both," she ordered. "Today. Also, use the word *motherfucker* at some point. You'll feel a lot better. Trust me."

And then she hung up without a good-bye.

I pulled the phone away from my ear, staring at it as confusion shredded my smile.

I'd said "motherfucker." Just never out loud.

"I'm sure you're probably very nervous, but after the first day it will be much easier." Principal Masters powered down the hallway at my old high school as I tried to keep up. "And after ten days," he continued, "it will be as comfortable as an old pair of shoes."

Inwardly, I admitted that I was never allowed to keep shoes long enough for them to get comfortable, but I'd take his word for it.

"I just don't understand," I said breathlessly as I jogged up to his side, trying to keep pace, "how someone with no teaching experience—no teaching education—is expected to bring eight kids up to speed for their senior year."

It was the dumbest thing I'd ever heard.

When I found out that I was going to be sent home to complete my community service, I was a little annoyed and whole lot relieved. While I certainly didn't want anyone finding out about the idiocy that got me arrested, I also had no place to live in Phoenix for the summer. Coming home had been a lucky turn of events.

Even when my mother told me I would be staying at the Brandts' empty house instead of shaming her with my presence at our home, I still thought it was better than hanging around Arizona, knowing that my ex was in *our* apartment with someone else.

But teaching? Whose brain fart was that?

"You're not teaching," Principal Masters shot back, turning his head only enough so I could see the side of his face. "You're tutoring. There's a difference." And then he stopped and spun around to face me. "Let me tell you something about teaching. You can have the best teachers in the world with the most scientifically proven resources that money can buy and a teacher will still fail. Students need attention. That's it." He sliced the air between us with his hands. "They need your one-on-one time, okay? You have eight seventeen-year-olds on your roster, and you will not be alone. There are other tutors and other teachers running summer sessions in the school. The cheerleaders and band members will be around here and there, and then we have our lacrosse boys on the field nearly every day. Believe me, the school will be packed this summer. You'll have lots of lifelines should you need them."

"Do you hold every tutor's hand like this?"

He smiled and turned to keep walking. "No. But then, I don't have any other tutors completing court-ordered community service."

Ugh. I'd blissfully forgotten about that for five seconds.

"I'm sorry." I winced. "I know this is an awkward situation."

"A very lucky situation."

I loved the pep in his voice. Our principal had always been easy to talk to.

"It must be ideal to be able to come home for the summer to fulfill your requirement. And in the comfort of a place you're familiar with."

Yeah, about that . . . "How did I get this project?" I ventured, clutching Tate's brown leather messenger bag from high school that I'd found in her closet this morning.

"I asked for you."

Yeah, but . . .

"Your information popped up in my e-mail," he offered. "I knew you, trusted you—for the most part—and knew that you shone at writing. Ms. Penley still uses some of your essays and reports to showcase to the other students. Did you know that?"

I shook my head and followed him up the stairs to the second floor, where my new classroom would be.

I loved writing. Always had. I was shit when it came to oral presentations, debates, or telling stories, but give me a pen, paper, and some time, and my thoughts came together perfectly.

If only life could be edited like a story, I'd rock.

He continued. "And I also knew that you had experience counseling kids at summer camps, so it seemed like a good fit."

My flip-flops slapped the smooth brick floors as we reached the second level. "But you said my information popped up in your e-mail?" I asked. "Who sent it to you?"

"I never knew." He scrunched his eyebrows at me, looking curious. "I figured it was just a paper pusher with the Corrections Department." And then he stopped in front of what used to be—or perhaps still was—Dr. Porter's chemistry lab. "And that reminds me"—he wagged a finger—"your special circumstances do not need to be broadcast. I trust I don't need to tell you that, but I want to make it clear. These kids are not to know why you are here. Do you understand?"

"Yes, sir. Of course." I fisted the strap of the bag hanging over my shoulder, feeling embarrassed. "And thank you for trusting me with this."

His blue eyes softened, and he shot me a small smile. "This will be your room." He nodded to Dr. Porter's lab and then handed me the file folders in his hand. "Diagnostic assessments telling you where each student stands, teacher notes, lesson plans, and worksheet master copies. Study up, and see you Monday, K.C."

And then he left, leaving me to look around and get the lay of the land. I had so many questions. These kids were seventeen. What if they didn't want to listen to someone who was only a few years older? What would I do with behavior problems? Of course, Jared and Jaxon Trent no longer went to school here, but I was sure other douche bags had replaced them. And why were we holding tutoring sessions for writing in the chemistry lab? Didn't I need to be fingerprinted to work with minors?

Oh, wait. I had been fingerprinted.

I laughed to myself, figuring it was better than crying. How shit changes.

When you're in high school, you think you're so smart and plans will always work out. You think you'll be on the road to success with money in your pocket and a busy schedule, because you're so important, having become exactly the person you always wanted to be as soon as you leave high school.

What they don't tell you is that you're more confused at twenty than you were at seventeen. And looking through the window on the door to the classroom, I rubbed the chills from my arms, wondering if I'd be even more confused at twenty-five than I was right now. The road had been clear before, and now it was so muddy that I could barely even walk.

But walking was all I was going to do this summer. Since I'd lost my license for a year, I let Nik take my car to San Diego with her and took comfort in the fact that I didn't have any friends in town—right now, at least—that would make it a burden for me not to be driving.

School and the gym. Occasionally the grocery store. Those were the only places I'd be going, and they were all a healthy, but manageable, hike from Tate's house.

I decided to head back there, opting out of stepping foot in the classroom until I had to. I deserved my punishment, but that still didn't make it easier to face spending all summer in a hot, musty building filled with people who didn't want to be there any more than I did.

Leaving the school, I dug out Tate's iPod and fit the earbuds into my ears. As I scrolled through the playlist, I couldn't help smiling as I realized I didn't recognize a single song she'd loaded.

I loved Tate's taste in music, even before I met her. But over the years I'd gotten tired of battling my mother on the songs she'd hear coming from my room, and so I gave up. On all music. I rarely listened to anything, because her voice would always invade my thoughts and ruin it.

Clicking on Chevelle's "Take Out the Gunman," I cranked up

the volume so loud my ears ached. But I still broke out in a huge smile when that sexy voice started and fireworks started going off in my chest. I couldn't hear my mother in my head or anything but the thunder of music, making me laugh, making my heart beat, and making my head bob as I walked home.

The neighborhood streets were calm, the occasional car breezing past, and the sun on my legs felt so warm I realized how much I had missed my hometown in the summer.

The lush green trees looming around me, their leaves dancing in the breeze. The smell of lawns being cut and barbecues grilling dinner. The children racing up to the ice cream truck as it pulled over to the curb.

I loved it all, and for the first moment in a very long time, I was at ease. Even despite the trouble I'd gotten into.

I realized no one was waiting for me, no one was watching me, and no one was bothering me. Eventually my mother would call. Eventually I'd have to go to tutoring on Monday. And eventually I'd have to return to my political science major in the fall.

But if only for this moment, I was free.

And damn hot. I ran my fingers across my hairline, wiping off a bit of sweat. That's one thing where Arizona wins out over Shelburne Falls. Less humidity there.

But I'd dressed as smart as I could. I'd worn a white crochet skirt that made my tanned legs look so much more awesome than they actually were, but I kept it conservative on top with a thin, button-up white blouse. The stickiness on my back was already too much. I unbuttoned the shirt and pulled it off, slinging it over the messenger bag and leaving me in my white cami.

My dark hair hung down past my shoulder blades, and now that it was getting windblown and sweaty from the walk, I wished I'd pulled it up.

Stepping over the curb, I walked across the empty street and suddenly felt my heart plummet into my stomach.

Oh, no.

Looking over the vast green lawn of the town park, I saw Liam's Camaro parked in front of Applebaum's Bagels. Liam. My ex-boyfriend who cheated on me twice and was supposed to be staying in Phoenix for the summer. *Shit!*

My head fell back, and I closed my eyes. *Fuck my luck.*

My teeth clenched, and every damn muscle in my body was charged.

But then I jumped, startled. A sudden jolt of vibrations tingled my feet and shot straight up my legs.

I opened my eyes and turned around to see that I'd stopped in the middle of the street I'd been attempting to cross before Liam's Camaro grabbed my attention. I blinked, staring wide-eyed at a car—actually, a ton of cars—as they just sat there, staring back at me and waiting for me to move my ass out of their way. How long had they been there before I noticed?

Chills ran up my spine, and I shivered, Liam forgotten. I barely noticed the other muscle cars. All I saw was the one in the lead. The black one staring at me through blacked-out windows.

The Mustang GT.

Jaxon Trent's Mustang GT.

CHAPTER 2

K.C.

I wasn't expecting that. Not for one minute did I think Jax would still be in town.

I hurried to the other side of the street, locked in a weird daze as Chevelle pounded in my ears. Turning around, I watched his Mustang just sit there.

What was he doing?

Finally he revved the engine and cruised past slowly, car after car, all tricked out, following in his wake.

My dry tongue suddenly felt like a scrub brush in my mouth. More cars zoomed by me, blowing my short skirt across my thighs, and I felt as if I'd gotten caught in the middle of a damn parade.

What the hell was this?

Some of the vehicles I recognized. Since Liam, Jared, and Tate all used to race at the Loop, I'd learned at least a few things. Like Jax's car was a Mustang, and I knew it was still Jax's car, because I noticed his license plate still read NATIVE on it. The car behind it was Sam's, a guy who graduated with me. It was a Dodge Challenger, but

I had no clue what year. There was another Mustang, a Chevy SS, and a couple of older Fords and Pontiacs.

And then there were some very out-of-place ones.

Subarus? Hyundais? Was that a MINI Cooper?

Jax's brother, Jared, would rather eat his own tongue than be seen with these cars. And they were all pimped out, too, with weird paint and huge spoilers on the back.

Wow.

But there were a shitload of them. I just stood there, staring, as car after car roared past me, all of them making their own distinct sounds as their engines sent vibrations down to the pavement at my feet, and up my body, making my belly hum.

I clenched my thighs and winced, disgusted with myself.

I was not wet.

No.

But I was. I was so completely turned on that I couldn't remember the last time my body had burned like this.

I looked over once more, watching Jaxon Trent's Mustang round the corner and disappear.

I spent the next few hours trying to keep as busy as possible. No friends, no car, not a lot of money, and I was restless as hell. And idle hands were the devil's plaything.

Boredom was the root of all trouble, and apparently trouble was still living right next door.

What the hell was wrong with me? I hadn't even seen the guy yet. He hadn't even stepped out of his car, and all my brain wanted to do was wonder about him. Picture him. In his car. Dressed in black as he usually was. Touching me to that Chevelle song. What did he look like now?

When I finally got home, I changed into workout clothes and

went to the gym, determined to kill some calories in kickboxing class. And then I stayed in the sauna, hoping to drain myself of every sexual impulse I'd had today.

For the most part, it worked. I was breathing evenly now at least.

As soon as I got back to the house, I showered, slapped on a little makeup and dried my hair, and then picked through my clothes for some sweatpants and a tank top.

Until I saw some of Tate's clothes still in the drawers.

I smiled, reaching in and snatching out a pair of cutoff jean shorts. I slid them on, loving the way they felt so comfortable and still looked cute as hell. They were baggy, hanging off my hip bones, but they weren't too long or too short, either. Pulling on my pink tank top, I looked in the mirror, wondering what my mother would say. She thought cutoffs were sloppy, and although she liked Tate, she stressed that her music and her style were not to be duplicated.

But she wasn't here, and if no one was going to see me, then no harm done.

I spent the rest of the night sprawled out on the living room floor, eating mac 'n' cheese and poring over the files Principal Masters had given me. Although he'd given me lesson plans, I typed up some K.C.–friendly instructions of my own on my laptop, adding a couple of journal activities I loved doing in my own classes at college. Sessions would be Monday through Thursday from eight fifteen to noon, and tutoring would end mid-July. After that, my hundred hours would be complete, and I'd be free for the rest of the summer.

I'd been staring at the same sentence for about five minutes when I let my head fall back and closed my eyes, completely pissed off at the noise outside.

The raucous party next door had begun as a dull hum two hours ago, but now it was a hodgepodge of laughter, squeals, thunderous engines roaring in and out of the neighborhood, and constant explosions of music that felt as if bombs might actually be detonating under Tate's house. I gritted my teeth together and grumbled to no one, "I can't believe no one in the neighborhood complains about this."

I shot off the area rug, heading for the windows in the dining room to take a look at what was going on, when I heard pounding on the front door.

"Juliet?" a singsong voice called. "What light through yonder window breaks?" The familiar words made my heart flutter, and I smiled.

"Romeo, Romeo," I called, doing an about-face for the front door. "Wherefore art thou, Romeo?"

I yanked open the door, reached for my cousin Shane's hand, and let her pull me into her body and then dip me backward so that my back arched and my hair caressed the hardwood floors.

She held me tight. "Your nose hairs need to be trimmed, cuz."

I popped my head up. "Your breath smells like a dead person."

She swooped me back up and plopped a kiss on my cheek before walking past me into the living room.

"How are you?" she asked, acting as if it hadn't been a year since we'd seen each other.

"Peachy. You?"

"Nothing that a few drinks or a bullet to the head won't cure."

I hesitated as I watched her crash into the armchair and slouch. Even though we rarely saw each other since college had started, we talked at least once a week and over time her jokes made me more and more uncomfortable. Those little comments were pretty constant.

Shane was my only cousin, and since we were both our parents' only children, we grew up close. I appreciated her way with words and her easy humor, but it still didn't erase the suspicion that she was aching to leave home and spread her wings.

"Careful," I warned. "I may actually start worrying about some-one other than myself."

"That would be new," she teased, folding her hands over her stomach. "So . . . are you really okay, Juliet?"

She was the only person who called me by my real name—Juliet Adrian Carter. Everyone else called me K.C.

"I'm fine." I nodded, sitting back down on the floor and spread-ing my legs around the laptop. "You?"

"Better now that you're home."

Shane graduated this year and would be off to college in Califor-nia in the fall. But even there, she wouldn't have much freedom. Her parents only agreed to pay the out-of-state tuition if she lived with her grandmother—on her father's side—in San Francisco.

Shane was less than happy, but she rolled with it. Although I think she liked Shelburne Falls—she had lots of friends—she was looking for an environment that had more than a ten percent African-American population.

Her dad was black. He loved it here and from what I gathered, he was comfortable, but Shane craved more diversity, more culture, more everything.

She cleared her throat and leaned on her knees. "What are you doing?" The question sounded like an accusation.

I looked up into her stunning hazel eyes. "Getting ready for my community service. I'm tutoring incoming seniors this summer."

"I heard." She still stared at me as if she were confused. "I meant why the hell are you holed up in the house when for once in your life Liam or Sandra Fucking Carter doesn't have you on a leash?"

"You know I love you," I started, "but I have a nice, peaceful house and a vibrator upstairs. I'm good," I joked. "Besides, do you really think I should go looking for trouble, Shane?"

"You won't have to look far." Her taunting voice sounded sexy. "Has it escaped your notice that a party has commenced next door?"

Ah. Now I got it. I looked at her attire, noticing the skintight black miniskirt and the white tank top. Unlike my tank, though, hers had sequins around the neckline and in one long strip down the front. With her café au lait skin, dark, straightened hair falling below her shoulder blades, and her legs that went on for days, she was stunningly beautiful.

I wondered if Jax ever noticed her, but I shook my head clear. I didn't care.

"No, it hasn't escaped my notice," I mumbled. "I think the vibrations of the music are shaking the foundations of this house, actually."

"Well, I'm going. And so are you."

"No, I'm not." I let out a bitter laugh and unwrapped a piece of spearmint gum, sticking it into my mouth. "Jax is trouble, and I have no desire to be over there."

"Yes, you do. Everyone wants to be over there. And every girl gets along with Jax."

I couldn't help it. I looked up and shot her what I was sure was a nasty little scowl. But I quickly looked back down again. Images of Jax screwing those two girls a couple of years ago flashed through my mind, and I thought of everyone else he'd probably had since then, and I . . .

I fisted the gum wrapper.

Why did he affect me so much? Jaxon Trent was just a cocky kid who had liked to push my buttons in high school—but for some reason my damn body had more of a reaction to him than the boyfriend I'd had for five years. And even though I didn't consider what he might or might not have been doing while I was gone, I damn well couldn't stop thinking about it now.

Oh, Christ. I hope Shane had never slept with him.

I almost asked.

"Well, I don't," I grumbled. "Jax was always bad news. Does he even go to college?"

"To Clarke," she answered quickly, and I blinked.

Clarke College?

It was local. Close enough for him to live in Shelburne Falls. But it was also private and had very high ratings for its academics. Shame warmed my cheeks for assuming he wasn't college material. He was, and he was in a much better school than I attended.

"So he still lives next door year-round with Katherine?" I ventured.

"No, she married Madoc's dad last year and moved into his apartment in the city. She gave Jax the house when he graduated from high school."

So that was Jax's house now.

I closed my laptop. "What's with all the cars outside?"

Her full lips, painted a glossy red, spread in a smile, showing off her perfect white teeth. "A lot's changed, Juliet."

"Trying to be cryptic? What the hell's changed?"

She shrugged. "It's hard to explain," she said, leaning back and resting her arms on the sides of the chair. "You just need to see. We're going to the party, and you're going to have fun."

I shook my head. "Neither of us is going over. I'm keeping my nose clean, and you're severely underage and without a party buddy."

Her eyes practically twinkled. "Oh, no," she gasped, putting her palm to her chest. "I can't be without a party buddy," she said as she stood up.

I stared at her. "What are you doing?"

She inched past the chair toward the entryway, smirking with her hand still on her chest. "Without a party buddy, I might do something moronic," she teased, still moving away, "like take a mysterious drink laced with GHB from a tattooed ex-con who wants to take me upstairs to introduce me to his buddies!" She opened the door as I scrambled off the floor. "Bye," she yelled.

And then she bolted out the front door, slamming it shut.

"Shane!" I growled, scurrying after her.

Damn, damn, damn! I pulled open the door, darted out to the porch, and . . . *shit!* Spinning around, I dived back into the house and shoved my feet into my black flip-flops that were lying in the entryway.

Yanking open the door again, I ran outside, leaping over all the steps on the porch and landing on the brick walkway.

Ugh, that girl!

She was gone. Twisting left and then right, I didn't see her sparkly white top anywhere. She was already at the party, and I sucked in breath after breath, trying to calm the tornado in my stomach.

Eighteen. Without a buddy. And the closest person I'd had to real family in a long time. All good reasons to go get her.

I looked down at my outfit. Sloppy and disheveled, in clothes that hung on me, hair kinky with the natural wave that I hadn't straightened out after my shower and barely any makeup on.

Well, the good thing was I'd push off any unwanted attention. That was for sure.

I stomped across the lawn, feeling the sharp blades of grass poke my ankles. The sun had set an hour ago, but the wet heat still hung in the air, and my back suddenly cooled with the light layer of sweat already coating it.

The long driveway was packed with cars—two rows, five deep—and the street was a damn parking lot. I recognized most of the cars I'd seen earlier. Different makes and models, some with loud paint and design work, others calm, clean, and sleek-looking. There were even cars parked in the middle of Fall Away Lane, as if the neighborhood residents wouldn't need their own street to drive on tonight.

I noticed that the garage—which sat on the other side of the house—had been extended from a two-car to a three-car, and the house had been refreshed with new white paint, although the shutters had been changed from navy blue to black.

My ears perked up when a new song started, and I actually recognized it. "Heaven Knows" by the Pretty Reckless. Nik had listened to it a lot at school.

Partygoers were scattered about as I walked onto the porch and stepped through the open doorway, trying not to think about the last time I was here.

But then I couldn't think about anything as I immediately deflated and gawked at the inside of the house.

Oh, my God. Wow.

More than the exterior had been upgraded. My eyes darted up, down, and all around as I took in new, bold paint making the house so much more inviting, and the carpet in the living room that had been torn away to reveal shiny hardwood floors. Everything in the rooms that I could get a glimpse of was made to accommodate a bachelor and his parties.

Three huge flat-screens lined the wall in the family room where the pool table still sat. The furniture in the living room had been replaced with deep leather couches and more flat-screens, and as I peered to the back of the house, I could see glimpses of a renovated kitchen as well.

"*A lot's changed, Juliet.*" Shane's voice came back to me. *Yeah, so it would seem.*

Katherine Trent—or Katherine Caruthers now—had kept a

nice house before, but this was . . . well, I didn't know how to describe it.

Loaded? Indulgent? Hot. Definitely hot.

I liked the red walls in the living room, the midnight blue walls in the family room, and the cappuccino-colored walls in the foyer. I liked the black-framed prints of Native Americans wearing various headdresses and jewelry on the walls leading up to the second floor, and even though black leather couches usually creeped me out, the ones in the living room weren't cheap. They were deep and lush, and expensive looking. Everything looked so well kept and clean.

"K.C.?"

I spun around, coming face-to-face with Liam.

And I swallowed my fucking gum.

I winced, not even trying to hide the look. The sight of his blue doe eyes and polite expression gave me a sudden urge to breathe fire in his stupid, fat face. Was this seriously happening to me right now?

He stood in the doorway, holding hands with the very same redhead I'd caught him with at the club last week. She had on a black, strapless dress, and her hair was full of volume and looking sexy as it fell around her.

Great. And I picked today to get rebellious with my appearance. I shook my head at the irony.

When he'd cheated on me in high school, I'd taken him back. Stupidly. I felt as if I'd done something wrong—something to push him away—and he'd honestly seemed sorry for what he'd done. After seeing how Jared had treated Tate through most of high school, I was actually grateful to have a boyfriend who brought me flowers when I was sick and who put up with my mother's attitude.

When I caught him cheating again a couple of weeks ago, I was done.

"Liam." I sighed, trying to look bored. "Doesn't Jax hate you? Why are you here?"

His face fell, and it was the first time I'd been glad for Jax's contempt toward Liam. Although I was also insinuating that Jax was fine with me being here, which might not be true, either.

"*Everyone's* here, K.C." Liam stuck his other hand in his pocket. "This is Megan, by the way."

"I'll let you know when I give a shit," I mumbled.

He continued, ignoring me. "I brought her home to meet my parents." *Don't care.* "We're moving in together, K.C."

My knees damn near buckled, and I let out a shocked laugh. "You're kidding, right?"

Megan arched an eyebrow, looking dissatisfied that she had to tolerate my presence, and Liam hooded his eyes, totally not laughing with me.

I immediately straightened. "Wow, I'm sorry."

"Excuse me?" Megan snipped.

"I mean, I'm sorry in advance. For when he cheats on you," I explained. "Do you really think that he won't?"

She smiled, looking smug, as if she knew something I didn't, and I locked my hands behind my back, fingering my scar.

"Men who are unsatisfied cheat," she taunted me. "And from what I hear, you were very unsatisfying."

And I stared dumbfounded as she pretended to take a dick into her mouth and start gagging.

I barely saw Liam give her a dirty look. All I could hear was my heart pounding in my ears while her pompous smirk leveled me. She was imitating me. Liam had told her . . .

No.

The room was too crowded, and I rubbed my upper arms, trying to erase the chill even though embarrassment warmed my cheeks.

They just stood there, staring at me, and it was my turn to act, but I locked my mouth shut, searching my blank mental arsenal for what I should do next.

But I had nothing. I was unsatisfying. I was pathetic to him. What was I supposed to do now? What was I supposed to say?

Tate. She would know what to do.

"You couldn't even give a decent blow job, huh?" Megan baited me. *Say something!*

Goose bumps broke out over my arms, I was so cold, and I blinked long and hard. So cold.

But then a rush of heat hit my back, and I gasped, my eyelids fluttering with the sudden warm relief.

"Liam," Jax's voice greeted him as he wrapped his arms around my waist and engulfed me in the soothing furnace of his skin.

"Jax," Liam muttered, his voice unfriendly. I opened my eyes to see his gaze shooting between me and the man behind me, probably wondering what the hell was going on.

Hell if I knew.

Glancing down, I saw Jax's same beautiful hands and long fingers, smeared with grease, locked in front of my waist. I brought up my hands and clasped his forearms, much thicker than they were last time I'd seen him.

I didn't know why he did it. All I knew was that I wasn't hurting right now, and I wasn't alone and feeling stupid.

He took my movement as an invitation and pulled me closer into his chest.

"How's it going?" he asked Liam.

"Fine," Liam answered, still looking between Jax and me suspiciously. "You?" he asked back.

I noticed Megan staring over my head at Jax, the hint of a smile on her lips.

"Fine," Jax answered in a flat tone. "But your new girlfriend is acting like a bitch, and it's pissing me off. If she upsets K.C. again, she's out."

A breathless laugh escaped my chest, and I clamped my hand over my mouth. *Oh, my God!*

Megan's eyes flared, and Liam just stared at Jax, shaking his head as though he wanted to lunge for him.

But he knew better. This was Jax's house, Jax's party, and Liam knew if it came to a fight, no one here would be on his side.

Heat spread across my face, and I dropped my eyes, knowing damn well they looked too pleased at what was happening. I wasn't supposed to like a guy throwing his weight around for me. I shouldn't want Jax to protect me. I should do this myself. But what the hell?

Liam looked between us and then grabbed Megan's hand, twisting around and leaving.

As they both disappeared out the front door, Jax dropped his arms slowly, his hands running down my bare arms before his touch disappeared altogether. I couldn't help feeling disappointment.

I was cold again.

Turning around, I folded my arms over my chest, putting on my game face. And forced down the sudden golf ball lodged in my damn throat.

Shit.

My eyes used to meet his neck, but now I stared at the wall of his chest. His strong-looking pecs and wide shoulders made me feel very, very small. No wonder I'd felt so warm a minute ago. His body would be like a blanket on mine.

And then my stomach flip-flopped, seeing that his nipples were pierced.

Well, that was definitely new.

He sported two barbells, one on each pec, and I suddenly felt as if I were on a roller coaster.

I scowled, wondering why I couldn't take my eyes off them. I didn't like nipple piercings, so what the hell?

Then I forced my eyes into a convincing—I hoped—little scowl and finally looked up.

Blue Hell arched an eyebrow at me, and I deflated. Not a damn thing had changed. And yet everything had changed.

While I was away, Jaxon Trent had become a man.

CHAPTER 3

K.C.

Only his hair was the same. Still as dark as black coffee but with a gorgeous shine. His face was still smooth and clean-shaven, but now it was more angular with chiseled cheekbones, a straight, narrow nose, and full, sculpted lips.

And his straight black eyebrows only emphasized the bluest eyes ever born to a human being. You could see those jewels from fifty yards away.

I knew that for a fact.

He was bare-chested, of course, and the cuts and dips of his abs and slim waist were hard to look away from. But I'd look away, scowl, glance back real quickly, and then look away again. His arms were a lot bigger than the last time I'd seen them.

He was huge.

And nineteen.

And a troublemaker.

And scary.

I dug in my eyebrows as deep as I could manage and met his gaze again.

His lips were tilted in a smile. "Don't worry. I know." He sighed, cutting me off before I could speak. "You're an independent woman who can fight her own battles, blah, blah, blah, and et cetera. Just say thank you."

Oh.

He thought I was mad about the Liam episode. That worked. I arched an angry eyebrow for extra effect, not saying thank you.

He smiled, probably amused by my defiance. "You looking for your cousin?" he asked.

I nodded.

"Come on." He took my hand.

The car grime on his hand rubbed into mine, and I held him firmly, a smile that I wouldn't set free tickling the corners of my mouth.

I liked how it felt. Sandy, gritty, alive.

Everything had always been clean for me. Every moment of my life had been manicured, pedicured, and scrubbed. My clothes always matched, my fingernails were always clean, and my biggest decision was whether I should buy the silver ballet flats or the black ones.

Now Jaxon Trent's dirty hands fused with my sweaty palms, and I wondered how good his dirt would feel everywhere else on my skin.

I glanced around me, noticing people noticing us. Their eyes visibly taking in the sight of Jax holding my hand behind him, at which point a confused look would appear on their faces. A couple of people seemed surprised, and a few others—women, mostly—scrunched up their noses or looked away, annoyed.

I squeezed his hand one last time—hard—because I never wanted to let it go, and then I yanked my hand quickly away. Jax only looked back for a second, probably to make sure I hadn't run off.

"This is ridiculous," I grumbled as I followed him through the kitchen. "Isn't there a maximum capacity in a house like they have for restaurants and elevators?"

Jax ignored me as if I'd asked a rhetorical question. We slithered through the crowd, stepping aside as three young men crashed through the back doorway.

"Shane comes around quite a bit," he said. "But don't worry. No one messes with her."

"Not even you?" I ventured, following him into the backyard.

Please say that you haven't screwed my cousin. Please, please, please.

He kept walking, turning his head only slightly. "Especially not me."

I exhaled, trying to keep my cool and my thoughts together. Until I took a look around. The backyard was insane, and I couldn't help gawking.

"Uh, I . . ." Was that a Jacuzzi? "I just came to take Shane home. Back to Tate's, I mean."

"I figured."

I couldn't see his face, but I knew he was nodding. His ponytail rose and fell on his spine. "See?" He turned and gestured through the gate. "She's fine."

But I barely registered my cousin sitting in a lawn chair, talking closely with another girl.

"What the hell?" I burst out, my eyes burning from not blinking.

No wonder it felt as if Tate's house was shaking! The party next door had spilled over into her backyard.

"K.C.!" Shane smiled with eyes full of mischief as she sat cross-legged on the lawn chair. I noticed that she had a Solo cup in her hand, but to be honest, my head was elsewhere now.

The old wooden fence that had separated Jared's and Tate's backyards was now gone.

It had been replaced with an awesome-looking wall of aged red bricks, pierced to leave small empty spaces for looking through. Each three-foot section of the brick wall was interrupted by a brick column, a lamppost sitting on top of each one. Where you would have to hop the old dowdy wooden fence before, you could now simply walk through a solid wooden gate to venture into the next backyard. Thus making two spaces into one.

Apparently Jax was using both yards for his party tonight. How had I not noticed the new fence when I got here? And how had I not noticed the party practically on top of me when I was inside Tate's house working? And how was Jax, who was only nineteen years old, getting all this liquor? And how the hell was he paying for all this stuff!

Shane had resumed her conversation with the girl she'd been talking to, so I let her sit tight as I followed Jax into Tate's backyard to the array of car parts spread out on a folding table. Several men sat looking over the machinery, inspecting, taking things apart, whatever.

I shook my head, in a daze. "Jax, what the hell do you have going on here?" I asked quietly.

It wasn't my intention to sound uptight or accusing, but I was concerned. All this took money. Lots of it.

I knew Jax was skilled and smart, especially with computers, so I'd never doubted that he'd do well for himself. I'd overheard him saying once that a person's entire life was online. You could control it or be vulnerable to it.

And you didn't have to know Jax well to know he liked control.

But to have all this? So young?

He picked up a tool and looked to be continuing work that he'd been in the middle of. "How do you mean?" he asked.

He was caging.

Jax had never confided in me. I'd never given him reason to think I cared, but I did know that his dad was in jail for abusing him, his mom wasn't in the picture, and he had spent much of his life in the system. Until, that is, his half brother, Jared, had started taking an active role in his life.

Shortly after, Jared's mom assumed custody of Jax, and they'd all been a family ever since.

But now she'd remarried, moved out of town, and from the looks of it, Jax was surviving very well on his own.

Noticing lots of people sitting close by in lawn chairs, I approached the table and spoke quietly. "This house has been renovated. You have a ton of expensive electronics in there, and you have to have close to a half million dollars' worth of cars sitting out on the street. Who the hell are all these people?"

His brother's parties used to boast only half as many guests. It had certainly been less impressive but a lot more comfortable than this chaos.

Jax threw down a tool, picking up a Phillips-head. "They're my friends' cars, not mine."

I stood there, studying him.

He looked up and locked eyes with me, letting out an annoyed sigh. "Okay, I'll slow down, K.C. First, a *friend* is someone you enjoy sharing time with. Someone you're nice to that you trust—"

"Screw you," I said, sneering, folding my arms over my chest again.

"She gets arrested," a girl off to the side laughed, "and she still thinks she's so superior."

What the hell?

I lost my breath, hearing snickers and snorts go off around the area as everyone reacted to what she'd said.

Everyone knew?

"We got a noise complaint!"

I jumped, twisting around to see two uniformed police officers standing in the open gate.

Chatter stopped, and everyone popped their heads up, eyeing the two officers dressed in black.

I swallowed the lump in my throat and felt the sweat on my forehead. Shane and I were underage at a party with alcohol. My mother would disown me if there was another call from the police.

Or maybe they'd just shut down the party. Hmm . . . that'd work for me. Shane safe, and me away from trouble.

"Hey," Jax greeted, and then turned back to his work.

I narrowed my eyes, watching his long fingers work.

"Okay, you can go back to your partying now." One of the cops waved everyone off, chuckling at his own joke, and others followed suit, laughing and beginning their conversations again.

"Hey, man." The same cop who had just spoken came up to the table and shook Jax's hand. "I brought Tim by to see the Evo." He jerked his thumb to the young-looking officer behind him.

Jax spoke lightly, gesturing with his chin. "In the garage. Go ahead."

The cops walked out, acting oblivious of the underage drinking, the packed street that had to be a fire hazard, and the huge amount of party noise coming from the house.

I turned to Jax, completely and totally confused. "What the hell is going on?"

"A lot's changed, Juliet."

Yeah, no shit, I thought. Jared got a ticket or two for noise complaints for his parties. Why not Jax?

He stopped working and cocked his head, taking me in. His gaze dropped down my body, over my tight pink tank top and Tate's shortish cutoffs. Suddenly feeling self-conscious, I tucked my hair behind my ear and then shoved my hands into my pockets, averting my eyes from his scrutinizing gaze.

But then I sucked in a breath as Jax reached over and pulled my hair back out from behind my ear.

"It was perfect before." His voice sounded gravelly as if his mouth was dry.

He held my eyes, and I swear I felt high from his presence. I wished he wouldn't look at me. I wished he hadn't touched me. I wished he didn't always knock me on my ass every time we were near each other.

Tossing down his tools, he spoke loudly. "Everyone clear out for a minute. Go get another drink."

And I watched as all the guys dropped their toys, and others stood up from their chairs, scraping the legs against the brick-paved ground. Looking over, I saw Shane watching me as she walked out, her eyebrows raised and licking her lips to hide a smile.

What did that mean?

I turned to leave, too, but Jax caught my arm. "Stay."

He let go and walked around, coming to stand in front of me and then leaning back on the table as he spoke.

"Do you remember when we met?" His soft voice reminded me of chocolate. "I told you that I was old enough to unravel you. Do you remember that?"

I swallowed and looked away. Yeah, I remembered. I'd played out that conversation so many times in my head.

How his eyes ate me up that night. How he wanted to give me a ride home. How I ignored Liam's calls and fell asleep thinking of the new kid in town. My body warmed as I thought about it. It was the first time I'd ever slept naked.

He gave a gentle smile and looked down. "Man, I wanted to unravel you, K.C.," he whispered, and then looked me straight in the eye. "I wanted inside you so badly."

No.

I reared back, but he caught my hand, holding me.

Please don't do this.

He caressed my fingers with his thumb, and my eyes fluttered at the tingles spreading up my arm. His soothing voice, his touch, his gentleness . . .

He barely whispered and my heart hurt, it was pounding so hard. "I wanted to make you come so hard that you'd lose that little sneer on your face forever," he said softly. "I wanted to taste how wet you were for me. I wanted you underneath me, writhing and sweaty and begging."

I closed my eyes, my chest tight. *Writhing. Sweaty.* That wasn't me. I'd never please him.

He continued, standing up and moving flush with my chest. "I used to fantasize about pinning you against the lockers at school and running my hand up the inside of your thigh, hearing your whimpers."

My knees shook, about to buckle, and I felt the warmth between my legs. He needed to stop.

"I wanted your mouth on mine," he whispered, his breath tickling my forehead. "And your legs wrapped around my waist as you rode me." *Oh, my God.* "Man, I wanted you, K.C. I wanted to undo you." His lips were so close to my face I could feel the moistness of his breath as he whispered, "I wanted to dirty you up."

And then he grabbed my wrist, and I gasped before clamping my mouth shut again. His hand was fire on my body, and my breath shook as he leaned in, almost touching my lips.

"But then I got to know you." His voice grew hard and clipped and my wrist ached where he squeezed. "You're gutless and helpless and I've never met anyone so desperate to get out of her own skin."

And then he yanked my wrist in between us, turning up the inside to reveal my two-inch scar. Running his thumb over it, he scowled down at me, looking disgusted.

Tears burned my eyes.

He knew. How did he know?

Pressing my teeth together so hard it hurt, I glared at him, yanking my hand out of his grasp.

Backing away, I pushed away the tears and hardened my jaw, determined never to show him defeat.

And as I walked out, back through Jax's house, I didn't even break pace as I grabbed an abandoned drink off the kitchen table and threw it on an amplifier before I left. I vaguely heard it fizzle, white static filling the room, as I walked out.

CHAPTER 4

K.C.

I sat on the edge of Tate's bed the next morning, running my thumb back and forth across the jagged scar on the inside of my wrist that lay in my lap. It was long and thin but well hidden, running diagonally on the inside of my wrist.

Gutless and helpless. I shook my head slowly, feeling a cold tear land on my arm.

Jaxon Trent was an asshole.

Everyone thought they had me figured out. Jax, Jared, Madoc, Liam, my mother . . . everyone.

Everyone except Tate and Shane. They were the only family I really had, because they were the only ones who knew everything.

"I've never met anyone so desperate to get out of her own skin."

I tucked my long hair behind my ear and sniffled. He was right about that. Immediately the memory hit me as if it had just happened yesterday.

"Katherina, come here," my father calls. He sits by the window, wearing blue lounge pants and a robe.

I chew on my nails, looking up at my mother, scared. But she doesn't look back. Why won't she look at me?

I'm four, and they don't tell me what's wrong, even though I keep asking. All I know is that my daddy can't live at home anymore. His hair is messy, and he never had a beard before.

"Katherina." He waves me in with his hand, wanting me to come.

"Daddy, I'm Juliet," I mumble, and my mother pinches my back.

My lip shakes, and my face hurts. I did something wrong. When I do bad things in public, she pinches me, because she says she can't yell at me.

I see my daddy's face look sad, and I drop my hands, because I want him to love me. "I'm just kidding." I smile as big as I can. "I am Katherina."

And I run to the safety and love of my daddy's arms, holding on tight, even though he thinks I'm my sister.

I couldn't believe it, and I hated to admit it, but the asshole was right. I wasn't my dead sister, Katherina, and what was worse, I didn't even know who the hell Juliet was anymore. I barely existed.

What ice cream did K.C. like? Because I'd just eat that so I wouldn't confuse my father's happy delusions. Did I have to wear Mary Janes to church every Sunday just because they were K.C.'s favorite shoes? I hated Mary Janes, but no, I was supposed to like them, so I decided just to like them and forget about it. What did I want to be when I grew up? Or, wait. What did K.C. want to be? Because Daddy liked to talk to her about that, and I had to try not to upset him.

In death, my sister was perfection. She never bit her nails, acted up, or listened to bad music. She was beautiful, perfect, and alive. Juliet was the dead one.

I trailed around in a daze, having slept barely at all the night before, and stripped off my pajama shorts and cami as I stepped into the bathroom. Turning on the shower, I climbed in, my heavy limbs moving only as much as they had to, weighted down with fucking defeat.

Gutless and helpless.

I dipped my head back and shivered as the hot water poured welcome heat all over my skin. The weather outside was hot and wet, and I kept the temperature inside at eighty degrees, not wanting to run up the Brandts' electric bill while I stayed here. But even though it seemed I was constantly wiping sweat off my brow, I wanted it hotter. I turned the faucet, increasing the temperature from a pleasant thaw to a fever, and I didn't care if it was almost too much. I wasn't cold anymore.

"*. . . writhing and sweaty and begging.*"

I tilted my head, leaning it on the shower wall and closing my eyes.

"*I wanted to taste how wet you were for me.*"

Sucking in my bottom lip, I felt the fire pool between my legs, and my head felt as if it were floating.

It could've been the heat of the shower. Or it could've been the memory of his breath on my face. It had smelled like apples and pears and rain.

Like summer. How could anyone's breath smell like summer?

"*I used to fantasize about pinning you against the lockers at school . . .*"

Reaching down, I slid my hand up the inside of my wet thigh, the urge undeniable. I should've let him have me in high school, but I was afraid he'd rip my life apart. I was afraid he'd confuse me. And here I was, just as confused as ever, and I should've let him screw me. Ten times a day, whenever he wanted, because at least I would've been Juliet again, and I would've felt something.

I brought my hand up between my legs and ran my middle finger along my slit, rolling my hips into my hand.

Oh, God, that felt good. I breathed hard, rubbing my hand faster.

I was at least grateful for one of the things my mother had encouraged. Waxing. I'd opted to get it all removed. I loved it, and I wondered if Jax liked that sort of thing. My fingers rubbed against the smooth skin, and the pressure built in my belly with the pleasure of skin on skin.

My fingers slipped inside my folds, and I reached up and held one of my breasts with the other hand, wishing it was his hands squeezing and kneading while his tongue swirled around my cunt.

Shit. I just said "cunt."

I never said words like that, but Nik constantly used them, and somehow it didn't seem out of place right now.

I groaned, swirling my fingers around my clit, feeling the hard nub pulse like an automatic weapon. I wanted him.

Jax's tongue was on me, and the hot spray of the shower doused his body in shimmering droplets. I wanted to lick them all.

But he was doing all the action right now. His tongue darted out to lick and play over my hip, up my stomach, and then stopping to French-kiss my breast before he stood up straight. Grabbing me by the back of my hair, he stared down at me as he whispered into my mouth.

I want your legs wrapped around my waist as you ride my cock.

"Oh, God," I cried out, swirling my clit faster and faster. "Yes."

I was throbbing and on fire, and I wanted what I had never wanted with Liam. Leaving the water running, I climbed out of the shower and hurried for the bedroom, dripping all over the rug. Yanking open the bedside drawer, I pulled out the vibrator and crashed onto the bed, lying on my back.

Spreading my legs, I turned the dial as far as it would go, and I heard the buzzing getting louder and louder. Working the head around my clit, I gasped at the swirls of pleasure filling my stomach.

Holy shit!

I started feeling little waves rolling through my belly. My eyes fluttered closed, and I arched my back off the bed, wanting more, needing more.

Oh, God.

Rubbing the vibrator over my entrance, I bit my bottom lip. The tantalizing vibrations felt so good.

"Oh," I groaned, feeling the quakes and quivers inside my body.

"I wanted to dirty you up."

"Jax." My voice shook as I pumped the cock around my entrance, never going in, but just massaging and teasing. My legs shook with the pleasure of what was happening inside me.

"Oh, God!" I screamed, spreading my legs wider.

Heat poured out of me, and I wanted this more than I'd ever wanted anything. The deep vibrations pulsed in quick hums inside my womb.

Oh, God. Faster, faster, faster . . .

I arched my back and moved the tool up and around, rougher and rougher, massaging my clit.

"Oh, God. Fuck!" I cried out, shaking and sucking in air as the cyclone between my legs racked through me. "Yes!"

I came, gasping and moaning as I reached up and fisted the hair at my scalp.

My arms ached with exhaustion, and I slowly relaxed my eyes that were squeezed shut.

Jesus. I blinked, seeing the white ceiling come into focus.

What did I just do?

"You know, if you could talk to me at some point in the foreseeable future, that'd be greeeeat, mkay?" Shane imitated the guy from *Office Space* as she trailed me in the school hallways Monday morning.

"Why are you even here?" I asked, sounding just as annoyed as I felt. It was eight o'clock in the morning on my first day of tutoring, but Shane was on summer vacation with no reason to be here other than to be a pain in my ass.

"I'm transitioning the new cheer captain." She smiled. "I'll be around tons." The snarky arched eyebrow was meant as a threat, and that was when I finally noticed the spandex shorts and sports bra she was wearing.

Ugh. *Damn. Damn, damn, damn, damn.* I thought I'd be safe at school at least.

Ever since the party last Thursday, she'd been on my case to give her the scoop on what had happened with Jax.

No comment.

I'd buckled down, prepared for tutoring, and spent my remaining days of freedom at the gym or lying out tanning in the backyard, although that was uncomfortable, since the brick wall made it easier to see through. Jax had come out in the backyard yesterday and immediately shoved all his friends back into the house when they interrupted my tanning. It wasn't like Jax to do anything to make me comfortable, but I appreciated it, even though I promptly got up and went inside anyway.

Luckily that was the only time I'd seen him, though. I'd heard his car in the mornings and in the middle of the night, coming and going at odd hours, but that was the thing. It was *constantly* coming and going. The guy hardly sat still and once he was home, he'd turn around and leave again minutes later.

I'd resisted the urge to peer out the windows, and I'd been avoiding Shane and texts from Tate and my roommate, Nik.

"Look," I said, grabbing the doorknob to the chem lab. "I'm sorry I've avoided you. I'm nervous, okay?" And that was true. I was practically squeezing the life out of the strap of Tate's messenger bag. "Just give me a couple of days to get settled in. We can do dinner Wednesday night. Sound good?"

Shane twisted her full lips to the side, looking displeased, but I couldn't help it. Jax's hateful words from the other night were still flowing through my mind, an ever-present whisper, and to make matters worse, I masturbated to him the very next day. Seriously?

Right now a nice, long walk with Tate's iPod sounded like heaven. It was really the only company I wanted.

"All right." Her mumbled answer took some weight off my shoulders. "Do you want a ride home? I get done at eleven. I'll stick around," she offered.

"No." I shook my head and smiled. "I'm actually enjoying the walks." Looking forward to them was more like it.

She gave me a playful sneer, her hazel eyes amused. "But it's so hot. Really?"

"I like the heat."

"Do you?" Her eyes twinkled with mischief as she backed up, walking away.

I smiled. Yeah, I guess it was weird. At first I thought that living in Phoenix got me used to the high temperatures, but Shelburne Falls was a different kind of heat. The thickness of the air saturated everything with moisture. It was wet, and it made every pore on my skin sensitive and aware. I was constantly conscious of the way the hem of my coral-colored skirt brushed across my thighs and the heat pouring off my chest made my shirt stick to my skin. The back of my neck was already damp, and although I was glad that I wore a light white sleeveless blouse, I wished I had pulled my hair up instead of leaving it down. Brushing it over one shoulder to lie on my chest, I turned the knob and walked into the classroom.

The smell hit me right away, causing me to stop. I hadn't been in a classroom in this school in two years, and that smell took me back to bittersweet memories. The whole school smelled the same. Like basketballs and construction paper. I inhaled, suddenly feeling alone but at home. I had nothing I had the last time I was here. No boy-friend. No best friend. But it was here that I was last happy.

"Hi, Ms. Penley," I said right away, trying to appear less nervous than I was.

"K.C.!" She smiled one of those smiles where you can see both rows of teeth. "It made my summer when I heard you'd be helping me out."

I nodded, looking around the nearly empty lab. A few other students—or possibly tutors, judging from the fact that they had files like mine—sat at tables around the room.

It was weird to see Ms. Penley in here, since her literature and writing classes were always in a standard classroom. This room made my legs stiffen with fear, whereas Ms. Penley's usual classroom made my toes curl with comfort. Chem lab was my least favorite place, because I hated science. Luckily I'd had Tate to get me through those classes.

"Well." I shrugged. "I just hope I can be of help."

She waved me off. "It'll be fine," she assured me. "I'll be in the room, and there are three other tutors here as well. That's why we're in the lab. Lots of room."

I nodded, it finally making sense.

She continued talking as she organized files on her desk. "You'll be sitting at a table with four students. We're going to spend the first half hour or so reviewing the basics: gathering and organizing their ideas, main idea and supporting details, and the revision process. Most of these students still need a lot of practice on forming a thesis state-ment. You already have their diagnostic assessments." She stopped to look at me. "So when we break into groups, I want them to each share a sample paragraph and discuss how it could be made better. I simply want them to analyze their work today, and I want them to see how their work compares to others'."

That sounded easy enough. "Got it."

Scanning the room again, I noticed all the other tutors seated on their own, so I headed for an empty table and unloaded my bag. I glanced up at the clock next to the door and counted down three hours and fifty minutes until I could leave. I'd have two sessions, each lasting an hour and forty-five minutes with four students in each session. Some kids were here for more than just writing, so they'd rotate to physics, English, or whatever math class they needed. And as icing on the cake, we'd all get our fifteen-minute snack or Facebook break.

One of the tutors—I think his name was Simon if I remembered him correctly from when we were in school together—smiled at me, and I nodded a greeting back.

Students trailed in, most of them later than the eight fifteen start time, and I let my eyes wander as some took their seats. I recognized a few kids, but I didn't know any of them. They had just been finishing their freshman year when I'd graduated.

Did I look that young only two years ago? Did I wear that much makeup?

As Ms. Penley began her lecture, showing examples over the classroom projector of what excellent papers looked like, I noticed that barely any of the kids paid attention.

This must be hard for her. Some of the kids clearly just didn't care. They covertly played on their phones under the table. They whispered to one another, ignoring Penley. They doodled in their notebooks.

And I remembered that that was what I did in my science classes in high school. It wasn't that I didn't care. I'd just gotten tired of struggling.

So I stopped trying. I did enough but no more.

Now I wished I tried more and wasn't so afraid to put myself out there. Maybe if I had reached out for new experiences, I'd know what I wanted to do with my life. Now my options felt limited, because I'd held myself back in high school, and I was two years into college political science classes that I couldn't just throw away.

I wanted these students to know that their education gave them choices. It was a valuable time.

Penley wrapped up her lesson and then directed the students to their tutors. I stayed where I was, leaning my elbows on the table and forcing a relaxed smile as one boy and three girls came to sit down.

"Hi, I'm K.C.," I greeted.

The guy held up his pointer finger but didn't make eye contact. "Jake." And then he buried his face in his hands and let out a loud yawn.

Jake might be on drugs.

I looked across the table to the three girls. I knew one of them. The younger sister of a somewhat friend from high school whom I no longer kept in touch with. The other two were strangers, but all three of them looked at me as if I were the hair in their soup.

That was one thing that didn't make me nervous. I had no trouble standing up to women in my own generation.

I kept staring at them, eyebrows raised in expectation.

The dark-haired girl finally spoke up. "I'm Ana. This is Christa and Sydney."

Sydney I knew. Her sister was sweet. She looked like a little shit, though.

She had long auburn hair, parted on the side and hanging in big, voluminous curls down her back and over her chest. Her stunning brown eyes brought out the red tint in her hair, and her makeup and nails were perfect.

Ana's beautiful Asian complexion glowed alabaster and her long, shiny black hair and dark eyes were flawless.

Christa had short blond hair cut in a bob with a severe angle. Although the wallflower out of the group, I knew from knowing Tate that those were usually the ones to show their awesomeness later.

All of the girls were dressed the same. Shorts and tank tops.

I smiled calmly. "Nice to meet all of you." I took out their diagnostic assessments—compositions they wrote at the end of the school year, including their outlines and rough drafts—and handed them their own papers. "So we're supposed to each share a sample paragraph and discuss what improvements we could make. Who would like to go first?"

No one budged. Jake sat next to me, looking as though he was ready to fall asleep. Ana looked away while Christa and Sydney smirked, challenging me.

"Anyone?" I asked, a grin tickling my face. I remembered my classes when no one would volunteer. Now I knew what being a teacher felt like.

I held up my hands. "I'll read it if someone wants to give me their paper. This time."

Jake shoved his paper in my face, still not making eye contact.

"Thank you, Jake." Relief flooded me.

I cleared my throat, reading out loud. "What do you do when you're hungry? You might go through a drive-through or hit the store. For eight hundred and forty-two million people in the world, they can't get food that easy."

I cleared my throat again, hearing the girls across from me snicker.

"That was a good opening paragraph." I nodded, keeping my voice light and looking at Jake even though he wasn't looking at me. "Asking a question right off the bat is a solid way to grab the reader. And I like your voice."

"He's barely talked since we sat down," Sydney joked. "How can you like his voice?"

"I meant the tone that comes through in his writing," I explained as if she didn't already know. "Expressions like 'hit the store' when most people would say 'go to the store' or 'drive to the store.' That's his personal voice. It makes the writing sound natural."

I caught Jake out of the corner of my eye, looking at me. I turned to him, wanting to be as kind as possible. The truth was, he needed a lot of work. His word choice was boring, he used adjectives when he should've used adverbs, and the sentences flowed like mud.

But I wasn't going to lay all that on him today.

"Two suggestions, though: The statistic you wrote wasn't cited. Readers won't know where you got that information and they won't trust it if you don't tell them the Web site, article, or text to which you're referring."

" 'To which you're referring,' " Sydney mimicked, and the paper crinkled in my hand.

"Is there a problem?" I asked, calling her out.

She rolled her eyes and whispered something to Christa.

"Another thing," I continued, trying to ignore her, "is that there is some passive language h-here," I stuttered, noticing Christa laughing into her hand and Sydney stealing glances at me. "You might want to spice it up," I tried to continue to Jake, "by saying—" And when all three of the girls laughed together, I stopped.

"What's going on?" I tried to keep my voice down.

The girls brought their hands down and folded their lips between their teeth to stifle smiles. Christa sighed sympathetically. "I'm just not sure why we're being tutored by someone that got arrested."

Son of a . . .

I narrowed my eyes and sat up straight. How the hell did everyone know? My mother definitely didn't tell anyone. And Principal Masters most certainly didn't tell anyone. What the hell?

"Everything okay here?" Penley stopped at our table as she circulated.

My chest fell with a hard sigh. "You might want to say 'For eight hundred and forty-two million people in the world,' " I continued to Jake, " 'the solution to hunger proves more difficult.' Using words like 'is,' 'was,' and 'am' is weak, so we try to use other verbs to make it sound better. Do you understand?"

Penley moved on to the next table, and I glared across the table to see that all the girls were concentrated on something out the window.

Jake shrugged. "I guess. So I have to go back and rewrite the whole thing?"

I shook my head, smiling. "Not today."

"Oh, my God!" Christa bounced off her chair and leaned across the counter underneath the window, peering out. "He's got his shirt off!" she whisper-yelled to her friends.

They scrambled out of their seats, Ana nearly falling in the process as they raced over to the window, giggling.

I shook my head, slightly amused, to be honest. I kind of missed being boy-crazy.

Sydney turned to her friends. "My sister says he's even better without his pants on."

One of them bounced up and down, while the other whimpered.

I wondered who they were talking about, and then I remembered Principal Masters saying something about the lacrosse team practicing every day.

Walking to the windows, I stood next to the girls and looked outside.

My shoulders sank, and I groaned. *Fuuuuuuck.* My heart suddenly felt as if it were too big for my rib cage as I watched a half-naked Jaxon Trent running around and rolling on the field as everyone horsed around with the water bottles.

"Damn, he's hot," Ana whispered, smoothing her hair as if Jax could actually see her. I felt like yanking her by her collar and sitting her ass down. He wasn't a piece of meat.

But I swallowed that urge. Gazing out the window, I watched Jax and the rest of the team grab their Gatorades and collapse on the grassy field, the sweat on their chests shiny from the sun's angry glare. His hair was wet, and he worked those long black shorts like a pro. I clamped my mouth shut before *I* whimpered.

He sat there, smiling and talking to a teammate, and I loved how even from here I could see his heart-stopping blue eyes.

He seemed oblivious that three teenage girls were gawking at him before he fell backward onto his back, resting.

"Girls," I choked out, my mouth as dry as jerky. "We've got work to do. You're here for a reason. And I'm here to help." I held out my arm, gesturing for them to come back to the table.

But Sydney didn't budge. "No, you're here because you're a fuckup, too," she shot back. "We're going to the bathroom."

And I watched as all three of them grabbed their purses and left. Scowling up at the clock, I gritted my teeth, noticing that I still had three whole hours left.

Luckily session two passed more smoothly. After Jake and the girls left, I got a group of three male students, and I relaxed right away, noticing that boys were a hell of a lot easier. Men simply wanted to do whatever you wanted them to do so you'd shut up. There was no arguing, no cattiness, and no chitchat. Other than some minor flirting, the only problem was disinterest.

It was going to be a long-ass summer.

At noon, all the students filtered out of the room to enjoy the rest of their summer day, and I finally reached into my bag to check my phone.

Four texts. No, five.

Tate: Jax not happy! You blew out his speakers? LOL!

Great. I'd given her hell about cutting Jared's electricity to shut down one of his parties. I was never going to hear the end of this.

Another from Tate. Heads up. Jared will be calling when he gets time. He needs to ask you something.

Hmm . . . okay.

Nik: Bored. Sooooo bored. Where are you?

I giggled quietly, missing my friend. I was about to dial her but decided to check my other messages first.

Mom: We need to meet for lunch this week. Call this evening.

Lunch? I grabbed the bag, swinging it over my shoulder as I walked out of the room, staring at my phone. Why did my mother want to have lunch?

When I got in trouble, she did nothing to help me. She had spoken to me only as much as she had to to let me know that I was not staying at home while I completed my community service. I'd felt alone and abandoned.

Now dread sat in my stomach like a ton of bricks, and the last thing I wanted to do was call her.

Checking the last message, I halted in the middle of the hallway.

Liam: Jax jumped me last night. Keep your new boyfriend away from me, or I go to the cops!!

Huh?

I dropped my arm and just stood in the empty hallway, probably looking as confused as I felt. Holding up the phone, I read the text again.

Jax jumped Liam?

Why? And why was Liam complaining to me about it?

Fisting the phone, I shook my head. Whatever. This was their problem. Not mine.

If Jax wanted to act like a child, that was on him. If Liam wanted to have the police laugh in his face, since they were obviously in the palm of Jax's hand, then let him.

Dumping the phone in my purse, I grabbed Tate's iPod, tuning it to Bananarama's "Cruel Summer," and stormed down the stairs and down the corridor to the rear of the school. Exiting through the back was a shortcut to Tate's house, and since I was already annoyed, I figured I might as well book back to the house and get changed for the one o'clock kickboxing class.

Looking down the hall, though, I stopped, seeing bodies scurrying through a door. I yanked out my earbuds.

"Hurry, hurry!" one of them whispered, but it was so loud I could still hear it yards away.

And even with the blur of short shorts and tank tops, I still recognized the girls.

Christa, Sydney, and Ana.

"Hey, are you all all right?" I headed up to the closed door that Sydney had just disappeared through and saw the sign that read ATH-LETICS.

Ana and Christa had spun around and were now staring at me wide-eyed, the blush of getting caught red all over their faces.

I smiled. "I'm not a teacher. Relax."

And they pinched their lips together, trying to hold back smiles while they snuck glances at each other.

"Where's Sydney?" I ventured, knowing damn well she'd gone through the door.

The sign didn't say that any specific gender was prohibited, but I did know that tutoring was over. The girls weren't supposed to be roaming the school.

"She's—," Christa started, but Ana nudged her with her elbow.

"She's . . . ?" I pressed.

When neither of them came clean, I turned to leave. "I think Ms. Penley is still here. . . ."

"She's in the weight room," Ana blurted out.

I turned around, narrowing my eyes. "Doing what?"

Both of the girls smirked, avoiding eye contact.

"Jaxon Trent," Christa deadpanned.

I froze. The softness from my face hardened into steel. "Go to the parking lot," I ordered. "I'll send her out." When they didn't move, I lost my cool. "Now," I ordered.

They covered smiles with their hands and veered around my immobile body, heading back down the corridor.

Heading through the ATHLETICS door, I walked down the dim, carpeted hallway with offices to my left and right. Coach Burns, the football coach and a history teacher. Coach McNally, the girls' tennis and soccer coach who also taught driver's ed. There were a few more offices, but I kept my eyes focused straight ahead on the big, heavy-looking wooden door that read WEIGHT ROOM.

I shook my head, trying to ignore the pounding of my heart in my chest. Jax wasn't really having sex with a seventeen-year-old girl in here. No, he was smarter than that, right?

And then I remembered the two girls I'd seen him with a couple of years ago. And I thought of Liam, who definitely wasn't as smart as I'd thought.

With my stomach clenching, I pushed lightly through the door and spotted both of them right away.

Separate and clothed. *Thank God.*

I let out a small breath and relaxed my shoulders. I didn't know why the hell I cared, but . . . I swallowed.

Just not her. He couldn't go for her.

The room was empty except for Jax and Sydney, and "Again" by Alice in Chains was playing on the CD player in the corner of the fully equipped room. I only knew the song because Tate listened to nothing but Alice in Chains when we'd first met. Two big fans were spinning from each side of the room, trying to keep it cool. The school had AC, but it was still stifling this time of year.

Jax was lying back on a black weight bench, a dumbbell in each hand as he spread his arms wide and then brought them back in and straight up over his body, flexing every muscle in his glowing, tanned arms, abs, shoulders, and pecs.

And I wanted her out of here.

He still wore the same knee-length black shorts as before, and his legs were spread, a foot resting on each side of the bench as a vision of me straddling him on that bench popped into my head.

I closed my eyes for a split second. *I'm so fucking warped.* I quickly swallowed the drool in my mouth before I accidentally drowned myself.

"You liked my sister."

I heard Sydney talking, with her back to me.

Jax's tone was clipped. "Your sister's cool."

"But not enough to come back for seconds," Sydney taunted in a sexy voice, stepping up to the weight bench. "Wanna see if I'm better?" she asked.

"Jesus Christ," Jax grumbled under his breath.

Dropping the dumbbells on the floor, he sat up and wiped his hand up his brow and over the top of his head, breathing hard.

Jax was pissed. I didn't know him well, but I knew that about him. Whenever I'd seen him angry, he always ran his hand through his hair. It was his tell.

"Sydney," I called, and watched both of their heads pop up to look at me. "Your friends are waiting in the parking lot. See you tomorrow."

Sydney paused, probably trying to figure out how she could get the upper hand. Jax was frozen, glaring at me under scary black eyebrows.

Sydney arched an eyebrow before walking past me out of the door. She almost brushed my shoulder, and I could smell the anger on her. I was going to pay for that tomorrow.

Cocking my head, I gave Jax an amused look.

He shook his head, grabbing his towel off the floor. "Don't give me that look. I didn't ask her to come in here."

"Like I care." I kept my voice casual, because I so totally did care. "Half the women in town have seen you naked."

He walked to a table, picking up a water bottle before turning his head to look at me. "That's an exaggeration." It sounded more like a warning instead of a statement.

And I watched him tilt his head back and gulp down mouthfuls of water.

Clearing my throat, I asked, "Why are you here? I thought you worked out at the gym."

He brought the bottle down and stood there, and I started to wonder if he was going to answer the question or not.

"I assist the coach with lacrosse practice."

Hmm. Well, that was cool. I hadn't pegged him for the volunteering type, but I wasn't sure why. He'd been in lacrosse in high school, and although he was cocky, he was also giving.

I'd noticed things like that in high school. He was generous. Generous with his time. Generous with his friends.

But shit. I let out a quiet sigh of frustration.

Jax was going to be around school a lot this summer. *Damn it.*

Walk. IPod. Escape. Remembering the quiet time I was looking forward to, I turned to leave, but then I remembered something.

I turned around and said, "I got a text from Liam, by the way."

"He texted you?" he asked, his eyes laughing. "Doesn't listen to directions very well, does he?"

"You told him not to contact me?" I crossed my arms over my chest. "I can handle him on my own, Jax. And he wasn't texting me before. Now he is, thanks to you, so just butt out."

A flush of anger spread down my body like a coat of paint.

"I didn't do it for you," he said matter-of-factly as he wiped down his body with the white towel. "Liam's had that coming for a long time now. He needed to be humbled."

Oh, what the . . .

"You've got some ego!" I yelled. "I mean, yeah, all of a sudden you have money. Where you get it from is too scary to even think about," I spouted off when I really should have just shut up. "And you seem to have the town's police in the palm of your hand. You're clearly running the Loop now. Congratulations, Jax." I smiled a big-ass, fake grin. "You're the most powerful man in Shelburne Falls, Illinois!"

I planted my hands on my hips, pretty damn pleased at how good I'd gotten at putting men in their place.

But then my smile dropped and my eyes rounded. Jax's eyes—full of challenge and amusement—narrowed on me, and he tossed his towel down, heading right for me.

Shit. I knew I should've listened to my mother. I talked too much.

He nodded, a grin playing at the corner of his mouth. "There she is."

I inched back to the wall as he advanced into my space. "What are you talking about?"

"The snarky girl I met at Madoc's house years ago."

Yeah, the one that was slightly drunk and hella confident? My head bobbed off the wall, signaling I was at a damn dead end, and a trickle of sweat skidded down my neck. I saw Jax's eyes flash to it, and all of a sudden I was too dumb to even remember my own name.

God, he was big. My chest vibrated with the heat of him only an inch away. He hovered over me, engulfing and consuming the space around me, making me feel as if I stood in the shadow of a tree.

Staring straight ahead, I made a conscious effort to keep my face straight. But it was almost impossible, and it was pointless. Out of all the reasons I could come up with for hating Jax—he always challenged and pushed me, and he always did whatever the hell he wanted—I could never claim that he wasn't smart. He knew I was affected. He knew my body liked him close.

"I love it when you get mouthy," he whispered down on me. "It makes me want to shut you up."

Son of a bitch. I clenched my thighs together, feeling about ready to scream at the moisture I felt there.

I needed to get out of here. "I have to go." I pushed off the wall but hit his chest, closing me in again.

"How do you like your community service?" he said low, trapping me by planting his hands on the wall on each side of my head.

Huh?

His smell was raw heat. Summer. Sticky cotton candy on a Ferris wheel and cool water on hot skin.

"What?" He'd asked me a question. What the fuck did he just ask?

He leaned on his hands, dipping his head close to mine. "Community service, K.C. How do you like it?"

I could hear the laughter in his voice. Little shit.

"I don't," I mumbled. "Teaching a bunch of kids who slacked off during the school year, because they didn't get the attitude adjustment they needed, isn't my idea of a good time."

His arms lowered a bit, and I could hear him inhaling through his nose, as if he was smelling me.

"Your idea of a good time got you here in the first place." His voice was calm but firm. "And those kids don't need an attitude adjustment. You do."

I smirked. "Well, I'm getting one, thanks to the great state of Arizona." Then I pinned him with hard eyes. "You don't know me, Jax." And I pushed him away and turned for the door.

But he hooked my arm, pulling me back.

"You're right," he said quickly. "I don't know you. So why don't you enlighten me? What does K.C. stand for? What did you do at college that got you arrested?"

When I just stood there, not answering his stupid questions, he backed me into the wall again. "Let's try something easier, shall we? Your favorite color. What is it?"

"Are you serious?"

"Are you stalling?"

I scowled. "Pink. It's pink."

"Is it?" he pressed. "How about music? Who's your favorite band? What about books? Your favorite genre? When was the last time you ate chocolate or stayed in your pajamas past eleven in the morning?"

I didn't know if the walls were closing in or if it was just Jax crowding me. "What are you getting at, you little shit?" I accused.

And he got in my face, smiling at the challenge of my condescending name-calling. "How about a shower, K.C.?" The sound of his deep, husky voice swirled in my stomach and shot downward.

I gulped, licking my sandpaper lips. "Huh?"

He stared at my mouth, looking hungry. "The little shit—who's not so little anymore—needs a shower," he whispered, still staring at my mouth. "Take a shower with me. Right now."

I flattened my hands against the wall, the cool white-painted concrete blocks relieving the heat in my chest. Where the hell was he going with this? He didn't want a shower with me.

I arched an eyebrow, trying to appear calmer than I was. "You called me gutless and helpless, Jax. Now you want to shower with me?"

"Show me, then." There was a sincere look in his eyes, serious, as if he was searching my face for something. "Show me you're not gutless. Take a chance." He narrowed his eyes, imploring me, and I think I swallowed my heart, because my whole damn body was throbbing.

"I'm being serious," he said quietly. "The team's gone. We'd be alone. Walk into the locker room with me. Get in the shower with me. Show me how bold you are."

I tried to say no, but the word was stuck in my throat. I wanted to say it, but I wouldn't have meant it.

He reached down and took my pinky, rolling it between his fingers.

Looking down, he continued in the softest whisper. "I won't touch you if you don't want me to." And then he raised his gaze, killing me with the hint of sadness in his blue eyes. "You only have to walk, K.C. That's it. I'll get you out of your clothes. All you have to do is follow me. I know you want to."

I dropped my eyes, and my face felt as if it would splinter in pain into a thousand cracks like paint on a China doll. Tears burned my eyes.

I did want to. I wanted someone to hold me and touch me, wanting to be with me.

He leaned in, the breath from his mouth fanning my lips. "Take a chance," he whispered.

I fisted my hands, then stretched my fingers and fisted them again. The urge was there. To reach out and touch him. Wrap my arm around his neck. Take his hand and let him lead me.

But I didn't even have the will to make my legs move. He'd laugh at me. He'd use me. He'd see nothing worth keeping around. Soon he'd hate me.

Blinking away the tears, I looked up, not caring that he saw my watery eyes. And I shook my head.

He studied me, searching my expression, and I couldn't tell if he was angry, disappointed, or disgusted.

He dropped his arms and stood up straight, the warm bubble his body created around me gone cold. "You're afraid of yourself," he said flatly. "Not me."

And then he backed up, looking down at me and down on me. "And that's why you're gutless, K.C."

Gutless. I bared my teeth, so fucking sick of him saying that.

"I have to shower." All the softness from his voice was now gone. "You need to leave."

And he turned around and strode for the men's locker room.

I shook my head. *I'm not gutless. I don't want to be gutless.*

I sniffled and cleared my throat, standing tall. "Maybe I just don't want you," I blurted out, and steeled my body when he spun around, looking surprised. "Maybe I just don't want you, Jax."

And I breathed out a small laugh as I spun around and headed for the door.

But before I even reached the handle, an arm circled my waist, yanking me back into his warm body, and I gasped just as my hair was swiped to the side and a hot mouth was on my neck.

Everything fell apart.

My knees buckled, my eyes closed, and my neck fell to the side, inviting him in.

Oh, my God.

I couldn't think. I couldn't pull away. I couldn't stop him. His scorching mouth spread over my neck, breathing hot air on my skin that was already on fire, and he barely moved, as if he'd lost control just like me. As if he had just craved the contact. His teeth grazed my skin, rough but not hard, and he slid his lips and teeth over the sensitive area under my ear, and I wasn't sure if he was kissing me or getting ready to eat me.

My chest shook, and I held on to his arm across my waist, but I didn't need to. He held me so tight I couldn't take in the deep breaths I hungered for.

But I could feel him, and that was all I cared about. His cock pressed into my back, and I writhed into him as his lips started moving on my skin. He scattered short kisses across my neck, at the base, and under my ear. His tongue flicked my earlobe right before his other hand reached around and turned my chin to him.

And then his mouth was on mine. I moaned, probably sounding as though I was in pain, but I couldn't help it. The tornado between my legs was powerful and sweet, and it made me feel like an animal. Wild and . . . just simply wild.

Jax's tongue found mine, and I groaned into his mouth, inhaling his scent while his powerful body held me. The heat, the wetness, the taste, everything was hard and fast as his lips worked mine.

As he kept an arm around my waist, his other hand left my face and went straight under my skirt into my underwear.

"Oh," I whimpered a muffled groan into his mouth that still held me hostage. What was he doing? I needed to stop this!

But my eyes fluttered as his smooth fingers dipped into my center, swirling the wetness already there around my clit.

And then his mouth left mine, and he yanked me up off my feet and growled in my ear.

"You're so wet for me, K.C." His voice was hard and threatening. "Gutless, helpless, and a fucking liar, too."

And then he dropped me, and I fell on my ass to the mats, shaking with confusion.

All I heard behind me was a door open and close, and I knew I was alone.

Bringing a shaky hand to my mouth, I sucked in air as if it were going out of style. *Holy shit.*

CHAPTER 5

K.C.

The air in the high school sat like a layer of wet clothes on my skin, dense and moist. It almost took effort to move through it on my way to the front office.

But I liked it.

Adding to the dimly lit hallways and the sound of rain threatening harder and harder against the roof, the atmosphere drowned out the evidence that anyone else lived in the world but me. And I needed that feeling right now.

More than just Jax's kiss had hit a nerve the other day, and I kept swirling his words around in my head. How was it that he knew me so well? He anticipated every argument that came out of my mouth and calculated my reactions, knowing the outcome beforehand, and I couldn't keep up. Now, a week later, he was still on my mind as much as food and breathing.

I really wanted to hit him, and I wasn't sure why.

Christ. I tucked my hair behind my ear as I continued down the hall.

It had started storming an hour ago. Since they kept most of the lights off in the school during the summer days—except for the ones in the classroom—to conserve electricity, the only reminder that it was late morning was the reflections of rain bouncing off the windows and their shadows dancing on the walls. We'd just finished both sessions, but you wouldn't know it. Already the school was nearly empty. Cheerleading and lacrosse never showed up, because of the weather, and at least a third of the tutoring students were absent as well.

Tutoring. I let out a sigh, moving down the steps.

Our progress had been slow during the past few days, the kids having mentally checked out because of summer break, I was sure. Although I had a few students I enjoyed—Ana was actually cooperative and apt with her skills—the lot of them were a struggle, and I knew I was doing something wrong. They wouldn't volunteer, they wouldn't answer questions, and they weren't happy. I sucked.

But when I looked around at the other tutors and their groups, I saw the same pattern. Disinterest and flat-out boredom. Of course, who would want to spend their summer break cooped up in a hot classroom when their friends were at Swansea Lake swimming, drinking, and making out? And why should I worry if they succeeded in school? If they didn't care, then neither should I.

But that was a shit response, and I knew it. I did care.

"Those kids don't need an attitude adjustment. You do."

Damn Jax.

Jax, whom I had barely seen since the kiss last Monday.

Jax, who had me stealing looks out the window as he ran, laughed, and sweated on the field.

Jax, who literally dumped me on my ass after kissing me breathless in the weight room.

Jax, who used to watch me in high school, and now I was the one watching him.

I dug in my heels, pulled open the main office door, and stepped through, looking around for a sign of anyone. The room was spooky, void of any light, life, or noise aside from the echoes of rain coming from every direction. The reflection of the storm created bubbles of light on all the countertops, and the sound of waterfalls surrounded me, hitting all four walls.

The storm was picking up, and I wondered how I was getting home, as I usually walked. I had to remember to call Shane.

"This isn't up for discussion." I twisted my head at the bark coming from the nurse's office.

Who . . . ?

But the voice continued. "As I said . . ."

Forgetting the reams of paper I was supposed to be collecting from under the counter, I inched toward the open door of the nurse's office a couple of doors down the hallway.

My short, layered black skirt wafted silently over my thighs, and I rubbed the chill from my arms, bare in their turquoise tank top.

"Yeah, Jared. I know who our father is."

I stopped, my stomach doing a somersault. It was Jax. And he was talking to his brother.

"I took a hell of a lot more beatings than you did," he growled. "So stop trying to protect me."

Beatings?

Stepping up to the open door, I tilted my head to peek inside, and instantly felt the butterflies take flight in my stomach.

Jax was a bloody mess. Literally.

He was dressed in long black mesh shorts with black running shoes. His hair was still pulled back tight to his scalp, but it stuck to his wet back, and I wasn't sure if it was sweat from working out in the weight room or rain from being outside. He held his cell phone between his ear and his shoulder as he stalked around the room, apparently looking for something. Clearly having a hard time, because he was holding a hand up to a scrape on his stomach even though the one on his elbow was dripping crimson blood on the tiled floor.

I could hear Jared's voice on the other end, but it was too faint to make out what he was saying.

Jax was swinging open cabinet doors and slamming them shut again, and while he appeared to be battered up, I got the feeling his irritation wasn't about the scrapes.

"If he gets out early, then he gets out!" he shouted, and I winced as he kicked a cabinet shut. "You get your fucking restraining order, and leave me out of it," he commanded. "If he comes near me, I'm putting a knife in his throat."

And I heard Jared's voice loud and clear this time. "Don't give me something else to worry about!"

Jax didn't respond. He yanked the phone away from his ear, pushed a button, and threw it on one of the cots.

"Son of a bitch," he grunted, bowing his head into the arm that he had propped against the cabinet.

His chest rose and fell quickly, his breathing labored, but I knew it wasn't from his injuries. I stood there, chewing the inside of my lip, knowing that I should just back away and get out of there. He'd been a total ass to me ever since I got back into town.

But instead of getting away from him, my instinct was to . . . *what?* Make sure that he was okay?

Truth was, I actually liked seeing him like this. Completely out of control—and I was in awe.

He was hunched forward slightly, and as the seconds passed, I heard his breathing turn slow and steady.

I'd never seen Jax really worked up. Jared sported his temper like a flare in the sky. He shot off bold and bright, blazing through the crowd so everyone within an easy distance knew when he was angry.

Jax always—always—moved with stealth and precision, as if all his decisions were premeditated and calculated. I often found myself wondering if Jax ever slept, or instead stayed up, planning his days to anticipate every conversation he might have or every turn he might have to take.

But really, what would it take for him to lose control? Kind of like the way he just did? And why was I hungry to see his temper again?

His father, I thought. That was definitely a twist of the screw that drove him close to the edge.

Just like me.

I licked my lips and spoke up. "Lie down."

He dropped his hand and swung around to pin me with angry eyes, as if he knew it was me right away.

Those azure jewels held me frozen for about two seconds, and I noticed the way the flawless caramel skin of his face tightened and his jaw hardened, bringing out smooth hollows in his cheeks and the severe slant of his black eyebrows.

Someday, I told myself. Someday we might look at each other when one of us wasn't scowling.

I used to be the one shooting daggers at him. Now he was looking at me as if I were a four-year-old who needed to be tolerated.

"Lie down," I urged, staying calm. "I'll find the saline wash and bandages."

I caught sight of his eyes narrowing, regarding me suspiciously, before I veered around him to the cabinets along the wall.

But then I felt a hand wrap around my upper arm, and I stopped to look up.

His whole face was a mask—nothing was getting out. I followed a trail of water that cascaded down his temple to his cheekbone, and I swear a tinge of salt hit the air. I licked my lips.

His Adam's apple moved up and then down before he spoke. "I can do this myself." His voice came out raspy.

I arched an eyebrow, and my eyes dropped to his fingers wrapped around my arm. "I never said you couldn't," I said, and peeled one of his fingers off my arm, bringing the rest with it.

Turning back around, I busied myself finding the wound wash and the bandages, and tried to keep myself from being aware of every move he made. My ears picked up his squeaky footsteps as he left my side and then the creak of the cot as he settled his weight.

I pulled my bottom lip in between my teeth, reaching up to grab the saline wash, and accidentally knocked a bottle of peroxide out of the cabinet. Thankfully the bottle was plastic, but I still fumbled as I dived down to snatch it off the floor.

Jax and I were alone, and it wasn't a fluke. I was a mess around him. Every time.

He was half-naked and lying on a bed. The school was dark, nearly deserted, and—damn it—I squeezed my eyes shut, releasing a long, smooth breath as I shoved all the items into my arms and powered over to the cots.

Jax was not lying down.

I stared at him, lying half on and half off the cot, and it was only when I heard something drop to the floor that I realized my muscles were failing me and I'd dropped something. Tightening my arms closed again, I blinked and averted my eyes before dumping the supplies on the bed next to him.

His black sneakers were planted to the floor, while the top half of his long body lay on the cot. Not so unusual. Maybe he felt vulnerable laying his whole body down.

No, the weird part was that he'd propped himself up on his elbows, and that was what got my arms pumping with liquid nerves.

He was going to watch.

I took a deep breath and leaned down to open up some bandages. "Lie back," I mumbled, feeling his eyes follow me.

"No."

What?

I shot my eyes over to him and immediately froze. Jax's eyes stared right through me, unblinking. They slid down my tank top, and as his gaze traveled back up to my face, I saw the corner of his mouth curl, looking relaxed and amused. And that was it.

Jaxon Trent was the goddamn devil.

I shook my head. "I'm trying to be nice. You could, too."

"Nice?" He laughed to himself. "I don't want your nice."

I clenched my teeth. What the hell was his problem?

Grabbing the bottle of peroxide I'd dropped on the floor, I unscrewed the cap and poured a short stream onto the gash on his stomach.

He hissed and grabbed some gauze, covering the wound. "What the hell?"

"Oops," I chirped, and screwed the cap back on.

I dumped the bottle on the cot, kicked his feet apart, and knelt between his legs. And I watched him watch me as I placed my hands on his thighs and slowly lowered my head to his wound. Peeling his hand away, I blew a cool, light breath over his bubbling cuts, soothing the sting I'd created.

Out of the corner of my eye, I saw his body jerk and then go completely still as if he weren't even breathing. I puckered my lips and blew soft breath after soft breath across his narrow abdomen, moving my head side to side along the short range of shallow cuts.

A hint of his scented body wash wafted around me, along with the rain and sweat, and I closed my eyes, losing myself to the fuzz in my brain.

"K.C.," he breathed out, and I looked up to see his head drop back as he closed his eyes. His chest rose and fell hard, and I couldn't look away. His torso went on for miles, and his Adam's apple bobbed up and down.

He loved this, and for fuck's sake, I was half tempted to kiss him better.

Leaning back on my heels, I looked up at him, my lips twitching with a smile. "You like my nice," I said, teasing.

I smirked and stood up on my knees, grabbing the saline solution and gauze as he brought his head back up to watch me.

"So, how did this happen?" I asked, holding the gauze on his skin, under the cuts, to catch the saline.

His abs flexed, probably from the cold fluid, since saline didn't sting, as I poured it over the cuts, cleaning them.

He sucked in air through his teeth. "Some of the science kids have greenhouses on the roof," he grunted, and I almost laughed out loud. "Masters asked me to go up and make sure the roofs were closed, but I slipped coming back down the stairs. Scraped myself on some bolts."

Ouch.

I used the rest of the gauze to wipe up the solution, and then ripped open a package with a wet wipe and made sure the blood was cleared up.

"You should be using gloves," he pointed out. "You know? Blood and all."

"I thought any girl was safe with you," I shot back, tearing open bandages. "Isn't that what you told me?"

Jax was silent for a minute, narrowing his eyes further and watching me as I placed three rectangular bandages on his stomach.

"I said any girlfriend of mine," he finally clarified. "But you shouldn't be so careless. Use gloves next time."

I ignored him, feeling weird on the occasions he acted like this.

Jax had a habit of scolding me, sometimes acting as though he was protecting me, and then following it all up with being an asshole. I finally figured out condescension was his way of gaining superiority. Making others feel stupid.

I sat back, looking him in the eye and changing the subject. "Is anything else hurt?"

He hesitated only a moment. And then folded his arm back, lifting his right elbow to reveal the scratches I'd noticed earlier.

Repeating the same procedure, I stood up and leaned over him, catching the saline wash as it cascaded over his wound and into the gauze.

He hissed, and I blinked.

"Blow on it," he ordered.

"It doesn't sting," I scoffed, knowing damn well that saline didn't hurt.

"K.C., Jesus," he barked, wincing.

I rolled my eyes but gave in. Holding the underside of his arm—his hard triceps—I leaned down and released a slow, cool breeze over the scratches. Jax's scent wafted over me again, and I desperately wanted to close my mouth so I could breathe him in through my nose.

But I didn't. I could tell his eyes were on me.

"Why are you watching me?" I asked, wiping up the rest of the solution and blood.

I didn't look at him, but I heard him swallow.

"This is just the first time you've ever made me feel good, is all," he replied in probably the most candid way I'd ever heard him speak.

I pinched my eyebrows together.

The first time I'd ever made him feel good. I didn't know what to say to that. Hell, I had nothing to say to that.

Keeping quiet, I finished applying his bandages as fast as I could and didn't meet his eyes again. He'd tried to be nice to me in high school. He'd tried to be a friend. Maybe friends with benefits but still a friend. Now here I was, forcing my attention on him, and he probably had no patience for me anymore.

"Can I ask you a question?" I ventured.

"What?"

"That night you drove Liam home . . ." I swallowed, smoothing my fingers over the bandage I'd fixed to his arm. "You said you had tattoos. Too many." I repeated his words, my eyes fixated on his forearm. "What did you mean?" I pressed, because clearly Jax didn't sport any tattoos. His statement hadn't made any sense.

Even though I hadn't looked at him, I noticed his head turn away as he inhaled a slow, deep breath. Kind of as though he was getting ready to dive deep underwater and knew he wouldn't be up for air for a while.

"Sorry," I said quietly, straightening up and crumpling the bandage wrappers in my fist. "I just . . . I don't know . . ." I trailed off. "I just want to understand."

I finally met his eyes, and he studied me silently. I didn't know if he was trying to figure out what to tell me or if he wanted to tell me anything at all. Funny thing was, I'd thought about what Jax said that night a lot over the years, and while I was curious, it wasn't until I'd overheard his conversation with Jared today that I knew it had something to do with his childhood.

And I realized that I didn't know Jaxon Trent at all.

He rubbed his forearm and narrowed his eyes briefly before relaxing. "If you could get a tattoo, what would it be?"

I blinked, shocked by his question. "Um." I laughed softly, thinking. "I thought about a set of angel wings, I guess. With one of the wings broken," I admitted.

"It has something to do with your past?"

I nodded. "Yes."

"And it's something you want to remember?" he pressed.

"Yes."

"That's why I don't have any tattoos," he concluded. "People get tattoos for all kinds of reasons, but they're always badges of what has made them who they are. I don't care to remember what and who made me this way. The people that gave me life. The people that brought me up . . ." He shook his head, defiant. "The places I've seen or anything I've done. It's all in my head, anyway. I don't want it on my body, too. I don't care about anything that much."

His sneer wasn't for me, but I knew I'd hit a sensitive area. And I kind of understood where he was coming from. The scars were on the inside—still doing their damage—and he didn't want reminders when he looked in the mirror.

Our friends had been lucky. Tate's mother—although deceased—had loved her. Her dad? Always there for her. Hell, even Jared's mom had turned out pretty awesome. And Shane's parents were overbearing, but they were compassionate.

And I finally saw what connected Jaxon Trent and me. How very different our lives would've been without our neglectful parents. Or with different parents.

"No mothers, no fathers," I whispered to myself.

"Huh?"

I blinked, shaking my head. "Nothing."

I barely noticed it, but when my lungs started to burn, I realized I wasn't breathing.

I took a deep breath and picked up the supplies, standing up. "Your brother is important to you, right?" I asked. "Jared, Madoc, Tate . . . Maybe someday you'll see how lucky you really are or find something or someone you do care enough about."

Maybe me, too, I thought as I walked to the cabinets, putting the materials away.

Nice and tidy, the way I had found them.

Light flashed through the room, and moments later I heard the thunder roll outside.

Shit. I still hadn't called Shane.

I heard the cot creak behind me and knew Jax had stood up. "It's raining," he said. "I'll give you a ride home. Come on."

I turned to find him standing in the doorway, filling up the frame and slipping his gray T-shirt over his head, a tear and bloodstains visible on the material.

Jesus. I damn near gulped at the way his ab muscles flexed and the V underneath disappeared into his shorts. The shirt draped loosely over his stomach, but the dips and curves of his biceps took up every spare bit of space in his short sleeves. Tall, with just the right amount of muscle, he was perfect. And I'd bet every woman thought the same damn thing when she looked at him.

Sex.

I turned back to the cabinets, trying to slow my breathing and not think of Jax and me alone in a car.

"I'll give you a ride home." I shook my head. *Yeah, hell to the no.*

"That's okay," I mumbled with my back to him. "I'll call Shane."

"If you even think of putting your cousin on the road in this weather," he threatened in a smooth, deep voice, "I may have to see what I can do to get you on your knees again today."

My face fell, and my tongue went dry. *Little shit.*

"Don't piss me off, K.C. I'll be in front of the building in five minutes."

And then he was gone.

Jax's car used to be Jared's. I'd seen it plenty over the years, and although it was older than Liam's Camaro, it was definitely a hell of a lot tougher. Or maybe it just felt more solid. I don't know. I remember being in Liam's car, waiting at a stoplight and feeling as if the car's engine was going to die or something. Just the way it puttered felt as though it was about to give out at any moment.

But, sitting in Jax's black Mustang GT, I felt as if I were sitting in a turbo jet as solid as a bullet the way it glided effortlessly through the torrential downpour. Inside, the spotless black interior was dark and narrow, like being in a cave. Outside, the wind blew sheets of rain across the windshield. I had to squint to see, because the windshield wipers could barely keep up with the downpour.

But the car provided a haven from the rain pounding on the rooftop outside, and the spray under the tires was a distant echo.

Even though I was safe and warm, I couldn't shake the nerves making the hair on my arms stand up. I clenched my skirt in my fists and looked at nothing out the window.

He was too close. And—I rubbed my fists down my warm thighs— he wasn't close enough.

"Here." Jax spoke up, startling me. He reached behind in the backseat and tossed me a towel. "It's clean."

Of course it was. Jax might get his hands dirty from time to time, but his clothes and his car—at least from what I'd seen on the outside—were always impeccably clean. Hell, even his house looked pristine when I'd been in there.

"Thanks," I said as I caught it at my chest.

Something to do. Anything . . .

I reached down and brushed off the droplets of rain that had drenched my legs, and then slipped out of my flip-flops to pat my feet dry.

I hadn't gotten completely soaked, and Jax had driven the car as close to the school as he could, but I still caught an onslaught of fat drops. My clothes were blotched with nickel-size circles, and some of my hair was sticking to my neck and shoulders.

Brushing up my thighs, I straightened my back against the seat and wiped the water off my bare arms.

But I was still shit out of luck.

He was watching me, and I could damn well feel it.

Turning around, I placed the towel in the backseat again and stilled when the grumbling of my stomach—evidence that I hadn't eaten since breakfast—burst forth in the otherwise quiet car.

Shit. I twisted back around and fastened my seat belt, hoping he hadn't heard it.

No such luck.

"Are you hungry?" Jax looked over at me. "I have some snacks if you want."

"No, I'm fine," I mumbled, not making eye contact.

But then my belly whirred again, and I closed my eyes and wrapped my arms around my stomach, melting into the seat.

"Oh, for Christ's sake," he chuckled, and I opened my eyes to see him reaching behind the seat again and digging a container out of his duffel bag. "Eat," he ordered, dumping a plastic Tupperware container in my lap.

I pursed my lips. Why did he have to sound so condescending all the time?

"I'm fine," I said flatly, turning my glare out the window. "I'll be home soon anyway."

"So I can give you a ride home, but you won't eat my food?"

My eyes widened, and I looked over at him. "You made me let you give me a ride home," I pointed out, and then added quietly, "Which I appreciate. Of course."

I shook my head, unable to keep the small smile from my lips.

"Fine," I grumbled. "I'll eat."

And it took me no damn time to peel the lid off the container and smile at the watermelon chunks inside. Picking one out with my thumb and index finger, I joked. "Fruit?" I asked. "I'd never pictured you chopping watermelon, Jax."

"But you pictured me," he deadpanned, his cocky lips twisting up as he pulled the shifter down, powering ahead as if he knew everything.

I rolled my eyes, not even entertaining the idea of walking into that one any further. Sliding a piece of watermelon between my teeth, I bit the red cube in half, loving the grainy texture against my tongue. Sweet juice filled my mouth, and my stomach growled again, in appreciation.

Sucking the nectar to the back of my tongue, I swallowed and placed a hand over my mouth. "This is really good." I nearly laughed, because I hadn't realized how hungry I was. "Thanks."

But glancing over at Jax, I lost my smile immediately. His straight face was focused out on the road, and he looked almost angry. The car had slowed, and an air of awkwardness had settled in his narrowed eyes.

"Am I eating your lunch?" I asked, all of a sudden feeling angry that he had bullied me into eating. "I told you I was fine—"

He cut me off. "Eat. Please."

And I saw his Adam's apple bob as he swallowed, looking unsettled.

Unsure about his change in mood, I couldn't figure out what to do. So I finally just continued munching, feeling the void in my stomach filling as Jax drove us through waterlogged streets.

Crossfade's "The Deep End" filled the space around us, and I was lost, barely trying to hide how I watched him.

He did the whole guy thing as he drove—body pressed into the seat back, arm steel-rod straight on the steering wheel at twelve o'clock, and chin down. But whenever he shifted up or down, my gaze flashed to his hand, reveling in the cords of his forearm and how they flexed when he changed speeds. And I loved how the car gained momentum and the engine roared and vibrated, making my thighs shake.

I wanted to be able to drive like that.

I'd never asked Liam to teach me, even though he probably would have. Aside from all the damn cheating, my boyfriend—er, ex-boyfriend—was actually a nice guy and easy to get along with.

But I never thought I could learn. Which was stupid. I held my own in school. It wasn't as though I was incapable of learning something new.

I kept eating, glancing down every time he shifted to watch him. Trying to memorize how he timed pressing in the clutch with shifting the gears and chewing as I studied his legs and arms all working to keep the car going.

My mother had taken me to the symphony in Chicago when I was little, and I remember watching the conductor while everyone else watched the musicians. The power of leading, of knowing when to push and pull, fascinated me. I was envious of having control like that. Of guiding so many instruments in a unified effort to create something so beautiful. It was like a magnificent puzzle, and you just had to find the right way—or maybe just your way—to fit them all together.

I chewed softly, watching Jax, my eyes moving up and down, following his movements, and I knew damn well that given the choice of the conductor or Jaxon Trent, I'd watch Jaxon Trent.

His long fingers clutching the shift, the muscular calves flexing every time they punched the clutch, the blue eyes that I swore turned black and intense as they stared out the window.

I could watch him work his car forever.

"You need to stop watching me like that." I heard his voice, and I jerked my attention up to his face.

Shit!

He was still staring out the windshield, lips slightly open and looking cautious.

"What?" I asked, trying to act as though I didn't know what he was talking about, and I wasn't just drooling over his driving. But it was useless. My cheeks had warmed, and I'm sure it showed.

"You're going to get us in a fucking accident," he scolded.

I scowled. "Me? What did I do?"

He shook his head, letting out a small laugh. "Do me a favor, would you?" His voice was soft and smooth, threatening in how quickly he turned sensual.

He shot his eyes to me, and I closed my mouth, gulping the bit of watermelon I'd been chewing. Why the hell was he looking at me like that?

He jerked his chin at me. "The watermelon juice spilling over your lip?" he indicated. "Lick it up or I will."

I dropped the piece in my hand and stared at him, stunned and hoping he was kidding. The dare in his eyes, the menace in his soft voice, the danger traveling from his side of the car over to mine—it was no joke. I blinked and turned my gaze back out the front windshield.

Fuck my life.

Darting out my tongue, I snatched up any remnants of juice from my lips and sealed the container back up.

My phone began chirping from my bag, and I reached down to retrieve it, thankful for the distraction. But looking at the screen, I winced.

My mother again. She'd called twice and had now sent another text.

Tate's house. Ten minutes.

I shook my head and stuffed the phone back into my bag, swallowing the bad taste in my mouth. What the hell did she want?

First she didn't even bother to make sure I made it home okay, and only a few days later she was calling and texting. Maybe she just couldn't stand the fact that I hadn't called her, but all I knew for sure was that I didn't want to see her. Not today and maybe not for a while.

"Who was that?" Jax questioned.

I sighed, still looking out the window. Why lie? "My mom. She's waiting at Tate's house."

"Why?"

I shrugged, feeling the sadness descend on me. It wasn't that I wouldn't talk to him. I couldn't. Who knew what would happen if I tried opening my mouth right now? And how easily the thought of her face, her voice, her presence had sucked dry the blissful little bubble I'd just been in?

"How am I supposed to know?" I griped. "You ask too many questions."

I didn't want to see her. I didn't want to hear her voice. I didn't want her hands on me.

I pursed my lips together, avoiding Jax's eyes that I could feel on the back of my head.

We rounded the corner onto Fall Away Lane, the weight of the rain barely affecting the speed at which Jax traveled.

I closed my eyes. *Please keep going. Please.* I clutched the door handle, the hollow ache in my stomach growing as he traveled closer and closer.

Three seconds.

Two.

And then one.

But he didn't stop.

He didn't stop! My eyes went wide, and I spun my head around to see his self-satisfied eyebrow arched.

"What are you doing? Where are you going?" I blurted out, planting my right hand on the dash to support myself as he picked up speed again.

"You want to go home?" he challenged.

No. "Uh . . . um," I stuttered.

"Good." He smiled at me and shifted into a higher gear—I could only tell because the speed picked up again. "I can relate," he sympathized. "I wouldn't want to see my parents, either."

"Okayyy," I drawled. "So, where do you think you're taking me?"

He didn't answer. He turned up the music and forged ahead through the dense storm and deserted streets.

CHAPTER 6

K.C.

The Loop was the town's unofficial racing ring. Frequented throughout high school by every guy with a car to race or money to bet, it was nothing more than a dirt track circling a very large pond on the Benson Farm property.

Or it used to be.

"Jax, I think you should just take me home," I said, trying to hide the bite from my voice as we turned onto the long driveway leading only one place.

I hated the Loop.

I hated cars. I hated not knowing about cars. I hated that my ex-boyfriend had met another girl here in high school. I hated that everyone was comfortable here except me.

And I hated that I was so insecure and ignorant that I was no more than wallpaper during events here.

"I've got you alone," Jax teased. "And you're not looking at me like I just pissed on your Prada for once," he continued. "Let's have some fun."

I scowled. "Um, unless your plan is to get me naked—which won't happen—I can't imagine why you thought this would be fun for either one of us. I mean, what am I supposed to do here?"

"Drive."

My heart pitter-pattered. "Excuse me?"

"You heard me."

What? But . . . how? I couldn't drive a stick! I tapped my feet, ready to dive out of the car, and I barely noticed that the crackle of gravel had disappeared under the tires.

I sucked in air, trying to fucking decide which battle to fight first. "Is the track paved now?" I blurted out.

The track now sported a concrete foundation, and it had been doubled in width. A few small sets of bleachers sat off to the side, and where viewers had once parked on the grass to the sides, now there was a set space.

"Jax?" I mumbled, taking in what I could through the blur of the rain. Were those stoplights at the finish line? And I looked off to the left. Was that a stand for the . . . announcer? Seriously?

"What's happened here?"

"Look at me," Jax ordered, ignoring my damn question.

I turned and met his eyes, forgetting my own damn question.

He pulled to a stop and set the parking brake. "How many guys have you had sex with other than Liam?"

My eyebrows did a nosedive. "Are you for real? Just get me out of here."

What the hell was he doing?

His voice stayed light, with the hint of a laugh, as he held up his hands in defense. "I'm not trying to piss you off, Precious," he teased, leaning his head back against the headrest and peering over at me. "I'm trying to make a point, okay? Driving a stick is like sex," he stated.

"Every person you're with is different. They're like a code that needs to be broken." He turned and ran his hands up both sides of the steering wheel, slow and smooth. "What parts like to be touched." His sensual voice started stirring its way through my body. "Licked. Sucked. Bitten."

Holy hell.

"Hell, some people don't even need to be touched," he pointed out. "Looking, teasing, playing mind games—everyone has that spot that jacks them into sixth gear, K.C." And I stared, watching his every move as he turned and looked at me, speaking softly. "And this car is no different."

"First, you have to find the clutch," he instructed, and I yelped when he slammed his foot down, pushing in the lever. *Jesus.*

Releasing the parking brake, he placed one hand on the wheel and the other on the stick in sweet, luscious perversion.

"Then you have the gas." He smirked, and his eyes stayed on me as he revved the engine but didn't go anywhere. "Working the two together, you find the sweet spot. The point where she lets you take control."

She?

"Push it." He tapped the leg pressing into the clutch, and I licked my lips frantically, because my mouth was so dry. "And then accelerate her slowly"—he tapped the gas leg, and I heard him rev the engine again—"as you release her clutch . . . slowly."

His legs moved, one coming up and the other moving down.

"Give-and-take," he continued, eyes still holding me. "If I push her too fast, she crumbles." He released the clutch, and I bobbed with the car as it died.

He pressed in the clutch and the brake and turned the key to the ignition again. "If I don't push her fast enough, she'll never move." And he held in the clutch, unmoving, as he revved the engine with no success. "Push and pull. Accelerate and release." I watched his legs work, releasing the clutch and accelerating the gas.

With my legs throbbing under me, I stared wide-eyed as Jax released the clutch and pressed the gas, vaulting down the track.

Grabbing hold of the dash, I peered outside at the vacant lane and let a small smile creep across my lips. It was definitely more fun being in the car than off to the side as a spectator. But I wanted to drive. I'd always been in awe of Jared and Tate, and I'd always wanted to learn, too.

"Eyes on me," Jax barked.

I twisted my head over to him and sat back.

"Manual transmissions are like sex to get them going, but they're also like sex to keep them going. Sometimes you have to change gears, speeding up or"—he turned his head to look at me—"slowing down when you need to."

He jammed in the clutch and yanked the shifter down, released the clutch, and gassed it again. As we powered ahead, he did the same thing again, only he shifted up and to the right this time.

"Every time you change gears, you simply need to press the right buttons and find the magic spot again. When you want to speed up, shift up. When you want to slow down, shift down." And he tapped the head of the shifter, indicating the diagram to where the levels were.

He circled the whole track, slowing down and shifting down when he rounded the corners and then speeding, shifting, and then speeding more when he accelerated. His legs, long and powerful, were in complete sync with whatever his arms were doing, and even though the car swerved in the rain and even spun out a little on the slick turns, Jax was like a conductor, pressing, releasing, shifting, and pushing.

Pressing, releasing, shifting, and pushing. Over and over again with my body jerking every time he yanked it up a notch.

My ass and thighs vibrated under me in time with the engine, and I warmed everywhere.

My gaze fell to his face, and a light sheen of sweat on the hollows of his cheeks made his olive skin even more beautiful.

I heard him laugh. "Stop looking at me like that, K.C.," he warned.

Shit. I blinked, clearing my throat. "My turn," I changed the subject.

Turning to look out the front windshield, I rubbed my thighs together to dull the burn between my legs.

"Well, that was easy." I could hear the laughter in his voice as he pulled to a stop at the finish/start line. "I'm actually honored that you let me teach you instead of Liam."

"Don't be," I shot back, my guard going up. "I never asked Liam. I don't want to go home, and you're here, so . . ."

His eyes narrowed. "For that, I'm half tempted to make you sit in my lap while you drive," he threatened.

I rolled my eyes and jerked my chin. "It's raining. You hop out, and I'll slide over."

He twisted up his lips in irritation. "Yes, Princess."

I ignored the barb as he opened the door, a flash of lightning and a roll of thunder filling the car. Biting my bottom lip to stifle the nervous tremble, I swung my legs over the console and grabbed the steering wheel, hauling myself into his seat, still warm from his body.

My fingers wrapped around his thick wheel, and the body heat he'd left behind on the seat spread through my belly and down my thighs. Rain pummeled the roof and hood, and I could barely see anything but his dark shadow rounding the car to the passenger side.

He opened the door and storm sounds flooded inside again.

"Thanks," he bit out, crashing into the seat and shaking water off his arms. His long black shorts shone with rain, and his gray T-shirt was now a little darker.

And suctioned to his skin, making every dip and ridge of his abs and chest completely visible.

"You okay, Princess?" I asked, trying to look innocent.

He slicked back his hair and put on his seat belt. "Seat belt," he prompted, ignoring me.

Pulling my belt on, I reached down and adjusted the seat and then reached for the ignition.

"Wait." Jax put his hand on mine to stop me. He was so warm. "Do you have the clutch pressed in?"

I shook my head.

"Hold down the clutch with your left foot and the brake with your right," he said. "When you're ready, turn the ignition, but keep your feet in place."

Doing as I was told, I kicked off my flip-flops and started the car. When the engine roared to life, I let out a smile even as a nervous heat weakened my arms and legs.

"Now." He took my hand and placed it on the stick. "This is first gear." And he held my hand in his as he shifted me out of neutral. "This is second." We slammed straight down into second as he fisted me, and my arm was getting weaker.

I didn't know why. I closed my eyes, feeling him move us.

"Third." Up and to the right.

"Fourth." Straight down.

"Fifth." His deep voice carried me up to the right again. "And sixth." He slammed me straight down, and my stomach fluttered as I lost breath.

"And this is reverse," he said just above a whisper. "And just a tip. It's better to drive with your eyes open, K.C."

I blinked them open. Yeah, so I didn't even know how to drive a stick yet, but I definitely wanted one as my next car.

I swallowed, scowling at him. "Can I go now?"

He smiled and leaned over to switch the music. Pop Evil's "Trenches." "A little inspiration for you, Tough Girl."

"Yeah, okay," I replied sarcastically. Releasing the clutch, I pressed the gas and sat stunned as the car sputtered to its death.

My face flooded with embarrassment, and I could hear Jax's snort and see his chest shaking with silent laughter out of the corner of my eye.

"Mmm . . . so that's your experience with men?" he joked. "I arrived just in time." He took my hand, placing it on the stick.

"Turn on the car," he prompted.

I did and sat with my foot on the clutch and my other on the brake.

"Put her in first," he ordered, keeping his palm against my knuckles.

Using all my might until the muscles in my arm burned, I pulled the stick to the left and pushed it up into first.

"Okay," he started. "Now, when I say go, I want you to—slowly—release pressure from the clutch as you apply pressure—slowly—to the gas. Give-and-take. Push and pull. You're going to feel the spot where they meet, when one is ready to be released and the other is ready to take over."

His azure eyes turned stormy, and his soft lips melted together as he studied me. "Are you ready?"

For what?

Oh, yeah. "Yes," I choked out, nodding.

"Go ahead. Don't release the clutch completely until you feel it." And he sat back but kept his hand on mine.

Slowly, I relinquished pressure from the clutch and felt him watching me as I applied pressure to the gas.

"Slowly," he reminded me.

As I pressed the gas, I felt the car start to move, and I looked to Jax, wide-eyed.

He grinned. "Do you feel it?" he asked. "She's ready. Release the clutch."

I took my foot off, and jiggled the steering wheel nervously as the car vaulted forward. My smile spread, and I laughed.

"What do I do now?" I shouted, excitement taking over.

"What do you think you do?"

"Shift?" I sucked in air and clutched the steering wheel.

He squeezed my hand. "When I say go, press in the clutch again, and we'll shift," he instructed me. "Go!"

"Jax!" I screamed at his lack of notice, and frantically pressed in the clutch. Jax grasped my hand and yanked us down into second.

"Again, release the clutch slowly as you apply the gas."

I could feel his fingers slide between mine, and my heart was pounding so loud I could hear it in my ears.

As I released and applied, I found the spot where they met in the middle and charged ahead, releasing the clutch again.

"I did it!" I burst out, smiling. "I did it!"

"Of course you did," Jax said. "You ready for me to let go?"

"No!" I gasped, laughing. "Don't you dare!"

I felt his hand tighten on mine, and his palm was so smooth and soft, his fingers fitting perfectly between mine.

The car reached thirty miles an hour and seemed to reach its peak. Pressing in the clutch, I looked down to the diagram on the stick—covered by Jax's and my hands—and remembered that the next gear was up and to the right. Jax's hand was light on mine as I shifted up and punched the stick into third, releasing the clutch as the gas took over.

I loved this. Even though I was stuttering my way down the track, and I could see Jax jerking with my rough transitions, I was filled with elation.

Driving a new car, the rest of the world blocked out by the rain out the window, and the delicious danger of Jaxon Trent sitting next to me. The boy my mother would never have approved of. The boy who was bad for me.

The boy who would do bad things to me if I let him.

Well, my mother had nothing to worry about after all. Jax might have wanted in my pants in high school, but this one saw the ten shades of wimp I was and was probably bored out of his mind right now.

"So, why did you get arrested?" Jax asked.

I took my hand out from underneath his and held the wheel as I rounded the first corner.

"I don't want to talk about it," I said quietly.

"Is it embarrassing?" he prodded.

"No." I winced. "Just . . . yeah, a little." I looked over at him. "I mean getting arrested is embarrassing, despite the reason, right?"

He arched an eyebrow.

I rolled my eyes. "Okay, never mind. In your world, wearing handcuffs is cool," I mocked.

But then my face fell, realizing what I'd just insinuated.

"I didn't mean that," I blurted, looking over at his grinning face.

His hot eyes smiled at me. "You in handcuffs would be cool, K.C."

Oh, shit.

I heard him laugh, but my eyes were blindly focused outside.

"Didn't mean to distract you," he sort of apologized. "Keep driving."

Clearing my throat, I forged ahead, getting all the way to fifth gear in between turns and coming down successfully when I rounded corners. I went around the track twice and eventually relaxed enough to sit back and smooth into the transitions from gear to gear.

And I loved it. Enticing the car to move when I wanted it to move. Propelling it forward, dragging it back down . . . It was almost obscene how much I liked it.

The small smile I allowed myself might have been barely visible, but I felt it all over my body. As I rounded the final turn. As I shifted down. And as I slowed to a stop at the finish line.

I definitely want one of these, I thought as I sat there.

Jax let out a pleased sigh. "Now you know how to drive a stick."

I bowed my head, hiding my smile from him. "Yeah," I said quietly.

"You driving us to school tomorrow?"

I laughed and put the car in neutral, setting the parking brake.

Running my fingers up the steering wheel, I nibbled on my bottom lip before speaking.

"I caught Liam at a bar with another woman," I started, not sure why. "I walked up to them—as they were making out—and grabbed a knife off the nearby bar and stabbed the table where they sat." I twisted my embarrassed smile to the side, feeling the blush heat my skin. "And then I proceeded to wave the knife in front of both of them and threaten his loss of genitals," I finished, closing my eyes, wincing at my idiocy. "Yeah." I nodded, knowing what he must've been thinking. "I did that."

"Badass." He sounded proud. "Good for you."

I opened my eyes and shrugged, still feeling stupid. "It was a butter knife," I mumbled.

And Jax lost it. He let out a huge snort and laughed, the wheezing sound coming from the pit of his stomach as he slapped his thigh once in appreciation.

"Funny thing is," I continued through his laughter, "I haven't cried." I looked over at him and narrowed my eyes. "I mean not about him. We were together for five years, and I don't feel like anything is missing. Isn't that weird?" I asked as Jax's face calmed, and he listened.

I had to admit it, even as terrible as it sounded. And Liam probably wasn't missing me, either. I wasn't the easiest girlfriend, and although I regretted him, I couldn't help feeling that he probably regretted me, too.

"You're going to be okay," Jax offered.

I shook my head, my voice turning sad. "I don't want be okay," I countered. "I want to be off the rails, Jax. I want to fight and scream and rage and lose myself. I want to be hungry." I dropped my voice to a whisper as I looked out the windshield. "I want to be a mess. For once."

Letting out a defeated sigh, I swung the car door open and stepped out into the rain. Slamming it shut, I turned around and placed my palms on the roof, bowing my head and closing my eyes. I breathed in and out, just wishing the rain would wash me away with the heat on my skin.

The fragrant smell of moss from the nearby pond coursed through my nostrils, and the pitter-patter of drops on the water drowned out the noise in my head. I smiled gratefully as thin lines of water spilled over my lips, and the cool rain plastered my clothes to my hot skin.

"So, why don't you do it?"

I popped my head up and spun around, seeing that Jax had come up behind me. "Do what?"

"Lose yourself." His deep voice and challenging eyes were hard on me. "Find what makes you hungry. Go off the rails. Fight, scream, rage . . . Why don't you just do it?"

I looked away. "It's so easy for you, isn't it?" I raised my voice, speaking over the downpour. "You don't answer to anyone, Jax."

He looked at me as if I was pathetic. "Oh, you're so full of shit," he chided. "You're fucking scared. And you're not going to realize it until you're saddled in the suburbs with two-point-five kids and married to some dick who'd rather let his secretary blow him than come home to you."

Tears welled and I swallowed them back, choking out my words. "You're such an asshole."

"And you're fucking gutless!" he taunted, his lips an inch from my face as he bore down on me.

I snapped my head up. "Stop saying that!" I raged.

"What?" He held a hand behind his ear, mocking me. "What was that? I can't hear you, Gutless. No one hears you."

My fingers fisted. "Fuck you!" I thundered, darting into his space.

"Get naked, and I will."

"Ugh!" I slammed him in the chest, baring my teeth. "You're a damn child. Grow up!"

And I gasped as he rushed me and snatched up my bottom lip between his teeth, sucking it into his mouth.

Holy shit. Fuck. Did he just bite me?

But I didn't have time to process any of it. He grabbed my ass, still holding my lip between his teeth, and hauled me up, slamming me back against the car door.

"This kid grew up," he threatened in a deep voice, grinding his hard-on between my legs. "And you're gonna fuckin' find out."

Oh. My. God.

He covered my mouth with his and moved slowly, like the tides of an ocean, in and out, in and out, drawing my bottom lip between his teeth and dragging it out like a threat. I think my stomach growled, and all of a sudden I wanted to eat him.

"Jax." I clutched his T-shirt in my fists, tensing as the tornado in my chest swooped down into my belly and then down between my thighs.

And just at that moment, he squeezed the back of my neck and pushed his tongue into my mouth.

I whimpered at the warm slickness of his tongue and moaned into his mouth.

"Oh, God," I gasped, dropping my head back and breathing hard as his mouth continued down my neck. I couldn't take his lips. It felt too good. Either that or I was too worked up. I clenched my thighs and groaned, the pulse between my legs pounding wildly.

"Jax, I'm ... I ... ," I stammered. "Shit." I couldn't help it. I grabbed his hard waist and rolled my hips into his, showing him how much I desired him as he licked and kissed my neck.

"Jesus." His breath tickled my ear. "You're ready to come already, aren't you?"

"But I still hate you," I insisted. "And in a minute, you're going to get your fucking hands off me."

Wrapping my arms around his neck and pressing my body to his, I sank my lips into his, which continued to move over mine as if they belonged to him.

And then I kissed his bottom lip, licked his top lip, kissed the corners of his mouth, and clutched the back of his damn neck as I stood on my tiptoes to meet him.

There was no escaping. Jax didn't give me time to think or to stop. Pulling up my skirt, he grabbed the backs of my thighs and hauled me off the ground. I didn't need instructions. I circled his waist, instantly feeling the thick ridge of his hard-on teasing me.

My eyes were closed, but I was sure I looked as if I was in pain.

"Jax, damn," I groaned. "What are you doing?"

It was like a goddamn roller-coaster ride of sensation every place his lips touched. How can anyone feel butterflies on her neck? In her mouth? On her cheeks?

His hands groped my ass, bringing me in rough and hard against him, grinding for more, and I even loved how the fabric of his shorts dug into my inner thighs. Jesus, I was so hungry. Sucking his tongue as hard as I could, I let go and snatched his bottom lip between my teeth, biting down.

"Shit." He pulled back, dropping me to my feet and bringing his fingers to his lip where I bit.

I dug my nails into my bare legs, the agony of his loss scaring me. I hadn't meant to bite him that hard. But I played it off.

"I told you you were going to take your fucking hands off me," I taunted him.

He pulled his fingers away from his mouth to inspect them, and I think he saw blood, because he yanked me by the arm, pulling me away from the car door.

"No, I'm not," he challenged. "Biting? You just kicked me into sixth gear. Get in the fucking car," he growled, swinging it open and pushing me toward it.

I clenched my teeth to keep the smile at bay. Climbing in, I scurried over the console, out of Jax's way, when I saw that he was following me in the same side.

I swallowed the dryness from my mouth, and I waited, feeling a need I'd never felt. Not even with Liam.

He slammed the door and looked over at me as if he wanted to beat me up or something.

But he didn't.

Grabbing me under the arms, he hauled me over onto his lap so that I straddled him. Taking my hand, he lowered it to his groin and panted into my lips. "Bite me, hit me, scream at me. I don't care. I want to feel it. Fucking hurt me, K.C. Let me see you."

And then he grabbed the back of my neck and brought my lips to his, immediately pushing his sweet tongue into my mouth and running his hands up my thighs under my skirt.

"Jax," I panted, moving back and forth, in and out, meeting his lips and pushing back. "I love how you feel."

I wanted this. I always wanted this. He was a carnival ride under my fucking skin, and there wasn't one inch of him I didn't want to taste.

Holding one side of his smooth face, I let my mind and my body slip into his warmth, and I forgot everything.

Just kiss him. That was all I heard—all my brain told me—as if it were just him and me in the world.

He held my ass in both of his hands, and I pulled my mouth away and looked down at him.

Placing my palms on his shoulders, I rubbed myself against him, really slow but really fucking hard, so I could feel every inch of him from the top of my clit to my entrance.

"Christ." He bared his teeth, looking up at me, our lips an inch apart. "I knew you were this beautiful."

Grasping my ass, his shoulders flexed under my hands as he pulled me into him and rolled his hips into mine.

Reaching back, I tried to pull his hands off my thong-clad ass. I couldn't let this go too far, but there was no way I wanted it to stop, either. I felt I should at least try, even though my effort was pathetic.

I just knew that it should stop. Sooner or later we were going to get to the point of no return, and the more his hands touched all the places he shouldn't, the more I wouldn't want it to end.

Touching his mouth with mine, I whispered, pleading, "I have to feel you, Jax. I need more," rolling my hips into his faster, again, again, and again. "More, Jax. Please," I moaned, loving the friction on my clit.

He reached down, and I heard a zipper, feeling my heart picking up pace, knowing that I was going to get closer. Shifting underneath me, he slid his shorts down just a little, grabbed my ass, dug his fingers in, and pressed me hard into his warm cock.

My underwear. The only thing separating me from him. The only thing keeping us apart.

"Jax," I whimpered, the heat flooding my pussy making me wet. "Oh, my God."

I swallowed again and again, the pleasure of him right there making me a mess of nerves.

"We have to stay on top of the clothes, okay?" I started dry-fucking him, loving what I was feeling but scared by it, too.

His head fell back against the seat, and he closed his eyes. "I don't care. Just don't stop touching me."

As if I wanted to stop! He loved what I was doing, and his ragged breathing, his muscles flexing under me, the sweat on his neck as we panted and moaned in the thick air of the humid car—I loved it, and I wanted to cry he felt so good.

With his hands gripping my hips, he rocked me into him, rubbing against his cock, over and over again, harder and harder until I didn't fucking care that the material separating us was causing rug burn.

He flicked my lobe with his tongue. "Mmmmm . . . you're so wet. I can feel it."

I sucked in a breath, wrapping my arms around his neck and leaning into his mouth. "And you're hard," I rasped, "so hard."

His tentative, slow fingers inched under my shirt, his thumbs rubbing circles on my stomach.

"Jax, no," I protested pathetically, sliding his hands back out of my shirt. "We can't go that far. We won't want to stop."

"If you only knew how much you saying no was turning me on . . ."

I licked his bottom lip, dragging the tip of my tongue across it. "Doesn't this feel good?"

He maneuvered under me, pulling his wet shirt over his head and tossing it on the floor. "Hell yes, it feels good." He grabbed my face and nibbled at my mouth. "But having you so close and not being able to move this one little piece of fabric"—he reached down and teased the elastic of my thong, his soft touch sending shivers down my arms—

"that keeps me from sinking inside you is fucking torture. I want you so bad, K.C.," he growled low. "I've always wanted you."

And I cried out, his hard-on all of a sudden jerking, pressuring my clit. I leaned into his lips, and we breathed each other in as I rode him.

"Oh, Jax," I cried out, the burn at my entrance making me want more.

God! I wanted more. I slammed my palm against the window, barely noticing the steam we'd created, but Jax held strong. Pushing me back, pulling me forward, sucking the breath out of me, and wanting it just as much as I did.

"Yo, Jax!"

Someone pounded on the driver's-side window, and Jax and I jerked, looking up.

"What the . . . ?" he bit out, gripping my shaky thighs. The orgasm that had been so close was now slowly ebbing away, and the throbbing between my legs turned vicious. I breathed hard, the need so bad it hurt. Did he feel it, too?

"Jax?" the guy called again, and I scurried back over to my seat.

Jax pounded the steering wheel once, growling. "Stay here," he ordered.

As he pushed the door open, Jax's body was rigid and noticeably hard. I groaned to myself, embarrassment warming my face.

"Hey, man."

"What the hell?" Jax chided, stepping out of the car and not hiding as he zipped up and buttoned his pants.

It had stopped raining, but I didn't know when.

"Oh, man." I saw the man's legs back away. "I'm really sorry. I didn't realize."

"What? Did the steamed-up windows confuse you?"

I dropped my face into my hands. *He did not just say that.*

Jax left the door open and took a step forward. "Just take off," he warned. "Seriously."

"Hey, baby," a woman's voice piped up, and I dropped my hands, straightening instantly. I hesitated only a moment before I threw open the door and peered over the roof to . . .

My shoulders sank. *No. Shit.*

It was one of the blondes I'd seen Jax with that night before college when he drove Liam home. I didn't want to, but my eyes darted to Jax to see if he moved or anything. Did I care if he was still close to her?

I definitely didn't want her near him.

She stood with a hand on her hip and a friendly smile on her lips, but it was weird. She looked at Jax more as if they grew up together rather than that they'd been naked together.

And then her blue eyes flashed to me and her eyebrows shot up.

"She's hot." She nodded her approval to Jax. "Call me later if you guys want company, okay?"

Huh?

"Excuse me?" I blurted out.

She hadn't just offered . . . I ran my tongue over my dry lips, not sure I'd heard her right. Her lazy smile played with me, and it was very clear that she wanted to . . . yeah.

"Honey." She laughed. "It usually takes two girls to wear this one out." She pointed to Jax.

"Cameron, Jesus." Jax ran a hand through this hair. "Use your filter. Please." And then he turned to look at me, concern in his eyes.

She held up her hands in defense. "Sorry. Okay? She's cute. You can't blame me for trying." And then she turned her eyes on me and made a telephone with her hand, mouthing, *Call me.*

"Your brother is waiting," Jax hinted, jerking his chin behind her to where her brother had climbed back into his car.

I barely saw her smile and walk off. I barely saw Jax turn around and look at me. All I thought about was whether to like her for having the courage to live how she wanted or whether to hate her for being with Jax.

I didn't like the image of her with him.

Jax stared at me, unmoving and waiting. "Cameron's a friend, okay?" he explained gently. "An old friend."

I hardened my jaw, the lump in my throat growing. "I see that."

"K.C. . . . ," he started, but I climbed back into the car before he could finish.

I didn't want to lose it in front of him. Was I mad? Was I upset? Shit, I didn't know. All I knew was what Cameron had said. Two girls. Two damn girls to wear him out. Which meant he did it regularly. How could I compete with that? What the hell did he want with someone like me?

I shook my head, going from sad to angry, and regaining my control just in time for him to climb back into the car.

"I'm tired," I said right away, lying. "I need to go home."

I stared out the window, but I still saw him. His grip so tight on the steering wheel that his tanned knuckles turned white. The long cord of his tensed arm. The lips closed tight, because I could hear him breathing through his nose.

But he slammed the door shut.

As he made his way back through town, the only sound we could hear was the water on the streets being kicked up under the tires. He'd silenced the radio, we weren't talking . . . and I felt as if he'd switched off.

Everything had felt alive when he kissed me. His heart under my palm. His breath in my mouth. His hands roaming over my skin as if they were trying to memorize every inch of me.

Now he was a bullet. Going from point A to point B without hesitation.

Until his flat tone finally filled the car. "Come home with me." It wasn't a question, and I couldn't hear a trace of emotion.

I turned to him, stunned. "Are you serious?" I asked. "I don't think I'd be enough for you."

"Don't do that," he shot back. "Don't ruin what happened between us. You were fire in my hands, and I want you to remember it, K.C."

I could feel his eyes on me as I clasped the strap of Tate's messenger bag sitting on the floor.

"Clothed, naked, I don't care . . . " He trailed off, sounding almost sad. "As long as your lips are on me again."

I shifted in the seat, trying to buy myself time. What I wanted and what I should do were two different things. I'd fought that battle with Liam, my mother, and hell, the list went on. It was true when I told Jax that I wanted to be a mess. But I didn't want to get hurt.

"Thanks for the lesson," I said. "And the ride. But I'm not like you, Jax. I don't just ignore the rules and take what I want."

"You don't know me." His tone turned defensive. "You know nothing about me."

"And what do you know about me?" I threw back. "Other than you wanted me to spread my legs in high school? You want to have fun with me and nothing more, Jax. Find someone else."

He jerked the steering wheel to the right, and I grabbed the door handle to keep from vaulting over to his side of the car as he sped up into his driveway.

My heart jumped into my throat, and I shot out my hand, grabbing the dash when he skidded to a quick halt in front of his garage.

"Jax!" I scolded.

He shut off the car, yanked the parking brake up, and turned to look at me, leaning his forearm on the steering wheel. "You think I don't know you?" he challenged.

I pursed my lips. "Other than that I'm gutless and helpless, no."

He shook his head. "You want to travel. To unusual and danger-ous places. You hid a binder full of *National Geographic* pages in your locker in high school because you didn't want your mom to see all the pictures you'd torn out to keep track of the places you wanted to visit."

My jaw dropped slightly, and I widened my eyes. *What?*

He continued. "You didn't eat lunch for an entire month senior year, because you saw Stu Levi not eating and found out his single mom was out of work and couldn't afford to put money on his lunch card. So you put your own money on it. Anonymously."

How did . . . ?

"You love dark chocolate," he kept going, "Ricky Gervais, and any movie with singing and dancing." His voice filled the car, and my heartbeat was in my ears. "Except *The Wizard of Oz*, because the witch freaks you out, right? And you've collected almost an entire set of vintage Nancy Drew books. You had the most badges in your troop in Girl Scouts, and you had to quit swimming when you were fourteen because your mom said that your shoulders were getting too muscular and you wouldn't look feminine. You loved swimming," he added.

I wrapped my arms around my stomach, the air turning cold. Tate and Liam didn't even know all that.

"I didn't drool all over you in high school, K.C. I listened to you. I paid attention to you. What the hell do you know about me?"

And he swung the car door open, climbed out, and slammed it shut, not waiting for an answer.

I sat there, watching him walk into his house and close the door.

Then the tears spilled over, and as much as I wanted to prove him wrong, I couldn't go after him. He didn't know that I'd watched him, too. He didn't know that I'd paid attention as well.

I always saw him.

"Music centers you," I whispered to an empty car, staring at his front door. "You listened to your iPod between classes and while you sat on the bleachers before school every morning." I smiled, letting more tears run down my cheeks and thinking back to him and his black hoodies, looking so dark. "You love popcorn. Almost every kind and flavor but especially with Tabasco sauce," I said, remembering the times he would come into the theater where I worked. "You hold the door open for women—students, teachers, and even old ladies coming out of Baskin-Robbins. You love movies about natural disasters, but they have to have some comedy in them. Your favorite one is *Armageddon*." I swallowed and thought about how little I'd ever seen Jax truly smile. "And while you love computers, it's not your passion," I concluded. "You love being outdoors. You love having space." My whole face hurt, the last words barely audible. "And you deserve someone who makes you happy. I'm just not that person."

CHAPTER 7

K.C.

"Hey, K.C." Simon, one of the other tutors, came up to me after the sessions ended on Friday. "Doing anything fun this week-end?"

"Probably not," I said, without looking at him as I loaded up my bag—or Tate's bag.

"Well, we're all going out for coffee. Wanna join us?"

I stopped what I was doing and looked up. Peering around him, I saw the other tutors gathering their materials and some waiting by the door.

Smiling softly, I apologized, "Sorry. It's kind of hot for coffee."

"Iced coffee, then?" he shot back, grinning playfully. "They have smoothies, too."

I swung the bag over my head, legs tensing with the urge to walk.

Simon seemed like a nice guy. And good-looking, too. I wasn't sure if he was feeling me out or just being friendly, but I clutched the strap over my chest, wishing he had just left me alone.

Not that he'd done anything wrong. I should spend time with

people. With a potentially nice guy, too. But last night—and nearly every night this week, actually—I'd opted to ignore Shane and texts from Nik and Tate and either take long, long walks or sit on a lawn chair in the backyard and zone out listening to the iPod. Alone but not really lonely.

How was that even possible?

Throughout high school and college, I was always lonely.

At parties. Lonely.

With Liam. Lonely.

Around my family. Lonely.

Standing in the middle of a group of friends. Completely lonely.

But it was weird. Now that I was alone more than I'd ever been in my life, the doubt and the anxiety were replaced with something else.

Time to think. Time to unwind. It unnerved me, but it also felt kind of good. I started putting my feet on the coffee table, drinking from the carton, and playing music every morning when I woke up. It was as though I was starting to meet myself.

I put my head down, feeling bad as I walked around him toward the door, but I just wasn't up for being social. "Thanks. Maybe another time, Simon."

As I walked into the hallway, turning right to head out the front doors, my phone rang from inside the bag.

Picking it out, I looked, only hoping to avoid calls from my mother, but I didn't recognize this number.

I held it to my ear. "Hello?"

"Hey, Trouble," a deep voice greeted me with humor.

Jared.

"Great," I mumbled. "You're teasing me, too? I seem to remember you getting arrested once."

I heard his quiet laugh on the other end. Jax's brother—also

Tate's boyfriend—and I were friendly but not particularly close. I hadn't seen him in forever.

"It's Tate's fault, you know?" I explained. "She's a bad influence."

"Yeah, no shit."

Tate was a ballbuster, and the whole town knew it. While she and Jared used to be childhood friends, he'd begun bullying her in high school for reasons I still didn't know. When Tate started fighting back, she *literally* started fighting back. There was a broken nose, a knee in the balls, some slaps, and a whole lot of damage to Jared's car.

Tate was awesome.

"So, how does everyone know?" I asked, remembering the principal's now useless advice of keeping my trouble a secret. "Was there a press release or something?"

"Tate doesn't keep things from me. You know that. And, yes," he continued, "there was a sort of press release. Liam, your asswipe ex, posted it on Facebook."

I halted in the middle of the parking lot.

"What?" I burst out, every muscle in my body tightening.

"Let it go." He tried to calm me. "Damage is done, and he got what was coming to him. Jax put a nice, fat fist in his gut."

Dropping my head back, I closed my eyes to the sky and felt my chest flood with emotions so strong my nerve endings felt like sparklers. Burning, sizzling, searing sparklers.

"Unbelievable." I sighed. So that was why Jax had jumped Liam last week. It wasn't about the incident between him and me at the party but about Liam humiliating me publicly on social media.

"Don't get mad at Jax," he scolded. "It would've been worse for Liam if Madoc and I had been there, too. Fuck," he continued, "if Tate had been there? Yeah."

Yeah. Tate would've done even worse to him.

I shook my head. People—hundreds of old classmates and Liam's family members—were now laughing at me.

Now I wanted to put a fat fist in his gut. Was this how Tate felt when she'd finally had enough? I suddenly felt as if I were five and wanted to push people.

I heaved out sigh after sigh, remembering that Jared was still sitting on the phone. Jared. Tate's boyfriend. A guy I'd kissed before they were together. Tate's boyfriend. Yeah.

"Why are you calling me?" I asked finally, getting to the point.

He was silent for a few moments, and my other hand started tapping my leg. Jared never called me.

I heard him suck in a long breath. "Relax. Tate knows I'm calling. I just want to know"—he trailed off, hesitating—"how my brother is doing," he finally finished.

Jax? Why would Jared be asking me that? And then I remembered Jared and Jax's fight when Jax was in the nurse's office.

"Um . . . ," I drawled out, trying to find an innocent reply but thinking about the weight room and the Loop. "I'm not sure how to answer that, actually."

"Does he look healthy?"

"Healthy?" I repeated. I thought of Jax's muscles that had seemed to double in size in the last two years and the bright white smiles he wore on the field when I tried not staring at him out the window. "Yes. Very," I said.

"What does he do with his days?"

"Jared, what's going on?" I prodded.

Jared calling me. Weird. Jared asking me about Jax. Weird. Jared acting worried about anyone other than Tate or himself. Very weird.

"Sorry," he offered, sounding unusually embarrassed. "It's just that you're right next door. I don't think it's escaped your notice how much weight he has to throw around, right? The changes at the house. The Loop. I just want to make sure he's okay."

"He's your brother. Ask him."

"I have," he shot out. "And I have no reason to suspect he's not okay. I'm just not there, and I . . . I . . ."

I raised my eyebrows, finding his stuttering amusing.

"I just hate not being there," he finished. "I need to make sure he's happy and taken care of, is all."

Hmm . . . I started walking again, thinking about how worried Jared must be if he resorted to calling me. "Well, everything seems fine." Not normal but fine.

"Fine." He started laughing. "You really have no idea, do you?"

I rounded the parking lot and stepped onto the sidewalk, my heels digging into the concrete. "What are you talking about?"

He paused long enough to piss me off. "Kind of convenient how the state of Arizona let you come all the way back to your hometown to complete your community service, huh?"

I pinched my eyebrows together. "Well, why wouldn't they?"

Yeah, why wouldn't they?

"Mmm-hmm," he teased. "And it's pretty awesome that you're sitting all comfy in your old high school tutoring a subject you love instead of cleaning up trash on the freeway, isn't it?"

I slowed to a stop on the sidewalk under a canopy of trees.

Principal Masters didn't know where the e-mail had come from to suggest me for the tutoring at the school.

I let out a breath.

And Arizona let me out without bail.

I clenched the phone.

And the judge let me off with no fines when the standard penalty for a first offense carried a minimum two-hundred-fifty-dollar penalty.

I could barely whisper the question. "What are you saying?"

"Nothing," he chirped. "I don't know shit. See you in a couple of weeks, Trouble."

And he hung up.

Rocks flew across the street as I kicked the gravel on my walk home.

Jared sucked.

What the hell was he trying to tell me?

Oh, I knew what he was trying to tell me. I wasn't an idiot. Sometimes I was a dipshit, but I definitely wasn't an idiot.

I mean, did Jax really have the pull to get my community service transferred from one state to the other? And then Jared suggested that Jax got my placement at the high school, too?

I shook my head, my eyes wandering as I tossed his words around in my head.

Yeah. No. For one, Jax didn't have that kind of power. Two, Jax wouldn't care. And three?

Jared sucked.

And Jax sucked, too. They both acted as if they had the whole damn world figured out, and everyone else was clueless.

"Okay," I thought out loud, letting out a sigh and ignoring the whistles from cars passing by.

"Jax could've suggested me to Principal Masters when he heard I was coming back to town. But . . ." I paused, mumbling to myself, as Fuel's "Hemorrhage" played through my earbuds. "Jax wouldn't have known I enjoyed writing. In fact, I'd be a hell of a lot happier picking up garbage on the side of the road," I grumbled.

"Hey, baby!" a male voice yelled out the passenger window of a car passing by.

I flipped him off without looking up.

I didn't know why guys thought cattle-calling was sexy. It wasn't as if I was dressed to impress or anything.

Even though all the other tutors dressed casually, I'd stuck to my skirts or dress shorts and nice blouses, hoping to at least look as though I hadn't been forced by the state to be there.

And even though I hadn't seen my mother, I knew she'd be disappointed if she saw me dressing unprofessionally in a professional situation.

But I had taken one risk.

Tate left behind some purple Chucks that went well with the white shorts and lavender peasant blouse I'd worn today, so I took a chance.

"And also," I continued out loud, talking to myself, "I definitely don't enjoy tutoring. No one that knew me would think I had the temperament to teach, and Jax had to know that much about me."

"Those kids don't need an attitude adjustment. You do."

I stuck my hands in my pockets, narrowing my eyes.

Kids. Those kids. Guilt crept up on me. I might have been only three years older than them, but technically speaking, I was the adult. They were youths needing direction, inspiration, and encouragement.

And I was failing them.

I walked and walked, thinking about Jax's words, thinking about Tate telling me to get wild, thinking about all the things I could've done differently the past two weeks in tutoring.

I walked up streets I'd only ever driven through and down lanes where I'd seen the seasons change so beautifully growing up. It was funny how much I enjoyed walking now. Even though I was sweating, and my hair, flatironed and shiny this morning, was now stuffed into a high, messy bun, my head felt clear.

And I'd finally come to a conclusion.

"Juliet? You could serve God, serve your country, or serve the ones you love, but to find true happiness you must always serve someone or something other than yourself."

My dad. He told me that one day when he was still in the hospital, on a rare occasion he didn't think I was my sister. One of the last times anyone other than Shane called me Juliet.

Walking past Tate's house, past Jax's house where I noticed Madoc's GTO parked, I continued the few blocks until I reached my house. My house that had never felt like a home once my dad left.

Looking up at the two-story redbrick Colonial, I clenched the fists in my pockets as my chest flooded with heat.

My mother wasn't going to be happy.

I reached for the door handle but pulled back, wondering if I was supposed to knock. Swallowing the sudden rush of saliva in my mouth, I fisted the handle and gritted my teeth.

And pushed through the unlocked door.

"Mother?" I called out, stepping calmly into the foyer.

The scent of lemon furniture polish hit me, and my nose started to sting. If I didn't know better, I'd say the light hardwood floors were soaked in it. Everything shone, from my left to my right. Up the sterile white walls of the staircase to the glimmering tabletops in the dining and living rooms.

Glancing up the wall along the stairs, I saw the same pictures of my sister and me that had been there forever. But the pictures never portrayed us as siblings but instead as a single child growing up. My sister's photos hung on the wall showing her growth until her death when she was five, and then photos of me after age five took over as if K.C.'s life continued.

All photos of K. C. Carter, a sister I never met. Not one photo of me as Juliet.

I had looked it up on the Internet once. A child conceived to replace another is called a ghost child.

Me.

I heard footfalls above me and looked up, my heart starting to pound double time.

"K.C.?" My mother's voice preceded her as she rounded the staircase and stopped at the top to peer down at me.

I peered back up, absentmindedly tapping my fingers on my leg from inside the pockets.

My mother looked like Mary Poppins. She always did. Thin and beautiful. Creamy skin that looked fantastic with red lipstick. And black hair always done up in some kind of twist or bun. Her clothes, even the casual ones she wore around the house, were always clean and pressed.

Today, she wore a yellow, flared, knee-length skirt and a white button-up cardigan. Lightweight, from the looks of it, but it still had to be hot as hell if she stepped outside.

"Take your hands out of your pockets," she instructed in a calm voice.

I obeyed, suddenly feeling as though I should've showered and cleaned up before I came here.

"Hello, Mother."

"It's nice to see you. I've been calling. And texting." She sounded annoyed as she clasped her hands in front of her.

I hadn't returned her calls, and I knew that would piss her off. That wasn't my intention. I just didn't want to talk to her.

Licking my lips, I clasped my hands in front of my body as well. "I apologize. Tutoring has kept me busy."

She nodded and began stepping down the stairs. "Now is a bad time. You should have called before showing up at someone's house unannounced. You know better."

Someone's house?

There was a time when my mother was a little warmer with me. Before my father started losing control. But she had always worried about appearances, and I wondered why. Her brother—the doctor—was very much like her as well. Clean and unemotional. But her sister—Shane's mother—was very loving. What was my mother like as a child? Did she laugh? Did she make messes? Did she make mistakes?

As she came closer, I straightened my back. "I was in the neighborhood, Mother."

"No, you wanted something."

I ran my hands down my shirt, noticing how wrinkly the linen was. I had thought I looked cute this morning, but now I felt uncomfortable. I looked ridiculous in this outfit. What was I thinking?

"I wanted to . . . I'd like . . . ," I stuttered, looking away from her gaze raking over my body, taking in my appearance.

"Do not speak until you are prepared, K.C." She spoke to me as if I were five.

I let out a breath and steadied my body, squeezing my interlocked fingers so tight the skin was stretched.

"May I please retrieve my journals? I'd like to use them in my tutoring lessons." And I evened out my expression to appear confident even though it took an effort to keep my knees locked.

Her bangs didn't even move as she cocked her head and regarded me.

"That sounds reasonable," she answered finally. "But first you need to shower."

"I'll take a shower at home," I said, and started to walk around her toward the stairs, but she grabbed my arm, causing me to wince.

"You are home," she said sternly. "That's what I wanted to talk to you about. It's time to come home."

I swallowed. Come home? Dread filled my stomach and spread through my system, slowly eating away at me.

"Why?" I could hear the crack in my own voice. I didn't want to come home now.

She raised her eyebrows as if I'd just asked a stupid question. "Because it's my responsibility to watch over you."

And it wasn't two weeks ago? When I needed her?

My jaw tightened. "Why now?" I accused.

And she slapped me.

My head flew to the side, tears sprang to my eyes, and I grabbed my face, trying to soothe the burn. I should've known that was coming. I was never supposed to mouth off.

"Now go shower," she ordered, and I could hear the smile in her voice. "Do your hair and your makeup, and then you'll join me and a few friends for dinner tonight."

I closed my eyes, feeling a tear run down my cheek as she walked around to my back and unwrapped my hair from its ratty nest.

No, no, no . . . I was twenty years old. I didn't need her to groom me anymore.

But everything needed to be in its place with her. Everything needed to look pristine on the outside, even as the dirt festered on the inside. Why did she worry about appearances so much? Did it make her feel so much better after the heartache of losing my sister— and my father, too, for that matter—for everyone to see us as perfect when we still felt like shit?

I heard her sigh, displeased. "Your hair needs to be trimmed. We'll give you bangs like me. But . . ." She walked back around to my front and grabbed my hand from my cheek. "There's no time for a manicure. We'll make sure you get fixed up good as new before the luncheon next week."

Gutless and helpless.

My mother continued on and on about waxing and coloring, but Jax's words were the only ones I latched on to.

"What's your favorite color? Your favorite band? When was the last time you ate chocolate?"

I squeezed my eyes shut, my scalp aching as my mother pulled and scanned my hair more closely, probably looking for loose ends.

I rubbed my hands together, remembering Jax's gritty, greasy hand in mine last week. Loving the way it felt. Wanting that feeling again.

"I wanted to dirty you up."

Gutless and helpless.

Gutless and helpless.

Gutless and helpless.

"Stop!" I yelled, feeling my mother jerk back and gasp at the exclamation.

Spinning around, I yanked open the door and jumped outside, sucking in lungfuls of air as I raced through the yard.

My mother didn't yell after me. She would never make a spectacle in front of the neighbors.

CHAPTER 8

K.C.

hane watched me pace Tate's living room like a caged animal. "What's the matter with you?" she asked.

"Nothing," I huffed, rubbing my thumbs across my fingertips and sucking in air that was getting me more worked up than calmed down.

"Obviously."

I stopped and turned to her. "My journals," I shot out, my chest shaking with . . . I didn't know what. Fear. Nerves. Anger. "You have to go to my mother's house and get my journals," I ordered her, and began pacing again.

"No, you need to go to your house and get your journals. You know your mother makes me twitch."

I barely heard her grumbles. Now I knew why I never wanted to come home. It wasn't my past behavior. It wasn't my mother.

It was me.

I let the abuse happen even long after I could've stopped it. I let her talk to me that way. I let her judge me.

I let it all happen. I hated her. I hated my father. I hated that house. I hated the grooming and the classes I was forced to take.

I hated my sister.

Sudden tears overtook me, and I stopped, breathing hard and my face aching with sadness. My five-year-old sister, who never knew me and wasn't perfect. She would've made mistakes, and she would've been hit. I hated her for escaping.

And I hated myself for thinking that.

She hadn't escaped. Not really. She'd died. I had the chance to live, and I was jealous of a sister simply because she no longer *had* to exist.

What the hell was wrong with me?

I wiped the tears from my cheeks before Shane could notice. Was I so scared to live? To take chances? To be anything other than gutless and helpless?

"I was actually upset when she wouldn't welcome me home," I told Shane, choking through the few tears I'd shed. "Now I feel nauseated that I was even in that house."

"Juliet, seriously." The concern in her eyes was true. "You need to confront her. You need to wig out. Get in her face. Scream. Throw shit. She deserves that and more."

There was no love lost between my mother and her sister's kid. In fact, my mother barely communicated with her sister and husband, since Sandra Carter was a closet racist. She'd hated that her sister had married someone nonwhite, and even though she never admitted it, she kept her distance and looked down on Shane's family. It didn't matter that her dad was a doctor, or that he'd attended Stanford. My bitch of a mother barely tolerated Shane.

Feeling the roll of nausea clench my insides, I began pacing again, slowing my breathing in an effort to calm myself.

It wasn't working.

The last thing I wanted to do was think about that woman, much less lay eyes on her again.

"I want my journals," I whispered, but it sounded like a prayer. As if they were going to magically fall into my lap.

"Then go get them," she urged, her voice stronger this time.

I shook my head. *No.* I couldn't. I'd rather stick my fingers in shit and make snowballs.

"Oh, of course."

I shot my eyes to Shane. "What does that mean?"

"It means you're a wimp, *Ju-li-et*." She dragged out my true name, making her point.

And I glared at her, curling my toes into the hardwood floors. "Piss off," I ordered.

And I flipped her off before spinning around to stomp upstairs.

I stared at Liam's Facebook page, and I could see why he'd never unfriended me. I would have unfriended him, but I had abandoned all my social networking lately.

There were pictures of him and Megan. Out at the Loop last weekend, selfies of them kissing, and a picture he posted recently of them at a Christmas party. A Christmas party last year, while we were still together.

He'd wanted me to see all this, and I bit my bottom lip to keep from giving in to the tears.

"How could he?" I whispered, realizing just how long he'd been going behind my back. And then I saw the post about how I'd gone off at him at the club, how I was mad that we'd broken up, and how I was arrested and carried from the club kicking and screaming.

Which was a lie. I was picked up outside the club on my way home.

And then I did what we should never, ever do on the Internet. I read the comments.

I realized that Tate and Shane were the only people I really had. Everyone else thought I was a joke.

I just stared at the computer, not noticing that I'd been digging my nails into Tate's wooden desk. Until I heard the scratching and looked down to see I'd left four abrasions where I'd dragged my nails across the wood.

And I slammed the laptop closed, hearing Jax's music pounding the foundations of the house again.

"Asshole."

Jared on the phone.

Liam in the Internet.

Mom in my head.

And Jaxon Trent in my ears!

Swinging open Tate's doors, I squeezed the railing as I hollered over the side. "Hey, hello?" I shouted to the people in his backyard. "Turn down the music!" I bellowed.

A few of the guys looked up from their worktable that had engines or some such shit and then turned back to their work, ignoring my request.

"Hey!" I hollered again, and a couple of girls looked up and started giggling.

Barreling back into the bedroom, I grabbed my cell and dialed the police. Again.

I'd already called twice. Once, an hour ago after Shane had left—probably to go to the party next door—and again forty-five minutes ago when the music, coincidentally, got louder.

"Yeah, hi. Me again," I chirped through my fake smile. "The music next door is so loud that I think my dead grandmother just shit her pants."

The lady paused, and I barely heard her babble as Pop Evil's

"Deal with the Devil" pounded and thundered out of the speakers next door.

Jesus. It was as if he knew every time I reported him!

I could feel the music in my chest, and I only knew the song because Tate had put it on the iPod.

Good song. But I needed quiet right now.

"What?" I jerked my attention back to the phone. "Um, yeah, I watched my language the first two times I called. I've listed my complaints. In English. You speak English, right?"

But then I heard a click.

"Hello?" I shouted into the phone. "Hello?"

Throwing my phone on Tate's bed, I didn't even watch where it bounced to.

"Jax wants music," I gritted out, exhaling. "Fine."

Darting around the room, I yanked Tate's surround-sound speakers off all four walls and dragged them, along with their thin gray cords, to the open French doors.

One down on the floor peeking out of the corner of the rails. Two and three down in the middle, and four down at the other corner.

All facing Asshole's house.

Stomping over to Tate's iPod dock in my red-and-white-pin-striped pajama shorts and red T-shirt, I curled my bare toes into the rug and punched buttons, looking for Katy Perry's "Firework."

The light tinkling started, and I smiled, jacking up the volume full fucking blast.

Bobbing my head, I scowled through the doors, seeking my revenge and hoping that my tunes were drowning out his. Peering over the railing, I gritted my teeth, smiling viciously hard at the wide eyes and looks of disgust.

Take that, asswipes.

Katy's voice rooted in my stomach and filled my chest, crowding the room like a thousand firecrackers in my heart.

And I started singing.

Hard.

I belted out lyrics, growling and shouting, feeling angry and sick. I squeezed my eyes shut, screaming the words throughout the room.

I can't hear you, Gutless. No one hears you!

Tears spilled down my cheeks.

Gutless. Helpless.

I screamed the lyrics, the pitch coming deep from the pit of my stomach.

I pounded my fists. I wasn't those things!

I was violent. I yelled so hard that my throat ached with rawness.

I was furious. I threw my head back and pounded the floor with my feet.

I was wild.

Violent. Furious. And *wild*.

And that was when I felt it.

The flutters.

In my stomach. In my chest. In my head. In my legs.

I broke out in a huge smile, gasping through my laughter.

I dropped my head and continued to let the rumble pour out of my lungs, and I let the tears fall, streaming down my face and making me a sloppy mess.

Because with every tear, every laugh, every breath, all the years of feeling powerless left my body, and I felt what I don't remember ever feeling before.

Freedom.

I just let go.

As I bobbed onto my knees, the words came out shaky.

"'You just gotta . . . ignite . . . the light,'" I stuttered, my voice growing stronger, "'and let it shine.'" I spread out my arms and belted out the goddamn lyrics.

"'Just own the night like the Fourth of Ju-ly!'"

And when the drums started pounding, I popped my knees up off the floor and jumped up and down like a crazy person, whipping my head front, back, side to side, and singing. Singing for me.

Laughing, smiling, throwing my arms in the air every which way, I leaped onto the bed and bounced back to the floor, twirling around the room and forgetting the party outside.

The song was inside me, and I was fucking happy for the first time in my life. Liam didn't do it. Neither did Jax. Nor my friends or my family.

When the song ended, I played it again. And again. And again. Dancing. Laughing. Living.

I guessed we've all built ourselves up through sadness, disappointment, and experience. It just happens at different times and in different ways.

Jared's parties pissed off Tate, so she beat him.

Jax's parties pissed me off, so I joined him.

CHAPTER 9

JAXON

I f there was one thing I craved day after day, it was the feeling of want.

We want a house, a car, a fancy fucking vacation, and prestige, so what do we do? We go to school, and we get jobs we hate to pay for the things we want. We deal with people we don't like and waste years of our lives sitting in stark, fluorescent-lit rooms and listening to coworkers who bore us so we can pay for a small amount of precious time to enjoy what makes us happy. To achieve a fraction of our lives just feeling as if it was all worth it.

We sacrifice to earn.

Well, I had a house. Not a mansion but a warm, clean home given to me by a woman who loved me and became the mother she didn't have to be.

I had a car. Not a Ferrari or some other coveted sports car but a loud and fast Mustang GT given to me by a brother I loved.

I had a fancy fucking vacation. I was still on it. Given to me by a new mother and a good brother who had rescued me from abuse and foster care.

I had prestige. Sure, it was in the small town of Shelburne Falls, and no one outside the county limits knew who the hell I was, but the people I saw every day and considered friends were the only ones who mattered.

I had everything everyone else sells their entire lives for.

I had everything except K. C. Carter, the one thing I wanted.

The first time I ever saw her, the ground flipped beneath my feet, and the world spun all around me. Even though I'd had girlfriends and had sex more times than I could count, I'd never had a crush on someone.

And I loved it. I loved the way she resisted me.

Wanting her was more addicting than the idea of actually getting her. I started to live for that feeling of knowing I was going to see her every day at school. *She's in the cafeteria. I can feel her.*

Standing in a group with her and feeling the pull to touch her as if we were two fucking magnets, and I had to fight the urge not to reach out. The hair on my body would stand on end as soon as she was near. Knowing her eyes were on me, and relishing the way she'd look away as soon as I caught her.

Every time she shot out some snotty insult or made a face at me, I nearly laughed, because she was going to be a fucking prize when I finally got her.

But I never pushed too hard. I never *really* tried. Wanting her was an addiction, and that was why I'd never made my move. I wanted her in my head more than I wanted her in my bed. I never wanted the chase to end.

Until I'd had a taste of her in the weight room. Then everything left my control.

"Are you serious?" she screamed, loud enough to hear over the party music.

I stood outside, leaning on my car with a group of people around me including Madoc and Fallon as we watched the two cops confront her about the noise as they all stood in the doorway of Tate's house.

I grinned, and everyone started laughing around me as she stormed past the cops in her cute little pajama shorts, short T-shirt that showed a sliver of her stomach, and bare feet.

Her arms swung back and forth as she stomped right toward us, growling the whole time. "Keeping me up for hours with your racket, and you file a noise complaint on me?" she shouted. "I'm going to make you hurt, Jaxon Trent!"

My chest shook with laughter. *Damn, she's so cute when she acts like she's five.*

She rushed up, straight toward me, swung her hand back, and I ducked just as she was about to slap me. Crashing myself into her thighs, I hauled her off her feet and swung her over my shoulder, her ass rubbing against my cheek.

"Whoa, Tiger," I chided, rubbing the back of her thigh.

She kicked her legs. "Put me down!"

I tightened my grip around her knees and looked at the cops. "Thanks, guys. I'll take it from here." And I jerked my chin, letting them know they could leave.

"Seriously abusing our friendship here, Jax," Wyatt, one of the officers, grumbled as he walked away with his partner.

"Put me down!" She slapped my T-shirt-clad back and I grunted, struggling to hold her as she thrashed.

Turning around, I walked up the steps and into the house, the tremors of the music pulsing through my feet and up my legs as we walked in the door.

"Listen up!" I called out, ignoring her shrieks. "This is K.C.

She's queen of the castle tonight. She tells you to fuck off, you fuck off. Got it?"

I didn't wait for responses as I swung K.C. back over my shoulder, plopping her on her feet again. Before she even had a chance to react, I circled her neck with my arm and yanked her in close, nose to nose.

"If you can't beat 'em, join 'em," I said, and reached over to yank a Seagram's Jamaican Me Happy wine cooler out of the tub of ice by the door. Twisting off the cap, I shoved it into her chest and turned to Fallon and Shane, having noticed that everyone had trailed in behind us.

"Fallon and K.C. You remember each other, right?" And I looked at K.C., hooding my eyes in a warning as I spoke to Fallon and Shane. "Get her drunk, ladies. But don't let her take any drinks from anyone other than you, Madoc, or me, okay?" I smirked at K.C.'s narrowed eyes and mouth hanging open. "Have fun," I whispered to her, and walked away.

Even though I knew she was pissed at me, I also knew she'd stay. Fallon and Shane were there to hold her hand if need be, and it just so happened that I had just planted her favorite alcoholic beverage in her grasp.

And even though I barely ever got wasted, I was very interested in seeing her get a little loose tonight. Maybe she'd finish what she had been doing to me in the car last week.

When Shane had finally trailed over a couple of hours ago, she mentioned K.C. being upset about seeing her mother, something about journals she wasn't able to get back, so I decided to lure her out. Every time she called to file a noise complaint, I got word of it and jacked up the music more.

Now here she was, friends at her side, drink in her hand, and—I looked over as she and the girls plopped down on the couch—a smile on her face.

Score. *God, I'm good.*

I tried not to grin as I played pool with Madoc and snuck glances at her from time to time. K.C. was such a little thing. Not so little that you'd mistake her for a child, but she was definitely more petite than Tate, Fallon, and Shane. Her small, flat waist would take absolutely no effort to circle using only one arm. Which I proved in the weight room. I swear her legs had absolutely no fat and she possessed the sexiest damn toned thighs I'd ever seen on a woman. Even her calves were toned, and her tanned feet and peach toenails had me drinking in every naked inch of her body.

I liked that she dressed colorfully, and I liked pretty things. I'd seen too much darkness growing up, and K.C. was like a red flag to a bull.

Her dark brown hair, the color of chocolate, spilled to the middle of her back and was parted in the middle, swinging in her eyes every so often. I'd never thought green eyes were attractive, but K.C.'s were beautiful. Like summer's first grass with the sun shining on it. Light green with gold glitter.

I squeezed the pool stick clutched in my fingers, having a sudden urge to haul her upstairs and take a shower with her.

What the fuck? That was random.

"So you're still into her, huh?" Madoc's voice broke into my head, bringing me back.

Turning back to him, I leaned on my upright pool cue and evened out my expression. "K.C.?" I clarified, trying to sound casual as I grinned. "I might still like to do a few things with her."

"That's what I thought about Fallon." He nodded. "It was like 'whoa, this is fun!' Now it's like 'whoa, I'm married!'" He gave a shaky laugh, and my chest shook with amusement.

I couldn't help being still shocked at Madoc and Fallon getting married when they were eighteen. First year in college, and they'd never even dated each other. But so far, so good. They kept an apartment in Chicago, where they lived while they attended Northwestern during the school year, and they spent their summers either traveling or at their house here in Shelburne Falls.

"Listen," Madoc started, looking between me and the table. "Fallon wanted me to talk to you about something."

I raised my eyebrows, noticing Madoc was staring at the table, mulling over a shot when he was already whipping my butt, because I was too preoccupied trying not to stare at K.C.

And when Madoc couldn't meet my eyes, I knew he was having trouble saying what needed to be said, which was also probably something I didn't want to hear.

So I waited.

He leaned down to take his shot. "She knows you're working for her father, Jax. Ciaran Pierce might be a nice guy, but he's a dangerous man. What are you doing?"

I hooded my eyes, bracing myself.

"Jax?" Madoc prompted, and I could tell he was looking at me. "Fallon doesn't like it. Hell, I don't like it. And Jared definitely won't like it."

I straightened my back, his chiding backing me into a fucking wall.

Of course Jared wouldn't understand. He was perfect. He did right even when he was doing wrong. He judged, laid down the law, and called the shots according to his assessment of how he thought things should be. There was no gray area with my brother.

So I had learned a long time ago not to tell him certain things. He didn't know what I did in Chicago on my nights alone in the city. He didn't know that I used my computer skills to hack and create illegal software for Fallon's father, who lived in Boston and worked outside the law.

And he didn't know what had happened in that basement at our father's house six years ago.

"Jared sees everything as black and white," I said, leaning down to take my shot. "There's just no talking to him about some things."

"He's your brother, and I'm your friend. We have your best interest at heart."

I let out a bitter laugh, shaking my head. "Because I'm too young to take care of myself?"

Walking to the wall, I sat down on a stool and slouched with my hands in my pockets.

"I may be a whole year younger," I explained, "but I'm also bigger and have taken more hits than the two of you combined. I've been feeding myself since I was five, and you don't even want to know how, so just stay off my back."

Awareness vibrated off my skin, and I knew others in the room had heard me, but I didn't give a shit. My brother and Madoc—as much as they tried to act otherwise—had no fucking clue how sick the world was. Who cared how I made my money as long as I ate?

When they were five they were raiding their refrigerators, trying to decide between the orange soda and the grape soda. I was rummaging through the trash for my father's leftover McDonald's and drinking beer because the water had been turned off.

And while Jared's mom—Katherine—was as close as I'd ever had to a mom, I wasn't about to be a burden on her even though I knew she didn't see it that way. She tried spoiling me with clothes and gadgets she thought I'd enjoy, but I spoiled her right back. I had to pay my way.

Madoc narrowed his eyes, probably stunned by my sudden irritation. He wasn't used to it, but I didn't feel bad. Questioning my decisions was an insult.

"Jax—," Madoc started.

"Don't," I cut him off. "I don't want your sympathy, and I don't want your concern, so fuck off." Every muscle in my face tightened.

"I just want you to shut your mouth and go back to worrying about what kind of board shorts you're going to wear for your next trip to Cancún, okay?"

He looked away, sucking in an angry breath and hardening his eyes. Placing the cue back on the rack, he stopped in front of me on his way out of the room.

"You're my brother," he pointed out in a low voice. "You have choices now. That's all I'm going to say."

And I watched him leave, knowing that he was right. I had opportunities, chances, and lifelines. I wasn't back in the foster homes I'd spent years in, and I wasn't living a nightmare in my father's twisted house anymore.

And that was why I did what I did for Fallon's father. To make sure I *never* lived like that again.

K.C. was AWOL.

Absent without leave, and she'd better not have left, because I'd damn well climb through Tate's French doors tonight if I had to.

Madoc had brought shit up I didn't want to think about tonight, and I really just wanted to see K.C.'s pouty little lips and pretty eyes right now.

Where the hell was she?

No lights were on next door.

Climbing the stairs, I saw a couple going at it in Katherine's old room, so I shut the door and checked my room. Not that she'd be in there, but it couldn't hurt to hope.

Empty. People knew my room was off-limits.

I heard a door behind me open up, and I turned around to see her stepping out of the bathroom down the hall.

She lifted her eyes, spotted me, and halted.

"I thought you left," I called out.

She stayed there, looking as if she'd stopped breathing and was afraid to meet my eyes. She rubbed the toes on one foot over the ankle of the other, scratching, and I had to clench my fists to keep from adjusting myself. Every fucking little gesture she did turned me on, and I was glad she didn't know her power.

I cleared my throat instead. "Are you drunk yet?" I asked, grinning.

She pinched her eyebrows together as if I were stupid. "No, just a little buzzed."

She walked toward me, tucking her hair behind her ear, but I caught her arm. "But you're happy?" I pressed, reaching over and pulling her hair back out from behind her ear and letting my fingertips graze her cheek.

Chills spread up my forearms. How could I not touch her? I wanted to grab her. Dig my hands into her soft skin.

"Yes," she whispered. "Feeling better." And then she tucked the hair back behind her ear.

I tilted up the corner of my mouth, pleased with her defiance.

And for the first time since knowing her, I didn't have the first clue what to do with this chance. She stood there—maybe waiting for me to make a move—and she wasn't scowling, sneering, or shouting at me.

But she broke the spell before I could decide how to react.

"What's in there?" She jerked her chin to the door in front of us.

It was my old room when Jared lived here, but now that I'd moved into his room, it housed my office. The door was secured with a padlock, and I kept the key on my key ring. Normally I didn't lock it if I was home, but during parties when anyone could venture in, it was off-limits.

"Porn," I replied flatly.

Her lips spread in a wide smile at my joke, and I felt my heartbeat throb in my neck as I flexed my jaw.

She'd never smiled at me before. Not like that.

Reaching into my jeans pocket for the key, I unlocked the room, having no clue why I was doing it. Hell, she asked, she was interested, and I wanted to prolong my time with her before she came up with a new corncob to lodge up her ass.

Opening the door, I waved her in ahead of me, but her eyebrows shot up and her eyes went wide.

"Wow," she blurted out before she'd even stepped into the room.

She inched in, and I followed behind, shaking my head at myself. Even still, the sensation of a bubble wrapping around us tighter and tighter, forcing us closer, was there.

I twisted the key out of the lock and threw it down on the table by the door, shutting it after we'd walked in.

I leaned back on the table, crossing my arms over my black T-shirt and watching her circle the room. "I don't let many people in here," I said.

I wasn't worried about the computers. They weren't important to me. The information I could use them to gain was. This room, and its contents, gave me the ability to protect myself and my family, make a living, and be aware of every stumble in the road before I even turned the corner.

When I was thirteen, and my father had been sentenced to prison time, I'd been sent to live with a family that had two computers. One of them was old, so they had let me tinker and explore with it. Once I discovered how to use it and the leverage that's at a person's fingertips if you're clever and diligent enough, I was hooked. I wanted to know everything.

She strolled down the wall, studying the six flat-screen monitors

I had mounted in two rows of three each. Two were shut off, two had updates and installations running, and the other two had accounts I was trying to crack. Not that she'd know what she was looking at.

There was a seventh flat-screen I had supported on a tripod that controlled the others. The room wasn't decorative. Instead of portraits or wall decals, I had bulletin boards and whiteboards with my scribble all over them, and desks lining the walls with electronics and computers sitting around.

In this room I was a god. I watched, and I swirled the paint every so often with no one the wiser.

K.C. passed each monitor and table, stopping to study a few things and swaying ever so slightly to the music coming from downstairs. Her thumbnail was in her mouth, but she looked relaxed.

"This is how you make your money, isn't it?" she said, turning away from my notes on the whiteboard to look at me. "Are you doing illegal things, Jax?"

I licked my lips, taunting her. "Would it get you hot if I said yes?"

"No," she grumbled, looking away again. "It gets me hot when you touch me."

My heart plummeted into my stomach, and I felt as if I were falling. What the hell did she just say?

She spun back around, her mouth hanging open. "I can't believe I just said that. Oh, my God."

I didn't blink, and her chest wasn't moving any oxygen.

I swallowed, standing up and stalking toward her. "Say it again."

"Damn wine coolers," she bit out, looking to the floor and retreating. "I never usually feel anything. How did you know they were my favorite?"

I smirked. How cute she was. I tipped my chin down, inching toward her and loving every backward step she took. Why did I like her being afraid of me?

"I didn't know they were your favorite," I lied. "And it's not the wine coolers you're feeling. It's me."

Her back hit the wall, and I came in front of her, bearing down on her. Her hair tickled my cheek.

"Say it again," I breathed into her ear.

Her hands went to my chest, trying to keep me away. "No."

"Coward."

She peered up at me, narrowing her eyes. "Now I'm a coward." She nodded sarcastically, pressing her hands into my chest with more force. "Gutless, helpless, and coward all because I won't sleep with you. Next, my girly pink wine coolers and peach nail polish will be under attack. Let me help you with some more names: princess, self-absorbed, weak, wimp, arrogant, snotty, sellout, conceited—"

Grabbing hold of the backs of her thighs, I heard her yelp as I hauled her off her feet and pressed her into the wall, forcing her legs around my waist. I cut her off, bringing us nose to nose. "I like your pink wine coolers, and I think your pretty toenails are sexy as hell."

Her chest rose and fell in silence, up and down, up and down, and the heat of her mouth was right on my lips as she stared at me, shocked.

Her soft lips.

Her fucking soft lips were panting and moist, and I stared at them, wanting to bite. Her hot cunt warmed my stomach, setting me on fire, and I loved how easy her body was to handle. "You're a pretty little thing, K. C. Carter," I whispered into her mouth, "and I like looking at you."

"Oh, G—," she moaned, but I cut her off, slamming my lips down on hers.

Three fucking years.

Three fucking years of desire for this girl, and I wanted that shit I claimed I didn't want days ago. I still wanted to pin her against the lockers at school. I still wanted her riding the shit out of me with her tits in my mouth.

And I still wanted to wipe the sneer off her face and see her smile.

K.C.'s full lips moved against mine, kissing me back, and while her mouth felt soft and moved fluidly like water, it also nipped and nibbled, bit and sucked.

She was good, and I gripped her ass in both hands, pressing her into my body so hard I could feel her heat through her clothes.

Her hands pressed into my chest again, and chills fanned against my skin as she pulled away. "Stop," she gasped.

Fuck no.

I gritted my teeth and slammed my ass down in the desk chair with her straddling me. Grabbing her wrists, I held them behind her back and jerked her chest into mine, forcing her fierce green eyes down on me.

"Say it," I ordered.

Her teeth were bared. "No."

Tough little shit.

I smiled, my lips threatening hers. "Your breath is shaking. You're scared to look at me." I sucked in air through my teeth. "And I know you feel me between your legs, don't you?"

Her eyebrows arched together, making her look even more vulnerable.

I jerked her into me again. "Don't you?"

And then she looked down, nodding quickly.

I swallowed, licking my dry lips. Old K.C. would never have been that brave.

She raised her timid eyes, speaking low and husky. "I liked your mouth on me in the weight room. And in the car."

My fucking head was floating, and I couldn't remember when I had wanted something so badly. Releasing her arms, I brought her hands in between us and then cupped her cheek, trying to get her to look at me.

My dick wanted me to bend her over every desk in this room, but my head liked her in my lap. I wanted her to be comfortable, so I let her ease into me.

Her throat moved up and down, and I saw that she was rubbing her thumb over the scar on her wrist.

"You think I tried to kill myself, don't you?" she asked, and I blinked. She'd changed the subject pretty damn fast.

"You noticed the scar at some point and assumed." Her eyes met mine, and she lifted her chin. "Well, I didn't, okay? I wouldn't try to hurt myself."

I narrowed my eyes on her. I had definitely referred to her wrist the other night when I said she'd been desperate to get out of her own skin, and even though I had no idea why she was bringing that up now, I sat back and let her talk.

"How did it happen?" I asked.

She shook her head. "It doesn't matter. I just wanted you to know that it wasn't that. I hate when people make assumptions about me."

I held her thighs. "Okay. Tell me what K.C. stands for, then."

She smiled, gesturing around the room. "I'm sure you have the capability to figure that out, don't you, Jax?"

Moving my hands up to her hips, I gripped her tight and eased her into me. Nipping at her lips in short, soft kisses, I glided my tongue along her top lip. "Tell me," I whispered, hearing her breath quicken again. "Or I'm going to lay you on my bed." I dug my fingers into her skin. "And eat your pussy so hard the whole damn house will hear you screaming."

I kissed through her excited little breaths.

"Katherina Chase." She pulled back, breathing hard. "It was my sister's name."

"Why do you have your sister's initials?" I asked quickly, trying to take my mind off her hands on my stomach.

"Because," she started, looking as if she didn't know where to begin. "Because she's dead."

I leveled my gaze on her, waiting, even though her weight on my cock was getting me so hard I could barely pay attention.

She swallowed, meeting my eyes. "My sister died before I was born. I was conceived shortly after. From what I remember, things seemed fine for a while, but then when I was four my dad was sent away to a hospital. A mental hospital."

I ran my hands down her thighs and up again, letting her know that I was listening. Truth was I cared more that she was opening up than about what she was telling me.

I already knew it all anyway.

She continued. "He'd been battling with coming to terms with my sister's death, and he finally started to lose his grip. He stayed in there for years. Winter of senior year, I went to visit him the same way I did every month. He freaked out, grabbed a pair of scissors, and slashed me." She ran her thumb down the long, diagonal scar on the inside of her wrist.

I stilled. "Why?" I asked, not remembering her wearing any bandages then. But it was winter, so long sleeves would've covered up the injury.

She shrugged. "Who knows?"

I sat up straight, pulling her closer to me. "So, why do you go by your sister's initials?"

"Well, that's how we knew my dad was wigging out." She nodded. "He started calling me K.C., thinking I was my sister. We tried to correct him, but it was more trouble than it was worth. So my mother called me K.C. in his presence to avoid his outbursts."

Fucking four-year-old little girl having to go through that. She must've been so confused.

"And then so did the rest of the family," she continued. "And eventually it started happening at home as well. My father would get a little better, come home for short spells, and we'd carry on the charade there. The practice eventually just became habit."

I ground my teeth together.

K. C. Carter was a dead little girl, and the woman in my lap was still living that lie. It pissed me off. She could've been someone different. Someone who knew herself and didn't follow what her boyfriend or her parents wanted. Instead K.C. was fearful, timid, and unsure. Until recently, anyway.

"What's your real name?" I pressed.

She grinned. "You're going to laugh."

The corner of my lips tipped up. "I won't ever laugh at you," I assured her. "Ever again, I mean."

She rolled her eyes and then let out a tired sigh. "Juliet." She winced, looking at me through embarrassed eyes. "Juliet Adrian Carter. My father liked Shakespeare, so he named my sister after the heroine in *The Taming of the Shrew* and me after . . . well, you know."

I dipped my head into her neck. "Juliet."

I felt her body shake with a shiver, and I threaded my fingers into her hair, nibbling her skin and eating up her scent.

"Jax, I can't," she breathed, placing her hands on my chest. "I . . . ," she stammered, "I don't exactly dislike you anymore, but this isn't a good idea. As much as I'd like to give in, I can't be that girl."

"What girl?"

She stared at me. "A one-night stand."

My fists tightened around her shirt. So that was what she thought I wanted?

My voice hardened. "What makes you think you'd be a one-night stand?"

"Because you're Jared Trent's brother. Because you're young. Why would you want more?" she asked, her tone light. "I'm not trying to be prissy, okay? You get to me. I like the way you feel. I'm just not ready for this." Her lips pursed, and she started to rise, but I pulled her back down.

"Ready for what?" I bit out, getting seriously fucking annoyed at her assumptions and the fact that she compared me to Jared. Two minutes ago she'd had her arms and legs wrapped around me.

Her eyebrows shot up, challenging me. "This," she spat out, and dug into my pocket, pulling out my knife. "It's been digging into the back of my thigh since I sat down. Why do you have so many computers? Why do the cops let you get away with anything? What do you do to make a living? And why do you carry a knife, Jax?"

My chest filled with delight at her anger. She was getting ballsier by the minute.

I shot her a smirk. "Because it's quiet."

And I almost laughed at her arched eyebrow. She was asking why I carried a knife, and I just answered why I carried a knife instead of a gun.

She averted her eyes, but I caught the annoyed expression as she raised the knife up to her face, studying it. She hit the button, and the blade shot out right between us.

I had only a moment to wonder what the hell she was doing before I reared back, seeing her jab the knife into my space.

"You think you scare me, don't you?" she taunted, holding the blade to my neck, playing with me.

I sucked in a few quick breaths and let out a startled laugh as my heart slammed against my ribs. Well, this was new.

I swallowed, meeting her triumphant little smile and leaning into the blade, feeling the sharp, cool steel bite into my neck. "You want to play? You don't know how to play my games, Juliet."

And I snatched the knife out of her scared hand and brought it down to the hem of her shirt, slicing it up the middle.

"Jax!" she screamed, fumbling with her now useless T-shirt as I threw the blade onto the floor. "What are you doing?"

Grabbing her around the waist, I stood up, whipped her around, and planted her in front of the window looking down onto the back-yard full of partiers.

I wrapped my arms around her shaking body and growled into her ear from behind her, "God, Juliet. You think I just wanna fuck? You think I wanna keep myself hidden and mysterious, because it's my play to get women into bed? Huh?" I pressed. "No, baby. I could fuck ten different girls tonight if I wanted to. I don't want to do that."

Her chest shook, and she squirmed against me, probably scared that we could be seen out the window.

"So, what do you want?" she cried. "If not a one-night stand?"

I closed my burning eyes, and buried my lips in her hair. "I want to terrorize you," I confessed. "I want to cut you without drawing blood. I want to break you." I pulled her into me. "And then I want to fuck you."

From the moment I laid eyes on her, I had wanted to break her out of her shell. I wanted to see her undone, and I wanted to take her over. For how long, I didn't know, but I knew it would be for more than one night.

I also knew it wouldn't be forever.

Her breathing slowed, and she stilled, staring out the window. I straightened behind her and peeled off the T-shirt she was holding closed.

"Jax," she whimpered, turning her face to me. "They can see us."

Reaching around, I turned her chin back toward the window.

"They can't see you. The window's tinted." The shirt, sliced up the front, fell down her arms and spilled to the floor. "But you can see them, Juliet," I pointed out, gently running my hands up her bare arms. "They drink. They laugh. They have meaningless conversations about what's trending on Twitter." I paused and dug my fingers into her hips, pulling her ass into me and breathing into her ear, "And I'm so jacked up I want you so bad."

My cock grew and swelled with the feel of her. The silk of her skin in my hands, the shape of her ass pressed to my cock, and the reflection of her hands covering her tits. She was so sweet and timid.

If I didn't know better, I'd think she was a virgin.

And she couldn't take it any more than I could. Dropping her hands, she turned her head to nuzzle into my chest, and I was tempted to slice off her shorts, too.

But I didn't. Instead I skimmed down her tight stomach and slid my hand into her bottoms, finding her hot, wet center.

I closed my eyes. She was fucking soaked. Her panties were wet, too. How long had she been like this? Since we got into the room?

Swirling my fingers around, I rubbed over her clit, feeling her body squirm against mine.

Slipping a finger inside her folds, I rubbed her small entrance in circles, alternating between that and massaging her clit.

"Jax," she gasped, crashing the palms of her hands against the glass and breathing hard. She leaned forward, and I bit down, clenching my jaw with the pressure in my jeans as she stuck her hips back at me, inviting me in.

Jesus. "That's it," I encouraged, taking my hand out of the front of her shorts and slipping in at the back instead.

I rubbed her pussy, stroking my hand forward and backward, forward and backward, my groans mixing with hers.

So wet. And so smooth.

She was clean-shaven. Or maybe waxed, because she was softer than any other girl I'd ever touched. And with her wetness it was as if my finger was touching silk.

But if she'd broken up with her asswipe boyfriend more than two weeks ago, why was she still keeping that area waxed? I didn't like the idea that she might be hooking up with someone else at all.

Arching her back, she moaned, "Yes."

And I closed my eyes as I bent down to kiss her naked back, my teeth grazing her skin. Reaching around with my other hand, I cupped and massaged her breasts, smiling through my kisses as she squirmed against me. I rolled her clit between my fingers, and her back jerked against my mouth.

"Fuck, Juliet," I breathed out. "No fucking way would you be a one-night stand."

Circling my arm around her, I pulled her back up against my chest and growled into her ear, "I'd need a lot more than one night to do everything I want to do to you."

I stuck my middle finger into her wet heat and held her tight as she gasped in sweet pain. Withdrawing it, I swirled her come over her clit and then dived back into her again, plunging the tip of my finger inside her.

Damn, she was tight. My finger wouldn't slide out easily, and the friction of her folds and skin along with her wetness had my dick jerking with need. I reached down and adjusted myself, feeling too fucking uncomfortable right now. She had to be able to feel me pressed against her back.

But I couldn't take her to bed now. Not with my house full of people.

We faced the window and saw everyone milling about the party, and it was such a turn-on to have Juliet reach behind and snake an arm around my neck and move her ass into my hand. She wanted this. She might even let me fuck her right now, but I couldn't take the chance. Not yet.

It would be in a bed. And in a fucking empty house where she could make as much noise as she wanted. Not tonight, but it was definitely going to be soon. Real fucking soon.

My hand fell to her tit, and I continued pumping her pussy with my finger faster and faster.

"Jax," she whimpered. "Jax, please. I can't."

I turned her around and pushed my body into hers against the wall perpendicular to the window. "Yes, you can," I said, staring into her eyes and moving my hand to the front, continuing to finger her.

I could feel her nipples pressing through my T-shirt, and I looked down to admire her. Everything below my stomach swirled in a storm of raw energy.

Damn, she was nice to look at. Her breasts were slightly bigger than average, and on her frame they were probably bigger than they should be.

"No." She shook her head, her eyes fluttering with what my finger was doing. "I can't. I can never come, Jax. Not with someone else."

I plastered my body to hers, forcing her mouth up to mine as I whispered against her lips, "I don't give a fuck about your asshole ex. You hear me?" And then I narrowed my eyes, looking down on her. "Wait. What do you mean 'someone else'? You can come by yourself. Is that what you meant?"

Oh, Jesus. Add that to the list of things I wanted her to do when we were in the bedroom.

She looked away out the window, but she didn't stop fucking my hand.

"Look at me." I pulled her head back to face me. "What do you think about when you touch yourself?"

Her eyes fell to the side, out the window again, and I could tell she was still loving the feel of my finger in her. She watched the people below us and grabbed my waist, continuing to grind into me.

"You like having them right there, don't you?" I asked, following her gaze outside. "It's okay, you know? There are no rules, Juliet. A pane of glass separates you from them seeing everything. It's okay if that gets you off. Now tell me, what do you think about when you finger yourself?"

Her eyes shot to mine. "Jax." She shook her head. "I . . ."

"Say it." My lips tightened. "You're driving me fucking crazy."

"I think about you," she rushed out, breathless. "I think about if I had let you give me a ride home two years ago, but you didn't take me home."

I closed my eyes, letting my forehead fall into the wall by her head.

"Jesus, keep going," I begged, rubbing her clit. "I want to see if your fantasy matches mine."

I'd thought about that night a lot over the years. I'd been disappointed when she wouldn't let me drive her home, and I definitely hadn't gone back to finish what I'd started with the two girls. I'd let them crash, and I went to shower and jerk off to the fantasy of K.C. peeling off that white summer dress in the backseat of my car.

I circled the hard nub of her clit faster and faster, feeling the pulse tap, tap, tap against my fingertips.

"You told me that you were going to kiss me," she started. "Just one time before I left for college, and I wanted you to," she whispered, her breaths shaky as I slid my finger into her pussy and came out to work her clit. "I wanted it so bad," she continued. "But I couldn't talk. The next thing I knew you took me to the falls. And you kissed me. Between my thighs."

Fucking hell.

Her voice grew stronger, bolder. "You lifted up my dress, Jax. And your tongue licked me up and down," she whimpered, sucking in a breath. "And I held your head there, because I didn't want you to stop."

She cried out and I knew she was coming. Her hips thrust into my hand, and she moved her hands up to my shoulders, digging her nails in.

I put my lips against her hot cheek. "And then what did I do to you?"

She let her head fall back as she moaned. "You turned me over the hood of the car onto my stomach," she cried, "you yanked up my dress, and then you fucked me."

Her mouth fell open, her eyes squeezed shut, and she cried out, moaning and gasping. I plunged my finger back inside her, feeling her body tighten and release around me, throbbing her quick pulse on my finger.

"Jesus," I groaned, kissing her forehead and absorbing her body shuddering and shaking.

Her head fell into my chest, and I held her as her breathing slowed down.

"Jax, I—" She sounded nervous.

"Shh. Relax," I said, even though my heart was still pounding like crazy, and my dick still hadn't come down.

I pulled my shirt over my head and slipped it onto her, since her shirt was useless now. Sliding her limp arms in, she didn't protest when I picked her up and carried her into my room.

"No more fun tonight." I tried to keep my voice gentle, but they were the hardest words I'd ever had to utter. I wanted to strip, crawl under the sheets with her, mold my body to hers, and bury myself deep in her warmth all night.

"I don't prey on girls that just ended five-year relationships, okay?" I said. "You've got time before I really start trying. Maybe to-morrow night."

"Great," she mumbled, sounding sarcastic but cute.

Laying her down, I shut off the light and kissed her lips. "Go to sleep. I just have some things to take care of, but I'll be back up soon."

Her eyes closed, and the two ever-present little wrinkles between her eyebrows disappeared as I watched her drift away.

"Jax!"

Someone pounded on my door, causing me to jerk. "Jax, you in there?"

CHAPTER 10

JULIET

I shot up in bed, fisting the sheet, as Jax strode for the door, whipping it open.

Looking over, I saw a young guy, nicely styled black hair, tattoos scaling down both arms, with several facial piercings. He peered around Jax, taking notice of me, and I immediately pulled the sheet up, embarrassed. I was fully clothed, but I was still trying not to be "that girl."

Yeah, I needed to get over that.

"A couple of the guys have someone cornered downstairs," he said to Jax. "Apparently someone saw him putting something in a girl's drink. You want to deal with this?" he asked Jax, and then looked at me again. "Or you want us to handle it?"

Meaning Jax looked busy.

This guy wasn't being snide or suggestive. He was asking Jax as though looking for orders. I turned away, shaking my head.

"Juliet, stay here," Jax commanded, and I jerked my stunned gaze over to him just as he slammed the door shut.

Um, what? My eyes burned like light sabers at the closed door, and I clenched the black sheet. Was he serious?

Yeah. No. I wasn't following orders like Jaxon Trent's latest toy.

Throwing off the covers, I went to the mirror and smoothed my messy hair, pushing away the delicious burn of him pulling it earlier. Then I tucked in the front and back hem of his T-shirt so it wouldn't make me look as though I had nothing on underneath. It wasn't particularly baggy, but it was long as hell.

I turned to leave but stopped, noticing two pictures peeking out from underneath a wooden box on top of his dresser. I reached over and pulled them up, studying the women in the images. One picture was old, an actual photograph of a girl—maybe sixteen or seventeen—wearing a defiant look on her face and a Cure T-shirt. Next to her sat an older guy—early twenties—with a cigarette in his hand. He had Jax's eyes.

The second photo was a rack card, advertising a club in Chicago that held some kind of show. The woman in the images was dark and beautiful, dressed in a black corset and top hat. She was hanging in the air above a full crowd, but I couldn't tell what was holding her up.

I looked between the two pictures, seeing the resemblance between the women.

I quickly stuffed the photos back where I found them and walked for the door.

Stepping out of the room, I turned the corner and descended the stairs. The party was still going strong—it was only a little after midnight after all—but the crowd had thinned. I didn't see Shane, Madoc, or Fallon anywhere, and I was little pissed off about that. My cousin, at least, should've checked in with me before she ditched me.

A few people lingered around the pool table, in the foyer, and I could hear voices coming from the kitchen. Everyone seemed heavily relaxed as they barely noticed me.

Five Finger Death Punch's "Battle Born" droned out of the speakers, and I walked out the front door in my bare feet, ready to just go home, when I reared back, planting my footstep back where it came from.

Holy shit!

"Jax! Whoo!" someone cheered, and I sucked in air and pinched my eyebrows together in horror.

Jax's naked back faced me as he hunched on the ground, slamming his fist into some poor guy's face. Well, not poor guy if he was the one slipping drugs to an unknowing girl, but poor guy because he was obviously down, and Jax wasn't stopping.

His arm shot back, the muscles in his triceps and back bulged, and his fist hammered down right on the guy's face. Again and again, and I fought against the pitching sensation in my stomach.

When Jax brought his fist back again, I saw blood, and I raced down to the walkway at the bottom of the steps, thinking it might be his.

Wiping his bloody fist on his jeans, he stepped up, bringing his victim with him by the collar.

I veered around the crowd that had gathered and hugged myself against a chill that didn't come from the air. Jax dug in the guy's pocket, bringing out a few small vials of liquid, and handed them to the same guy who'd come to Jax's room.

The dealer wobbled back and forth, blood dripping down his lips and chin, and Jax hovered down on him, damn near pressing the guy into the ground with the anger in his eyes. His lips moved, and he whispered something in the dealer's face, but I couldn't hear it. I doubted anyone could, and I knew there was a reason for that.

People shouted threats they never intended to keep. Others whispered threats they didn't want witnesses to hear.

Dropping his hands, Jax talked to Tattoo Guy while everyone started to disperse. Then he turned around and locked eyes with me.

"I told you to stay upstairs." His voice was quiet but hard and annoyed.

I dropped my eyes, trying not to see all the blood. "I think I'll go home. I'm not even sure I want to know you right now."

Some girls may want a tough guy. An alpha dog who pushes them around. Someone who beats up drug dealers on their front lawn. It struck me that I'd simply like someone who didn't attract drug dealers in the first place.

"You already know me. Intimately." He smirked.

Several bystanders laughed, and I glared at Jax.

"That doesn't mean you know me," I bit out.

He stepped into my face. "And witnessing me pummel a nineteen-year-old guy who gave a sixteen-year-old girl GHB so he could do who knows what to her body doesn't mean you know me, either, K. C. Carter." He drawled out my sister's name, trying to piss me off. "You can leave now."

"Ohs" filled the air around me, and I stared at Jax as I ran my tongue along the back of my teeth, fuming.

I could say it was the fight that had pissed me off. Or I could say it was the plethora of questions without answers that had made the bug crawl up my butt.

But it wasn't either one.

If he had come up to me and put his arms around me, looking at me as if I were the Christmas present he'd been waiting for as he had done in that room, I would've folded. I wouldn't have cared that he got into fights or that he was a complete mystery.

What shut me down was the fact that I was disposable to him. Just like to my mother. To Liam. To most people who looked through me as if I were a piece of glass.

Fuck him.

I walked past him, not saying a word as I headed toward Tate's house.

"Are you okay?" Fallon rushed up and touched my shoulder. "I just came out and caught the tail end of that. Anything I can do?"

I nodded, still walking. "Yeah. Get Madoc's car keys, and get Shane. We're going on a midnight run."

Homicides occur more frequently during the summer. Little-known fact, but it's true.

The irritation of the heat drives people to lose their cool—no pun intended—and they end up reacting in ways they might not in more temperate conditions. Sunshine blinds you, sweat trickles down your back, and your body heat rises, making you uncomfortable. Given the right circumstance—the right person getting in your face—your brain is pushed beyond the breaking point, and you snap.

All you want is to feel better, and all it takes is a twist of the screw to drive you over the edge.

Well, all I wanted was to feel.

Not feel better or feel good. Just feel *something*. And while I definitely wasn't itching to kill anyone, I could understand how a little thing like the weather drove people to do things that were out of character.

It might've been Jax who got my blood pumping again, or it might have been being on my own, without my mother or Liam. All I knew was that something was twisting my brain tighter and tighter, and I couldn't *not* react anymore. Almost as if it was all out of my control.

"How many times have you driven a stick?" Fallon asked beside me as we both bobbed forward in Madoc's car.

I licked my lips, tasting the sweat on my upper lip and Jaxon

Trent still in my mouth. My stomach growled again, but I ignored it, punching into fourth gear.

"Shut it," I warned, joking. "I'm still learning."

"Madoc's going to kill me," she complained, and I saw her cradle her forehead in her hand out of the corner of my eye. "You should've let me drive, K.C."

"Leave her alone, Fal," Shane piped up from the backseat as I rounded onto my street. "And her name's Juliet."

I glanced at Fallon, who looked over at me, her light brown hair fanning around her eyes. "Juliet?"

I arched an eyebrow at her. "No jokes," I ordered. "It's my real name."

"Why don't you go by it?" Fallon asked.

A smile played at the corners of my lips. "I do now."

Pressing in the clutch and downshifting, I cruised to an easy stop in front of my—my mother's—brick Colonial. Looking past Fallon out the window, I found it hard to believe I was only here this afternoon.

"So, what's the plan?" Shane asked.

"You don't have to come in," I explained. It was too much to ask them to get involved with this. "I just need to get my journals out of my room. It's more than I can carry in one trip. If you're willing, I thought we could all do it quickly," I said as more of an apology but quickly added, "But you definitely don't have to. My mother will be a pain the ass."

"Ooooh." Fallon rubbed her hands together, smiling. "Pain-in-the-ass moms. My specialty."

"I'm down." Shane leaned over the seat, looking at me. "Let's do this."

I inhaled a deep breath and tucked my chin down to calm my nervousness. Climbing out of the car, I stared at the dark house as I waited for Fallon and Shane to follow me out and then started around the car toward the front lawn. I smiled to myself, kind of liking the feeling of them behind me. Kind of as though they'd catch me if I fell.

It reminded me of Tate, and I wished she was here.

"How's your dad doing?" Tate asks me as we walk home from school.

I shrug, holding on to my backpack straps. "The same. Sometimes he remembers me. Sometimes he doesn't."

It's Monday afternoon, and we've just finished our last class, freshman PE. And thank goodness for that! If I had PE earlier in the day, my mother just might show up to ensure that I showered, and then she'd bring me a freshly pressed set of clothes. At least this way, I can just come straight home, shower, and never have my friends find out what a spaz my mom is.

"It's hard to think of you as Juliet," Tate teases. I'd only just told her about my dad and the deal with my name a week ago.

"Just stick with K.C.," I tell her. "It's what I'm used to."

"Out of the way!" someone growls, and we both jump, huddling together, as Jared Trent zooms past on his dirt bike. He stands up, pedaling and scowling back at Tate. His deep brown hair blows in his eyes, but you can still see the hatred blazing out of them.

"Jared Trent!" I belt out. "You're so dumb you'd trip over a cordless phone!"

I hear Tate snort, but then she chides, "Don't piss him off. He takes it out on me." But then her eyes dart up. "Oh, crap."

I look up the street to see Jared swerving his bike in a circle and coming back at us.

My eyes go round. "Run," I order.

And Tate and I shoot off, up the sidewalk and into the grass, as my backpack bounces against my tailbone and Tate grabs my hand, squealing.

I start laughing as we scurry, and I don't even look back to see where

Jared is. Vaulting up the steps, we crash through my front door and slam it shut, gasping for breath and laughing.

"Stop antagonizing him," Tate commands, but her face glows with amusement.

I drop my backpack to the floor, my chest rising and falling hard. "He's an asshole, and you're awesome."

"K.C.!"

I jerk to the stairs, straightening my back immediately.

"Yes, Mother." I look up and then to the floor. My mother descends the stairs, and I can already smell her perfume.

She doesn't have to say anything. I used vulgar language, and it was unacceptable.

"Tatum, honey," my mother greets as she comes up in front of us. "Nice to see you. What a darling little tank top."

And I turn my head away from them, cringing as my eyes fill with tears. My mother hates her tank top, and Tate knows it. Embarrassment heats my face, and I clench my fists, wanting to shove my mother away.

But I grit my teeth and turn back. Tate wears a tight white cami underneath a loose black tank top. The top features a white skull with a Native American headdress of beads and feathers.

"Yeah." I swallow. "I like the skull on it. I was hoping I could borrow it."

Tate's uncomfortable eyes shift to me, and my mother arches an eyebrow. If we were alone, I would've been hit.

When we are alone, I will be hit.

"Tatum?" my mother starts, her voice dripping with sweetness. "K.C. has a doctor's appointment. Are you okay to make it home on your own?"

Doctor's appointment?

Tate glances at me, looking as if she's holding her breath, and then smiles, nodding. "Of course." She leans in for a hug. "See you tomorrow, K.C." And then whispers in my ear, "Love you."

"You, too," I mumble, because my mom is watching.

Tate walks out the door, and my mother steps in front of me, cocking her head. "Upstairs," she orders.

I'm not sure what she wants, but my stomach rolls anyway. I'm tired of being afraid of her.

I still remember my dad being home and cuddling on the couch with him, watching Barney. *He hated the show, but he'd sit with me for hours, because he knew it was the only way I was allowed to watch TV.*

My mother never takes me anywhere unless it's to pretty me up shopping or to the salon, or to smarten me up at a museum. She rarely laughs with me, and I don't remember ever being squeeze-hugged, tickled, or gushed over.

I wish she loved me. Like K.C. I hear her cry sometimes in her room, but I don't dare tell her. She'd get mad.

I walk upstairs, glancing back out of the corner of my eye every so often to see her behind me. I'm afraid to turn my back on her.

Opening the door to my bedroom, I stop.

Our family doctor is standing by the window in his suit minus the jacket.

"No," I choke out, and turn for the door again.

But my mother grabs me, yanks me into the room, and slams the door.

"No!" I cry.

The tears that pooled at the memory didn't spill over. I wouldn't allow it. This twisted house wasn't mine anymore, and I didn't have to stay once I got my journals. I would forget the slaps. I would forget the harsh words. I would forget the doctor's visits.

I wouldn't spend another day giving any of it more attention than I already had done.

I rang the doorbell.

Moments later, a light came on inside and then the front porch light. I shifted, immediately wondering how I looked, but then I stilled again. I was still dressed in my pajama shorts and Jax's T-shirt, looking completely out of sorts, and it didn't fucking matter.

My mother opened the door slowly, eyes narrowed as she took us in. "K.C.?" She looked between me and Shane and Fallon. "What is the meaning of this?"

"I need my journals."

Her confused and annoyed expression turned to a scowl. "You will most certainly not get your journals right now. How dare—"

I pushed past her, barging through the front door, and spun around.

"Fallon? Shane?" I crossed my arms over my chest. "My journals are tucked in a secret compartment at the bottom of my hope chest. Would you mind?" I asked, and then looked to my mother. "My mother has things to say to me in private."

I knew the word "private" would buy me some time. My mother's back straightened, and her gaze barely flickered to them as they darted past her and up the stairs.

My mother closed the door and walked toward me. "How dare you? It is the middle of the night, and I told you you could have your journals when you came home."

"I'm not coming home." I hoped I sounded defiant.

"K.C.—"

"My name is Juliet."

And I sucked in air as she grabbed my upper arm. "You will do as you're told," she growled, jerking me closer.

My skin burned where she buried her nails, and I clamped my mouth shut and held her eyes. I wouldn't let her see me falter.

I got in her face. "No," I countered.

Her eyes flickered upstairs, and I knew she was gauging whether or not to hit me.

I dropped my voice to a whisper. "You can't hurt me anymore."

Her mouth twisted up, and she went for it. She dropped the hand from my arm and whipped it across my face, sending me stumbling back into the wall.

But I shot back up. "Again," I demanded, holding out my arms, inviting her.

Her eyebrows dug deep, and she looked at me, searching my eyes for what—I don't know.

Her hand came down again, this time her fingernails catching my lip, and I squeezed my eyes shut, wincing.

My breath poured out of me shakily, but I pulled myself up straight. "Come on. You can do better," I challenged, my eyes pooling with tears, but I wasn't sad or angry or even hurt. The more she hit me, the more powerful I felt. This was all she had.

"Juliet, what—" I heard Shane at the top of the stairs, and I darted out my hand, signaling her to stop.

I sucked in breath after breath, shaking my head at my mother as I cried. "You can't hurt me."

The hardness in her face was like steel, but her voice shook. "I'm calling the police," she warned, and turned to walk to the living room.

"And tell them what?" I taunted.

I cocked my head and continued. "Sandra Carter. Vice president of the Rotary Club, president of the Shelburne Falls Garden Association, and School Board chairperson?" I listed the many forums on which she could potentially be embarrassed. "What will you tell them that I can't?"

And she stopped. I knew I had her.

The woman didn't like unsavory attention, and even though I would never talk about her, my sister, or my father, she thought that I might. And that was enough.

She kept her back to me. "Get out."

"So you can be alone?" I asked quietly.

She didn't turn around.

She didn't look at me.

She just stood there, waiting for me to disappear, so she could sink back into her delusions as if none of this ever happened.

I looked to Fallon and Shane, their arms loaded down with my black-and-white composition books, staring at me wide-eyed.

"Let's go," I urged.

As we left the house and walked to the car, Shane sped up next to me. "Are you okay?"

"No." But I smiled. "Not in the least."

CHAPTER 11

JAXON

"*D*ad?" *I call, coming into the living room.* "*Do you want to go to the park?*" *I hold in my breath and hope I sound nice and quiet. Please, please, please, I pray. I want to go to the park and play someplace pretty.*

"*No,*" *he grumbles, not even looking at me.* "*Not today.*"

I stand in the doorway, watching him and a girl play with sugar on the table. They slice it with something sharp, and then they laugh right before they suck it into their noses. They don't see me, and I don't know what they're doing, but I know that I don't like it. There's something wrong.

Music comes out of the radio, and it bounces off the walls, hitting me. The blaring sunlight blasts through the windows and warms the garbage in the kitchen, making it stink really bad.

And I know that my dad and the girl will be like this for a while, and I will be alone for the rest of the day.

I don't like it here, and I want to go home. To my foster family. I lived with them all five years since I was a baby, and I don't like my dad.

I inch toward them. "*What are you doing?*" *I ask in a quiet voice.*

"*Nothing.*" *My father's voice turns hard.* "*Go play.*"

I don't know where to play. We don't have any toys, and there's no yard. Only a dirty old street outside.

The girl stands up and starts dancing, and my dad smiles at her before sniffling more of the powder.

My eyes ache and burn with tears. I want to scream that I don't like it here. That I want to go home, but my dad says he'll hit me again if I say anything bad. I thought I wanted to live with him when he came for me. I thought I'd meet my mom.

But I'm alone, and I'm sad all the time. It's dirty here, and I don't like the people that come around. No one cooks. No one plays with me. I cry every day I wake up and remember where I am.

Tears drip down my face, and I try to whisper. "Dad, I'm hungry."

He looks at me mean, and I back up, my face hurting, because I can't stop crying. More tears fall, and my shoulders shake.

"Aw, go get the kid some food," the girl says in a nice voice. "I'll stay with him."

"Kid can wait," my dad grumbles, coming up behind her and putting his hands on her privates. "Show me how good you suck first."

I stood in the shower, my head bowed and my forearm propped up on the wall. Running my hand over the top of my head, I exhaled breath after breath, releasing shit memories I'd spent day after day trying to forget.

This was why I stayed busy.

School. The Loop. Lacrosse. The club. My computers. My friends. There was hardly any time when I stayed at home—especially alone—and this was why I didn't get close to people.

Especially women.

I rubbed my hands down my face, feeling the familiar comfort of my hair resting against my back.

To hell with K. C. Carter. She just had to go and get all bitchy again, and why was I even surprised? Jared had warned me, saying she was uptight and whiny, but I still wanted her.

And why? What made her so damn special? I didn't indulge in nearly as many girls as she probably thought I did, but I could. I could have anyone. Hell, Cameron and I were always on call for each other, so why did I crave K.C.'s piss and vinegar all the time?

Every one of her looks was worth a thousand words. Why did it fill me up so good when she smiled at me or looked at me as if she needed me?

And then last night when I looked into her scared eyes and saw, for once, all the feelings she was so desperate to have but afraid to experience, I knew without a doubt that there was a hell of a lot more to her than what she let people see.

And I knew she'd bring me past the edges of my control.

I swallowed the lump in my throat and shut off the water. Stepping out of the shower, I grabbed a towel, wrapped it around my waist, and walked to the vanity. I wiped off the condensation and leaned in, trying to see what I wanted others to see.

I was good enough. I was strong enough. I was powerful enough. And I was worthy enough. I was clean, and no one looked down on me.

I stood up straight and steeled my jaw. Screw her. Why the fuck did I even care?

Sure, last night was the best sex I'd ever had, and I didn't even get to come. But then she'd looked at me when we stood outside like the dirty shit son of Thomas Trent, and for the first time in a long while, I felt as if I were back in his house. Unclean. Unsafe. And unworthy.

I didn't let anyone make me feel like that. Not ever again.

Grabbing a rubber band off the sink, I tied back my hair and walked into the office, where the speakers droned on with Three Days Grace's "The High Road." Logging in to Skype, I called my boss, Fallon's father, and after a few seconds, he picked up.

"Ciaran," I greeted, opting to stay standing and lean over to the screen.

"Jaxon."

Ciaran Pierce was late forties, early fifties, but he still looked like a James Bond type. You know, the type who ages like a fine wine, whose personality has just as much style as his clothes, and who has chicks on every continent? That was Ciaran.

Fallon's father was Irish but wore his heritage like an Italian, all suave and confident and shit. We'd met a couple of years ago when Madoc and Fallon first got together, and as soon as I graduated from high school, he approached me.

No guns. No drugs. No meetings. Those were my stipulations.

I could still get arrested. What I was doing for him was still illegal. But I didn't have any moral hang-ups about what I was doing. I still felt as though I was coming out on the right side of things. Researching shady campaign donations so Ciaran could blackmail a senator for prime real estate or feeding fake info to his competitors was slightly dangerous, and could get me into trouble, but it wasn't putting drugs on the street or putting me in situations where I'd be a recognized target.

For the most part it was a small-time game with big-time rewards. The work didn't take up too much of my day, and I was saving enough to make sure I was safe.

"Doc 17?" Ciaran inquired.

"Tomorrow night."

"Llien?"

"Uploading now." And I punched a few buttons, finishing the task.

Ciaran and I kept our online conversations short, simple, and in code. Just in case. Doc 17 referred to a warehouse Ciaran bought whose permits needed to be pushed through, and Llien was the last name spelled backward of someone for whom he'd requested the personal and financial history. The jobs weren't hard, but they were numerous. He kept me pretty busy.

"Good." He nodded. "I'll be in town soon. We can catch up then."

"Sounds good."

He brought a glass to his lips, which I knew was Scotch, because the first thing I'd done when I met him was research him.

"My accountant will send payment today," he stated.

"Don't bother," I teased. "I already took it out of your account."

"You little shit." The hint of a smile tugged at his lips as he plopped his drink down.

I laughed, shaking my head. "You should trust me better. I wouldn't do that to you. I can do that to you," I pointed out. "But I won't."

He let out a sigh, and I took a moment to observe how much he looked like Fallon. Light brown hair, dark green eyes, skin that always looked tanned, even in winter. Even the small sprinkle of freckles across their noses.

But whereas Fallon sported some discreet tattoos, Ciaran sported scars from bullet holes.

"You look tired," he observed. "Someone keep you up last night?"

I wish. "You could say that," I caged, not wanting to talk about Juliet with him.

"To be young again," he mused. "Have fun while you can, son. Sooner or later one will come along that has the power to fuck you up."

Yeah, no shit. "I'll watch myself."

He jerked his chin at me. "Take care, kid."

"You, too."

Logging back off, I walked out of the office and into my room, throwing on some loose black pants. I usually wore jeans, but since I'd be in the garage today, I knew I'd get stained. Black pants it was.

After working out at the gym earlier this morning, finishing a few of the other projects Ciaran had sent me, and showering, I only had about an hour before my house would be packed with people again. I had two cars, other than my own, running tonight with different drivers, and then a few friends usually brought their cars over here on race day to prep. And they usually brought friends and girlfriends with them. It was part of our warm-up. Hang out, chat, borrow one another's tools . . . Since Jared had left all of his here, and I'd acquired lots of my own, I had a decent selection.

And while hostilities still ran hot at the Loop, some of us kept it cool enough to stay friends and still race one another.

I ripped my rubber band out and had grabbed my brush off the dresser, about to head out of the room, when a blast of music hit my ear.

What the hell?

I stalked to the window and yanked it up to peer outside. "We played that game last night, remember?" I yelled at Juliet through Tate's open French doors. "I won!"

I could just make her out through the trees, frantically hitting buttons on the stereo. "I'm trying to turn it off! Just leave me alone," she hollered, not looking up.

Sliding out the window, I scaled through the tree, trying to step lightly and quickly, since my weight was making the thick branches creak. Leaves swayed as I grabbed onto parts of the tree, and I made it to Tate's only-for-show balcony and swung my legs over the bars, hopping into the room.

"Get out." Juliet's wide-eyed, defiant expression zoned in on me. "I can handle this, Jax."

Reaching behind the TV stand, I yanked the cord out of the wall, and the room fell silent. My heart thumped in my chest, and Juliet's chest rose and fell in heavy breaths. I didn't know what it was about her, but my blood always rushed hot whenever she was near me. I wanted to either break shit or fuck her crazy, and it weirded me out. Not the fuck-her-crazy part, but the break-shit part. There was a violent urge around her, and I wasn't sure why. I wasn't sure if I should be scared of it, either.

I stood up straight and flipped my loose hair back over the top of my head, out of my face. I clenched the brush in my hand, watching her watch me with wary eyes. Her mouth hung open a little, and she didn't exactly look mad. I couldn't figure out what she was thinking.

Dropping the cord, I arched an eyebrow. "Use your head," I ordered. "Just kill the power next time."

She crossed her arms over her see-through white pullover, and I could make out a white bikini top underneath. "Well, maybe if you hadn't rushed to stick your nose into things, I would've figured it out," she snarled, tipping her chin up.

I shook my head, letting out a bitter laugh. "You stuck your nose into my business last night. And I was just trying to help," I said angrily, yanking the brush through the back of my hair.

"By being condescending and telling me to use my head?" she shot back. "I don't need that kind of help, Jax."

"Yeah." I got in her face. "I was nice to you for years, and what did it get me? You start behaving yourself, and I'll do the same."

"Then stop looking down on me!" she shouted.

"Ditto!" I growled back, turning around.

I yanked the brush through my hair again and tied the rubber band back in it, getting ready to climb out the window.

"Stop," Juliet groaned behind me.

I spun around. "What?"

"You're . . ." She pinched her lips together and ran her hands down her face. "You're ripping your hair apart," she blurted out. "I can't watch it anymore. You're not brushing it right."

I rolled my eyes and turned to crawl back out the window. "Yeah, I know how to brush my hair, Mom."

"Sit down," she commanded, and I heard furniture move behind me.

Turning back to her, I saw that she had moved Tate's desk chair to the center of the room, and my mouth went dry. "Why?" I asked, my voice barely above a whisper.

She stood behind the chair, her shoulders relaxed, and a nice view of her tight stomach peeked out between her shirt and jean shorts. Her hair was in a messy bun, her face glowed with a thin layer of sweat, and she had on no makeup, obviously having been in the backyard lying out. I wanted to touch her. I wanted to pass the whole afternoon in bed, with her, just us alone.

"Just sit down." She nodded, her tone firm but patient. "Please?"

I narrowed my eyes. She didn't want to . . . My shoulders slumped, and my eyes widened. *Oh, hell no.*

I shook my head, my pulse throbbing in my neck.

"Go get the poor kid some food. I'll stay with him."

No, no, no . . . I bit down so hard my jaw ached. No one touched my hair. No one.

"Jax, if you're going to keep your hair long, you have to take care of it." Her voice was so gentle, and her summer green eyes were patient.

I looked down to the floor, suddenly feeling five years old again. "I know how to take care of it."

"Yeah," she sighed. "Using ninety-nine-cent shampoo?" she joked, not realizing that I barely heard her.

How the hell had she switched gears so fast? She was mad, and now she wanted to brush my hair?

My knees felt damn near about to buckle, and my stomach hollowed. This was what it had felt like being at my father's house, lying in bed, and watching the shadows under my closed bedroom door from the party going on the other side. Wondering if someone was coming in. Wondering if I could sleep and being too scared to close my eyes. Wondering why no one ever helped me.

Juliet wasn't right for me, and I clenched my fists, reminding myself of that. She made me feel unsafe again.

"No." I tried to swallow past the tight ache in my throat.

She narrowed her eyes slightly, looking confused, and I hated myself. She got me jacked up, and she jerked me around, and on these rare occasions when she was sweet, I was turning her away. I wanted to sit down. I wanted her to touch me, and fuck, I didn't want to leave!

She continued to wait, and my fists clenched with the urge to hit something. "I don't like people touching my hair, okay?" I explained, trying honesty.

"Then why do you keep it long?" she asked.

"Because I don't like it touched," I repeated. "Not even by a stylist. I can either shave my head or grow it out, so I grew it out."

Now, please fucking God, don't ask any more questions.

She squinted at me, thinking. "You wanted me to trust you last night. Did you think that was a one-way street?" She tapped the back of the chair with both hands. "It's your turn. Come on."

I swallowed, wanting and not wanting the same exact thing.

I wanted what my brother had and what Madoc had. I wanted to be close to someone.

I saw the way my brother loved Tate. How he smiled at her even though she was walking away and couldn't see him. How he was always looking for a reason to touch her. And how when he held her, he closed his eyes and looked as if he'd just found a life raft in the middle of the ocean.

I saw Madoc and how he loved Fallon. How he couldn't keep his eyes off her. How every time he had to walk away to talk to someone, to go get a drink, to do anything, he had to grab her hand and drag her everywhere as if she were attached to his body. How he'd stop in the middle of a conversation and kiss the shit out of her.

Juliet wouldn't hurt me. Juliet couldn't hurt me. I was in control. I was powerful. I was worthy. And I was strong.

I exhaled. Fucking fine. I inched toward the chair. "Take off your shirt," I ordered.

Her eyebrows shot up, and she plastered her hands to her hips as I came to stand right in front of the chair.

If she wanted me vulnerable, then I needed something to distract me. I didn't think she'd do it.

But then she crossed her arms, grabbed the hem of the shirt in her hands, and lifted it over her head, revealing her smooth, golden skin in a white halter-top bikini featuring a hole in the center to display her ample cleavage.

"And take down your hair." I kept my face even, but my voice turned deep. I couldn't help it. She unwrapped her bun, and all her deep brown locks tumbled down around her shoulders.

The ten-ton weight in my stomach turned into a full-blown hard-on in my pants, and I imagined her and her hot little body straddling me on the chair.

Good enough.

I cleared my throat. "Just try to be quick, okay?"

CHAPTER 12

JULIET

I was shameless. Absolutely without any pride, and I should lock myself up until I stopped going into heat every time this guy was around. Every damn time.

Tate's older-than-dirt CD player had some kind of alarm clock on it, and I accidentally hit a button and then the damn thing wouldn't shut off when I jammed the power button. Several times. And then I started hitting other buttons. And then I turned the volume down. And turned it. And turned it. And turned it. And nothing.

And then Jax had climbed over, his long hair hanging in his face and looking straight off the cover of one of those romance novels where the superhot savage is ripping off the petticoats of the pampered city girl, and I froze.

Frickin' froze, and I didn't want him to leave.

He picked up the chair with one hand and moved it into the bathroom.

"What are you doing?" I asked, following him.

He sat down, facing the mirror. "I need to be able to see you."

See me? What was he so afraid of? I thought to myself. But I kept quiet, knowing he wouldn't tell me even if I asked.

From the moment I'd offered to do his hair, he'd stilled and looked scared, and for the second time, Jaxon Trent backed away from me. The first being two years ago when I'd asked about his lack of tattoos.

I came up behind him, trying not to smile at his huge frame in Tate's small bathroom—but one look at his wary eyes staring back at me through the mirror, and I stopped. He looked as if he was ready to bolt at any sign of danger.

I placed my hands on his bare shoulders, wanting to show him that I understood his apprehension. I didn't like to be groomed, either.

"Do you know I purposely failed a test senior year so you would have to tutor me?" I blurted out, trying to distract him as I gently pulled out his hair from his brown rubber band—the ones you get in the office supply section that are terrible for hair.

I looked up and met his eyes again, keeping my face even. He watched me like a hawk, his heavy breaths making it very clear that he was still uncomfortable.

"We shared a math class," I said, setting down the rubber band and threading my fingers through his gorgeous black-brown hair that was longer than mine. "You tutored kids in the morning, and I wanted to spend time with you, so I failed a test on the chance that you'd have to help me."

He leaned back in the chair, relaxing a little more, and my stomach fluttered with the sexy little smile curling his lips.

"Yeah, but it blew up in my face," I laughed nervously, spraying some detangler in his hair. "My mom found out and hired a personal tutor at home." I held his cold locks in my hand, piece by piece, spraying. "So that sucked. I had to waste an extra hour three times a week for a month for a test I could've passed. It was embarrassing."

Reaching down, I took his brush out of his hand, and gathering up all the hair, I started lightly brushing through it from the bottom up. He didn't speak, and I was surprised he didn't comment on my story. I figured Jax would gloat about something like that.

"Even more embarrassing was the first guy I ever kissed," I continued. "Yeah, I thought it was a guy, but it wasn't. He was a girl. A very boyish-looking girl at a party when I was fourteen . . ." I rambled, trying to keep his mind on me.

He listened as I told him about the Barbie skates that I could still fit into as I brushed through all of his hair and put some product in for styling. He kept his eyes glued to me as I told him about the time I was eighteen and too drunk to notice that I hadn't taken my underwear down before peeing on the toilet. He followed my every movement as I dragged the edge of a comb along the sides and parted pieces of it for braiding and kept talking.

Through the layer of sweat on his back and with his fists clenching the fabric of his pants on his thighs, he listened and didn't take his eyes off me for a single moment, listening to my ramblings as if they were the most interesting stories in the world.

And the whole time, I just wanted to wrap my arms around him and hold him. He didn't feel safe, and I didn't wonder about the cause.

I simply wanted to know where they were, whoever had done this to him, so I could choke the shit out of them.

Reaching down, I placed my hand on his as I used the other to dig in the drawer for some small clear rubber bands.

I didn't look at him, and I didn't touch him unnecessarily. I just wanted him to know that I was there.

I'd seen him wear his hair in ponytails and braided ponytails, but my favorite styles were where he braided three small strips above each ear, so I decided to do three braids to the scalp instead of the traditional ones he usually did.

Braiding three rows on each side, securing them with rubber bands as I went, I then took all the bands out and pulled everything back into his usual ponytail midskull. Twisting the rubber band, I threaded his thick black hair through, squeezing the soft, cool locks in my fist.

Running my hand over his scalp to pull back any flyaways, I slowed when I saw him close his eyes. He looked relaxed. Peaceful. Maybe soothed.

Spraying some hair spray to keep everything in place, I put my hands back on his shoulders and waited for him to open his eyes again. He could stay like that all damn day for all I cared.

Fireworks popped under my skin and exploded in my chest at the sight of him. We were close to each other and we weren't shouting for a change. Damn, he was beautiful.

"I'm sorry I wasn't nicer in high school." My voice came out raspy, and when he opened his eyes they almost seemed to glow in the dark.

"Every morning you'd sit on the bleachers with your iPod and stare off onto the field. Staring at nothing. I wondered all the time what you were doing. What you were thinking about. You scared me."

"Why?" he asked, sounding calm. "I would never have hurt you, Juliet."

I shrugged, not sure how to answer that. "I don't know. Liam was safe, I guess. He pissed me off and hurt my feelings, but he never got under my skin."

Liam never made me cry. Forgetting me, disrespecting me, humiliating me—that all made me cry. But losing him to another woman never hurt. It wasn't a loss. But Jax . . .

I looked down, swallowing. "First time I saw you I knew . . ."

"Knew what?"

I met his eyes on the mirror. "That you'd mean more."

Jax's chest filled with a deep breath, and his gaze turned heated. He pushed out of his chair, and I jumped back at his sudden movement. Looking up, I watched as he advanced on me, backing me into the bathroom wall.

"Jax—" But before I could say anything more, he leaned down and cupped my cheek, and butterflies swarmed in massive circles in my stomach when his lips crashed down on mine.

I moaned, his tongue flicked mine, and I jerked with the rush of heat spreading through me and then sinking right down between my legs.

Shit, he felt good.

I opened my lips more and kissed him back, wrapping my arms around his neck, standing on my tiptoes, and leaning into his body. His arm circled my waist, and his other hand went straight for my ass, pressing me into him harder.

I felt my bikini top give way, and that was when I noticed he had pulled the ties at my neck and back.

I reached up, trying to catch my top before he snatched it away from my body and tossed it to the floor.

"Jax, no." I pinched my face up in worry. "Shane will be back—"

"You want me to stop?" he said, cutting me off, lifting me up by the backs of my thighs and pressing me into the wall with his body. "There's no stopping," he warned, covering my nipple with his mouth.

I groaned, letting my eyes roll back. *Oh, shit*. Everything he did hit a nerve straight down to my center, and I squeezed my thighs around him.

"Jax, please," I begged. I wanted this.

But I wasn't ready.

"Please what?" he taunted, his scorching breath making me shiver as he swirled my hard nipple with his tongue.

"Please stop," I gasped, wanting him to do everything but stop. *More.*

"Stop what?" he asked, still kissing me. "Stop this?" He sucked my whole nipple into his mouth, fast and fucking hard, and then drew it out between his teeth while looking up at me with those devil blue eyes. I sucked in air, watching him suck and release, kiss and drag, making me throb so hard I started grinding against him.

Lowering me just a bit, he crushed my lips to his and held me tight as he walked us to the bedroom and laid me back on the bed.

He broke the kiss, and I inhaled a sharp breath at the sudden coldness I felt. He leaned over me, looking down into my eyes.

Grazing the back of his hand over my cheek, he dragged it down my neck and then my torso, spreading the heat of his touch down my body. My stomach shook as he slid past and dived into my shorts.

I arched my back and groaned when his finger slipped inside me.

He closed his eyes, looking as though he was reveling in what he felt there.

"Jesus Christ," he swore, baring his teeth.

He came down and sucked my bottom lip between his teeth as he worked the button and zipper of my shorts.

I held on to his face, kissing him back. "Jax," I breathed out, "I need you to stop. I don't want you to stop"—I laughed a little—"but I . . ."

My thoughts were a jumbled mess. My body knew what it wanted. I was on fire for him. But I didn't want a one-night stand, and I was scared.

I might not please him.

He bowed his forehead to mine. "Shh," he soothed. "I'm not going to make love to you, okay? I have no expectations. Yet. I just want to see you."

He hesitated for a moment, searching my eyes, and then hooked his fingers in the loops of my jean shorts and slid them down my legs, bringing my bikini bottoms with them.

The cool air touched between my legs, and I felt his eyes on every inch of my skin. I shot up, grabbing his face for a kiss, trying to cover my body. But he was too smart for that.

"I want to look at you," he whispered between kisses, slowly pushing me back onto the bed. "Do you feel safe with me?" he asked.

I looked up at him, knowing immediately that I didn't trust Jax. Not completely.

But I also knew he wasn't going to laugh at me. I knew he thought I was pretty. And I knew that he always looked me in the eye when he spoke to me.

So I nodded.

"Your mother's not in this room, Juliet." His voice was thoughtful as his eyes stayed glued to mine. I clenched the sheets at my side.

"Jared sees Tate like this," he continued. "Madoc sees Fallon like this. And I would've tossed any girl aside over the years to see you beautiful like this."

I licked my lips, breathing in and breathing out, watching him, trying to stay calm. I wasn't sure I wanted him to see how much his words touched me.

Holding my eyes, he stood up straight and backed away. I only had a moment to wonder what he was doing before he switched on the iPod and "Torn to Pieces" by Pop Evil came on.

My body sank into the bed, and I felt myself relaxing. The noise helped. I couldn't hear my thoughts so much now.

He turned around and gazed at me. "I can't wait to have my mouth on you, Juliet."

The drums started, and my whole body tensed with the pounding in my heart and in my ears. And I was ready. With a smile, I sat up and rose to my feet, folding my lips between my teeth.

"In my fantasy," I said in a small voice, "I was standing up."

Walking over to him, I circled both of my arms around his neck and plastered my naked body to his. My lips found his, and I felt his body jerk when I slid my tongue into his hot mouth that tasted like summer.

"You smell so good," I breathed into his lips. "I want it all over me, Jax." And I grabbed his bottom lip between my teeth and then kissed him before nibbling more. Reaching down, I slid my hand over his thigh, rubbing the hardness in his pants. I had no idea what the hell I was doing or how far I wanted to carry this, but that was the thing—I wasn't thinking. And it felt so good.

My hands tingled with the urge to explore him. Everywhere. My mouth wanted to be on him just as much as he wanted his on mine. And I wanted more than his mouth. My nipples hardened against his warm chest, and the pool of heat between my legs flooded with the friction of his pants rubbing against me.

"You're such a little shit," I teased, breathing into his mouth.

And all hell broke loose.

Jax pulled his mouth away and jerked my hips into his hard cock. "You feel that?" he threatened, leaning his forehead into mine. "Don't fucking push me, Juliet, or in a minute, you won't feel safe."

And I sucked in a breath, my jaw dropping as he grabbed my hand and dragged me back to the bed. Swinging forward, I toppled onto Tate's gray and black comforter, probably looking as though I was about to do a crab walk escape from the big, bad shark. I stared as Jax stood at the end of the bed, grabbed my ankle, and yanked me down to the end.

"Jax!" I cried out. But I was too late.

He planted both hands on my waist, holding fast so I couldn't move.

And then he lowered himself in between my legs and ran his tongue along the length of me.

I stopped breathing, and my mouth fell open.

"Fuck, I knew you'd taste good," he breathed against my skin.

I could only watch as he flattened his tongue and licked oh so slowly up my folds to the top of my clit and then dragged his tongue back down over the hood all the way to my entrance. Up and then down, up again and then slowly, all the way down. I could feel my clit throbbing a mile a minute, and my pussy clenched with his agonizing slow speed. Up and then down, licking and tasting, and I cried out, slamming the palm of my hand down on my thigh.

"Jax," I whimpered, and I felt a tear spill out the corner of my eye.

Relaxing my legs, I let my thighs fall wider apart, and I dropped my head back to the bed as he increased the speed.

I throbbed, and my belly swarmed with heat like hot water gushing over my skin.

I arched my back. "I never want you to stop," I groaned.

His teeth pinched my clit, and I grabbed his hair at the scalp as my back bent off the bed. The blood rushed through my arms and legs like liquid heat, and I released one of my hands and brought it up to my breast, massaging it.

"Jesus, Juliet," Jax growled into my pussy. I looked down to see him watching me. "Keep doing that," he ordered.

And I obeyed.

I rubbed my hand over my breast and across my nipple slowly, loving the feel of my body and loving how he watched me. Every hair stood on end, and my cheeks warmed with a small smile at how alive I felt.

But then he grabbed my clit in his mouth and sucked.

"Oh," I cried out, feeling a new surge of need. "Jax, don't stop. That feels so good."

Squeezing my tit in my hand, I jerked my hips up against his lips, holding his head there with my other hand. He looked as if he were sucking fruit, the way his lips surrounded me and stretched my skin with how hard he tasted me. He dragged my tender flesh out through his teeth only to recapture the erect nub and suck me again. My chest shook with my shaky breaths, and I started rolling my hips into him gently.

"Baby, you should never have let me taste you," he choked out, dipping his tongue to lick my clit and then suck, lick and then suck. "I'm going to come at you tonight. Tomorrow. At school. Hell, I may just have you spread these legs at the dinner table so I can eat."

I narrowed my eyes in painful desire, thinking about him sitting in a high-back chair at a twelve-foot-long dining room table with my legs spread for him like a goddamn meal.

Holy shit.

I licked my sandpaper lips. "I want you in my mouth, too."

And then he plunged his tongue inside me, and I shot off the bed, throwing my head back.

"Jax, fuck!" I screamed, squirming under his assault. "It's too much!"

"Juliet?" I heard my name being called from somewhere, but I didn't care.

Grabbing Jax's hair, I held him to my seriously overheated and throbbing clit, seeing the flesh of my nipples pebble and my breasts bob back and forth with my movements. He dipped his tongue inside me, making me contract and release. I needed more. I needed him.

He trailed his tongue out of my pussy and started French-kissing my clit right before he slid a finger inside me.

My head dropped to one side, and I started gasping and fucking his finger, not fucking caring that I was shameless or that Jax wasn't even my boyfriend.

"Jax," I moaned. "Oh, my God."

"Jax?" I heard someone repeat. "Juliet, are you okay?"

My eyes snapped open, and my face flushed with heat.

"Oh, my God," I whispered, looking down at Jax's laughing eyes as he kissed my clit.

"Juliet?" Shane called again from the other side of the locked door.

Jax arched an amused eyebrow. "Come on. Let her hear how wild you are. How much you're fucking enjoying this."

In and out, his finger plunged, back and forth. So good, and the itch was right there hanging on the edge. I was almost there. His tongue was tireless, going at me, licking and sucking me. In, out, lick, taste, bite.

"Ah," I gasped. "Oh, God!"

Then I came, shocks exploding below my belly as I grappled the comforter over my head. I jerked into him, sucking in air and rolling my hips into his fingers, needing everything he had to give me.

More. I swallowed and looked down at him with blurry eyes.

I wanted more. More of him.

"Juliet!" The doorknob jiggled, and I grabbed the T-shirt I slept in off the top of the bed.

Sitting up and slipping it on, I caught Jax just as he pulled me into him for a kiss. Kneeling between my legs, he cupped my face and held my mouth to his. Slow and sweet.

Pulling back and tilting his forehead into mine, he closed his eyes. I watched in silence as his eyebrows pinched together, and he looked as though he was sad about something or thinking about something important.

He pulled back, shaking his head and letting out a sigh. "Shit," he mumbled, barely a whisper.

"What?" I asked quietly, suddenly feeling as if I'd done something wrong.

"Nothing," he breathed out, running his hand through his hair.

"I just . . ." He hesitated, looking away and then back at me. "I just never thought the real thing would live up to the fantasy, you know?" He tipped up the corner of his mouth in a smile. "Hope you like summer fun, Juliet, because it's just getting started."

And I watched as he stood up, unlocked the bedroom door, and walked past Shane's stunned face and frozen body.

Summer fun? I felt a mischievous smile cross my lips. So he thought he pulled all the strings, and that he had me.

I almost snorted.

CHAPTER 13

JAXON

I threw the shop cloth down and gestured with my chin at Sam to help me with the tire. He rolled it over, and we lifted it onto the axle.

My house had been flooded with people as soon as I left Juliet only a few hours ago, and we were all prepping for races tonight.

They were here, their heads under their hoods, but mine was still between her legs.

Jesus.

I reached over, jacking up Korn's "Falling Away from Me," and ran my hand over my hair just above my ear where her braids still stretched my scalp.

I smiled, remembering her doing my hair. She hadn't touched too long in any one place. She hadn't fallen all over me or petted me. And when she reached out and touched my hand, just letting me know that she understood, and that I didn't have to talk about it, I'd closed my eyes, feeling safer. I didn't like to be groomed, but I'd liked her touching me, and I'd happily let her do it again.

FALLING AWAY

She took care of me today.

And what did I do? I spread her legs and ate her out as if she were a whore.

I still hadn't taken her on a date, a nice dinner, or a walk in the goddamn park the way girls wanted. Over the past couple of weeks, I'd fought with her, threatened her, and then tried to get my hands on her every time we were alone. I'd pushed her, grabbed her, and yelled at her.

I was an asshole, and I wasn't gentle.

Fuck me. Sweat trickled down my temple, and the bugs buzzing outside in the summer sun had me itching to turn the music up. Drown out all these thoughts.

I wasn't going to stick around long enough to see her push me away when she realized the mistake she'd made in getting close, but every time I thought I could pull away, her defiance and fight drew me back in.

"Shit!" Sam barked, being dragged to the ground by my end of the tire I hadn't realized I'd dropped.

I fisted my hair at the top of my head and turned around, kicking the toolbox against the wall. The tools crashed together inside, some of the drawers popping out.

"Um," I heard Sam venture. "Overreact much?"

I turned around, seeing his confused expression, and let out a shaky laugh. "Sorry. My head's preoccupied, man."

"Since when?" he mumbled, bending to lift the tire back up. "That was the first time you ever reminded me of Jared."

"Yeah," I grunted, bending to lift the tire with him, "what's wrong with that?"

He struggled with the weight, gritting his teeth. "Nothing at all, if you're the tornado," he joked. "It's everything in its way that gets destroyed."

Okay. Solid point.

My phone vibrated in my pocket, and I let out a hard breath as I slipped the tire on its axle.

I looked at my phone, seeing Jared's name, and rubbed my hand down my face.

Great.

"What?" I answered, knowing he was going to bug me about that damn restraining order again.

"Jesus Christ," he swore. "What's crawled up your ass this summer? Every time I call you you're bitchy."

"Nothing. I'm nice to everyone except you."

"Lovely," he shot back. "Sue me for caring about you."

"Bullying me is more like it." I walked out of the garage, away from the half dozen other guys and their girlfriends in my driveway.

"Funny," he said. I could hear the fake humor in his voice. "So, what's wrong with you?"

I tightened my lips. "Nothing," I lied. "Just busy."

"You're always busy." He hesitated. "And we need to talk."

"It's not a good time."

"Dad's getting out of jail soon," he shot out. "We need to talk."

I squeezed the phone in my hand and calmed my voice. "My answer about the restraining order hasn't changed."

My father still had three years left on his sentence for drug possession and child abuse, but his time had been whittled down for good behavior and ratting out two old contacts in the drug trade.

Jared was talking to his mom's new husband—Madoc's dad—about getting a restraining order in place for when our father was released from prison. He wanted Thomas Trent away from him, his mom, and Tate—and I, on the other hand, welcomed my father.

I wanted to face him, and I had a contact on the inside keeping me well-informed of everything that was going on with him. His friends, his visitors, and his enemies.

"I'll be home Friday, and we're taking care of business." He was telling me, not asking.

The anger warmed my whole body, but I didn't want to get into it with him again. He was away a lot, and I loved him.

But he had to fucking stop already.

Madoc's GTO pulled up in front of Tate's house, and I narrowed my gaze, seeing a red Nissan 370Z cruise to a sudden halt right behind it.

Jared rambled on in my ear, but I couldn't hear him. Why was Madoc at Tate's house? And whose Nissan was that?

Madoc and Fallon climbed out of his car, followed by the driver of the Nissan, a tall blond yuppie who dressed a lot like Madoc with navy blue cargo shorts, an expensive-looking T-shirt, and flip-flops.

Jesus. They were walking up Tate's walkway. Why were they walking up Tate's walkway?

I hung up on Jared as Madoc headed my way and Fallon and the yuppie continued to Tate's door.

"What's up?" I jerked my chin at Madoc and gave him the usual casual handshake.

"Nothing," he chirped innocently.

"Cut the crap. What's with One Direction over there?"

He laughed. "Oh, you mean my buddy from Northwestern?" *Asshole's enjoying this.* "His name's Adam Larson. He's in town visiting. Fallon and I are taking K.C. to the carnival and thought . . ."

But I'd stopped listening.

Peering around Madoc, I saw Juliet emerge with Shane, and it looked as though Fallon was introducing them all.

Juliet reached out her hand, shaking his, and I saw her smile.

My phone cracked in my fist, and I blinked, bringing it up to see that I'd splintered the case.

Fuck.

"Oops," Madoc said, jeering, laughing at my cracked phone. "Someone's mad."

I shook my head. "What are you up to?"

He held up his hands in defense. "Nothing. I saw what happened at the party last night, and I figured you weren't interested anymore. Adam's a good guy. I just didn't want K.C. to feel like a third wheel with Fallon and me at the carnival."

"She has her cousin," I growled through clenched teeth. "How would she be the third wheel? And her name's Juliet. And I don't want him anywhere near her!" I got in his face.

"Hmm . . ." He regarded me for a few seconds and turned to look at everyone coming down the stairs. Juliet glanced at me, looking slightly uncomfortable before turning away and letting *Adam* open the door for her.

She looked hot as hell, and I wanted to see her eyes again. She wore frayed jean shorts with one of Fallon's specialty T-shirts. Black Def Lepperd logo on the front, with her smooth, tanned back peeking out of twenty or so slits running horizontally across her back. I also made out long earrings—feathers, I think. Her hair was straightened, her makeup made her glow, and my hands wanted those legs.

And she was leaving with another guy.

Madoc turned back to look at me. "If she knew she was yours, she wouldn't have gotten in that car."

Motherfucker.

"Took Jared eight years to pounce on Tate," he challenged. "Thought you had more game."

He narrowed his eyes, his point made, and stuffed his hands into his pockets before walking away. Shane climbed into Madoc's car with Fallon, and that meant Juliet was alone with that guy.

And I watched as all of them sped away.

I tightened my fists and reached in my pocket for my keys.

"Sam." I grabbed my T-shirt off the worktable. "Can you lock up when everyone's gone? I need to head out for a while."

He nodded. "Sure. Where are you going?"

I ignored him, Madoc's words still floating in the air.

"If she knew she was yours, she wouldn't have gotten in that car."

No, I thought. She knew she was mine, and she *shouldn't* have gotten in that car.

CHAPTER 14

JULIET

When I get my hands on you . . .

I texted my threat to Shane and Fallon and stuffed my phone back into my purse.

"Sorry if you were ambushed." Adam shot me an apologetic look as he drove. "It wasn't my idea."

"I'm sure." I didn't know Fallon extremely well, but I got the impression that this was probably more Madoc's brainchild anyway.

"But I'm kind of glad." He flashed me an honest grin. "As long as you don't have a boyfriend that's going to come and beat my ass."

I sucked in a shaky breath, immediately thinking of Jax, which was strange, since I'd just broken up with Liam. Shouldn't I have thought of Liam when Adam said "boyfriend?"

"Nope," I rushed out. "No boyfriend."

"Good." He relaxed into his seat, doing the guy thing like Jax. But not doing it nearly as well.

Adam's body wasn't long, and it didn't fill the space the same way. His car was more compact, and I didn't feel the quivers in my thighs the way I did when Jax's Mustang vibrated under my body.

Adam's car was fun. Jax's car was a threat.

Oh, my God. Why was I comparing them? Jax wasn't making me any promises. And Adam was only here for a few days.

Both were unavailable, in my opinion, and I was a free agent.

Just have fun at the carnival, Juliet.

We pulled into the fairgrounds and parked on the grassy field, right next to Madoc's car.

As soon as I stepped out of the car, I smiled.

County fairs were held at the town's established fairgrounds, not far from the Loop, and today was probably the best day to come. Being that it was midafternoon, the temperature had to be pushing a hundred degrees already, and I was already sticky. While some hated that, I loved it.

The fuzzy lights in the distance cast a spectacular glow of reds, greens, yellows, and blues, and the sounds of carnival life filled the thick, hot air, making me want to smile.

Eighties music crackled over cheap speakers, riders screamed as their roller coasters whipped them through the air, and intercoms blared names of the latest winners of the ring toss and duck pond, while the sharp pop of the balloon-and-dart game cut through my ears.

I inhaled the hot scent of funnel cake, mixed with sickly sweet cotton candy, and clutched the hem of my shorts at my sides as we traipsed through the high grass to the entrance. With the sun beating down on my shoulders, and the sweat already dripping down my back, I licked my lips, tasting the dirt in the air.

Cheap carnivals grossed a lot of people out. They were grungy and dilapidated, and they attracted deviants.

At least, that was what my mother had told me.

The only reason she ever came was to work a stand, signing up people for the Garden Club, the Rotary Club, or whatever election candidate she was supporting that year.

I never wanted to be a part of that, though. I never wanted to be stuck inside the old banquet hall at the fairgounds with the air-conditioning. There was just something completely raw about the atmosphere outside. About the sweat, the heat, and the dirt.

I couldn't explain it, and I was always ashamed of it, but I felt primal here. I loved the carnival. For all the reasons my mother hated it.

Walking in, we purchased bracelets that would allow us to ride as much as we wanted until closing, and then we went for food.

"Hot dog," Fallon ordered, digging in her purse.

Madoc came up behind her, sucking on her neck. "Save your appetite. I've got a foot-long for later."

"Ugh." She shoved him away but still smiled.

I grinned, Madoc laughed, and Adam and Shane were helping each other with their wristbands.

I turned to the girl working the concession stand. "I'd like a cherry Popsicle, please." And I raised my eyebrows to Shane. "You?"

"Hot dog, too!" She barely glanced up as she fastened the band at Adam's wrist.

"Adam? You want anything?" Madoc asked.

"Nah, I'm good."

We paid and ate and chatted about everything that had been going on. Shane's brilliant notion to change her major again for a college career she hadn't even started yet. Fallon trying to decide which piercing she'd get, and Madoc trying to stick his hand between her legs to indicate where he wanted her to get pierced. Adam talking about the latest research on vegan diets.

And me trying not to think about how fast I'd fallen in the last twenty-four hours.

I'd threatened my mom, let Jaxon Trent stick his fingers and tongue inside me, and now I wasn't sure where I was going to end up for college in the fall, since Sandra Carter would no doubt disallow access to my college fund.

And I laughed.

The smile spread my lips wide, and my skin hummed just under the surface as everyone chatted away, and I kept laughing.

My head bowed, and my stomach tingled.

"Um . . . ," Shane started. "You okay?"

I looked at her, my eyes blurry with happiness. *Yep. Not okay. Kind of okay. Feel okay. But not okay. Isn't it wonderful?* I just smiled at their wide-eyed expressions.

"K.C.?"

And then my smile faded.

I halted, seeing my mother standing a few feet away, carrying a tray of pies.

She wore a wispy, lavender summer dress and high heels, looking absolutely pristine with her hair curled and tied back in a low ponytail. Suddenly I was very aware of every inch of my sweaty skin.

I saw her eyes sweep up and down the length of me, taking in my appearance, and then her eyes narrowed like bullets. She didn't say anything before she turned and walked away, back into the banquet hall.

I stood there, looking after her, trying to figure out what was going through her head. Did she really hate me so much?

Madoc and Adam had walked ahead, but I turned to Fallon and Shane at my side. "I don't look inappropriate, do I?" I asked.

The corner of Fallon's mouth turned up. "How do you feel?"

I looked down, amusement tickling my face. I wasn't wearing anything special, but it was skimpy, slightly see-through with the slits on my back, and suggestive. The three terrible *S*'s.

"Loud," I confessed. "I feel loud. Like everyone can hear me."

"But comfortable?" she pressed.

I nodded. *Yeah.*

"Then that's good enough," she shot back. "You make your own rules, Juliet. Girls dress for others. Women dress for themselves."

And those were the truest words I'd heard in a long time.

I liked being aware of my body.

"So, what's it going to be?" Shane ran her fingers through her hair, flopping it to one side. "The Gravitron, the Tilt-A-Whirl, or the Kamikaze?"

I looked around and spotted a haunted fun house. My guilty pleasure.

"That." I pointed to the small warehouse with a huge blowup dragon seated at the front entrance with its mouth open. It was a staple every year that I'd been here. You walk into the dragon's breath and into the warehouse/converted fun house for the regular kind of carnival fare.

I led the way, Shane and Fallon giggling behind me as Adam and Madoc stayed behind with the water gun game.

We left the bright smells and sounds of the carnival, and I gasped at gusts of wind hitting my body as we stepped through the dragon's mouth. Fans blew from several directions, cooling the light layer of sweat on my legs, stomach, and arms, and the fog machine rolled soft clouds around my feet.

Looking around, I inhaled the darkness, taking in the hot smell of dirt and depth. Kind of like being in a basement.

Juice from the Popsicle dripped on my hand, and I blinked, looking down and licking the sweet red stickiness from my hand.

The ceiling gave way, rising, and we entered the fun house.

Veering through the maze of clear plastic panels, I bumped into walls I didn't see and laughed through turns I had to blindly hold my hand out to make sure were there. Sucking on my Popsicle, I wobbled across the bridge, through the spinning barrel, and across the plank with the neon carnival masks zooming past. My equilibrium was lost, and I bit my lip to stifle my laughter. I liked not knowing which direction to turn or which way was up.

My eyes moved everywhere, taking in all the sights, and I took my time, strolling into the haunted house part of the tour.

Biting off a piece of my Popsicle, I stepped up to the different displays around the large room. The lights cast a soft glow, and the little playhouses decorated with bare trees, gargoyles, and zombies almost made it feel like Halloween.

Almost. If not for the heat.

I heard laughter in the distance and twisted my head away from the cemetery scene to see that I was alone.

I lowered the Popsicle, licking my lips and darting my eyes all around me. Where were Shane and Fallon? The fun house hadn't been busy. It never was, but . . .

I felt my heartbeat pounding harder, and my senses kicked into high gear. It was dark in here, I was alone, and . . .

Yeah. I circled the corner and climbed the stairs. If I remembered correctly, there was a slide that took you to the bottom level and exit.

Running up the spiral staircase, I speed-walked past the row of carnival mirrors, kicking up dust and dirt with my flip-flops as I jetted for the tunnel slide leading back to the outside.

But I didn't make it.

Someone snaked an arm around my waist, and I screamed as he growled in my ear, "Did you think"—his hot breath scorched my skin—"that I was kidding when I said that there was no stopping, Juliet?"

Jax.

His hard chest pressed against my back, and I closed my eyes, feeling safe and threatened at the same time.

My heart thundered against my sternum, and my chest burned.

"What do you think you're doing?" I asked, pinching the Popsicle stick between my fingers, not caring that the juice was spilling down.

He ran his tongue from the bottom of my neck up to my ear and caught my lobe in his teeth. "I don't know." He sounded playful. "Do you want me to stop?"

I twisted my head, and the air between our lips charged with heat before he lifted his head, threaded his fingers through my hair, and covered my mouth with his. Cinnamon touched my tongue, and I pressed my lips into his, darting my tongue out to lick him.

Then his mouth left mine, and I blinked as he dropped to his knees, reached around to unfasten my shorts, and yanked them down, underwear and all, then sank his teeth into my flesh.

"Jax!" I yelped.

Oh, my God! We were in public! Shit!

He held my waist, kissing and biting my lower back and ass.

I groaned, a fucking inferno blazing between my legs. "Jax, Jesus," I whimpered. "Someone could come in."

He stood up, lifted me into his arms, and carried me to the wall, leaving my shorts in a pile on the dusty floor.

Planting me back on my feet, he reached down and lifted my shirt over my head.

He was still wearing his straight-leg black pants, sitting low but secured with a black belt. He had taken off his T-shirt, though, and it hung out of his back pocket, swinging against his leg as he moved.

Hovering over me, he stared down in what felt like a dare. "No one's coming in." And he flattened his hand on my chest and ran it slowly down, stopping to knead my breast, and I closed my eyes, letting my head fall back as he claimed it in his fingers.

"Your Popsicle's melting." His voice held a hint of humor. And then I watched wide-eyed as he brought my hand up, peeled the Popsicle stick away and licked all my fingers one by one.

Lowering his hand, he swirled my nipple in his mouth, and I sucked in a breath through my teeth with the shock. My already hard nipples puckered even more, and the cold juice in his mouth contrasting with the sweltering heat wave down below made for a nice cyclone in my stomach.

"You like that." He sounded surprised. "Bet you'll love this."

And I grabbed his shoulders, digging my nails in when he slid the Popsicle between my legs, gliding it along my slit.

I moaned. "You're such a little shit." But holy hell, I loved it. "Please stop," I begged.

He sank his lips into mine, molding our naked chests together, and I kissed him as if he were the last meal I'd ever eat. I held him close, going at him and rolling my hips into the Popsicle he still held there.

Fuck, I wanted him.

"I hated the idea that guy might touch you." He slid the Popsicle in and out of my folds.

Oh, God. I squeezed my eyes shut. It felt so good.

I shook my head. "He didn't touch me," I gasped. "Is that what you're worried about?"

He ignored the question as he continued kneading my hip and working the Popsicle.

"Jax," I whispered into his lips. "You're the one I think about."

The next thing I knew the Popsicle was gone, and Jax was between my legs, licking up the red juice that had melted all over my skin.

"Oh, God." I gripped his hair.

His lips sucked my clit, and I let him swing one of my legs over his shoulder as he ate me.

The dirt on the wall behind me ground into my back, and the heat burned my nostrils as I breathed hard.

"Jax, it's so hot." My hair was stuck to my neck and face. "Baby . . ." I fisted his hair harder, ready to ride his damn face if he didn't give me what I needed.

He kissed my clit, my folds, my thigh where it met my hip . . .

"Your sweat . . ." He darted out his tongue, licking my hip and stomach. "Damn, you're fun to play with."

I swallowed and took my leg down. Gripping his ponytail at his scalp, I forced his eyes on mine. "I'm done playing."

My eyes burned, and I didn't know if it was from the ache of my pussy throbbing or knowing that his eyes, his tongue, or his fucking defiance was twisting me so hard and tight that I was ready to scream.

"Please. Fuck me," I whispered. I could feel the wetness pouring out of me. I was ready. I needed this!

His eyes flared, and he, for once in his life, looked stunned.

His chest rose and fell in silence, but inch by inch, he rose to stand over me. My hands fell to his chest, and I held his eyes as he unfastened his belt. I smoothed his hair back above his ear, smelling tires and grease on him as he took out a condom and then let his pants fall to the floor, kicking everything off.

And I even held his eyes, sucking in a breath when he smoothed on the condom and lifted me, pressing my body into the steel wall behind me.

I hung off his neck, my head falling back as his nipple rings teased my breasts, and his lips bore down on mine.

"I want you," I whispered. "I want your sweat on my skin, your tongue in my mouth, and your cock filling me up. Jax, I'm yours," I rasped out, my throat dry. "I was only ever yours."

He grabbed my neck, planting a hard kiss on my lips, and I gave it back full force.

And when he reached down between us and worked himself into

my entrance and into my body, I pressed my lips to his so hard that I could feel his teeth cut into me.

"Oh, God," I gasped and whimpered, my eyes squeezed shut and my whole body shaking as he sank into me, inch by hot inch.

"Ah," I moaned, stilling and feeling him stretch me.

The searing heat shot through my womb and down my thighs as his steel thickness pushed deeper, and I let my head fall back as I clasped Jax's neck with both hands.

We were joined, and I was on fire.

And I was his now.

CHAPTER 15

JAXON

I slid the rest of the way inside her, feeling her body stiffen and relax as she opened for me.

Jesus Christ.

I eased out, bringing my hips back slowly and then sliding back into her tight heat.

"Fuck, you feel good." Her slick pussy surrounded my cock, holding it like a fucking glove, and I squeezed her hips, forcing myself to go slow.

I should've stopped. We were in public, and I should've fucking stopped, but I couldn't.

My lungs ached, because I couldn't take in a goddamn breath, and I hid my face in her neck, sure that she could see the sweet agony written all over it.

"Jesus, baby," I said in a pained voice. "So tight. And so fucking wet." And I groaned, sinking back into her slowly and gripping her ass in my fingers.

"Jax?" She raised her head back upright and wetted her lips. "I'm not a doll," she panted, pleading with me. "I won't break, so don't hold back. I'm ready."

I let out a shaky laugh, feeling sweat pouring down my back as I sucked on her heated skin, really loving how good she'd gotten at being heard.

Straightening up, I lifted her just enough to make sure I had a good hold and pressed her against the wall. "I hope you've been working out," I warned. "You're going to need stamina for this."

Her arms tightened around my neck, and her face sat cheek-to-cheek with mine as I started fucking her the way I knew she wanted.

Her mouth in my ear was torture, her moans and cries surrounded us, and I sank my lips into hers, eating up all her cries. I fucking wanted it all. Everything she had to give me. Feeling her moans and whimpers in my mouth vibrate down into my throat was a fucking rush.

While my hips rolled into hers, shivers covered my skin with the warmth and frenzy burning inside me.

Her hard nipples kept rubbing against my chest, her long black-and-white feather earrings teased her shoulders, and with her glowing skin and petite frame . . . She was killing me. So beautiful it hurt.

"Jax," she gasped against my lips, and tilted her head back to look up at me. She looked about two seconds from passing out. "I'm sorry I don't know what I'm doing," she said in a shaky voice. "I want to be good for you."

And I flexed my muscles, squeezing her ass harder.

"Baby." I shook my head, gazing down into those lovely eyes as she moved up and down my cock, her pussy grinding on me. "Nobody's ever been sweeter than you. You're fucking perfect."

Her eyes flashed to the side, and I followed her gaze, seeing Madoc, Fallon, Shane, and Ken Doll roaming outside. The walls of the fun house only rose halfway, leaving the top half open. We were high enough and far back enough that we wouldn't be noticed, but we could see them.

And they were looking for her.

Poison's "Talk Dirty to Me" was playing over the speakers outside, the hot air blew across our skin, and I grinned my ass off. "They're coming in," I said. "I wonder how long it will take for them to find us."

"No." She bit her bottom lip, a worried look crossing her eyes. "I thought you said no one was coming. My mom is out there." And then she moaned, closing her eyes. "Oh, God. Keep that pace. Keep doing that," she panted.

I straightened my back, pulling her hips into me faster and faster. "Don't worry. Mom won't find out."

I dipped down, kissing her breast and continuing to move inside her. I licked the salty sweat from her skin and shifted my attention to the other breast, taking her nipple in my mouth.

Fucking hell. Her skin was sugar.

"It's so hot," she breathed, and that was the goddamn truth. Her hair still looked sexy as hell, but strands were sticking to her, and I could feel mine sticking to my skin as well.

"I'm coming," she moaned. "Just keep that pace, Jax. Please. Just like that," she urged.

I stood up straight, looked down at her tight stomach, and grabbed her hips. "Like this, baby." And I guided her hips in a figure-eight motion into me and then back down.

Her stomach moved in waves toward me, and I groaned as she caught on and found her rhythm. In and then out. Rolling in and rolling back out. Over and over again, she was driving me fucking crazy.

Her eyebrows pinched together as she took over, working me faster and faster.

"Oh, Jax," she cried, rolling quicker and harder. More and more. Again and again her hips slammed into me, pushing my cock deep inside her.

I sucked in air, feeling the pressure build as if I were ready to implode. "Come on," I grunted, gripping her hips and yanking her into me. "Fuck that shit, baby." And then I dropped my head back. "Jesus, you're killing me."

And we were going to bruise my goddamn hips, but I couldn't care less.

"You feel so good," she whimpered. "Ah, ah, ah . . ."

I plastered us to the wall, chest-to-chest, and held my hand over her mouth, drowning out her cries.

Her moans vibrated through my hand, and her body went limp with her orgasm as I powered through my own. All my muscles tensed with the wave of euphoria in my dick, and I dropped my head back and groaned. "Fuck, Juliet. Fuck." I clenched my teeth, thrusting hard and spilling inside her as she came down.

Fucking hell. My heart was pounding so hard I could hear it in my ears, and I had to tense every damn muscle in my body to make sure I stayed standing. My abs were tight as hell, but my arms were far from tired.

I kneaded her ass, my teeth bared and my chest going a mile a minute.

She was hanging on by a thread. Her limp head bobbed against her skinny arms that were still wrapped around my neck.

And then she lifted her head, meeting my eyes. And I stilled.

K. C. Carter, naked and glowing, stripped and wild, was smiling at me.

"Juliet!" someone shouted. "Where are you?"

She jerked, but I brought her back, holding her tight and whispering into her lips, "I think I like you." And I sank into her mouth, kissing her soft and long until we were both breathless. I pulled back, letting my forehead fall to hers as I tried to catch my breath.

There was just too much shit to process. She constantly looked at me as if she expected better behavior, we always fought, and to top it all off, there was a ton of things she would never know about me. But . . . I liked her. I definitely liked her.

She pulled back, weightless in my arms as she looked up at me. "I like you, too." She smiled. "Was I okay?"

My jaw itched with a smile that I didn't let show. "I'll let you know when we're done," I replied in a cocky tone, and jerked her into me again.

"You're still hard?" she blurted out, looking scared. "But . . . but," she stuttered, "they're coming!"

I thrust my hips into her, shutting her up.

"Look at me," I urged, pressing my forehead to hers and sliding my cock in fast and hard, again and again.

She raised her eyes, her chest rising and falling a mile a minute.

"Juliet!" Fallon called from somewhere in the building.

"Oh, God, Jax!" Juliet called out, and I didn't care who heard her.

"Say it again," I gritted out, running my thumb over her lips, all the while fucking her like a machine. "Say it, baby. Say it."

"Oh, God?"

I shook my head, laughing. "Not that."

Her eyes narrowed on me, and then realization dawned in her eyes, and she sucked my bottom lip into her mouth, drawing it out slow. "Only ever you," she whispered.

"Again." I thrust harder, her moans vibrating through my skin as her tits bounced up and down.

"Only ever you."

"Again." I leaned down to her lips. "Who do you want?"

"Only ever you, Jax," she whimpered. "Ah! Oh, Jax." Her eyes stayed fixed to mine, her summer green burning against my blue. "Only ever you," she barely whispered.

My lips covered hers and we both came, swallowing each other's moans.

Fallon burst in. "Oh, my God!"

"Out!" I yelled, buttoning up my pants. "Tell everyone she's in line for the Porta Pottis or something."

"Jax!" Juliet scolded, still naked and hiding behind me. "Gross."

I rolled my eyes and Fallon snorted.

"Okaaay," she choked out. "Just send her out soon. It's getting weird."

And she barely waited until she was out of the room before she started laughing her ass off.

I grabbed my shirt off the floor, the one I'd used to clean Juliet up and then myself before getting dressed. It was a disaster, and I kind of felt bad.

I'd told Katherine not to buy me expensive shit, but she reveled in it. When she tried to do nice things for my brother, he simply scowled and then rolled his eyes. Graciousness with gifts was not his strong suit.

So, in turn, she spoiled me, because I, at least, knew how to pretend. Even though I didn't need nice stuff—and could certainly buy it for myself if I wanted to—I liked having someone dote on me the way she did. I took her gifts, and while I didn't need them, I loved that she gave me things.

I rolled the shirt, covering up the evidence, and stuck it in my back pocket before I fastened my belt.

Juliet looked shaky. I stepped over, snatching up her shorts.

"Here, baby," I offered, handing them to her and then asking, "Are you okay? Did I hurt you?"

She shook her head, a smile in her eyes. "I'm okay. Just a little sore."

I bent down to pick up her shirt, dusting it off.

Everything was dirty in this place, and there were wet spots on her shorts. Looking down at the floor, I saw small puddles of water, probably from a rainstorm, and that was when I noticed the cobwebs in the corner where the wall met the ceiling.

I looked down at Juliet, her smooth chocolate hair now matted and stringy, and there were red blotches on her hips from where I'd gripped her.

She flipped her hair over the top of her head, and I offered a small smile that I wasn't feeling.

What the hell was the matter with me? This was what I wanted. What I'd dreamed about for years. But she deserved better.

I ground my thumb across the insides of my fingers, feeling the grime that I'd wiped all over her, and taking in this filthy place, I couldn't shake the feeling that this all should've happened differently. "You've only ever been with Liam?" I looked down at her, the sweat on my skin becoming a weight in my stomach. We needed a fucking shower.

She nodded slightly. "Could you tell?" she ventured, looking embarrassed. "I can't say that I had a lot of experience. Even with him, it wasn't like this."

I touched her cheek. "You don't have to say that. It's okay if you loved him."

She shook her head, tears pooling. "I didn't. That's what I mean. It should've been you. This—right here—should've been my first time."

I stared at her, knowing exactly what she meant.

"Come here." I hooked a hand around her neck and brought her into my chest, forcing her chin up. "I didn't push you, did I?"

"Yes."

"I'm being serious," I chastised. "Our first time should've been in a bed. In a clean bed without people around. I pushed you too hard."

A wicked smile cross her lips, and she trailed them along my jaw, finally catching it in her teeth.

I sucked in a breath, feeling my dick jolt to attention again.

"Maybe I pushed you," she teased. "Anyway, I like it when you push me."

And then she pulled back, slipping into her shirt.

"I've got the Loop tonight." I pulled out my hair and refastened the tie. "Tell me you're coming."

She slipped her feet back into her flip-flops, not looking at me. "Depends on how late my date goes."

I rushed her, using my body to bully her into the wall again, and she laughed. "Watch it," I threatened with a smile.

Her little grin was so cute. "I'm teasing," she said sweetly, kissing my lips.

"For your sake, I hope so."

There was no way in hell she was still on a fucking date.

But she nodded her answer. "Yes, I'm coming. Of course."

I pushed off the wall, sliding my feet back into my shoes. "Just come with me now. We'll shower, get something to eat, and go together."

Her sigh was thoughtful. "I want to."

"But?"

"Shane's leaving for California soon," she explained, sounding apologetic. "I should spend the afternoon with her."

And I just wanted to chuck the whole damn day and crawl into bed with her. Turn off phones, strip off clothes, abandon food . . .

"Not to mention," she continued, "that I want to get pretty again before I ogle you tonight." She came up, clutching my belt in her fingers. "If I go home with you to get cleaned up, you'll just get me all messy again."

I laughed. "True."

As much as I'd like to claim that I wouldn't prey on a barely experienced girl who was on the rebound and probably sore, I wouldn't be able to take a shower with her and not . . . *yeah*.

I held the side of her face, arching an eyebrow. "I don't want you in his fucking car. You got that?"

She saluted, clearly biting back her smile.

After about five more minutes of making out, I led her down the stairs—no way was I doing the slide—before we really got caught. I'd paid the kid taking tickets not to let anyone else in, but if Fallon slipped through his fingers, we didn't have long.

We headed out into the late-afternoon heat, hand in hand and smiling. The blush covering her face, her long brown hair shining in the sun, her body glistening with my sweat . . . Without a doubt, I fucking liked her.

Too damn much.

"K.C.?" I heard a woman call, and my gaze shifted to the side as Juliet halted and her fingers tightened around mine.

"Mother," she replied flatly, and I turned wide-eyed at the older version of Juliet. The hair was a vibrant black, but the eyes were the same.

She was beautiful. And very fucking clean.

Her face stiffened in anger. "What have you done?" she accused, taking in her daughter's appearance. The dirty, smudged clothes, the sweaty hair, and the owner of the hand she held. Her pained eyes left her daughter's and flashed to me, raking her eyes up and down my body.

Only, with me, her lips turned down in disgust. I wasn't sure if it was the way I was dressed, the way I wasn't dressed, my long hair, my piercings, or the clear evidence that we'd just been all over each other, but one thing I did know.

It was definitely the sight of her daughter's hand in mine that made her worried eyes turn angry and her fists clench.

"What have you done?" She looked straight at me, accusing. "What have you done to her?"

I gritted my teeth together, remembering those same words on another day. The same words spoken by my father. By Jared.

Those fucking words that told me I was a dirty, shit kid who had blood on his hands and skeletons in the closet.

"What have you done?"

CHAPTER 16

JAXON

sat on the hood of my car, earbuds in and listening to Apocalyptica's "I'm Not Jesus," while I stared at the layout of the tracks on the iPad.

The dirt and sweat were gone. I'd showered when I got home from the carnival, scrubbed my skin till it was red and washed my hair twice, but I still couldn't sit still. There was still dirt under my nails.

"What have you done?"

I tapped my foot, feeling the weight of my phone in my pocket.

Don't call her. Don't text her. She's coming. She said she would.

And as soon as I saw her, got a chance to wrap my arms around her little frame, I'd forget the way her mother had looked at me. I'd forget the knife in my other pocket, the one that said I'd hurt anyone who made me feel dirty again.

She could touch me. She could touch any part of me, and that was it. Just her.

So I swallowed the jagged pill in my throat and gripped the iPad, forcing myself to focus. The Loop. The track. The money.

"Heads up!"

I jerked my head, seeing Fallon just in time to catch the water bottle she tossed. Holding it up and offering a tight smile, I watched her smile in return and walk back to Madoc, who leaned against his car, waiting for the races to start.

About a year ago, I had started working with Zack Hager, the Racemaster, who'd run races here on Friday and Saturday nights. Things were amateur back then. Mostly local high school kids racing their fancy toys that Mommy and Daddy had bought them around an unstable dirt track. My brother, Madoc, and Tate had all raced here during that time. They were illegal events on private property that everyone knew about but no one cared to stop.

And why would they? It was boring as hell.

For me, anyway. It was like watching NASCAR. Left turn, left turn, left turn. Guess what's next. Yeah, left turn.

But cars interested me. Racing definitely interested me. So Zack and I had pooled our resources and stepped up the game. High school races Friday nights. College-and-beyond races Saturday nights. We struck a deal with Dirk Benson, the farmer on whose land the track sat, and got permission to pave it. Only instead of being a rounded square circling a pond, the track now had kind of a Hershey's Kiss–looking top. We'd included the long driveway leading into the track as part of the race now. Drivers did their turn around the track and ended by racing to the end of the driveway, skidding to a turn, and racing back to the finish line.

We'd also constructed another dirt track through the forest between his farm and the highway and incorporated off-roading races as well. Sometimes they ran simultaneously, but we usually tried to keep them separate.

Best of all, the races were almost fully legal—except for the betting—and now they were wired in as well. GoPro cameras were installed on all the vehicles before the races so viewers could access footage on their phones and iPads with the Web Site I'd created. This feature was especially important for the off-road races where the viewers couldn't venture.

Zack took care of scheduling drivers, making sure they signed our disclaimer forms, and the money. I took care of the tech stuff, planning new events, and alterations to the track.

After all, this would eventually get boring, too, so things had to keep changing.

And thankfully this kept me busy. During the school year, when I attended college, my class load, plus the track, was enough to keep me out of trouble. The fall and spring were my safest times. School was in session, and the weather was good for racing. The winter and summer were shaky. Either school was out or the track was dead.

My leg vibrated, and I inhaled a deep breath before looking down.

I blinked long and hard, my stomach turning as I dug out my phone.

Yeah.

My father called regularly, and I did nothing to stop him. Jared didn't know, his mom, Katherine, didn't know, and I wasn't running from the bastard.

I answered the phone. "You're boring me," I said right away. "Come find me when you get out, and we'll have a real conversation then."

"That may be sooner than you think."

A bad taste filled my mouth, but I tried to keep my face even as I swallowed.

"Good," I replied. "I still play with knives."

I heard his quiet laugh on the other end of the phone line.

I had no idea how he called me. I could find out if I wanted to, but for some reason, I didn't want to keep him away. I'd never try to avoid him. I wanted him to avoid me.

"I only want what I've always wanted," he stated. "A chance to make amends. I raised you, Jax. I'd like to show you that I'm better than I was."

"No, you want me to take care of you," I shot back. "You're not using me to pay your way. Not anymore, you sick fuck."

When I was little, my father used me—and Jared—to make money. Stealing, breaking and entering . . . A kid could get in where an adult couldn't, and my father knew that.

"You forget, you little shit," he growled, and my stomach rolled with the memories his insults invoked. "I know where your mess is buried."

But his threat didn't hit home, because I made damn sure I'd always have the upper hand.

"And you forget," I countered, "that I'm not a kid anymore." I jumped off the hood and strolled around to the door, tossing the iPad through the open window onto a seat. "There's a guy in there with you. Christian Dooley. You got a beating from him, right?"

The phone was silent, so I continued. "Just happened to be right after the last time you threatened me?" I taunted, knowing my meaning was clear. "Threaten me again, and you won't make it out of those doors alive."

And I hung up, putting my palms down on the roof of my Mustang and lowering my head.

He wasn't a man, I told myself. I was strong. I was worthy. And I was clean.

I could feel the sweat on my brow cooling me as the light wind hit it, but now my back was nearly drenched, and I wanted to rip off my shirt.

It was after eight, but the day's sunlight still warmed the air. It had to be over ninety degrees.

"I know where your mess is buried." My hands shook, and I clenched my fists.

The mess I'd made the day I'd had enough. Enough of the hands touching me. Enough of people looking at me and hurting me. Enough of being weak. My only regret was that I didn't bury my father with them.

I had come a long way from that scared kid. I never wanted to be weak or surprised in any relationship or situation, and so I'd assumed absolute control over everything in my life.

But as much as I'd never wanted to feel like that unclean kid again, I couldn't shake the feeling of dirt on my skin. I took two showers a day. I had someone clean my house twice a week. I always counteracted one shitty thing I said or did with two decent things, like volunteering or donating money, but I still felt unclean.

Nothing was clean enough.

"Well, you got me here."

I raised my head at the sound of her voice and twisted around to see Juliet.

She stuck her hands in the pockets of her seriously faded, ripped, and tight jeans, and my chest filled with amusement at the sight of her loose black tank top that hung low in the back but showed off her belly button in the front. It had one of those "Keep Calm" logos, but instead it said "I will not keep calm. I will raise hell and break shit."

My father was forgotten.

"I'm not a fan of this scene," she admitted with a glint of humor in her eyes, "so if I'm still bored in an hour, Shane and Fallon promised me we could leave and go back to the carnival."

"You think that's more fun?" I challenged, sauntering over to her. She nodded. "Oh, yes."

I smiled, unable not to touch her anymore. Reaching out and taking her hand, I pulled her into me as I leaned back against the car.

"I've got a carnival ride for you." I leaned into her lips. "Open all night," I whispered, taking her lips in mine and wrapping my arms around her waist.

I heard her snort at my lame joke, but I was smiling, too.

She tasted like water. Every time I'd kissed her it had been like that. As if I was so thirsty I sucked in gulp after gulp, realizing how much my body needed this and how I felt soothed the more I drank.

I reached up and cupped her face with one hand, diving into her mouth and working my tongue around hers. Holding on to her, I molded her hips to mine and felt her moan against my lips. I slipped my hand inside her shirt under her arm, feeling the bare skin of her back. So smooth. Like cream.

"Jax," she gasped, trying to pull away, "we're in public." I knew she didn't want to stop, but she was embarrassed.

I normally would have been, too. I didn't do PDAs, but with her? Hell yeah.

I looked down at her, not letting go. "I know. I just want to touch you all the time. Now that you're letting me, it's hard to stop."

Her hair hung loose and smooth, straightened and parted in the middle. Her green eyes sparkled under dark eye shadow, and I was glad her lips were clear of lipstick. She had full light pink lips, and they were perfect the way they were.

She smirked happily. *"Touch me all the time,"* she repeated. "But we don't get along."

"We get along great." I grinned. "As long as you don't talk." And I leaned down, snatching up her lips again.

She laughed and tried to push away from me, her back bending and her head falling back, but I held tight.

"Stop!" She giggled and squirmed as I kissed a trail up her neck. I loved seeing her giddy.

"Stop talking," I scolded, still kissing her. "We get into trouble when you speak." And I took her earlobe in my teeth, sucking hard, and she went limp.

"I feel like I'm falling," she admitted through her breathlessness, standing up straight and taking my hands away. "But it feels good."

I cocked my head and folded my arms over my chest. "Are we putting K.C. away so Juliet can come out to play?" I joked.

She mock-scowled at me. "Juliet's not any more docile, if that's what you're hoping."

I licked my lips. "I don't care who it is that gets naked for me, just as long as I get her again."

Her eyebrows did a nosedive, she let out a disgusted breath, and whipped around, stalking off, and I was sure my face was red with laughing so hard.

Man, I loved to piss her off. I loved the foreplay. And I was going to enjoy backing her into a wall later on and convincing her she wanted to spend the night.

Madoc stalked over, holding Fallon's hand, looking back at Juliet and then to me.

And he started singing Foreigner. " 'I want to know what love is! I want you to show me!' "

"It's scary that you know that song," Fallon grumbled.

I watched as Juliet walked over to Shane. They were looking at a car that had its hood propped up, but I saw her peek over at me out of the corner of her eye. She couldn't hide it. She pursed her lips together in a smile and rolled her eyes at me.

She was taking me as I was and loosening up—and I wasn't thinking about my father, the Loop, or anything but her.

We were both falling.

Walking down the line, I checked cars off on the roster on my iPad, making sure they were present and ready.

"Suited up?" I inquired, looking down at Derek Roman, who was fixing a GoPro on the trunk of a Raptor.

He stood up, gesturing. "You tell me. Can you access it?"

These cameras couldn't stream footage live from long distances, but I could access it on my phone. I waved, picking myself up on the screen of my cell.

"You got it," I said. "You're getting pretty fast at that."

He smiled, looking too much like a five-year-old who just got a pat on the head.

"Faster means more races," he pointed out. "More races mean more bets. And more bets—"

"Mean more money," I finished, shaking my head. "Yeah, I know where your heart lies." I jerked my head and walked off. "I need to check in with Zack. See you in a minute."

He turned back to his work, and I grinned, actually surprised that he was becoming an asset.

Derek Roman was a couple of years older, but you wouldn't have known it in high school. He used to race the Loop, but his antics got him in a lot of trouble. He didn't get along with Jared, when they raced, or anyone else. He was careless, sloppy, and aggressive, exactly the kind of driver I didn't want here.

So instead of banning him and waiting for the retaliation that would eventually come, I played it smart.

I kissed his ass.

Bullies want to matter. They act the way they do because they don't feel important.

So I gave him that. Told him how much we had planned and what kind of undertaking it all was. How much I needed help, and how much I needed someone who knew the Loop inside and out, and then I gave him jobs.

He stayed busy, got special perks, and got his name officially listed on our Web site, any advertising, and he was involved in decisions. Now, if he decided to be stupid, he'd have a lot to lose.

"So." Madoc ran up next to me, throwing an arm over my shoulder. "Could you possibly fit me into the schedule?"

"Tonight?"

I could feel his eyes roll as I worked my way through the crowd up to the announcer's stage, and he fell in behind me.

"Yeah," he answered. "I want to do that couples race you've got going on. Fallon loved riding with Jared that time he and Tate raced, and I want to take my wife out."

I ran my hand over the top of my head, letting out a frustrated sigh as I stopped next to the stairs.

I turned, looking at him. "Do you have any idea how far in advance these races are scheduled now? It's not high school anymore."

He narrowed his eyes. "Do I need to kick your ass?"

I dropped my gaze, smirking. Yeah, Madoc and Jared were old favorites here, but things were a hell of a lot different now. Whereas they had to contend with three or four races a night, we now had ten to fifteen, and some going simultaneously.

"I'm not saying that." I moved away from the stairs, seeing Zack— the Racemaster—climb down from the podium.

"Hey," I greeted Zack, and gestured over toward the track. "Roman's going to send off the rally race, so can you make sure Sam knows to get his ass out first with the camera before they take off this time?"

"Sure." He nodded and slapped Madoc on the arm. "Hey, man."

"Hey," Madoc answered but kept his eyes on me, waiting for me to get my reality check.

"Okay." I laughed after Zack had walked off. "Of course I can fit you in." I lowered my voice and arched an eyebrow before continuing. "Even though *everything* is scheduled down to the *minute*, and you're messing with my timetable right now. But okaaaay."

He smiled, teeth flashing bright white, nudging my arm. "Thanks, dude!" And then walked off.

"You need an opponent," I called after him.

He turned, slipping his hands into his jeans. "I know," he replied. But I didn't like his smile as he walked away.

For the next half hour, we got through five races—two rallies off track and three on. Once the cars were suited up and races began, my job got easier. I sat up in the podium running the cameras, alternating angles for the viewers so they always had exciting perspectives when they were on the site. Once in a while, I'd have to go and help with the cameras or the cars, because something wasn't working, but Zack handled setting off the cars, and he, Roman, and a few others handled the bets.

It was easy and comfortable. Up here. Alone. With a clear view of the action below.

"Hey."

I turned around and saw Cameron, stepping up the last stair, carrying a red Solo cup. She was dressed in a black miniskirt and a red flannel shirt tied above her belly button with the sleeves rolled up.

"Hey." I leaned back against the small table, crossing my arms over my chest.

She came up next to me, looking down at the crowd silently. Everyone was enjoying whatever they'd brought in their coolers while Rob Zombie's "Never Gonna Stop" played over the speakers.

I rubbed my fingers against my palms as I clenched my fists. My hands were actually sweating, and I didn't understand why—after five years of knowing Cameron—I was suddenly uncomfortable.

The thick silence hung there between us, and I searched my

brain for something to ask her. College? No, she wasn't going. Her old foster parents? Maybe.

She broke the silence before I could. "Well, this is fun." Her nervous laugh seemed so out of place.

"Yeah," I muttered, wondering why the hell I felt uneasy.

She looked at me, her eyes serious. "So I've finally lost you, haven't I?"

I swallowed, not knowing exactly what she meant but definitely noticing the difference.

"Never," I said thoughtfully. "I'm always your friend."

"But I'm not the only woman you love anymore."

I dropped my eyes, my lips curling on a hidden smile. I did love Cameron. She was the only girl I'd really talked to. But while we were very much the same, my heart never held her close. She was a friend. Someone I could trust and someone who would stand up for me.

But after she'd leave for the night, I didn't think about her, and I didn't count the minutes until I could see her again.

She stood up straight, shrugging. "I know it's not like that with us. Not love-love, per se," she clarified. "But we were each other's firsts. No matter who I hooked up with, you were always ten times more important."

I flattened my lips, feeling guilty that it was different for me.

We'd both lost our virginity long before we met each other, but we always considered each other our real first.

Since our first sexual experiences weren't something we wanted to remember.

We were there for each other, and I loved her.

But there was a girl who was more important for me, and it had been that way for a long time. A very long time.

She continued. "It never even occurred to me that it would be hard when you finally replaced me in your heart."

I looked down to the track, seeing Juliet sitting on the bleachers with Shane, Fallon, and . . . One Direction.

I blew out a breath. "I have no heart. You know that."

She shook her head, tears pooling. "You suck," she joked.

"Why?" I grinned. "Because I'm letting another girl have some summer fun with me?"

"No," she blurted out. "Because you're keeping her to yourself."

My chest shook with laughter as I yanked her in by the neck and kissed her forehead. Her blond hair, hanging in a high ponytail, smelled like overripe strawberries. I glanced down at Juliet, thinking of her hair that smelled like a crisp fall morning.

And she was looking up at me.

Shit.

Her eyes were narrowed as she rested her elbows on her knees and watched me with my arm around Cameron.

I sighed, pulling away. "I'll see you, okay?"

I left Cameron and climbed down the ladder, facing forward as I jumped the last five steps to the ground.

Girls liked to make a mountain out of a molehill, so now I had to go put out the damn fire she'd no doubt started in her head.

As I approached the bleachers—where she sat two rows up—I noticed Shane sitting next to her, talking to friends on her other side, while Madoc, Fallon, and Adam stood up, talking to a group of people.

She saw me and looked away, straightening her back. I set my foot on the bottom bleacher and leaned in next to her face.

"Don't," I cautioned, looking in her eyes.

She dropped her chin, looking almost sad. God, I wanted to wrap my arms around her.

"Don't what?" she mumbled.

"Don't be jealous."

"I'm not," she maintained, looking defiant.

I nearly whispered. "Three years ago, I laid eyes on you for the first time," I said, "and every time I've looked at another girl since then, I've compared her to you. Every time."

She raised her eyes hesitantly.

I gave a half smile. "Your big green eyes that give away everything you're feeling. Your pouty little mouth that tells me when you're happy or pissed." I leaned in, close to her lips. "And your tight little body that I finally got my fucking hands on after years of waiting for you."

Her throat moved up and down as she listened.

"I have lots of energy for you, Juliet—only you—so don't go imagining shit that's not true."

No more bullshit. I always knew what I wanted, and I never failed at getting it. I had an appetite for a lot, but when I found my niche, I knew it. Lacrosse, computers, the Loop . . .

And Juliet. She was my niche, too.

When her lips pursed against a smile she desperately tried to hold back, I knew she'd relaxed.

"Keep your eyes open," I whispered.

A confused look crossed her face right before I dived in, caught her lips in mine, and kissed her deep and soft. My tongue flicked over hers, owning her mouth. She was helpless against me, and I was absolutely fine with that.

I pulled away to nuzzle in her ear. "You drive me crazy."

She shivered, breathing hard. "Good."

I smiled, continuing to trail my lips over her jaw.

"Jax." I heard Madoc's voice off to the side. "Adam's going to race me in his 370Z, okay?"

I stopped, my lips hovering over Juliet's skin.

Standing up, I turned and saw all three of them looking at me and waiting. "What's the point of that?" I scoffed.

Madoc's face fell, and I saw the eyebrow shoot up as he realized I was insulting his friend's car. A GTO against a 370Z? He knew better.

"Juliet?" Madoc averted his eyes to her, ignoring me. "It's a couple's race. You want to ride with him?"

I turned around completely, facing him. "Enough already," I growled low. "I'm sick of your bullshit."

Everyone clammed up, and I struggled between feeling bad that I was getting pissy with my friends, feeling shitty that I was determining for Juliet what she would and would not be doing, and being angry that every time I felt fucking high on life, someone or something messed with it.

Adam stepped forward. "If I'm supposed to have a girl in the car—"

"You can have a guy, too," I shot back. "Love is love. We don't discriminate."

Fallon snorted, and Madoc scowled down at her.

I bit back my smile, locking eyes with Madoc. "She's not going."

I heard Juliet clearing her throat behind me, but I ignored it. Would she be okay with me taking another girl for a drive?

Madoc held out his hands. "Shane won't do it. I asked," he explained. "I'm honestly not trying to get under your skin, okay?"

"Relax." Adam stepped forward, and I folded my arms over my chest. "It's obvious Madoc set me up with a girl who's already taken. I'll keep my hands off. I promise."

"That's right." I nodded. "Because she won't be in the car. You're not a screened driver, and she could get hurt. You want to mess up your ride. Go ahead. But not with her in it."

"Jax," Juliet said under her breath behind me, and I could tell she was trying to rein me in.

Yeah, no.

Fallon spoke up. "So, how about Madoc takes K.C. . . ." She paused, shaking her head clear. "Juliet, I mean—and I'll go with Adam."

"No," Madoc maintained. "This is supposed to be you and me riding together."

Fallon pulled her hair up in a ponytail. "Baby, if this is the only way, he'll let her—"

"I'll go," Juliet groaned, climbing down from the bleachers. "I'll go with Adam."

I dropped my arms, staring down at her like a warning.

She cut me off before I started. "Just be quiet for a minute. It's a three-minute race." She peered up at me, handling me. "Let Madoc have his fun and calm down. The guy's car is pretty intense. I'm sure he knows how to handle it."

I steeled my jaw, not liking her talking about his ride. "You're trying to make me feel better, right?" I joked. "I mean, that is your goal? Because it's not working."

She laughed into my chest. "You're not jealous, are you?"

"He can go alone," I said, annoyed. "I make the rules, and I choose when to break them."

"You're being silly." She started to back away toward the cars. "Especially when you're the one I might let take me home tonight," she teased.

"*Might?*" I shot out. " I really don't like you sometimes."

"I don't like you, either," she singsonged, walking toward Adam's car.

"Shit," I breathed out, raking a hand through my hair and watching her head to Adam's car. Was I being silly?

He wouldn't touch her if he knew what was good for him, and she wouldn't let him. I trusted that.

And I'd be absolutely fine with Jared or Madoc driving with her. It wasn't that I never wanted her to be on the track.

No, I was simply worried he'd get her hurt. I didn't know him or his driving, and I was real damn unhappy about this.

Both cars roared to life, filling the air with the whir of Adam's high-pitched 3.7-liter engine and the heavy rumble of Madoc's 6.0 LS2. I didn't breathe as I watched Juliet buckle herself in, her black-and-white feather earrings dangling against her neck.

I breathed out a sigh, heading back down the track. I swung myself around the stairs and jogged up to where Zack already stood, ready to announce the next race. Both cars traveled slowly down the track, coming to a stop below us, revving their engines.

"We need to meet this week," Zack said to me as he inspected the scene below. "I want to talk about your plans to expand to street racing. I'm concerned."

I gripped the railing, watching every movement of Adam's ride. "Not now." I shook my head. "That's at least a year out. We'll talk later."

The crowd cheered, welcoming one of their favorite sons home. So many people remembered Madoc, and everyone flooded the night with noise. The crowd at the Loop used to be mainly high school students, but now it was more eclectic, and since it was summer, a lot of our high school friends were here.

"Announce it," I said to Zack. "Madoc Caruthers and Adam One Direction."

He laughed under his breath. "This is an odd matchup."

I nodded, knowing it wasn't really a race. Madoc had to know he was going to win.

Zack leaned on the railing, microphone in hand, booming voice hitting the crowd. "I know you all remember him!" he taunted, and the crowd cheered.

"If you don't, then I know you've heard of him!" Zack's deep voice echoed through the night air, and they shouted louder.

People held up their cups and cans, howling over the track. The GTO shook as it revved, while the 370Z's high-pitched hum matched it, both drowning out any coherent thought in my head.

"Give it up for Madoc and Fallon Caruthers," he sang out, going long, "going up against K. C. Carter and Adam One Direction!" he yelled.

The sea of spectators cheered, holding up their phones and iPads, probably taking either pictures or video. Since the couples' races were only once around the paved track, we never installed GoPros. No reason to dumb down the audience. They had a perfect view anyway, so it worked.

"Come on," I nudged. "Get this over with."

He walked around me to my other side, lining up with the starting line. "Ready!" he shouted, and the stoplight stayed on red. "Set!" And the stoplight switched to yellow, the engines revving over and over again as the crowd went wild. "Go!" he roared, and my heart leaped into my throat as both cars saw the light change to green and spun their tires, trying to take off so quickly.

I swallowed, seeing Madoc shoot off first, and I gripped the railing, watching the 370Z speed after him. Both cars gained speed, and I listened for the change of gears, hearing when each shifted up, increasing its pace.

Madoc knew the track, knew when to speed up, and knew at exactly which point he needed to lay off the gas to round the turn effectively. He spun around, drifting into a slight skid, but I gritted my teeth, seeing Adam fishtail left and then right as he corrected himself.

I rubbed my hand over my face, walking around the stand, following them with my eyes as they circled the track. Adam would speed forward, and Madoc would swerve on the track, joking around to stay in his way.

I'm going to kill him.

Zack laughed next to me. "Madoc's back."

"He's being stupid," I bit out. "Pulling that shit with his wife in the car . . ."

"And Madoc's never been in an accident. Calm down."

Madoc straightened out after that, so I let it go. He was stupid, but I guessed not that stupid.

But my stomach tightened every time Adam tried to get around Madoc but lost time spinning out. He could never get ahead, simply because he was flooring it between turns.

As he rounded the third turn and swerved to a gentle right up the driveway that served as the extended track, I narrowed my eyes, watching like a hawk.

Almost over.

They'd go down to the end, skid to a turn, and race back down to the finish line.

But then my chest flooded with fear, and I could barely breathe.

"Son of a bitch!" I raged, seeing that Adam's car had lurched forward, twice the speed it had just been going.

"Fuck!" I spun around, barreling down the stairs and pushing through people. "Get out of the way!"

I raced down the track, empty except for the hundred or so spectators lining the sides. I could hear some guys behind me, running with me, but we all stopped when we got in view of the driveway. Madoc's car had halted at the end of the lane while Adam's back end sank into a ditch.

I took off, pounding down the track, full speed, until I came to the car and caught him climbing out.

"Are you insane!" I bellowed, grabbing him by the shirt and holding him up to me.

"Jax, stop!" Juliet urged, stepping out of the car. "I'm okay."

But when I looked at her, she was rubbing her neck. I didn't see blood.

"No, you're not," I growled, throwing Adam to Zack and Derek. "I knew this was a stupid idea. Hold him."

They secured both of his arms, holding him, and I shook my head at Madoc, who'd come up with Fallon. I didn't want one word from him right now. He'd said enough tonight.

I dived into Adam's car, took his keys out of the ignition and popped the hood. Lifting it up, I reached down and grabbed hold of the red-and-blue nozzles I knew I was going to find there.

"Son of a bitch," I cursed, anger flooding my body.

Zack and Derek dragged Adam over.

"Nitrous," Zack mumbled to himself, sounding just as pissed at seeing the nozzles. Somewhere in the car, probably the trunk, a tank of the chemical was hidden.

I arched an eyebrow at Adam. "Failed to mention that?"

He shook his head, blowing me off. "I've done it lots of times, man. I just didn't expect it to take so long to slow back down. I'm sorry."

I reared back, hammering my fist across his face. He crumbled, Zack and Derek holding him up by his limp arms.

"Jesus Christ," Madoc sighed, sounding done for the night.

I slammed the hood shut, throwing the keys against his chest, where they fell to the ground. "Get out of here."

"Are you okay?" I heard Fallon ask behind me.

I turned to see her grab Juliet's shoulders, looking at her neck.

"I'm fine," she muttered, dropping her hand. "Just . . ." She looked at me and then spoke to Fallon. "Can you guys take me to Tate's, please?"

I walked over. "I'm taking her home."

She shook her head, walking away. "No, you're not."

"He almost got you killed," I pointed out. "His stunt could have hurt others. I have every right to be pissed off."

"Then send him off the track. Yell at him," she threw out. "But your first order of business wasn't to make sure I was okay. You threw your weight around and acted like a caveman. You were looking for a reason to be mad at him. If you were concerned about me, you would've checked on me first."

I grabbed her arm, stopping her. "I always put you first."

She narrowed her eyes, confused, and I looked away.

"Are you okay?" I asked, not seeing any damage on her.

She cocked her head. "I've seen you beat up two guys in twenty-four hours, Jax." She shook her head at me and then looked around the scene. "I don't want any of this."

"Any of what?"

Her expression turned vulnerable. "I don't want to be scared," she admitted. "And you scare me."

I studied her, not knowing what to say.

She inched toward me, lowering her voice. "What did you say to that guy on the front lawn last night? How deep are you in with Fallon's father? And what's the Skull and Feather?" I narrowed my eyes and stared down at her. How the hell did she . . . ?

My room. I blinked long and hard. She'd seen the card in my room for the club in Chicago.

My heart pumped double time. "What do you want from me?" I pressed.

She shook her head, turning away. "Nothing."

But I grabbed her arm, pulling her back. "What?" I growled. "What the fuck do you want?"

"I want you to be better!"

CHAPTER 17

JULIET

He squeezed the steering wheel and scowled at the road as Stone Sour's "Tired" played on the stereo.

"Why won't you look at me?" I whispered, staring at my lap.

He stayed frozen, not breaking pace as he drove us home and answered, "Because I should never have touched you."

I quickly twisted my head, looking out the window to hide my tears. My jaw ached, my throat felt as if it were being pierced in a hundred different places, and I wanted to run.

Away. Far away.

Everything had been beautiful this afternoon. Hot, sticky, sweaty, dirty, and completely beautiful when I was in his arms. Now . . . now he acted as though he hated me, and I felt stupid.

Was it so bad that I wanted him safe? I didn't know the details of what he did with computers, but I knew it wasn't on the up-and-up. And I definitely wanted inside his head. But now his exterior was harder than ever, and he was pulling away from me.

K.C. would get upset. She was weak, and she would cry. Juliet would hold her fucking tears in front of assholes.

My body swayed to the left, and I grabbed the door handle as he barreled into Tate's driveway.

Looking over at him, I watched as he yanked up the parking brake and turned off the ignition.

He sat there, and after a few moments of refusing to look at me, I was ready to scream.

"Jax," I started, swallowing the lump in my throat. "I—"

"It's fine, Juliet," he shot out, his tone flat. "It was a mistake. You want 'better'? Go find 'better.' "

"What?" I asked, shocked. "Jax, I didn't mean—"

I stopped, seeing his fist tighten around the steering wheel so hard that I could hear the leather twisting.

What the hell was wrong with him? I never meant that he wasn't good enough.

But right now cool and calm Jaxon Trent was pissed, and he was barely tolerating me.

He opened the car door to get out, but I reached out and grabbed his arm. "Don't bother," I said, before he had a chance to throw me out of the car. "I can open my own door."

I stepped out of the car and slammed the door shut.

I looked up, seeing a light was on in the downstairs of Tate's house, but I didn't remember leaving one on. I was about to turn around and say good-bye, hoping maybe I would see the Jax who had spoken to me on the bleachers before, but I decided not to. Without turning back, I started for the house.

"Juliet?" Jax called, and I stopped in the middle of the walkway up to the porch.

Turning around, I crossed my arms over my chest to keep from shivering.

He'd stepped out of the car, leaned over the hood, and studied me. He opened his mouth, looking as though he wanted to say something but then just closed it, steeling his jaw again.

I waited for a second longer than I should've, wishing he'd say the things he said to me in his car last week. Or in his office last night. Or the fun house today.

Tears pooled before I could stop them, and I turned around, walking as calmly as I could for the front door. Unlocking it, I slipped in and slammed it shut, sliding down to the floor.

"Hey, you," I heard a familiar voice chirp.

My stomach lurched into my throat as if I were falling, and I looked up to see Tate standing between the dining room and foyer, holding a can of Coke in her hand with her little dog, Madman, hovering between her legs.

The tears instantly spilled over. "Tate?" I choked out.

Pushing off the floor, I launched myself at her, wrapping my arms around her and burying my face in her neck.

It was too late. The sobs couldn't be stopped. I clutched her T-shirt, probably digging my nails into her skin, too, as my body shook with relief.

"Hey, hey," she soothed. "What the hell happened?"

But I couldn't speak. The shakes, the relief, the loss of the loneliness—everything overtook me, and I held her tight for a long time, thankful that she didn't ask again.

I sat on the edge of Tate's bed, curling my toes into her rug and letting the morning chill cover my arms as I stared into the distance out her French doors.

Tate had opted to let me keep her room and sleep in her father's room, and from the lack of sound, I gathered she was still sleeping. It was early, after all.

I had spent all of yesterday curled up in my pj's in the chair by the window reading through my journals, and trying not to look outside every time I heard a thunderous engine roar down the street.

Jax hadn't been home, and since I hadn't left the house, I hadn't seen him or asked Tate about him. She had seen him drop me off, and she knew I was upset.

There was no doubt she'd pieced it all together, but she didn't push. I just wanted to be left alone.

My body felt as if I'd just done a BodyPump class after a five-year hiatus. My muscles were sore, and I ached between my legs. Even today, I could still feel where Jax had been.

With Liam I hadn't felt any of that. Not in my body or in my heart.

I'd given my virginity to him when I was fifteen, because I needed to get rid of it. My mother tortured me to protect it by having our family doctor come every month to look for signs of sexual activity.

So to make the visits stop, I rushed to have sex. I let Liam have me not long after we started dating, and I suffered the repercussions. I was put on the pill, and in the end she let me keep seeing Liam, because if I was sleeping with him, then I wasn't "spreading myself around." That was how much she thought of me.

But the truth was, I barely connected with Liam. I tried to keep him happy, because I had wanted someone to love me, but every time we were together, something was missing. I knew it, and so did he.

Everything I struggled to hang on to, whether it was love or perfection, ended up failing me in the end. It was an impossible expectation that weighted me down.

And now I didn't have Liam. I didn't have family. I didn't have anyone putting expectations on me, and somehow I was lighter.

Whereas the fear of mistakes had weighted me to the earth, falling away from listening to everyone else had me floating. It was addicting.

Liam didn't want me. My mother didn't want me. Jax didn't want me.

I had Tate. I had Shane. I had Fallon. I wasn't perfect, but I also wasn't alone.

Taking one last deep breath, I stood up and grabbed my box of journals out from under the bed. Picking out four, I stuffed them into Tate's messenger bag and got ready for school.

"Morning, Ms. Penley," I said, offering a smile.

"K.C.," she chirped, looking up from the papers she was organizing. I saw her do a double take at my attire.

I wore white shorts and Tate's native headdress skull shirt that I'd finally found after digging through her drawers this morning. I'd washed and straightened my hair, but I'd also braided little pieces of it, making it look a little punk. And I had on less makeup than usual.

She finally found her tongue. "Did you have a good weekend?" she asked.

I pulled out my earbuds. "Eh, the usual," I joked. "Booze, broads, and bank robberies."

She laughed. "Typical, then," she agreed.

I leaned on the lab table she used as a desk. "You?"

She smiled and shrugged as if apologizing. "Reading."

I narrowed my eyes on her as she pretended to work. It seemed sad that she spent her weekends reading alone. Penley was hot.

She was middle-aged—early forties—but still very beautiful. She had a great figure, a fantastic personality, and a steady career.

She needed a boyfriend.

I shook my head, smiling at myself. Yeah, right. Now that I was soooo happy, I thought I'd set everybody up, right?

I slapped the lab table, changing the subject. "So, do you mind if I do something different today?" I asked.

She peered at me through her glasses. "Such as?"

"I'd like to take them outside for a writing project."

She twisted her lips to the side, thinking.

Tutoring was like pulling teeth. None of the students wanted to be here, and all the tutors were complaining. I was worried Penley wouldn't like me diverging from the lesson plan, but other than a change of pace, I didn't know what else to try. I needed to get their attention.

But then, to my surprise, she agreed. "That sounds fine." She nodded, returning to her work. "Just make sure you stay on school grounds."

I let out a breath. "Great. Thanks."

I stuck my earbuds back in, bobbing my head to "Bones" by Young Guns, thankful to Tate. She seemed to know exactly what music selection I needed, and while most of it was angry rock, some of it was fun, girl music. "Cruel Summer," Katy Perry, and a couple of eighties hits from Madonna and Joan Jett were on the playlist, too. The perfect mix of "hey, I really want to kick you in the balls right now" and "hey, I really just want to jump around and dance right now" type of music.

Sitting down at my usual table, I dug out a file folder of copies I'd made that morning and left my journals in the bag. I pulled out the packets of papers for each of the students in my group and waited for everyone to filter into the room.

Once Penley was done with her group lesson, she let us divide into groups, and that was when I stood up.

"Follow me," I instructed as soon as my four had come over.

Not waiting for them to ask questions and ignoring their confused faces, I walked past them and out of the room. After about three seconds, I heard their scurried footsteps behind me, and I continued down the hallway, out the side door, and all the way to the outside amphitheater.

"K.C.?" I recognized Christa's voice. "What are we doing?"

I took a step down into the Coliseum-like venue, and continued climbing down, bench after bench, until I got to the concrete stage.

"Taking class outside today," I answered, looking up. "I wanted us to have some privacy."

I gestured for them to take a seat, and other than the swelling balloon in my throat, I felt fine.

Someone tsked. "But it's so hot," Sydney whined. "I'm sure this is illegal."

I smirked. "Cheer up. Lacrosse is practicing today. Maybe you'll get a show for your trouble."

She pursed her lips, looking snotty, but she sat down between Ana and Christa. Jake plopped down on the steps and then took his glasses from his bag and slid them on his face.

I set my bag down and clutched the papers in my arms.

"For now," I started, walking toward them, "I'd like you to raise your hands. Who here likes to write?"

I looked around as I handed the first packet to Ana. "No one?" My eyebrows shot up with my surprised smile.

"Okay." I handed the next packets to Sydney and Christa. "How many of you like to talk?"

The girls immediately raised their hands, giggling at one another. Jake was asleep, I think.

I smiled. "Well, writing is like talking, only it's to yourself. I talk to myself all the time." I looked around, handing the last packet to Jake. "And so do all of you. Admit it."

Christa smiled to her herself while Sydney rolled her eyes.

"Come on," I begged. "You talk to yourself in the shower, in the car, when you're mad at your parents, or when you're trying to pump yourself up. Right?"

I raised my hand. "I do."

Jake raised his hand, giving me a lazy smile. Eventually Ana and Christa joined.

"So, if we like talking, we like writing. What we don't like about writing is being judged. We don't like the format, the rules, the editing, the need to make everything perfect. But writing can be a way to formulate your thoughts when you can't say what you need to say or you don't know how to say what you need to say on the spot. Writing lets you take time. Find the words. And express yourself exactly how you wish. And when we're young, it's a way to lose yourself as well as find yourself. When we get older, we find that drugs, alcohol, and sex can do that for us, but with higher consequences. Writing is always safe."

They watched me, leaning back against the concrete benches.

I held my packet by the staple. "Take a look at page one."

They held up their papers, squinting at them, beginning to read.

I swallowed. "Christa? Would you read the first entry, please?" My pulse raced just beneath my skin.

She cleared her throat, sat up, and started.

11/16/2003

Dear Juliet,

I'm sorry that Mother took away your toys. Please don't be sad. Everything is going to be good someday. If you practice you will get better. It took me a long time to make sure my shoes were lined up straight, too. You're already so much better than I was! And I thought your hair looked super. Don't worry about what Mother said. You're so good at braiding. I'm sorry she spanked you. Go give her a hug and say how nice her perfume smells. Maybe she'll let you borrow some!

I love you!

Katherina

Her voice was chipper and happy, and you could hear the exclamation points. She'd picked up the voice of an eight-year-old easily.

She looked up and pinched her eyebrows together. "This is a letter from a child," she guessed.

I smiled gently and nodded.

"Ana?" I gestured, and she sat up. "Next one, please?"

Ana leaned forward, setting her elbows on her knees, and started.

7/14/2004

Dear Juliet,

Mother is right. You are no good! You can't even keep your shirt from getting wrinkly before family pictures! You are worthless, and I hate you! Everyone hates you! I wish I had a different sister! You're ugly and stupid! Everyone laughs at you, and Daddy doesn't even want you. He only wants me! I wish you were dead!

I pressed my lips between my teeth and breathed in. I didn't want to look up, so I just kept going.

"Sydney, turn the page. Read the next one, please," I said, flipping the page over.

Sydney hesitated and then cleared her throat.

9/2/2010

Dear Juliet,

I made a new friend today. Her name is Tate, and she

doesn't have a mom. I wish we didn't have a mom. Maybe you would be safe then. I love you, Juliet, and I think Tate will love you, too. She's so beautiful and cool and kind. She makes me laugh, and I wish I could introduce her to Dad. He talked to me today, you know? Well, of course you do.

I hate that he can't remember you most of the time, and I hate that he's in that hospital, but at least he gives me hugs. Even if he can't remember me, he's the only person that gives me hugs. I wish I could see you. I wish I could look in the mirror and still see you there. I'll bet you look awesome, and I miss your music. Why did you leave? Why won't you come home?

Katherina

Sydney's voice fell raspy and soft. "These are a child's diary entries, aren't they? To her sister," she assumed.

I sighed. "Perhaps," I said, looking around at the girls' troubled faces. Jake hid behind his sunglasses, but I could tell he was listening.

"What's the child feeling?" I asked.

"Anger," Jake ventured. "Innocence. And a lot of sadness."

I nodded, strolling down the row of seats past each student. "This child has no one to talk to," I pointed out. "She's hurting, and she has nowhere to turn to." I tipped my chin down, swallowing the lump in my throat. "Jake, will you read the next one, please?"

He stayed back, leaning against the concrete but turning his attention to the paper.

3/24/2011

Dear Mother,

I can't wait to leave you. It's all I think about. Three more years, and I'm going to college, and I never want to see you again. I feel guilty every time Liam kisses me. I feel like I'm doing something wrong. I'm not doing anything wrong! Everyone kisses their boyfriend and does more! I want to feel. I want to laugh and let go. I want to be happy. Were you ever happy? Did you ever love my father? Me? I feel like I could sink to the bottom of the ocean and never need air. I'm dead.

Katherina

Jake sat up, studying the paper, and then looked up at me. "Juliet is her alter ego," he stated. "When she writes to Juliet, she's angry at her. Disappointed. Condescending." He took off his glasses and squinted at me. "But when she writes to her mother, she's angry and disappointed in herself. Juliet and Katherina are the same girl."

My chest flooded with icy heat, and my heart jackhammered through my chest. *Jesus.* Jake might not be on drugs after all.

I inhaled a breath and looked down. "It's possible," I offered, and looked to the girls. "Christa, will you read the next one, please?"

Christa rushed to flip the page.

12/11/13

Dear Juliet,

There's a new guy at school. He keeps looking at me. Mother would never approve of him, but I can't help it. I can't wait to get to school every day and feel him watching me. He makes me feel beautiful, and I love the way my heart rushes. I hide it, but I love it. Being inside my head these days is a lot more fun than it used to be!

Christa smiled wide, and I saw the others try to bite back theirs. "I like that feeling." She laughed, and I remembered loving it, too. Jax was something I looked forward to, and he gave me tunnel vision. Catching him looking at me always made me feel beautiful.

I cleared my throat of the tears I'd been holding back. "I'll read the last one."

6/16/2014

Dear Juliet,

I'm sorry that I let others make you feel bad. I'm sorry that I hurt you, and I'm sorry that I didn't fight for you. I should've saved you a long time ago, but I wasn't strong enough. You are beautiful. You were the best at making friendship bracelets at camp in fourth grade, Shane thinks you make the best deviled eggs, and Tate loves your crazy stories. You are worthy of all the love the world has to offer. Your friends stay by your side, and someday you will find a man who thinks the world of you, and you'll both have children that will be so lucky to have you as a mother. If you want to scale waterfalls in Ecuador and kayak off the coasts of Alaska, then you have to do it. Toss the umbrella and enjoy the rain. Roll down the window and stick your head out. Take off your shoes and go barefoot.

I love you.

I pursed my lips, trying desperately to hold back the tears threatening at the corners of my eyes. Looking around, I noticed Christa wiping tears away and Sydney staring at the paper and clutching the sides in both of her fists. Ana rested her head in her hand, looking touched.

And Jake. Jake flipped back to the front page and looked to be re-reading the whole thing again. Amusement tickled my lips, and I smiled.

"Wait a minute," Ana called. "That last entry is dated today."

I nodded. "Yes, it was. So"—I quickly changed the subject—"Jake has suggested that Juliet and Katherina are the same person. Who agrees with him?"

I waited, looking between the girls and Jake. One by one they began raising their hands, and I wasn't sure if they really thought that or they weren't sure what to think and just agreed. It didn't matter. The answers weren't as important as the process.

"Okay," I started. "Let's run with that. If Katherina is writing to herself—a girl she calls Juliet—why does she do it instead of just writing 'Dear Diary'? Or instead of just sharing her thoughts on a page? Why is she writing to herself?"

"Because she feels alone." Ana shrugged.

"Maybe she's got a personality disorder?" Christa offered a timid smile, and I nodded in response to their responses, trying not to grin.

"Because," Sydney piped up, "she can be whoever she wants on the page."

I narrowed my eyes on her. "What do you mean?"

She licked her lips, sitting up straighter. "In the first entry, she's supportive but a little condescending, like she's taking care of Juliet. Like Juliet's the little sister in need of guidance. Then she gets angry at her, acting like she's perfect and not the disgrace Juliet is. In both entries, Juliet is portrayed as sad and not good enough. When she writes as Katherina, she gets to be more than that. She gets to be strong and confident."

I continued, listening and drifting down the aisle.

"Then," Sydney kept going. "You see her transfer her anger to her mother, saying things she wouldn't say to her face. She's also kinder to Juliet as if she begins to realize not everything is her fault."

And she glanced at Jake and then back at me. "Juliet's not her alter ego. Katherina is."

My heart tightened in my chest.

Wow.

"So," I prompted. "Journaling did what for her?"

"Gave her an outlet," someone said.

Jake spoke up. "Let her say what needed to be said when no one else would listen."

"It was a release."

"It saved her life." And I looked over at Sydney, the girl I didn't see eye to eye with, but all of a sudden she seemed to get it.

"Writing can be very public and also very private. I want you to forget the rules today," I said. "I'm going to give you twenty or so minutes. Go put in your iPods, spread out, go to the grass, and write. This isn't graded. I don't care about grammar or conventions. I want you to write to yourself as if you're going to read this twenty years from now. Share who you are right now. What you want. Where you want to go. What you hope to accomplish and what you hope to gain from friends and family. There are no rules. Just write to an older you."

As they began to dig in their backpacks, I walked back to the stage and grabbed the last journal I'd used. Flipping it open, I sat down on a bench and completed the assignment, too.

CHAPTER 18

JAXON

"*Jared!*" *I call.* "*Catch!*"

My new brother throws his hands up in the air and runs to capture the old, faded football. A car honks, and he twists around, dashing off the street to get out of the way.

"*You trying to get me killed?*" *he jokes, smiling at me, and I run to throw my shoulder into his stomach.*

"*Ahhhhhh!*" *I tackle him to the sidewalk.*

He laughs, grunting as he hits the concrete. We've gotten tons of scrapes already today, but we don't care.

Ever since my half brother showed up last week to visit for the summer, we've spent every waking minute together. Almost, anyway. We've played football and gone to the movies, and he's taught me how to climb trees, even though we have to walk a lot of blocks to get to the nearest park.

Jared lives with his mom a few hours away, and this is the first time he's met our dad.

I know he hates it here. I'm sure it's not as pretty as his mom's house. But I feel safe with him here. My dad's friends haven't bothered me since he showed up, and even though I know he can't, I keep hoping that he'll take me with him when he goes home. I don't want to be alone again, and I know that he'll protect me.

I let myself dream it, for a little while, anyway.

"When you come to visit me, you'll get to play on the grass and climb trees right in your yard," he tells me, ruffling my hair.

I nudge away, grinning. "Stop it. I'm not a baby."

We rise to our feet, and he looks at me, shaking his head. "Does Dad have those parties a lot?" he asks me about all the noise last night.

I nod, leading the way back toward the house. "Yeah, but it's best to stay out of the way."

"Why?"

I shrug and stare off down the street. "Some of the people don't like kids." Or they like them too much.

I'm thirteen now, and even though I barely remember what it was like to live with my foster family, I know how bad things make me feel.

And what I feel now is a lot worse than what I felt when I was five. No one should have to see the dirty things I see going on at my house. I thought it was normal, but I don't think it is. My friends at school don't have dirty houses that smell bad.

During the parties, I usually leave and camp out on the wood chips underneath the playground. When I get home in the morning, everyone is passed out or too out of it to be bothered with me.

I see the old gray car coming down the road, and my stomach flips.

I turn to Jared. "Let's go to the park," I urge.

"It's almost dinnertime," he points out. "Plus, I wanted to see if I could use Dad's phone to call my mom and Tate."

My cheeks ache, because I'm trying not to cry, and I want to bury myself in his T-shirt. It's such a stupid feeling, and I feel dumb, but it would make me feel better.

Jared is bigger, and he always wears black. If I can wrap my arms *around him, I can dive into where it's dark, and I feel as if maybe I can hide.*

I see them get out of the car, my father's friend Gordon and my father's girlfriend, Sherilynn. I turn toward Jared, giving them my back.

"Jax!" Gordon calls, and I wince.

Jared's eyes flash over my head, and then he looks down to me. "Who is that?"

I try to calm my breathing, but my stomach is lurching. "That's Gordon. Dad's friend."

"Jax!" he calls again, and pain shoots through my stomach. I reach out, wrap my arms around my brother's waist, squeezing the wind out of him as I bury my face in his shirt.

Jared's here. Jared's here. Jared's here. He'll protect me.

But Jared was only fourteen. He couldn't help me.

It was then that I knew my days as a child were over. There was no one coming to save me, and I was simply a prisoner by choice. I was on my own, and I was done being helpless.

I punched the black bag, jabbing my fist at it again and again, swinging my right and then my left. My fists, wrapped in tape, threw blow after blow. Right, right, left. Right, right, left, rear back, kick, right fist again.

Sweat drenched my chest and back, and my hair stuck to my body as I whipped around and threw four uppercuts on the bag behind me and darted out my leg again, jabbing the bag to my right.

"I want you to be better."

I growled, throwing punch after punch, blow after blow, until my knuckles burned.

"So, are you hiding?"

I jerked up and spun around to see Tate in the doorway.

My chest rose and fell as fast as my heartbeat. "Hello to you, too," I mumbled sarcastically before turning to continue my attack on the bags.

We hadn't seen each other in weeks, and I knew my brother's girlfriend was going to start in on me about Juliet.

I knew it, because she'd tracked me down. After dropping Juliet off the other night, I'd come straight to Madoc's house to stay awhile and get my head straight with some distance. After five days of being here, I was still working on that.

"Look, I'm not going to pry," she continued. "K.C.'s not talking about it, but I saw you drop her off last weekend, and I know something is wrong. Katherine called, too. You haven't returned her texts, and she was worried. I said I would check on you."

I punched the bag, zoning in on the small tear in the leather. I hadn't meant to worry Jared's mom.

"I know you want to be alone, but Jared's coming home this afternoon," she said, "and I want you there." She circled around to stand on the other side of the bag, holding it for me. "Please come home."

I hesitated, blinking, and then continued lighter punches. Jared would kill me if I hurt her, after all.

"Her name's Juliet," I reminded her.

"I know."

"I can't come home, Tate."

Her long blond hair swayed as I jabbed the bag harder and harder.

"Yes, you can," she implored, grunting every time I hit the heavy bag. "You can always come home."

I looked down at her. "She must hate me," I whispered, more to myself. "I can just picture her nose turned up so high that she's probably getting nosebleeds." I punched the bag harder, feeling guilty at Tate's wince.

But then she laughed. "Actually she hasn't talked about you."

I stopped and stood up straight. After what had happened at the fun house and at the Loop, I was sure she'd have to talk to somebody.

But she wasn't talking about me? Like at all?

"Yeah." Tate nodded. "She's fine. Hasn't said one word about you. She's getting busy applying for her student loans. She's thinking about changing her major to education to be a teacher, and she's getting her job back at the movie theater for the summer."

"Loans?" I pinched my eyebrows together. "Why would she have to do that?"

Tate folded her lips between her teeth, thinking. "Well, her mother has withdrawn her support. K.C.—" She shook her head. "Juliet, I mean, will probably have to get loans to finish school."

I scowled, turning away and wiping the sweat off my forehead. What a vindictive bitch. Her mother was almost as bad as my father.

No mothers. No fathers. I couldn't help the grin that escaped, remembering her words.

"She's fine, Jax," Tate said behind me as I grabbed a towel to wipe off. "In fact, I've never seen her so centered. Like she knows who she is and what she wants now."

"That's great, Tate," I bit out, throwing the towel down. "Glad to hear it. I've got a workout to finish."

Awesome. I was coming apart without her, and she was ready to take on the world without me.

I felt Tate move behind me, and I didn't look at her as she made her way to the door.

But she stopped before she left the room. "She got a tattoo as well." Tate's eyes were on me, her voice light and inquiring. "Angel wings on the back of her neck. Both of them broken," she said. "Underneath, it reads 'Only Ever You.'"

I closed my eyes.

I wasn't sure when Tate left the room. All I remember is lowering myself into the chair and burying my head in my hands, feeling as if I were falling and would never hit the ground.

"I don't like having to chase you down," Ciaran said.

I let out an aggravated sigh, ignoring my employer's scowl across the computer screen. Pulling out a half dozen flash drives, I dumped them on my desk in my room at Madoc's house. When Jared's mom—my mom now, too—had married Madoc's dad, she made sure I had a room of my own here, even though this was technically Madoc and Fallon's house now, and my own home was only a twenty-minute drive away.

Thankfully she hadn't insisted on decorating it. Still, it was convenient when Madoc had parties. I had a place of my own off-limits to guests.

"Relax, old man," I griped. "I haven't taken a day off since you hired me."

"And I pay you to be available."

I stopped and shot him a dark look. "Are you whining?" I accused. "Jesus, what's her name?"

"Shut it," he shot back with his heavy Irish accent.

I rolled my eyes. "Fine. Here." And I punched a few buttons, starting to send files as they loaded from my flash drives. "As soon as you get this shit, leave me alone for a few days, okay?"

"Why?" He sipped coffee, starting to look more relaxed now that he was getting what he wanted.

"Nothing major." I didn't want my employer to see that I was distracted and lose faith in me. The less information, the better. "I just need to focus on a side project."

"What's her name?"

I heard the laughter in his voice as he repeated my words, and I glowered at the screen.

"Her name," I started, "is none of your fucking business, and she hates me, okay?"

"I doubt it."

I loaded the last flash drive, dragging files into the Ciaran folder, and sent it. "I made love to her for the first time in a dirty carnival fun house and haven't talked to her in five days. Trust me, she hates me."

He shook his head. "Son, women are easy. They simply want everything. It's not difficult."

I let out a shaky laugh. "Yeah, not difficult." And then I looked at him. "And what if she wants to know things I don't want to tell her?"

"You're asking the wrong question," he said flatly. "The question is, would you rather keep your secrets or keep her?"

My eyes dropped, and I closed my mouth.

"If you want a woman," he started, "then you have to start acting like a man."

I nodded, understanding.

"And that means," he continued, "you start looking like one, too."

I narrowed my eyes, looking down at my workout pants and sneakers. "What's that supposed to mean?"

"It means grow up, kid."

I stared at him wide-eyed, and when I spoke, my tone sounded like a warning. "You know? Plenty of girls like the way I look, old man."

"Yeah. Girls," he deadpanned. "They may like those T-shirts with all the writing on them, and those wallet chains and badass braids, but I bet you don't feel like a real presence in those clothes, do you?"

I arched an eyebrow.

"Take more pride in yourself, Jaxon. You'll be surprised how it transfers into your behavior. You're going to be a father someday, for Christ's sake."

"What the fuck?"

"Probably," he added. "Is that how you want to look at parent conferences?"

Whoa! What the hell? I let out a nervous laugh. "Yeah, this conversation escalated quickly. Damn."

Why was my appearance suddenly under attack? I'd never gotten any complaints before. Jeans, black pants, nice T-shirts that fit great . . . My clothes didn't attract attention, but they certainly weren't Salvation Army, either.

Jesus, why was he making me feel as if I looked like a bum all of a sudden?

He cleared his throat. "My son-in-law is a bit of a Barbie." He jerked his chin at me. "Have him take you shopping."

Madoc and me? Shopping?

I inhaled a deep breath, trying to figure out what the hell was happening. Okay, yeah. Maybe Madoc fit in places Jared and I didn't. We weren't about clothes and appearances, and that worked for us.

But on the other hand, people showed Madoc just a little more respect, too. Their initial impression of him was different from what it was of me. I could see it, even though they were polite. He looked as though he took pride in himself and that he cared enough to put in the effort. People appreciated that.

"Shopping?" I repeated to myself.

"Yeah, shopping," Ciaran mimicked. "And cut that fucking hair, too." And then he hung up.

I stared dumbfounded at the now blank laptop screen and slowly fell back in my chair, feeling more confused now than I did after Tate left.

What the hell just happened? How do you go from talking business, to talking about women, to talking about me as a father, to me getting a make-over?

I raked my hand over the top of my head, unable to catch my breath. *A father?*

And then I caught my reflection in the laptop screen and stilled. I continued to stare at myself. *I might be a father someday. Someone's father.*

Was I unhappy with my appearance? I'd never really thought about it. Women came easily, I was clean, and I was healthy. That was as much as I cared about how I looked.

And I loved how Juliet looked at me. As though she couldn't see the shit inside. And she certainly didn't seem to care about my clothes or hair.

Madoc said once that the clothes didn't make the man; the man made the clothes.

I reached back and grabbed my ponytail, running the length through my fist, feeling years and years of growth, some from when I lived with my father. I didn't know about clothing, but my hair definitely owned me, and I was sick of it.

The lump lodged in my throat, and I didn't even try to swallow it down.

Shooting out of my chair, I stalked out of the room and down the stairs. Swinging myself around the banister, I leaped onto the tiled floor and toward the kitchen. I made my way to the patio door— Madoc and Fallon had been swimming a while ago—but then I heard piano keys tinkling, and I pulled up short.

Basement.

I turned around and almost jogged for the basement door. Madoc had a classic Steinway that he kept down there so he could play in private. Fallon and he talked about bringing it up, but it never happened. I wasn't sure why.

And right now I didn't care. Thundering down the stairs, I skipped the last few, jumping to the bottom, and looked up, my mouth dropping and my eyes damn near bugging out of my fucking head.

Uh . . .

Fallon sat on the top of the huge piano with her legs wrapped around Madoc and her head fallen back. Even though he stood in front of her with his head buried in her neck, I could tell she was naked except for her shorts.

"Oh, shit," I whispered.

Fallon shot her head back upright and screamed, and Madoc spun around, putting his body in front of her.

I held up my hands. "So sorry." I guess I knew why they hadn't brought the piano upstairs now.

"What's the matter with you?" Madoc seethed, his blue eyes turning fierce. "Get out!"

Fallon cowered behind Madoc, peeking over his shoulder.

"No," I shot back. "You should be in your room if you're going to do that, and I need help. Now."

Madoc rolled his eyes and looked to the ceiling, exasperated. "God, I miss being an only child."

"Baby," Fallon whined behind him, taking offense to that remark. They used to be stepsiblings.

I stared, waiting.

"What?" Madoc held out his palms, shaking them with annoyance. "What do you need help with?"

I straightened, feeling embarrassed as I hooded my eyes. My voice was barely a mumble. "I need to go shopping."

"Shopping?"

I looked at him as if it was no big deal. "Yeah, so? I need some clothes, and you're girlie like that, so . . ." I trailed off, hoping he'd just do it and shut up.

I saw Fallon kind of grin behind him while Madoc looked at me suspiciously. "You want new clothes." He said it as if he was trying to understand Latin.

"No pastel shit," I commanded. "Just stuff that's more grown-up."

Why was he pinching his eyebrows together? *Yes, I want new clothes. Soak in the idea. Breathe, Madoc. The world hasn't ended.*

He finally grumbled, "Fine. I'll be upstairs in a few."

I nodded once and turned to leave. "I need a haircut, too," I called behind me, and slammed the door.

CHAPTER 19

JULIET

Tate paced the living room, smoothing down her loose light gray blouse that fell off one shoulder and over her short white shorts. "Do I look okay?" she worried, stopping and standing stiff in front of me.

I looked up from my laptop, and smiled at how the soft glow of the lamps made her skin look like fine cream.

"You look amazing," I replied.

Her face scrunched up. "I should wear a skirt." She sounded utterly tormented. "I'm probably going to wrap my legs around him as soon as I see him, so I thought shorts would be easier to work with."

I shook my head, amused. "If Jared can see your legs, then he's sold." I started typing again, working on loan applications that were probably far too late to be considered.

I'd thought about switching schools for something cheaper—Arizona was out-of-state tuition, after all—but it was so late, and I definitely didn't want to get stuck having to take a semester off school to get in elsewhere, so I'd decided to just stay where I was for convenience's sake. I'd put in an application at the local community college just in case these loans didn't come through, but to be honest, I couldn't stay in town even if I had to.

Jax would be everywhere.

I cried the night he dropped me off, several times the next day, and in the shower practically every morning. But no one saw it, and no one would.

I missed him, and everything ached, and . . .

I caught the tear at the corner of my eye and cleared my throat, typing faster. Financial information, references, names, addresses. *Just go. Don't stop. You. Will. Be. Fine.*

Why wasn't he home? Why wasn't he at lacrosse practice this week? Why wasn't he calling? And screw him! I punched the keys harder.

"I went to Madoc's today," Tate piped up, peering out the window, "to talk to Jax."

I looked up, my fingers still planted on the keyboard. Madoc's. So that was where he was.

She continued. "He'll probably be here soon to welcome Jared home."

I squeezed my eyes shut for a second and then quickly dropped my gaze back down to my computer screen.

They were all supposed to be going to dinner.

I'd been invited but had the good sense to decline, knowing Jax would probably be at the pizzeria.

"K.C.?" Tate pressed, sitting down next to me.

"Juliet?" I corrected her, mimicking her tone.

She laughed. "Sorry. Old habits die hard, I guess."

She continued to sit there, staring at me, so I finally looked up. "I'm okay, Tate," I assured her.

"If it's any consolation, he looked miserable."

I scrunched up my lips and looked back to the laptop. "I doubt that." Jaxon Trent never looked bad. Freshly showered? He was gorgeous. Sweaty? He was sublime. Happy? Stunning. Angry? Brilliant. And when that man was dirty? Holy. Shit.

"He looks completely twisted up. He never loses control," she ventured.

"Except with me," I replied. "He's always fighting with me."

"Mm-hmm," she agreed, a cocky hint to her tone.

I looked over at her suggestive eyes. "What?"

She held my gaze, and I watched as her eyes turned from playful to serious.

"He's falling in love with you." I could hear the emotion in her voice. "If he hasn't already."

I sat there, stunned by her words.

Falling in love?

I clenched my fists, my heartbeat drumming in my chest. *No.* He wouldn't have pushed me away if that were true. He wouldn't have stayed away. That was what had hurt more than anything these past few days. Jax didn't care the way I did.

His words came back to me. *"I just never thought the real thing would live up to the fantasy."*

I dropped my eyes, my head suddenly too damn heavy to hold up. *Jesus.*

Tate nearly whispered, "It's impossible not to love them, isn't it?" and my resolve cracked. I had to look away, taking deep breaths.

She was talking about the Trent brothers. Her Jared . . . and my Jaxon.

"I love you," she said sweetly, probably seeing that I was in pain.

I nodded. "I know." I looked over at her. "And I don't know why. How come you're so good to me?"

She narrowed her eyes, confused.

"Three years ago, I pretended to date your high school bully who is now your boyfriend so I could get even with Liam. For cheating. The first time." I admitted the whole sordid mess. "Why didn't you kick my ass?"

She offered a small smile. "Because you took Liam back," she said. "I knew you were going to need a friend." Tears sprang into my eyes, and I wanted to hug her.

As she got up, I followed her with my eyes, realizing how much I loved her and how much I wanted to deserve her.

"Tate?" I choked out. "I'm—"

"Oh, good God," she said, cutting me off, staring wide-eyed out the window.

"What?"

She shook her head, a surprised grin on her face as she looked out the window. "You better come see this."

I picked up the laptop, leaving it open as I carried it to stand beside her. Looking through the sheer curtains, I sucked in a breath, my arms shaking so bad that the laptop tumbled out of my grasp.

"Shit!" It shot out of my hands. I tried to clutch it as it bobbled against my weak arms and finally collapsed to the floor.

Tate covered her snort with her hand, and I breathed a mile a minute as I dived down to pick it up again.

"Damn it," I yelled.

The battery pack had come out, and the screen had gone blank. I clenched my teeth so hard my jaw ached. "Damn him," I growled, trying to fit the battery back in and glancing up out of the window repeatedly.

Jax stood next to his car, parked at the curb just behind Madoc's GTO, and I kept scaling my eyes up and down his body, trying to take everything in.

Nothing had really changed and yet so much was different about him. Damn . . .

I licked my lips.

He wore straight-leg black pants. Not skinny but definitely slim, and my eyes widened when he turned around to talk to Madoc and Fallon. I knew what he looked like naked, even though I hadn't had time to explore, but I hadn't realized how much his baggy pants had covered up his form. Nice ass. He still wore clothes that fit his style—dark and low on flash—but they fit him better now. Almost too good. You could see how big he really was through his white V-neck T-shirt that draped just loosely enough to be comfortable but tight enough to show off his muscular shoulders, tight chest, and toned back. Hell, I could even see his shoulder blades.

And his hair. I let out a breath, my shoulders slumping a little. His hair was gone. I wasn't sure how I felt about that.

He looked more beautiful. Definitely. I hadn't realized how much the hair took focus from everything else, and now that it was gone, you could see the whole picture. The mouth, the nose, the eyes, everything all together.

And his body, too, looked bigger without it.

But I had also loved his long hair. It was a sign of his defiance.

The hair was now cropped short and styled on the top. He made my mouth water, and I gritted my teeth, knowing just how much other women would be looking at him now, too. As if they hadn't looked at him enough before.

Jesus.

Watching him, Madoc, and Fallon talk on the front lawn as Jax crossed his arms, pushing out his chest, I brought myself back to reality, and I suddenly didn't care that the hair was gone. And I didn't care about his new clothes, either.

So what?

Even if his appearance had changed, it was still Jax. The same one who had kicked me to the curb five days ago.

"Go on." Tate nudged me. "Get cleaned up."

Huh?

"What?" I asked, standing tall. "No. Screw him. After the way he acted, it's going to take more than new clothes and a haircut."

Tate let out a condescending chuckle and turned to face me. "Juliet, I'm speaking from personal experience, so pay attention."

She grabbed my shoulders, and I sucked in a breath as she turned my body to face her, running her hands up and down my arms in a maternal manner. "When he comes in here, honey, he's going to fix his eyes on you and look at you all intense. He'll look mad," she pointed out, talking down to me, "but what he's really contemplating is whether or not to rip off all your clothes, slam you into a wall, and fuck the daylights out of you . . . from behind."

My jaw dropped, and I clutched my laptop tighter.

"Then," she continued, "he'll corner you somewhere where you least expect it. He'll lean in close"—Tate stepped up to me so our bodies were touching—"touch his lips to yours without actually kissing you, and you'll feel how tortured he is simply by the heat on his skin." She took my face in her hands, getting nose-to-nose, and her voice dropped. "Then, in barely a whisper that will have your thighs quivering, he'll say, 'Baby,' and you will melt without him even having to apologize."

I gulped, my mouth completely parched.

"Now, Juliet?" Tate hardened her voice. "That aqua and gold miniskirt I bought you in Tokyo? Go get it on. You look like shit."

"Ugh," I whispered.

She snatched the laptop out of my hand, slammed it shut, and tossed it on the couch. "He's coming."

After that I didn't hesitate. I darted past her, racing up the stairs two at a time, and crashed through her bedroom door, slamming it shut. Hitting the power on the iPod dock, I dashed into the bathroom as Joan Jett & the Blackhearts started with "I Hate Myself for Loving You." Music made me work faster.

Whipping off my tank top, I pulled my hair out of my ponytail and hastily applied eyeliner and mascara. Dabbing a little red on my lips—not lip gloss, because Jax hated it—I ran the straightener through my hair, smoothing it over with the brush, and then scurried for Tate's walk-in closet.

Joan's guitars kept my blood boiling, and my muscles were pumped. I sang along, suddenly very fucking hungry for pizza.

"'I hate myself for loving you,'" I sang, bobbing my head.

I grabbed my long-sleeved, loose black silk top. High collar in the front, but draped low in the back, showing off ample skin.

If I was going to tell him to screw off, at least I wanted to look hot doing it.

I dropped my shorts, and then I unclipped the skirt from the hanger.

The drums vibrated in my chest as I stepped into the miniskirt and slid it up my legs. "'Can't break free from the things that you do.'"

But just then a shadow fell over me.

I gasped, looked up, and jerked the zipper up, staring wide-eyed at Jax.

Shit.

He had both hands pressed against the doorframe, leaning in slightly, and cocking his head at me like a challenge.

His eyes were like fire, and his jaw was hard. I swallowed and held his eyes, but the combination of his silence and stare had me so jacked up I wanted to scream.

Say something!

"Fuck off," I choked out.

Then he rushed me, grabbing my face with one hand, my waist with the other, and sank his lips into mine.

"No," I cried into his mouth.

But it was useless.

I immediately took his face in my hands and held his lips tight with mine as he hoisted me up and guided my legs around his body.

His arm was like a steel band around me, and I wrapped my arms around his neck and tightened my thighs around him, unable to get fucking close enough to him.

His lips were everywhere, moving fast and hard, and we groaned, filling the small space with our heavy breaths and moans.

He tore his lips away, and I let my head fall back as he dived for my neck, licking, kissing, and biting a trail up to my ear.

"Holy shit," I panted.

His hard shoulders flexed under my fingers, and the next thing I knew I was spinning around in his arms and entering the light of the bedroom as his heavy footsteps pounded on the hardwood floors.

"Fuck," he growled, and dropped me to the bed, falling on top of me.

I moaned, diving for his lips again, so damn hungry for the taste of him. "You're an asshole," I breathed out in between kisses.

"I know." His lips curled, and he reached down between us, unfastening his belt.

I twisted my lips away, and reaching up, I put my hands on both sides of his face, forcing his eyes on me. "Don't you ever ignore me for five days again," I gritted out.

He ripped through the button on his pants, tore down the zipper, and freed his cock, seating himself between my legs.

"Never again," he promised, looking down at me with fire in his eyes as he tore the condom from its wrapper and rolled it on. "You've owned me since I was seventeen." And he slid his greedy hand under my ass, held me tight, and thrust his cock inside me, spearing me.

"Ah," I sucked in a hard breath, throwing my head back.

"God, baby . . . I missed you." He squeezed his eyes shut, and I released my grip on his face, taking his neck instead and bringing him down to my mouth.

"Always wet for you," I whispered into his mouth.

He thrust hard, fucking me fast and rough. Just the way I wanted it from him. We both moaned loud, not caring that there were probably people downstairs.

He was mine, and I was his, and the next time the little shit threw his temper around or shut down on me, I was going to either push him harder or pull away for good.

Push and pull.

Give and take.

Accelerate. Release.

Jax's finger traced the lines of my profile, gliding over my nose and brushing down my lips. I let out a blissful sigh.

I loved to be touched. With kindness, that is. And it felt so good that I wanted to close my eyes, but I couldn't. I'd waited years to just be able to look at him, without fear of him seeing me, and now I couldn't get enough.

"You're so beautiful," he said, lying next to me with his head propped up on an elbow.

I reached up to touch him, too, but halted and jerked my head toward the door, hearing Tate's squeal from downstairs.

"He's here!" she shouted, and I grinned, turning back to Jax.

"Guess that means Jared's home."

Jax let out a sigh next to me. "Oh, joy."

I rubbed the tip of my nose on his. "What's going on with you two?" I asked, concerned.

He kissed me softly on the lips. "Nothing," he whispered. "He just likes to get on my ass like you."

I laughed. "Hopefully not just like me," I joked.

Sitting up, I grabbed my brush off the nightstand and fixed my hair. "Jax?" I licked my lips, my mouth suddenly dry.

"Yeah." He sat up, dipping his head into my neck.

Tingles spread like a swarm of butterflies under my skin, and I pushed him away, smiling.

"I overheard your call with him the day you gave me driving lessons," I confessed. "Your father is getting out of jail soon?"

Jax leaned back on his hands, looking down. "Maybe." He shook his head. "Don't worry about it."

I rose off the bed and straightened my skirt.

"I want to, Jax," I said. "I mean," I rushed to add, "I don't want to worry, but I want to know about you. I want you to tell me things."

"Jax! Get your ass down here!"

We both jumped at Madoc's bellow, and I let out a nervous laugh. *The king of bad timing.*

I leaned down, cupping his face.

And once I was staring into those blue eyes, I couldn't stop. I kissed his forehead, then his nose, and when he closed his eyes, I kissed those, too.

"I like you," I admitted. *A lot.* "I want to know you."

He pulled me down into his lap and wrapped his arms around me as my feet dangled above the floor. I closed my eyes, feeling his light fingers brush my hair over my shoulder and kiss the sore skin on the back of my neck.

He knew I had a tattoo. *Fuckin' Tate.*

"All you need to know," he whispered in my ear, "is that there's still shit that bleeds when you're not around."

My throat tightened.

He continued. "Do what you want with me, Juliet. Just don't leave. Not yet."

I narrowed my eyes, the sting at his words causing me to blink.
Not yet?

"Leave?" I repeated. "You piss me off, you make me cry, you make me crazy . . . but you make me better, Jax."

"And you make me happier," he finished, and I got lost in his eyes.

The shadow of the tree's leaves outside swayed across his face, and I smiled, hearing thunder rumble. The room dimmed with the loss of sunlight.

"Now!" a bellow came from downstairs, and we both shot up, knowing it was Jared this time.

Jax gave me a quick kiss and jetted out the door while I swiped Tate's comforter off her bed and tossed it in the corner to be washed later, just in case.

Powering down the stairs, I smoothed my blouse, skirt, and hair as I walked into the living room.

"Hey." Jared was turning and pulling his arms from around Tate to walk to his brother. "Jesus, look at you." He smiled, grabbing Jax's neck and looking over his hair and clothes.

"Glad you're home," Jax said, and they pulled each other in for a hug.

"I missed you," I heard Jared say quietly as Madman yelped and circled his feet.

"Yeah, me, too."

Looking at Jared and Jax together, you would think you could see the brotherly resemblance. You couldn't. The only thing they shared was charisma. You know? That invisible power some people possess that draws others to them? Both of the Trents had it.

But that was where the similarities ended.

Jared looked like his mother. Chocolate brown hair, now buzzed close to the scalp on the back and sides and cropped short on the top for the military. Deep brown eyes. Coloring similar to my own. He was slightly shorter than Jax, maybe an inch, but his build was just as big. He'd put on a lot of muscle since the last time I saw him.

I'd never seen pictures of their father or Jax's mother, so I didn't know who Jax took after, but I did know that Jax was part Native American, which accounted for his darker skin and hair.

And in personality, they were very different. Both were volatile. Both could be angry. But whereas Jared raged, Jax waited. Where Jared charged, Jax assessed. Very different.

I couldn't help wondering about the man who fathered them both.

Everyone sat or stood in the living room—Tate by the fireplace, Madoc and Fallon curled up on the couch, and Jared and Jax standing in the middle.

And me, trying to melt into the carpet, feeling intimidated all of a sudden.

Jared always treated me somewhat decent, but he also looked at me as if I were the five-year-old at the big kids' table. Better seen than heard.

And as I stood there, trying to find a comfortable place to rest my eyes and wondering what the hell to do with my hands, I realized that I was not my mother's daughter anymore. I was not the hair in the soup, the fly in the ointment, or the stain on the sheets. I might not be Jared Trent's favorite person, but he certainly wasn't mine, either. It was past time that I stopped wondering if I was good enough for others and started wondering if they were good enough for me.

I dropped my hands and stepped up next to Jax.

He immediately looked down at me, smiled, and put his arm around my shoulder, tucking me in.

Jared stopped talking. As he glanced between Jax and me, his deep brown eyes narrowed, and I saw the wheels start to turn. Jax and I were silent as Jared's eyes went from confused to sudden realization.

"Trust me," I shot out before he had a chance to speak. "I've got his back. I promise."

Jared looked stunned, his eyebrows shooting up, and then he finally just shook his head, blinking. "Okay, then."

And that was it. Jax squeezed me tighter, and Jared went back to Tate, where their hands were all over each other.

"Okay, shower up!" Madoc urged, looking at Jared. "Pizza. I'm hungry."

But Jared shook his head. "No way."

"Huh?" Madoc asked.

Jared dropped his arms from Tate and started unbuttoning his camouflage utility jacket. "Look, everyone." He spoke to all of us. "I love you, but you have to go."

Everyone just stood or sat there.

"I haven't seen Tate in weeks. We need alone time. Sorry." Jared tossed his jacket on the chair, leaving him in his camo pants and T-shirt.

"Jared?" Tate complained, blushing with embarrassment.

But he shot her a warning look. "It's been weeks, babe."

She straightened, and I almost laughed as her expression changed. "Yeah, okay." She clapped her hands, ushering everyone to the front door. "Everyone out. We need to be alone."

"For how long?" Madoc protested, standing up with Fallon.

"Like three days," Jared said.

"Three days!" Madoc shot back.

Fallon pulled him toward the door. "Let's go, Madoc."

He grumbled, and I laughed to myself as Jax took my hand, leading me out. The door slammed behind us, and the four of us filtered down the steps toward the cars.

"Seriously?" Madoc was practically whining now. "You guys are coming, right?"

Jax patted his pant legs. "Shit," he cursed, turning back around. "I left my phone on the coffee table."

"I'll get it." I held my hand up to stop him. "I forgot my purse, too."

I darted back up the stairs and quietly slipped back through the front door, hoping to God they weren't already naked.

The foyer was empty, and I crept on tiptoe into the living room to grab my bag off the couch and Jax's phone off the coffee table.

I heard Jared's deep but muffled voice. "I missed you like crazy. God, baby. I love you."

Kisses, shuffling, moans . . . *yeah*. I slipped my bag over my head and prepared to make a quick exit.

"Me, too." Tate was crying. "I hate this so much, Jared. How are we going to be okay for months with you away if it's like this after only a few weeks?"

I stopped, knowing they were in the kitchen, just on the other side of the door, and my eyes teared up for her. As much of a pain in the ass as Jared was, I knew he adored Tate. He'd invade hell for her. And yet with all of my own ups and downs, I hadn't noticed that she was unhappy. I'd never thought they wouldn't be okay, and I'd been so buried under my own bullshit that I wasn't there for her.

I heard a thud and more groans. "It's thundering," Jared said to her.

I heard her sniffle, then laugh. "You thinking what I'm thinking?"

"Chaise longue?" His voice turned cocky. "Backyard? Just like our first time."

And then I bit my bottom lip to stifle a laugh as she squealed and they opened and closed the back door, gone in a flash.

Poor Tate. Well, not poor Tate. She was titanium. But she was missing him. Terribly.

I walked for the door but stopped, hearing an unfamiliar voice.

"Hello?" A male's voice, distant yet deep and calm, got my heart racing with fear.

Creepy.

And I jumped, suddenly remembering the phone in my hand. I brought it up to my ear.

"Hello?" I answered back.

"And who is this?" the smooth, light voice asked.

"Oh, I'm sorry." I shook my head at myself. "I must've accidentally answered. You're looking for Jax? Hang on." And I opened the door and stepped out onto the porch.

"And you are?" the man asked.

"Oh, Juliet," I answered. "I'm a . . ." I hesitated, thinking. "A friend of his, I guess."

"Mmm, Juliet. Pretty name. I'm his father."

I stopped, my face falling.

"Tell me," he started, "how many times a day does he fuck you?"

My eyes widened. *Oh, my God.*

My lips quivered as I stared at Jax across the lawn talking to Madoc and Fallon.

Jax.

"Women love him, you know? Such energy," his father's silk voice taunted. "You can't count the amount of cunt that boy can go through."

My mouth was like a desert, and I clutched the phone, afraid my shaky hands would drop it.

"And I'm guessing," his father continued, "that since you're answering his phone, your pussy must taste pretty damn sweet for him to let you stick around."

My eyes blurred. "What the hell is the matter with you?" I choked out.

"I'm enlightening you, sweetheart," he said, his voice turning rigid. "He won't keep you. Not for long. You can count on that."

Jax looked over at me, his smile disappearing the moment he saw me.

"Has he told you about the basement yet? The knife he carries? His bitch mother that abandoned him to foster care when he was an infant?"

I swallowed, seeing Jax start to walk over to me. How could a father talk this way about his son?

"If he hasn't let you inside his head, then he's not yours, Juliet."

Jax held my eyes, his expression turning more worried the closer he got.

"He doesn't trust you enough," his father warned.

I sucked in a breath, tears pooling as I handed the phone to Jax. "Your father."

His blue eyes turned to ice, and he grabbed the phone. "What did you say to her?" he growled into the phone. "Hello?" He tightened his lips and gritted his teeth. "Hello?"

"Fuck!" he yelled, staring at the phone.

I wiped the tears, only wanting one thing from Jax.

He had to talk to me. About everything.

His back was to me, but I saw him run his hand through his hair. "Jax?"

He shook his head, turning around. "Juliet, I'm sorry. My father is . . ." He trailed off, looking as though he was at a loss for words. "My father is evil. Whatever he said to you is bullshit. He can't do anything. He can't hurt you."

"He didn't threaten me. He talked about you."

"He hasn't seen me since I was thirteen," Jax gritted out, getting angrier. "He knows nothing. He's just talking."

I tipped my chin up. "I want to know."

"What?"

"Everything!" I held Jax's hard stare as Madoc's GTO started and pulled away.

Jax looked at me as if I were the enemy, as if I were the one who was hurting him. He shook his head, defiant, and turned to walk off.

"Stop!" I ordered as he stepped off the porch and made his way home.

I stomped after him. "What about my community service? You can start there."

"What about it?" he barked over his shoulder.

"You fixed it, didn't you?" I accused. "To get me back to town. To get me the position in school. How did you know? How did you know about my trouble?"

He didn't answer me. He didn't even look at me. He walked through his front door, and I followed him as he headed for the stairs.

"Answer me!" I cried, slamming the door shut and stopping at the bottom of the stairs. "How did you know?"

He spun around, his face twisted in anger. "Because I know everything that happens with you."

CHAPTER 20

JAXON

I descended the stairs, stopping just one up from the bottom, and loomed over her.

"The speeding ticket your freshman year at college that magically disappeared?" I hinted and continued. "The finite math test you were unprepared for that coincidentally got delayed because the sprinklers went off?"

I could see the wheels turning in her head.

"All the books reserved for you at the library to research Oliver Cromwell's England? The bookstore job that just landed in your lap when your mother cut off your credit card for switching your minor to creative writing?"

I bared my teeth, getting in her face. "Every time you needed something during the past two years, I was there."

Her chest rose and fell, and she looked as if she could barely catch her breath. "You stalked me?"

"Yeah, get over yourself," I shot back, swinging myself around the banister and heading for the kitchen. "I didn't read your e-mails or steal your underwear."

"Why?" I heard her footsteps behind me. "Why did you do it?"

I let out a bitter laugh, heading for the refrigerator. "It really bugs you, doesn't it?" I grabbed a bottle of water and slammed the door shut. "You're so insecure about what others think that you can't stand that I had my hands in your business without your knowledge, right? You're worried. 'What does he know? What did he see?'"

Her fists were little, but they were clenched tight, and her face was flushed with anger. "Why?" she repeated.

"Leave it—"

"Answer a fucking question for once!"

"Because I was worried about you!" I shouted, vaulting the water bottle down the hallway.

I stood there, watching her pull back and stand up straight, shock written all over her face.

Running a rough hand through my hair, I fisted the short locks, all of a sudden missing the long ones I'd had just this morning.

The sweat on my scalp had cooled, and I reached back and pulled my shirt over my head. Tossing it on a chair, I stood with my hands at my hips, trying to calm down.

I walked toward her, seeing her inch back to the wall.

"About a month after you left for college," I started, "we were getting things going at the Loop. Renovations, construction . . . " I trailed off, licking my dry lips. "Your mother filed a petition with the city trying to stop us. She hated the Loop, thought it attracted trouble, so she got some support behind her and ran with it."

Juliet looked up me, seeming so small. I'd wanted to protect her. I'd wanted to make sure she was happy.

I continued. "She wouldn't have won. Most of the town looks at the Loop as a commodity," I assured her. "But she could have stalled things, so I investigated her."

"For skeletons in the closet," Juliet inferred. "To blackmail her."

"For leverage," I corrected. "To persuade her."

Juliet crossed her arms over her chest, waiting for me to continue.

I took a deep breath. "She had a daughter listed in her personal information. No surprise, except the daughter was named Juliet Adrian Carter. This confused me, because K. C. Carter or any name starting with a *K* didn't show up." I eyed her. "So I started digging. And when you told me your story, I—"

"You already knew." She cut me off, her eyes pooling with tears. "You just let me confide in you like an idiot while you sat there listening to the same sordid shit you already knew."

"No." I tipped her chin back to look at me, but she jerked away. "I didn't listen to the story. I listened to you, okay? You were talking to me. You were trusting me. I didn't know shit about you—not really—until I heard it from your lips. I read about you, but I didn't know you."

She looked away, shaking her head. She didn't believe me.

"The more I found out about you," I continued, trying to make her understand, "the more I couldn't let you go. One thing led to another, and I . . ." I hesitated and swallowed. "I wanted to be there for you. I accessed your class schedule to see how you were doing."

She ran her hands over her face, turning away, but I grabbed her shoulders and turned her back to me.

"I found out you were struggling in a math class, so I set off the sprinklers the morning of the midterm. Shitty thing to do, I know. But I figured extra time to study was welcome. After that, I . . . I just kept an eye on you, okay?"

I'd never intended to invade her privacy, and as easy as it would've been or as much as I wanted to, I never went into her e-mail, social networks, or medical records. I actually tried to talk myself into it.

Lots of times. Sure, I'd just be making sure she was healthy. I'd just be making sure no one was harassing her. I'd just be making sure her asshole boyfriend wasn't screwing around. But I never did any of that. I wasn't trying to control her. I just wanted to take care of her.

At least, that was all I hoped it was.

"I didn't feel like you had anyone," I admitted. "It wasn't pity. It was actually kind of a relief to know your life wasn't perfect. I felt like we had one thing that connected us, that made us different from our friends, and I didn't want you to be alone." And I rushed to add, "I knew that being away at school was probably more freedom than you'd ever had. I wanted you to love it. I wanted to make things easier for you. That's all."

She squeezed her eyes shut, tears running down her cheeks as she bowed her head into her hand.

"So you know everything," she cried. "You knew about my father. That the day after he cut me, he slashed his wrists. Because he could never forgive himself for my sister."

Yeah, I knew that, too. How could a father forgive himself for causing the death of his own child?

I nodded. "It was the middle of the night," I almost whispered. "Your sister had gotten out of bed. He thought she was an intruder. It was a terrible accident."

Her head hung low, and she wiped her tears.

"He killed himself to protect you," I said. "He thought he was going to hurt another daughter."

She looked up. "He did anyway, didn't he?" Her voice grew strong again. "He left me with her. Wouldn't you resent him for that? I mean, what about your mother, huh?" she asked. "She left you with your father."

I slid my hand into my pocket, instantly feeling the comfort of the knife. "Yeah. So?"

"Well, don't you hate her?"

I wrapped my fingers around the thick plastic of the handle. "I don't know," I mumbled.

She smiled angrily, shaking her head. "Neither do I. I know nothing about you. You give me nothing."

"Because it's all just shit!" I barked, running my hands through my hair. "I don't want you to know those things about me. I don't want it dirtying anything I have with you." I leaned in, cupping her face, but she slapped my hands away again.

"You won't have anything with me!" she spat out, turning to leave.

"The fuck I won't." I yanked her back, every fucking muscle in my body solid stone as I pressed my body into hers, pushing her into the wall. "Come on. Admit it. This is all you really want from me anyway, isn't it?" I seethed, forcing my mouth on hers in a rough, angry kiss. "Yeah," I whispered hard. "It's what they all want from me, Juliet."

"Jax!" Her voice trembled as her arms tried to push me away. "Stop it!"

I yanked her loose top down over her shoulders, exposing her in her bra. "Oh, come on, Juliet." I held her tight. "I'll fuck you so good. You can go tell all your friends that you finally had your turn, and that I was such a good time," I growled. "They can all get their places in line."

I pulled the knife out of my pocket and hit the button, the blade shooting out. "You're going to love this. They all do." And with the speed of a bullet, I slipped the knife under her bra, between her breasts, and sliced the material.

"Stop!" She brought up her hands, covering herself and crying.

"Isn't this what you wanted?" I bellowed, getting in her face and pushing her and pushing myself, falling over the edge and knowing that I was going to hit bottom sooner or later.

Fuck!

I gripped the blade in my fist. "Aren't you finally fucking happy now?" I yelled, and reached up, punching the wall above us, sinking the blade into the plaster.

She cried out, and I nearly fell on my ass when she launched off the wall and wrapped her arms around me, stunning me silent.

I stood there, wide-eyed and not breathing. Her arms tightened around my neck, blanketing me in warmth, and I closed my eyes, my rabid heartbeat pounding in my ears.

Juliet. A tear spilled out of the corner of my eye, falling over my cheekbone. Fuck, what was I doing?

"It's okay," she whispered, her shaking lips wet against my chest. "It's okay."

I wasn't sure if she was trying to assure herself or me, but she wasn't running. Why wasn't she running?

I stayed, unable to open my eyes, unable to move. The world spun around me, and I felt like I was swaying and about to fall. *What the hell's wrong with me?* I might've hurt her. I'd never hurt a woman. Except one.

I squeezed my eyes tighter. *Oh, Jesus.* I wrapped an arm around her waist and put my other hand on her face, holding her to my chest.

"Shh," I soothed, running my hand down her hair. "I'm sorry."

Her body trembled in my arms as she tried to catch her breath, but she quieted and slowly relaxed her hold around my neck. All I felt was the heat of her lips against my skin, and I knew one thing.

I wanted her more than I wanted my secrets.

"I like knives, Juliet," I confessed, still stroking her hair. "When you see someone getting shot on TV, they look shocked. It's over too quickly." I forced my raspy voice to stay steady. "A cut is different. As you know. It's pain, followed by fear."

She pulled back, covering her naked chest as she looked up at me and listened.

I reached up and pulled the knife out of the wall, making sure to hold it gently.

"I don't even need to use it," I pointed out. "People know that I have it, and that's enough."

Her pained green eyes looked between me and the knife.

"But there was one time when I needed to use a knife, Juliet. One time when I was tired of being hungry, tired of bleeding, tired of them touching me where they weren't supposed to . . . tired of being afraid and being alone."

Her lips trembled, but she stood strong as she whispered, "What did you do?"

I let out a small laugh. "Yeah, that's what people want to know, isn't it? What happened? How did they hurt you? How did they touch you? Where did they touch you? How many times did it happen? Fuck." I laughed to myself, my eyes blurring and my jaw aching with tears I wouldn't let go.

But I swallowed down the pain and locked eyes with her. "I need to remember how I survived. Not what I suffered," I said. "How I fought, and not how I hurt."

She looked up at me, trying to understand.

"I'm not the kid wearing filthy clothes to school anymore." I sheathed the blade and stuck it in my pocket. "I stopped throwing up half of what I eat. I don't beg for them to stop. I don't cower in corners, hide in closets, or fear coming home."

That was all I needed to remember. All that was important.

"I'm not cold," I said. "I'm not hungry. I'm not helpless. I'm not scared. And I'm not always alone anymore."

That was what I wanted her to understand about what I'd been through. About what she'd been through. The more you suffered, the more you survived. It shaped people in different ways, and what broke one person could empower another.

We were the lucky ones.

She looked at me with weary eyes and nodded, finally understanding.

Bringing her hands up, she held my face, rubbing circles with her thumbs. "What did you do, Jax?" she asked.

I closed my eyes, bowing my forehead to hers. "I made them stop."

She nodded, accepting. "Good."

"What are you doing?"

I sat at the kitchen table, watching Juliet walk from one end of the kitchen to the other, gathering food out of the refrigerator as well as pots and pans from the cabinets.

"Making you dinner," she replied. "We didn't get to go out for pizza, remember?"

I let out a sigh, rolling my eyes. "I don't give a damn about food," I said, watching her in her bare feet. "You're wearing my T-shirt. You may as well be naked, for Christ's sake. I want to touch you."

"You can have dessert if you finish your supper."

I dropped my head back, clutching the armrests. This was ridiculous.

Ten minutes ago we were screaming at each other, five minutes ago I had my knife out, and now she was acting all calm as if we'd both just woken from a peaceful nap.

It was insane.

After I'd told her that I'd rid the planet of two child abusers, she kissed me, sat me down, and stripped out of her ruined clothes to put on my white V-neck. All calm. As if I'd just told her that I'd stolen a candy bar instead of stabbing two people when I was thirteen. She was either losing her fucking mind or trying to distract me.

And if that was her goal, it was working. The T-shirt hung down to just below her ass, and I couldn't take my eyes off her.

"What are you making?" I pressed, getting irritated.

"Steak."

"I don't want a steak." I shot out of the chair.

Walking over to her, I held her hips from behind as she worked at the stove. "Stop acting weird. Either fuck me or yell at me. You have to have something to say about what I just told you."

She turned around, arched a mama eyebrow, and shot out her pointed finger, directing me to my chair like a child.

"Now," she ordered.

I groaned, raked my hand through my hair again, and plopped my ass back down in my seat.

And then my heart lodged in my throat when she leaned over to grab rubber bands off the window sill and her thong-clad ass peeked out from beneath the shirt.

I chewed the corner of my mouth as I watched her tie back her hair in two low pigtails under each ear. My dick swelled, crowding the slim fucking pants Madoc had told me to buy.

"Oh, my God," I groaned. "Pigtails?" I blurted out. "Baby, please." And I stood up to go to her again, but she spun around with a murderous look in her eyes.

"Sit!" she commanded, and I dropped my ass back in the chair, letting out a growl.

So I waited. Silent and docile for once in my life. Fifteen minutes of absolute torture before she was done.

She grilled some steak on the stove, steamed some vegetables, and chopped everything up, piling it into a large bowl.

But as hard as it was and as much as my mouth watered for something other than the food, I loved watching her in my house. I'd had the kitchen remodeled along with much of the rest of the place, and now I was glad. I wanted her to be happy here. To cook here. To sleep here. To feel good here.

Her slender feet padded along the dark slate tile that I'd picked out myself, and she explored the insides of the new dark cherry cabinets I'd put in. The stainless steel appliances and the granite countertops were the best money could buy, but for the first time I was wondering if someone else liked it other than me. Did she feel at home here?

Jared had liked the renovations, but his taste was different. He and Tate kept trying to talk me into black this and black that, but I wasn't feeling it. I loved black, but my home was a different matter. It had to be warm.

Juliet came over, set down two bottles of water, and then grabbed the bowl with a fork. She parked her ass on the table in front of me and started stirring up the food.

Yeah. No.

I grabbed her hips, slid her off the table, and sat her in my lap, straddling me.

She grinned to herself, her tone amused. "Okay, now you can touch me."

She stabbed a piece of steak and broccoli and held it up to me.

I pulled back. "With your fingers."

She nodded, stuck the food in her mouth, and put the fork down on the table as she chewed. Reaching into the bowl, she took a chunk of meat and held it up to my mouth.

I opened, taking the bite and closing my lips around her soft fingers. Her eyelids fluttered, and her throat bobbed up and down as she slid them out. I barely tasted the food.

I wished I could touch her and not feel what was happening in my chest. I wished I could look at her and know that it would be easy to let her go at some point.

But as she sat there feeding me with her fingers, wearing my T-shirt, sporting her pigtails, her legs spread over my thighs, and her feet dangling six inches above the floor, I knew that I was completely at the mercy of someone nearly half my size.

I was hers.

She fed me another bite and leaned into my hand when I caressed her face.

"Do the police know about what you did?" She spoke softly.

I nodded. "Yes. It's been taken care of," I assured her. "I didn't want that hanging over my head."

That was the perk of having connections. Ciaran—a gunrunner and drug dealer with resources. Madoc's dad—one of the best defensive attorneys in the state. And the police—whom I'd worked with supplying favors and getting them in return. No one was going to come after a kid who did what he had to do in a horrific situation.

Of course, my father thought the bodies were still buried in an unmarked grave. And for now, I'd let him think that.

"Will your father come here when he gets out?" she asked, and I ran my hands up and down her thighs, understanding her worry.

"It's possible," I said. "Very possible."

She put the bowl down, and I pulled her into me, kissing her beautiful soft lips. I couldn't let my father show up here. Now I understood what Jared's worry was. He wasn't concerned about himself. He needed to protect Tate and me. The people he loved.

And I needed to protect Juliet. Even the idea of my father seeing her . . .

I wrapped my arms around her waist, squeezing tight.

"They mean nothing, you know?" she said into my neck. "They don't deserve us."

Meaning, our parents.

"Nothing," I repeated.

Her arms circled my neck, and I dived into the kiss, wanting to get happily lost. She rolled her hips into me, and I grabbed her ass as I ate up her taste and smell. God, she was incredible.

Breathing hard, I lifted the shirt over her head and dumped it on the floor. I kissed my way up her warm neck and splayed my hands across her back. My fingertips touched the silkiest skin I'd ever felt.

But I sucked in air, trying to calm down.

I hadn't made love to her properly yet. In a bed. But fuck . . . She was irresistible on this chair, moving on top of me, her skin against mine.

She'd moved her hands, holding them clasped under her chin, keeping her arms up to cover her breasts. When I brought my hands around to open her up, she tore away from the kiss, shaking her head. "Mmm, nope. Sorry," she insisted. "You have to do the dishes."

Huh?

She pried herself free from my grasp and stood up, still holding her arms over her chest for modesty's sake.

I pinched my eyebrows together in disbelief. "Dishes?"

She nodded, biting back a smile. "Dishes," she repeated, and turned to walk out of the kitchen.

Her round little ass had my handprints on it, and I shifted, in pain, at that lacy black thong I wanted to rip off her.

"I pay someone to do the dishes," I growled.

She stopped in the doorway, peering back at me with humor in her eyes. "I cooked. You clean. Fair's fair. I'll be upstairs."

She left the room.

And I had never cleaned anything so fucking fast in my entire life.

CHAPTER 21

JULIET

Jax had turned on me.

He'd morphed into a loose cannon, and I saw the same fierce temper I'd seen on Jared. The same temper I'd seen on my father. But strangely, neither of them had come to mind.

The moment he pulled the knife, all I thought about was how to get him back. I didn't think about running. I was scared *for* him, not *of* him.

All I saw was Jax. What had happened to him, and how was I going to catch him when he fell?

I walked up the stairs, smiling at the sound of dishes clanking and a pan crashing to the floor.

Someone was in a rush.

I liked him. Man, did I like him!

I remembered Tate's dad sitting both of us down to talk about the birds and bees. We were fourteen or fifteen, and someone at school had taught us what a blow job was. Mr. Brandt deemed it high time to give us the talk, even though I wasn't his daughter and it wasn't his call to educate me. He'd said when my mother emerged from 1958 she could come and kick his butt. Until then . . .

Anyway, he gave us three irrefutible pieces of advice about the male species:

1. Boys will lie, cheat, and steal to get into your pants. A man will stand the test of time. Make him wait, and you'll see which one he is.
2. They will try to tell you that it feels better without a condom. You just tell me where they live.
3. And relationships are supposed to make your life better. You don't drag each other down. You hold each other up.

When we're little, we think true love is Romeo and Juliet, together in life or together in death. They couldn't stand not to have each other, and when you're young it's romantic to think of suicide as the answer. Better not to live at all, etc.

When you grow up, you realize that that's bullshit. I mean, who really wins there, right ?

Jax was happy to see me happy. I didn't need him to survive, but I liked him. He made my life better. Happier. He also challenged me to grow.

Coming to the second floor and turning for his bedroom, I glanced behind me, noticing the padlock on the office door.

I walked into his bedroom, still uneasy about everything he'd done in my life without my knowledge. And everything he was doing. He was mistaken if he thought he was going to continue to keep an eye on me.

And the people who'd hurt him and what he'd done to them? I knew I should be nervous or even scared that he was capable of violence, but I knew he didn't rush to react. The only thing I was worried about was how far Jax had to be pushed to do it. And would he do it again if he were pushed hard enough?

I didn't fear being on the receiving end, but I didn't want to worry about him in trouble, either.

I stopped in the middle of the bedroom, taking a minute to look at my surroundings. The only other time I'd been in here was the night he'd gotten in the fight on the front lawn. It had been dark and I hadn't wasted time exploring. Now, as I looked around, my eyes fluttered at the warmth pooling in my stomach and farther down.

His bedroom.

Everything was dark. I loved how the cherrywood furniture made the black bedding and curtains seem warm. And with the drapes drawn and a small lamp lighting the desk in the corner, the whole room glowed like an old chapel, lush and elegant with its carved furniture but cozy and secluded as if it were some room lost in the middle of a thousand other rooms buried deep in a mansion, never to be discovered.

I felt as though if we closed the door, I'd never want to leave. I'd never want to be found.

Jax had a king-size bed, and I instantly sucked in a breath at the thoughts of him. There. With me. For hours.

Running my hand down his dresser, I savored the cool, smooth wood beneath my fingertips, reminding me of him. His skin, so fluid but so hard under my fingers, and I closed my eyes as the desire swamped me.

My chest rose and fell hard, and I reached up, running a hand over one of my breasts. My core started pulsating, and I touched the hard flesh of my nipple.

Jax.

Warmth hit my back, and I opened my mouth to speak but was cut off.

"Don't open your eyes."

I could hear the smile in his voice.

He was behind me, his breath warm on my neck. His musk scent made me want to bury my nose in his skin and crush my chest to his. I kept my hand on my breast, but my head started floating away from me.

"I'd rather be touching you." I smiled, keeping my eyes closed.

"You still like me?" he asked.

"Yes."

"Good," he replied calmly. "I like you, too."

"I know."

I felt his laugh on my shoulder and leaned my head back against him as I reached behind me and took his hands, placing them on my breasts.

He instantly cupped them and started moving them in circles.

"You're so incredible," he said, nipping at my earlobe. "I look at you, and I can't think about anything else beyond having you."

And he took a hand off my breast and grabbed hold between my legs.

"Oh, my God," I groaned, excited at the possessive feel of his hand there. Touching me. Taking it. "Jax," I gasped.

"Fucking mine," he whispered in my ear.

"Yes." I licked my dry lips, panting.

His hand got more demanding, urging my whole body backward flush with his as he rubbed me hard and kneaded my breast.

"I have lots of fantasies about you, Juliet."

I heard the edge to his voice. The one that told me he was trying not to lose control.

"Lots of different ways I want to see your body move," he said. "And I want to do lots of it tonight."

It sounded like a warning. A warning I was definitely going to ignore.

I opened my eyes, seeing his head bowed down next to mine, staring at me with that fucking intensity as if I were his favorite toy.

His hands moved behind me, and the next thing I knew he'd unfastened his belt and yanked it free of the loops of his pants, startling me as it whipped through the air.

I laughed nervously.

"You okay?" he taunted, still holding the belt at his side.

I nodded, speaking softly. "That, um . . . it makes me . . ."

"What?"

I shifted my eyes, searching for the word. "A little excited?" I confessed.

His amused eyes narrowed. "She likes belts," he said to himself. "Duly noted."

My faced warmed, embarrassed, but I arched an eyebrow.

"We're going to need water," I advised. "I have my own fantasies, too, so hydrate."

Pulling out of his grasp, I took him by the hand and led him to the bed. Sitting on the end with my feet on the floor, I put my hands on his hips, holding him in place in front of me and dropping my head back slowly to look up at him.

"Jax?" I whispered, smiling a small, playful smile. "I want to show you how good I can move." I nipped soft and slow at the button of his pants. "I want you in my mouth." I licked my lips, looking up at him and rubbing my cheek against his pants. "I want to taste you." And I slipped my tongue out, licking his pants with the tip, watching his eyes flare and turn intense. "I want you down my throat." I bared my teeth, nipping at the bulge in his pants. "I want you everywhere."

He clasped my pigtails at the back of my head, and I continued to rub him with my face and lips, feeling him grow thick and hard through his pants.

I loved watching him watch me. His abs flexing, his thick biceps tightening, his nipple rings gleaming at me, and even though I wanted that body all over me, I loved this view. I could appreciate his beauty, touch him where I wanted, make him feel good . . .

And that was what I wanted. I wanted to know that I made him feel good.

Moving slowly, I unfastened his pants and slid my fingers under the waistband, gently pulling down his clothes.

I could feel my eyes widen, seeing his erection spring free, standing hard, full, and ready for me.

I knew it was long. I'd felt him through his pants before. But the thickness kind of shocked me.

He wasn't my first—even though I wished he had been—but I couldn't say it was fair to compare him to Liam, either. Jax felt so much better. They were on different planets.

He started running his fingers back and forth in my hair, and I looked up at him and wetted my lips.

"I want it." I darted out my tongue and licked his tip. Again and again, so slow, enjoying the hot taste of him.

His head dropped back. "Oh, fuck, Juliet," he murmured, gripping my pigtails tighter. "More."

I took him in my hand, running my palm up and down his shaft as I sucked his tip into my mouth, getting him wet.

And then I dived down, taking him to the back of my throat and holding his hips.

I held him there, trying to ease down and take it all. I wanted him to love this, and I wanted to give it to him. It was almost funny. I never liked doing this for Liam, because it had felt like an obligation. I wanted to keep him, so when my heart wasn't in it, he could tell.

But I really wanted to do this for Jax.

I moaned, already so wet from just the idea of him in my mouth, filling me up thick and hard.

I worked him up and down, taking him in slowly, knowing that if I eased into it, I could take him all the way, and then back out, running my tongue back and forth on the underside of him.

"Baby, you feel so good," I groaned, licking him from base to tip, and then taking him back into my mouth.

"Juliet," he gasped, his faced pinched as I started bobbing up and down on him faster and faster. "What are you doing to me?"

His hands stroked my face, and I looked up, locking eyes with him. Dragging my lips slowly off his cock, I teased the tip with my tongue, holding his gaze as I licked, kissed, sucked, and nipped.

And when I lifted up his cock and sucked the flesh underneath into my mouth, he cried out.

"Fuck, baby," he exclaimed, pulling away from me and looking at me as if I had done something wrong.

"Wh . . . ," I choked out. "Wh-what's wrong?" My clit was throbbing so hard, and I groaned, rubbing my thighs together.

What the hell?

"Nothing's wrong," he barked, yanking his clothes completely off and standing there erect and ready.

I stood up. "Then why did you stop me?"

He pulled me into him, crushing our bodies together and growling with his mouth an inch from my lips. "Because I don't want to come that way yet. I wanted to make love to you in a bed tonight. Slowly," he said, holding me firm.

"You liked it, didn't you?" I pressed.

"But you got me too excited," he complained. "You're fucking with my plans."

He snatched up my lips, and I arched up on my tiptoes to meet his mouth head-on. His strong arms wrapped around me tightly, and before I could control it, I started rolling my hips into his erection that had slipped between my thighs.

"Oh, God," I breathed out, the tease of him there making me shiver. "I can't wait, Jax. Please," I begged.

He pulled his mouth away, looked down at me, scowling with his sweaty hair sticking up in all directions and his fire blue eyes looking at me like the calm before the storm.

His hand dipped under the string of my thong at my waist, and my heart jumped when he yanked, ripping the material clean away from my body.

The pathetic black lace scrap fell to the floor, and I had enough time to wrap my arms around his neck before he picked me up and started carrying me for the bed.

We crashed down onto the mattress, and he wasted no time in nestling himself between my thighs and sinking his lips into mine. His hands were everywhere as he leaned over me, keeping his chest just a few inches above me.

"I love to look at you," he whispered between kisses, grazing a hand over my nipple and down to my stomach.

I lifted my head off the mattress. "I want to fucking feel you inside me, Jax." I squirmed, bending my knees up.

"Do you?"

I closed my eyes, trailing kisses up his neck. "Yes."

"Tell me what I want to hear," he demanded, thrusting his hips and making me groan.

"You're driving me crazy," I cried, the rod between his legs relentless where it pressed against me.

"That's not what I want to hear." His teasing voice laughed at me.

"You're an asshole?" I ventured, dragging my nails over the soft skin of his ass.

"No," he grunted, grabbing my hands and pinning them over my head. "Say it."

I smiled, loving how worked up he got. Loving how much he

wanted to hear it. And as I looked over his face, falling into him with my heart swelling in my chest, I felt more at home, more safe and more cared for, than ever before in my life.

I swallowed down the tears in my throat, trying to whisper, but it came out barely audible. "Only. Ever. You. Jaxon Trent."

Peace settled in his eyes, and his jaw twitched with a smile.

Holding my gaze, he reached over and grabbed a condom out of the bedside drawer, ripped it open, and slipped it on. And my eyes fluttered as he positioned himself between my legs and slowly sank into me, inch by agonizing inch.

The vein in his neck bulged, and I closed my eyes against the on-slaught of sensation, feeling him stretch and fill me and then ease back out slowly.

"Keep your eyes on me," he ordered.

Holding himself up on one arm, he reached down to cup my ass with the other and brought me in tight as he sank back into me, hard and deep.

"Please," I gasped out. "Again."

He slid out, gripped me hard, and dived back in deeper and deeper every time.

I planted my palms on his chest, rubbing my fingers over his rings, and arching my neck as he drove deep again and again, my back burning from being rubbed against the sheets so hard, but I didn't care.

His hips started working faster, shallow thrusts and then a deep one, keeping the same rhythm until I was clenching around his cock, feeling the heat swarming in my belly like a storm.

Reaching down, I grabbed his hips and then leaned up and took his mouth.

His lips. God, his fucking lips. I lifted my chest off the bed to wrap my arms around him and held his mouth, not letting go as he fucked me harder and faster.

I rolled my hips, urging him on as we kissed and tasted each other. Our sweat mixed together, molding his chest to mine, and my clit throbbed at the feeling of his rings against my nipples.

I tore my mouth away, holding on for dear life. "Fuck me, Jax," I cried. "God, don't stop."

He growled against my lips, his body working like a demon on mine. "I haven't even fucking started."

His hips pounded against me, taking me, and I moaned, feeling him sink so deep, hitting that spot again and again.

"Harder, Jax." I sucked in air fast and hard, the orgasm building in my womb, and I couldn't control myself anymore. Throwing myself back down on the bed, I rolled my hips, meeting his thrusts until the orgasm crashed over me, making my center clench and tighten, pulse and throb. I cried out, stilling as he kept fucking me, not stopping or slowing down.

"Jesus," I moaned. "I love you."

Wait. What?

I snapped my eyes open, seeing him smiling down at me.

"I . . . no . . . I . . . I." *Fuck!*

"Don't worry." He chuckled. "I don't trust postorgasmic *I love yous.*"

He stopped thrusting, pulled out of me, and got off the bed. I instantly covered myself, confused. But before I had a chance to question him, he pulled me up, picked me up, and guided my legs around his body.

"What are we doing?" I asked, kissing him.

"I need to watch you." He looked so desperate, as if he needed more and more.

And feeling his hardness rub the sensitive area between my legs was making me needy again.

He led us to the low lounge chair in the corner of the room. Slight recline on the back and no armrests to get in the way, the dark wooden chair with black cushions looked like something that might sit outside, but it was perfectly at home in his room.

Sitting down, I took his cue and unlocked my legs from behind him, and straddling him, I hung my legs over his thighs, planting my feet on the floor.

"Oh." I let out a nervous laugh, grabbing his face for a kiss. "This is going to feel good."

He sat back, looking relaxed and holding my hips. "You're going to look good, too."

I didn't waste any time.

Lifting myself up, I held his eyes as I lowered myself back down, taking him back inside me.

His eyes drifted closed. "How can you still be so tight?"

"This feels different," I said, moving up and down, finding a steady pace.

"It's deeper."

I bobbed faster, my breasts bouncing against his chest as I let my head fall back.

"Damn, look at you," he mused, and I grabbed his face, covering his sweet lips with mine.

But I needed more. More contact.

I started rolling my hips into him, feeling his length massage my insides, making me groan as I withdrew, reveling in the skin on skin.

I whimpered thoughfully. "I like this," I taunted. "I'll have to ride you more."

His eyes closed, his head fell back, and his white teeth peeked out with his little smile. "Now, that was a mistake."

And I yelped when he wrapped his arms around me and shot off the chair—surprisingly easy since he was carrying an extra hundred twenty pounds—and he stomped to the bed, dumping me on my ass.

"Jax! What . . . ?" I trailed off, confused.

His devilish grin pinned me for two seconds before he hooked my knees, yanked me down to the end of the bed, and flipped me over.

"Jax!" And I gasped as his cock crowned my entrance and his shadow loomed over me.

Oh, shit. My muscles clenched, and I could feel the warmth pouring out of me. "I'll never hurt you," he whispered in my ear. "But you'll ride me when I say you can ride me."

And he pushed into me, sinking deep and fucking fast.

"Oh, Jax," I moaned, the thick heat of him filling me, giving me what I needed.

He pumped his hips, going rough and fast, spearing me, and all I could do was sit there and take it.

Or not. I turned out one knee and planted my hands on the bed, arching up.

"Damn, Juliet," Jax grunted, driving into me. "You feel so good."

The orgasm was starting to rock my insides, and I just held on, loving the feel of his fist gripping my hair.

I squeezed my eyes shut, my sex tightening and then slowly exploding in waves. "Oh," I cried out. "Oh, God!"

And I let it go, feeling Jax's arms wrap around me, holding me as I shook.

"Juliet . . ." He fell apart, jerking into me and breathing hard on my neck. "Only ever you."

CHAPTER 22

JAXON

I grip my arms tight, huddling in a ball and squeezing my eyes shut so hard tears seep through the lids. The blasts of cold air cut into my ears as the fans blow around my face.

I'm in a freezer.

A deep freezer in my dad's house, and this isn't the first time.

"Please." I can only whisper, my teeth chatter so hard. "Let me out."

How long have I been in here? It feels like an hour, but I don't think it's been that long. I can still hear my father yelling at Jared outside in the kitchen. Oh, God, it hurts! I rock back and forth.

He'd hit our father. That's why I'm in here.

Jared knows how I'm being hurt, and he's mad. He lunged for our father as he sat on the couch, and it took them no time to get him under control. I don't even want to think about what they're doing to him out there. Jared's angry about what our father makes us do, he's mad about what happens to me, and I saw my father bring out the belt to punish him. I'm scared.

My brother. He tried to protect me.

The cold air burns my nose, so I inhale through my mouth and feel my lungs fill with ice. I cough, gasping in shallow breaths.

Reaching up, I press my hand against the lid and push harder and harder, the muscles in my arm stretching and aching as I hunch over and cough. It hurts to breathe, my ears sting like a million needles, and I'm shaking with the frozen air on my skin.

"Please," I cry. "Please!"

Two thuds pound on the lid, and I try to open my eyes to see if they've opened it. "Dad?" I quaver.

But my eyes open, and the freezer is still black. No light.

I shake my head, my long hair coated with frost. "Please, please, please!" I scream, my throat hoarse from the roar.

"Please!" I scream, clasping my hands over my frigid ears. Burning, aching, air . . .

"Please!" I shout again. "Jared! Jared, please!"

My body shakes with the cry, the wail coming from much deeper than my stomach. It's sick, like an animal's. "Please!"

I thrash, throwing my arms against the walls of the freezer, slamming and jabbing my fists again and again and again. "Let me out!" I roar, pounding the walls left, right, left, right, again, and again. "Let me out!"

Light brightens the inside of my cage, and I clench my fists and grit my teeth. Down, down, down, the rage sinks back down my throat, swirling in my stomach.

I look up, eyes burning with fury.

My father's girlfriend and his friend peer down at me, smiling at what they, no doubt, have planned.

Sherilynn reaches down and caresses my hair, and I let her. Strangely, it doesn't scare me. She doesn't scare me.

Why don't they scare me?

Gordon licks his lips. "Basement, Jax," he orders.

I nod.

I know what's going to happen. As if there's no other choice.

It felt like that at the time. There was no choice. No other way for me to survive. It was as if a curtain had fallen in my brain, signaling that the show was now over. I didn't descend those stairs to the basement knowing what would happen. I simply knew what I wasn't going to let happen.

With every muscle in my body, I knew it would never happen again.

I looked over at Juliet, making no sound as she slept beside me. The room was black, but with the glow of the alarm clock, I could make out her form. Legs curled and lying to one side. Back flat on the mattress with her head facing me. Her arms bent at the elbows and hands resting on her stomach.

And my heart firmly lodged in my throat.

I let out a sigh and ran my hands through my hair. Why had I chased her?

I knew it was going to be like this, after all. I knew once I got under her attitude, I would find someone who was my match and drove me crazy. I'd cut my hair, stepped foot in an Abercrombie & Fitch, and made love for the first time. All in one day.

She was breaking my routine. The routine that kept me safe.

I swallowed, looking over at her sweet, peaceful form again. There was simply no choice. I had to have her.

Leaning over, I ran my fingers down her hair, kissed her forehead, her nose, and then her lips.

My dick jerked, but I ignored it. We'd gone through four condoms already. She was the first thing I was going to want in the morning, so I let her rest.

I got out of bed, dug some black lounge pants out of the dresser, and slipped them on, before grabbing my spare keys off the dresser.

Leaving the room as quietly as possible, I unlocked my office door and tossed the keys on the worktable, rounding the room as I switched on all the monitors. I tipped my head left and then right, cracking the tension out of my neck.

I was behind.

E-mails were backed up, people wanting to sponsor operations at the Loop, not to mention communications about lacrosse, and favors I'd guaranteed to this person and that for shit I didn't feel I had time to do now.

Things I did have time to do until recently.

I plopped my ass down in the chair, watching light slowly hit all the surfaces of the room as the monitors sparked to life.

And all of a sudden, I wasn't interested in any of it. I sat back, running my finger over my lips, trying to work up the gumption to get back to business. To get caught up. But all I kept thinking about was Juliet, curled up in my sheets, always warm for me, and I let my head fall back as I nudged my cock back down.

"Shit," I breathed out, my heart jacking up again as I stared at the ceiling.

I wanted to go to her, but I had things to do.

"Jax?"

I jerked up, seeing Juliet standing in the doorway.

A smile played at the corner of my lips. She looked like a damn meal.

Her hair was knotted up, falling in her face and down her shoulders. Her naked body looked smooth and tan. And her face was sleepy, eyes barely open. Completely fuckable.

"I'm here." I held out my hand, and she started walking in as she rubbed the sleep from her eyes.

"Sorry." She yawned. "I just didn't know where you were. You have work to do?" she mumbled.

PENELOPE DOUGLAS

"Yeah." But I took her by the waist and guided her legs around me, bringing her down to straddle me.

Her head immediately fell to my shoulder—she had to be exhausted and still half-asleep.

Her arms circled my neck, and I smiled at her peaceful little moan.

"Didn't mean to disturb you," she mumbled sweetly into my neck. "Your cell phone was ringing in the bedroom."

I ran my hands down her side, the taste of her skin already in my mouth as I breathed her in. "Oh, yeah," I responded, not giving a shit about my phone.

Her head nudged mine as she nodded sleepily. My hands drifted down to her smooth bottom, and I closed my eyes, feeling her slowly start to grind on my cock.

Her head stayed buried in my neck, almost as if she'd fallen asleep. But those little whimpers were vibrating out of her lips onto my skin, and I gripped her hips, pulling her closer . . .

"What are doing to me, girl?" I dragged my lips, keeping it soft and gentle, against her shoulder, feeling her grinding grow more urgent.

She reached her hand down, into my pants, and pulled my cock free, running her fingers up and down it.

I reached over and grabbed a condom out of the desk drawer, and watched—amazed—as she leaned back, slipped it on me with her eyes still looking sleepy, and slid me right into her hot and tight little body.

Her head fell back, and she moaned, placing her hands on my shoulders for support.

She was soft but fast, bobbing up and down on my cock, driving me nuts how she never broke pace or had to slow down. She never opened her eyes, and her sweet little moans filled the room, almost as if she were having a nice wet dream. I palmed her breasts, scooting down in the seat so I could see her better, and damn, I loved everything I was seeing. I could watch her all day.

She was using my body, and I didn't care.

I didn't care that she was in charge.

I didn't care that she was riding me as if I was there to service her. I didn't care.

She came in here as if it was the most natural thing in the world, and thank God for that. She liked sex.

The smooth, flawless curves of her breasts stood proud right before me, nipples hard as my cock, and as she started to come, I took one in my mouth.

She cried out, bringing up her knees as she spasmed.

I held on tight, feeling her come apart and closing my eyes, because I loved it so much. Every shake, every shiver, every whimper was mine.

My bed was hers. My T-shirts were hers. My house was hers. My dick was hers.

I squeezed my arms around her, breathing into her neck. And this was mine.

Her pussy pulsed, tightening around me as she shook through the rest of it.

I finally leaned back, taking control as she went limp, and I pulled her hips into me, grinding harder and harder until I felt every muscle in my body burning. I reached down, pulling myself out, ripping the condom off, and spilling onto her stomach, baring my teeth as I breathed hard.

Her stomach moved with her breaths and I looked up into her eyes that were now open, hoping she wasn't put off. I kept having to remind myself that she wasn't that experienced. Everything we did might be the first time she'd done it.

But she smiled and leaned her head in to kiss me. "I'd say you dirtied me up, Mr. Trent." She laughed against my mouth, and I nibbled her lip.

"Happy now?" she asked.

"Not nearly."

Her face lit up, and she shook her head, climbing off me. "You had a phone call," she reminded me. "When you're done, come back to bed."

She walked off to the bathroom, and I got up, grabbing some tissues from the box and cleaning myself up before heading back to the bedroom.

My body felt loose again. The release helped. I might actually be able to get some work down now as long as she didn't mind me waking her up in another two hours for round six.

Snatching my pants from earlier off the bedroom floor, I dug my phone out of my pocket and looked through the missed calls.

Three. All from a number I recognized.

Dialing back, I waited for him to answer.

"Jax?" Corvin, my police officer contact at the prison, answered.

"What do you got?" I asked.

"Sorry, man. I called as soon as I heard. Judge approved your father's release. Tomorrow. Noon."

I crossed the room, slamming the door shut. "Tomorrow!" I seethed, gritting my teeth. "That's not the notice I paid for."

"I called as soon as I heard," he maintained. "This is your last chance. Ciaran already said it's taken care of if you want to—"

"Fuck you." And I hung up, slamming my hands down on the dresser and bowing my head into my arm.

I closed my eyes. *Shit.*

I was supposed to have more notice. That was what I paid him for, for Christ's sake!

Corvin was Ciaran's man on the inside, and when I'd started working for Fallon's father a year ago, I made him my contact as well. Through him, I knew my father had been speaking to lawyers, turning on old contacts, and working out a deal. This had been happening for a while, and even though I expected the inevitable, I also expected more than twelve hours to prepare myself.

"Noon," I whispered, sweat already coating my forehead.

He was going to be free. Three years early when he should've been put down, not let go.

For six years I'd known exactly where he slept and ate. Somewhere where he wasn't a threat to me. And now, in a matter of hours, I would have no idea if he was a hundred miles away or right outside the window.

I heard the soft spray of the shower running, and my head filled with dread.

Juliet.

My Juliet.

I dialed Jared.

"It's late. What's up?" he answered.

I stood up straight, clearing my throat. "Meet me in the backyard. We have to talk."

"Wh—"

And I hung up.

"Stop fucking hanging up on me!" Jared whisper-yelled, walking out the back door of Tate's house and zipping up his jeans. "You're always doing that, and it pisses me off."

I rolled my eyes. "Yeah, I'll pencil in time to cry about that later, Princess."

I walked through the garden door, meeting him before he'd even stepped off her back porch.

"Yeah." He barked out a laugh. "I'm not the pretty one who now shops at the mall. Nice haircut," he jabbed.

"Nice buzz cut," I shot back, teasing. "You trading in the Boss for a minivan next?"

He dropped his head back, sighing. I crossed my arms over my chest, trying to keep the smile off my face.

My brother and I had always gotten along before we lived in the same house. Since then, you could mistake us for five-year-old girls.

We argued, constantly challenged each other, and neither backed down in a difference of opinion. The shit was getting thicker, too, and it was going to get worse before it got better.

There can't be two alphas in the pack, after all.

He looked at me, annoyance written all over his face as he put his hands on his hips. "So, what do you want?"

I tipped my chin up, getting serious again. "I have a contact at the prison. Just got a call from them," I said. "He's being released tomorrow at noon."

His eyebrows nose-dived. "No, we would've been notified."

I nodded. *Yeah, you would think.*

"Sounds like it happened pretty quickly," I offered as he stepped down the stairs, coming closer.

His brown eyes searched the ground and then eyed me with obvious concern. "Are you sure?"

"Sure enough."

Corvin might've given me shit notice, but he was giving me accurate info. I trusted him, and I knew that if I called right now and gave him the go-ahead, my father would never wake up in the morning.

When I began working for Ciaran, he'd found out about my father. Even offered to "take care" of him for me, but I'd shot him down.

I didn't know if Jared and I were still scared of our father or just worried, but neither of us wanted to wonder where he was or what he was doing.

Jared shook his head, in denial. "He won't come here."

"He'll definitely come here," I countered in a calm voice.

"How do you know?"

"He calls," I admitted without hesitation.

He cocked his head, peering at me. "You're talking to him?"

I breathed out a laugh. "Yeah, for hours," I taunted. "We share gluten-free recipes and gossip about *Pretty Little Liars*."

Jared cocked an eyebrow.

"He calls," I said flatly, "I issue a few nicely placed threats, and we do it all over again the next week, Jared. Don't get your panties in a twist."

He ran a hand through his short hair, shaking his head at me. "You should've told me."

"Why?" I shrugged. "So you can lose your mind over shit you can't control?"

I knew my brother loved me. I knew he'd do anything to protect me. And that was the problem. Jared could be sloppy, and he always advanced without thinking first. He worried too much, and while I knew he did everything in my best interest, I didn't want to have to clean up whatever mess he made as well as deal with the problem he'd still failed to solve.

"We need that restraining order," I pointed out.

He narrowed his eyes. "I thought you didn't want it."

"Yeah, well"—I ran my hand over the top of my head, glancing up to my bedroom window—"I'll take every measure possible to protect her."

He nodded, looking at me knowingly. "Now you see."

I didn't nod or say anything. He knew he was right. A restraining order might not do any good, but every precaution that could be taken needed to be taken.

"It's the weekend," he pointed out, thinking. "Jason might not be able to do shit until Monday."

His mother's new husband—and Madoc's father, Jason Caruthers—should be able to get us a restraining order quickly. But it being Friday night, he might not be able to reach a judge.

"All right," he blurted out, looking as though he'd just come to a decision. "Let's just go. Tate and Fallon were planning a camping trip for next week. Let's just go now until we can get the restraining order in place."

He dug his phone out of his jeans, continuing. "Let the girls sleep. I'll call Madoc to warn him to start getting the gear together first thing in the morning, and you and I will go for provisions. We'll head to the falls and stay off the radar for a few days."

I thought about it, knowing a long weekend was doable. I could get caught up on e-mails and other business tonight, and Ciaran hadn't sent me any new work, so it should be fine.

"It's a plan," I agreed. "We'll hit the store at eight."

I turned to leave, but he grabbed my arm.

"You should've told me," he repeated, worry clear in his eyes.

I knew he wasn't trying to get on my case. Despite our bickering, my brother wanted to be there for me, and I knew he didn't appreciate me keeping him in the dark.

I gave him a thoughtful nod, understanding his concern.

I cleared my throat. "And you should tell Tate," I advised.

"Tell her what?"

"That you hate ROTC," I replied. "That you have absolutely no idea what you want to do with your life, and that you're suffocating."

His back straightened, and he looked angry. But I knew I was speaking the truth. On the occasions I was in Chicago and saw him with his classmates, he looked out of sorts. Completely uncomfortable and out of place. He wasn't in his element, and from certain things he'd said, I knew he wished he was home instead.

He turned to leave, and it was me grabbing his arm this time. "She'd want you to be happy," I pressed.

"She's going to medical school, Jax," he said as if I were an idiot. "I love her, okay? It's the only thing I do know for sure."

And I watched as he climbed the steps and disappeared back into her house.

Okay, so she was going to medical school. So what? Did he think he had to do something profound or more respectable with his life? To be good enough for her?

Tate wasn't like that, and she had never encouraged him to join the military in the first place. Her father had, but even Mr. Brandt would support a full-grown man going after the life he really wanted. What was Jared thinking?

I traipsed back over to my yard and into the house, running through the whole downstairs and double-checking locks.

Heading upstairs, I was about to go for the office but went for the bedroom instead. Juliet was sleeping soundly again, and I caught sight of the tattoo on the back of her neck.

Crawling in behind her, I threw my arm over her waist and kissed the tattoo.

Only Ever You.

We hadn't talked about it, and I didn't know if she wanted to, but I knew those words were mine. She might have thought them up and spoken them, but they were for me and no one else.

I nuzzled into her neck, remembering how I would nuzzle into Jared's shirt when we were kids.

I wasn't holding on to Juliet. I was hanging on to her. For dear life.

"Jax?" Her low voice was sleepy.

I moved my nose out of her hair. "Yeah?"

"My freshman year of college, did you replace my music appreciation teacher's playlist of baroque composers with 2 Live Crew's 'Me So Horny'?"

My body shook silently as I laughed my ass off.

Oh, shit. I chuckled. I'd forgotten all about that.

"You're laughing," she accused. "You did do it."

Yep, I did it, I thought, smiling to myself.

"That's just so wrong," she replied playfully.

I squeezed her tight, smiling into her hair, my father momentarily forgotten. "You're welcome."

CHAPTER 23

JULIET

"Jax! Now!"

We both jerked our heads to the door, hearing Jared's bellow from downstairs.

Jax smiled, gave me one last peck on the lips, and hopped off the bed.

His hair was still wet from the shower he took while I was asleep, and he already had jeans on, but he was only half-dressed.

When he'd stepped back into the room this morning, saying he and Jared were leaving to get supplies, and we were all going camping, we got sidetracked. Again.

Jared had been honking his horn for five minutes.

Digging into one of his clothing bags—I assumed from the shopping trip with Madoc yesterday—he grabbed a black T-shirt and slipped it on.

"Be ready when I get back, okay?" He grabbed his phone, keys, and wallet, shoving them in his pockets. "Pack a bikini and some of my T-shirts to wear. You don't need anything else."

Smiling, I sat up, covering myself with the sheet. "I'll be ready."

I knew he wanted to get out of here soon, and I was glad he'd confided in me. I didn't know how concerned to be about his father or
whether or not he was a genuine threat, but I trusted Jax's and Jared's
instincts to keep a safe distance until they were prepared.

And hey, if it meant sharing a tent with Jax for three days, then I
was cool with that. Tutoring was on a one-week hiatus for the Fourth
of July next week, and I wasn't starting my theater job until after that
was completed mid-July.

He dived back down for a quick kiss and then headed for the
door. "And don't comb your hair," he ordered, looking back at me and
winking.

I saluted, watching him leave.

Swinging my legs over the edge of the bed, I kept the sheet
wrapped around me and rotated my ankles and feet back to life. I'd
practically been fucked into the mattress, although I vaguely remembered going into his office last night, riding him in his chair, and
then returning to bed as if I'd just gotten up to get a drink of water.

The bedroom door swung open, and I looked up to see Fallon
pulling to a sudden halt and peering down at me wide-eyed.

"Oh, wow," she said.

I bowed my head, groaning. I didn't even want to know what I
looked like.

I heard a second set of footsteps and glanced up to see Tate.

"Well," she drawled out, grinning. "You're a mess. Sorry to barge
in"—she stepped into the room—"but there's no time to lose."

I nodded, tightening the sheet. "Sorry for the delay. Jax . . . um,"
I mumbled. "Energy. Lots of energy."

Fallon stayed in the doorway while Tate sat down beside me.
"I . . . I'll . . . um . . ." Fallon stumbled over her words. "I'll go back
over to your place and run her a bath."

She walked out, and Tate called after her as she started to rub circles on my back.

"My soothing salts are under the sink!" she shouted.

I shrugged her hand off, letting out a nervous laugh. "It's not my first time, Tate. Stop fussing."

She dropped her hand to her lap, speaking sternly. "You ever done it so many times in one night before?" she asked, looking around the floor, probably referring to the condom wrappers.

I stared at my feet, smiling to myself and shaking my head.

She continued. "And if Jax is anything like his brother, then I'm sure he's no gentleman in the bedroom."

I bit my lip, trying not to laugh and look as though I was losing my mind. I was mortified, delirious, and happy all at the same time, and I probably looked as if I'd been attacked by an animal. *But definitely not by a gentleman.*

Shelburne Falls wasn't actually in Shelburne Falls. The town was named after the three roaring rapids that all merged into a single river that fed our small city. Even though the actual falls were a good distance away, no town was closer than ours.

After about forty-five minutes of plain highway driving with a barely noticeable incline, the lush green grasslands of the Midwest gave way to denser forest and narrower roads. All leading up to Blackhawk Lake—also known as Party Cove—and the three Shelburne waterfalls.

I'd rarely ever been up there. My mother wasn't an outdoor person, and by the time I was old enough to fish or hike, my father was in and out of hospitals. The only times I'd ventured here were once with Tate and her dad, and another time for a party.

Madoc led the way in his silver GTO, Jared and Tate followed in Jared's Boss, and Jax and I trailed in his Mustang. I'd texted Shane, telling her I'd be back in a few days and would see her before she left for college, but I didn't bother letting my mother know anything. She hadn't even attempted contact.

Jax tapped his fingers on the steering wheel to Starset's "My Demons" while I attempted journaling through his *The Fast and the Furious* driving.

"What do you write in there?" He peered over at me, shoving his thick biceps in my face as he tried to snatch the notebook.

"Stop." I laughed, twisting away. "It's nothing about you. I promise."

"It better be about me," he teased, feigning insult and going back to driving.

I smirked. "I can't put you into words. It's impossible."

When he didn't say anything, I looked up to see him smiling to himself.

Yeah. There was no way to put him into words yet. Every time I *thought* of him, all I wanted to shout was "I love you!" Every time I opened my mouth to *speak* to him, all I wanted to say was "I love you!"

So not very coherent at this point. What the hell is love anyway? Did I love him already? Should I love him already?

Or was it just attraction? I mean, he looked like a demigod. I wanted to touch him and crawl on top of him at every opportunity. His smell, his personality, his body, everything intoxicated me.

But that wasn't love. I was smart enough to know that. So why did I always want to say it?

"Thanks for the watch." I spoke up, trying to get my mind off the subject of love. I looked down, rubbing my thumb over the white Samsung Gear fitted to my wrist. He'd picked it up while he and Jared were out getting supplies, but it wasn't just a watch. It was a phone, a camera, and a pedometer, and I could do almost anything with it that I could do with my phone.

"You haven't GPS'd me, have you?" I teased.

"Maybe." He smiled. "No, it's simply a phone you'll always have on you, if you need it. It's safe."

I noticed he hadn't gotten one for himself, though. He worried about me too much, and I wished he wouldn't.

For the next ten minutes, I wrote a whole page of my name, Juliet Adrian Carter, over and over again in my journal.

For years, I'd been writing and signing my sister's name, even though Juliet had always stayed my legal name. School, doctors' offices, and such treated K.C. as a nickname, so I'd signed Juliet on official occasions, but rarely for anything else. I needed to get used to using it full-time again.

We pulled off the main road, taking a short trip through a dense brush to a clearing right on the banks of the lake. Tate had booked the campgrounds for next week, but we got lucky and got in early. There were other campers, and I could hear boat engines, squealing girls, and music already, hence the name "Party Cove."

Although the beach ahead looked rocky, nothing was more beautiful. The panoramic view of evergreens surrounding the midnight blue lake, disturbed only by the havoc of Jet Skis and a few kayaks, was the epitome of summer fun. Fresh air, clear skies, and the laughter and music signaling good, clean fun. I couldn't wait.

I just had no idea what to do first. Dive into the lake or get lost in the woods.

After we'd parked in the lot, we hauled our gear to the campground surrounding the beach and started setting up. The other campers in the area, about ten or so, already had a party going, and I caught sight of an old wooden rowboat completely filled with ice, soda, and an assortment of beers.

Even though it was early, the partying had commenced. I didn't worry, though. Madoc would have a ball, but Fallon would rein him in. Jared had stopped overindulging in high school, so Tate would be relaxed, and they'd enjoy their time together. I got drunk once in my life, wasted an entire day on a hangover, and vowed never to do it again.

And Jax? I'd heard about a time or two that Madoc got him loaded, but I'd never seen it, and now I think I knew why.

Jax hated any dependencies. He didn't smoke, do drugs, and I'd rarely ever seen him drink alcohol. Probably because of his father.

Maybe the shit he went through had served a purpose after all. It helped shaped the man he became. Survival, not suffering.

"Tent's almost ready." He came behind me and helped lift the air mattress I was hauling from the car. Tate, Fallon, and I had inflated the mattresses using the vacuum that attached to a car's cigarette lighter. Easy peasy.

I felt a hand on my tush and glanced around, nearly stumbling over a log, to see Jax reaching out, pawing me through my short black shorts.

"How'd you like it if I felt you up in public?" I teased. I heard him laugh.

"You're lucky I'm not yanking that bikini string loose. Red is my favorite color on you," he teased.

"Well, don't get too excited, mister," I advised, pulling down the visor on my baseball hat. "I want to hike to the falls after we're down here."

"Your ass is vibrating." He changed the subject as he picked my cell phone out of my back pocket.

"Hey," I scolded, dropping the mattress next to the tent and turning around. "Phone, please."

I held out my hand, smirking and tapping my foot, but I stopped when I saw Jax scowling at the screen.

"Why is Liam calling you?" he asked as the phone stopped vibrating in his hand.

I dropped my hand and narrowed my gaze thoughtfully. "I don't know."

He held on to the phone, straightening his back and looking down at me. "How often does he call?"

I took a deep breath, not liking his tone. "Why don't you check my call log to see for yourself, Jax?"

Dropping my gaze, I put my hands on my hips and waited. I had no idea why Liam was calling. It was the first time, and if he'd left a message, I had no interest in hearing it.

But Jax wasn't inquiring. He was interrogating, and he had no reason not to trust me.

He handed me my phone. "I don't want to invade your privacy."

"Too late," I mumbled, bending down to pick up the mattress again.

But he hooked my arm with his, bringing me back up. "Hey," he soothed. "I'm sorry. I trust you, okay?" He tipped my chin up. "Other guys shouldn't be calling my girl, though. What would you do if Cameron or another past hookup was calling me?"

I pursed my lips to hide the smile, but he still saw it.

"Oh, that's funny?" he joked.

"No." I wrapped my arms around his waist. "You called me your girl." I nodded, waggling my eyebrows. "And," I continued, "you'd better believe this little wallflower will cut a bitch with that knife of yours if anyone lays a hand on you." I darted out, catching one of his nipple rings in my teeth and sucking.

He gasped in surprise and then chuckled, wrapping his arms around me. "I never would've thought."

"What?" I played, holding the barbell between my teeth.

"I don't like aggressive women." His voice was low and thoughtful. "I never have. I'm sure you know why."

I stopped and tilted my head back, looking up at him. *Yeah.* I knew why. And I could understand it.

"But you?" He ran his finger over my cheek. "It's different. I like it when you're nice, but I love it when you're rough." He leaned down to whisper in my ear, sending shivers down my spine, "So, just a warning . . . if you bite my nipple piercings one more time, the thin walls of the tent will do nothing to drown out how hard I'm fucking you."

And then he backed away, everything in his eyes telling me that his threat for today was a promise tonight.

"I don't think we're going the right way," Madoc whined as we wound our way through the forest, traveling steadily uphill.

"We're following a trail, Einstein," Jared called back. "I'm not carving this baby out for the first time. Relax."

The intimate hike I'd been hoping for consisting of just Jax and me didn't happen. Instead of a quiet jaunt into the woods and maybe a sexy swim in one of the pools at the bottom of the falls, we were a group six strong with Jared in the lead, followed by Tate, Fallon, Madoc—because he wanted to stare at his wife's butt—and then Jax and me.

"Well, Jax should be leading," Madoc called out. "His people have skills. Like bear whispering and understanding messages in the wind and shit."

"Nah," Jax joked. "But I can weave a damn nice basket."

Everyone chuckled, but I simply smiled. I was feeling more and more a part of the group as time wore on, but they'd all spent loads of time together, and I was still trying to find my place.

And—looking up—I smiled, liking my place so far.

Jax was wearing long black cargo shorts, hiking shoes, and a dark gray backpack on his naked back. I looked much the same, except I had my red bikini top with my black shorts and backpack. My white baseball cap was pulled over my hair, which I'd stupidly left down, and I was sweating already.

We needed a swim. The temperature at this elevation wasn't stifling, but the exertion certainly helped toward making it unbearable.

"Well, I'm getting tired," Madoc carried on. "I was told we were doing water sports. On the beach. Beer and Jet Skis. That's my thing."

"Fallon, take care of your baby," Tate called back. "He needs a breast to suck on."

"Madoc, stop whining," Fallon scolded. "We haven't even gotten to the switchbacks yet. You think this is tough?"

"What the hell is a switchback?" Madoc shot out. "It sounds like a snake."

We laughed, but then Jared called out, "K.C., you still with us?"

"Juliet," everyone shouted, correcting him.

I laughed. "I'm here," I assured him. "I did my nails and makeup waiting on you slowpokes."

"Ooooh." I heard some taunts at my joke and looked up to see Jax smiling back at me.

An hour later and we'd finally reached our destination. Shelburne Falls was three waterfalls, but they ran in succession. One fell, poured into a pool, and fed another waterfall. That fell into another pool, which fed the final waterfall. We ended up at the pool that fed the lowest waterfall.

Looking up, I saw the second fall cascading down, narrow but roaring, and could feel the lovely cool spray blow across my body. Boulders and rocks surrounded the calm little lake, and I clutched my backpack straps as I took in the high walls of the cliffs around us.

I smiled, feeling gloriously small. *I think I might like the outdoors.*

"Wow." I stopped at the edge of the pool, looking up at the high fall. "This is amazing. Can we swim in it?" I asked Tate, who stood at my side.

She started stripping out of her shorts and tank. "Yeah, it's safe."

"Hey, there's tire swings!" I pointed to the low cliffs and started over that way.

"Juliet, don't," Jared warned. "You have no idea how long that shit's been up there. Let me check it out."

My eyebrows shot up, and I looked over at Tate, who was shaking her head and smirking.

"The military is making him very authoritative," she explained. "Safety first."

"You like it," he called back, obviously hearing what she'd said.

She eyed him, nodding. "Yes, I like it."

Jared climbed up the wall like a pro, coming onto the landing about fifteen feet up and yanking on the rope, checking the weight and making sure the swing was safe to use. Fallon and Madoc were already in the pool, and Tate started walking for the tire swing.

I looked around. "Jax?" I called, circling a three-sixty and looking to the others. "Where's Jax?"

"Over here," I heard him call, and I whipped around to see him kneeling on the far edge of the pool. Where it dropped into the waterfall.

Climbing across some stones, I wiggled out of my backpack and set it down right as I came up next to him. He stood on one knee, peering over the edge where the final waterfall was pouring into the last pool. After that, the water followed a steady stream that eventually fed into our town's river.

Inching to the edge, I peered down the long drop to the pool below until my heart filled my throat and the ground tipped up toward me.

"Whoa." I backed up, letting out a nervous laugh. "That's a drop."

"Yeah," he agreed, sounding dreamy as he stared over the side.

"Oh, don't fall!" Madoc came over, knocking Jax's shoulder, but he pushed himself back.

"Jackass." He smiled, righting himself again.

Everyone else started trailing over to catch the view, but my eyes stayed on Jax. I didn't like how he was looking over the side. It seemed to me as though he was trying to muster up courage.

"Jax, no." I shook my head, reading his mind. "It's too high."

He twisted his lips, still peering over, and my hands started to tingle.

"It is tempting, though," he whispered.

"No, it's not," Jared countered. "This waterfall has an eighty-five-foot drop, and we don't know how deep that pool is."

"You don't," Jax taunted. "But I do."

Jared loomed over him, and I swallowed when I saw Jax's mouth curl up in a cocky grin.

"No." Jared's deep voice issued his order.

"I've never heard of anyone jumping from up here, Jax," Tate added, heading back to the pool.

Jared followed her. "And no one will." He glanced back at Jax, his warning clear.

"Woo-hoo!" Madoc howled, and I turned to see everyone dive from the rocks into the cool black water. "Come on!" He waved me in, and I smiled.

But turning back to Jax, I felt my heart drop into my stomach, and I stared at the now empty space where he had just been standing.

"Jax?" I breathed out, my mouth falling open.

And then seeing his backpack lying on the rocks at the edge, I screamed, "Jax!"

I rushed for the edge, dropping to my hands and knees, gulping in air as I peered over the side.

But all I saw were the concentric circles rippling the water, telling me that someone had entered the pool.

My hands shot to my hair, holding my head, as I frantically searched the water for signs of him.

No, no, no . . .

"What happened?" Jared shouted behind me. "Did he jump? Goddamn it!"

"Where are you, baby? Where are you?" I prayed, scanning the water, seeing only the black of the depth and the white of the spray. My eyes flew left to right, seeing nothing.

"Shit, where are you?" I whispered to myself, my voice cracking.

I squeezed my eyes shut, fisted my fingers, and shot off the ground, standing up straight and tightening every muscle in my body.

"Jaxon Hawkins Trent!" I bellowed, my face on fire with anger, remembering a teacher calling him by his full name in high school.

And then, as if summoned, he popped out of the water, smoothing his hand over his hair and looking up at all of us as he treaded calmly.

My body relaxed, and even though relief flooded me, my head swelled with anger. What was he thinking? What if he'd been hurt?

It was too far away to tell, but I think he was smiling as he did the backstroke to the edge as if he hadn't just scared the shit out of all of us.

"Oh, thank God," Tate exclaimed, coming up next to me. "He's okay!" she shouted to the rest of the group.

I dug my nails into my palm. "No, he's not," I retorted, watching him climb out of the pool and onto the rocks.

"What do you mean?" I heard Tate ask.

But it was too late. I was gone.

I leaped over the side, sucking in a breath and my heart stopping as I shot out from the ground and plunged feetfirst through the air to the depths below.

Oh, shit!

My arms and legs tingled, and my heart started jackhammering through my chest as adrenaline raced through me.

Air rushed up at me, sending my hair flying, and that thrill feeling crept up my throat, making me want to laugh out of fear. The kind of fear you get on a roller coaster.

I vaguely heard someone yelling at me or after me, but before I knew it, the pool flew up at me and I had just enough time to suck in a breath before plunging through the ice-cold water and into the silent darkness.

My arms and legs fanned out, stopping me in a weightless suspension, but I didn't take time to look around.

I didn't care that I'd made it. I didn't care that I just made an eighty-five-foot jump.

Kicking my legs, I pushed myself back up through the surface, sucking in a deep breath as I swam to the side.

"Juliet!" I heard Jax's voice. "Jesus, what are you doing?"

I crawled up the rocks and stepped out of the water, furious breaths pouring in and out of me.

Jax grabbed my waist. "Baby, are you okay?"

I looked up into his heavenly blue eyes, pushed my wet hair back over the top of my head, and slammed both palms into his chest, shoving him away and causing him to stumble backward.

I didn't care that he looked confused. I didn't care that he almost fell. I only hoped that he felt the pain in his chest that I'd felt when I thought he might be gone.

Motherfucker.

CHAPTER 24

JAXON

What the hell did I do now? I just stood there, wide-eyed and completely fucking clueless as she stomped off, pissed at me yet again.

Was it impossible for us to get through a twenty-four-hour period without getting into a fight?

She'd just jumped off a cliff like she was eating a sandwich, but when she'd slammed her fists into me, I could feel her fury, and I didn't know why I felt bad all of a sudden.

I didn't wait for the rest of the gang to climb back down the mountain. I could already hear Madoc's laughter, so as soon as I got my head clear enough to move, I traipsed back down the trail.

Going downhill was a lot faster than going uphill, but she had to be jogging, because my long legs carried me fast, and I never caught up to her.

By the time I got back to camp, I could already smell the meat, charcoal, and lighter fluid in the air, not to mention that the music had kicked up a few notches, and people were in real good moods.

I yanked open the flaps on our tent, and bent down to poke my head in, but she wasn't in there. I searched Tate and Jared's tent and Fallon and Madoc's, but no sign of her. I headed straight for the woods, toward the parking lot, but stopped halfway.

She was sitting on a log, leaning forward, with her head resting in her hand.

Her hair, still stringy from the water, covered her arms and back, and I noticed the quick and heavy rise and fall of her body as she breathed hard.

"What's wrong?" I shouted, and saw her back instantly straighten. "What did I do now?"

She shot up off the log and spun around, stomping toward me without meeting my eyes. I thought she was coming to hit me again, but her straight face and defiant expression told me she didn't even want to have anything to do with me right now.

She marched past me, but I quickly grabbed her shoulders, stopping her. "What the hell is the matter with you? What did I do?"

She swiped my hands away, looking up to glare at me. "You could've hurt yourself! Why did you want to scare everyone and just disappear like that? Why?" she shouted, her face flushed with anger and red from tears. "You pulled a stupid prank, and I was afraid. Why did you do that?" Her voice shook as she tried to hold back more tears.

I pulled up straight, looking down at her, confused. I didn't understand. I jumped off a cliff. It wasn't as though I didn't know I'd be fine. She had to know I wouldn't have done something that would get me hurt.

"I'm sorry," she choked out, sniffling. "But you just can't do things like that. I worry about you. Jared wouldn't have scared Tate like that. And Madoc would've thought of Fallon first. You left me alone up there, and you didn't think of me. It wasn't fair."

I stared down, trying to understand.

She didn't know the drop was safe as I did. And I guess I would've been mad if she'd done it with no warning. In fact, I was. When I saw her leap, even though I knew she'd land okay, my heart still jumped into my throat, because for a moment, as she sprang into the air, she wasn't safe.

But I also didn't like people worrying about me. Telling me what to do. Having an opinion about how I lived my life. I'd done fine on my own for so long. She was inching in, and I wasn't used to this.

This was just summer fun. For both of us.

I dropped my hands from her shoulders, lowering my voice to a whisper. "I told you a long time ago that my brother and I are nothing alike. Don't get your hopes up." Better she get that through her head now.

She nodded, her furious eyes focused to the side. "Yeah, don't worry. I got it," she bit out, backing away. "And I won't forget again."

The puddle between us immediately spread into a vast ocean, and even if I reached out my arms, I would never be able to reach her.

What the hell was the matter with me? I wanted her—I wanted today, and I wanted tomorrow, but I couldn't think about next year or even next week. I wanted her curled up next to me, between the sheets, warm and safe, but I had to know when to let go. I had to do it before she did.

She pushed past me. "I'll stay in Tate's or Fallon's tent."

My shoulders fell. *No.*

I darted out and circled my arms around her from behind, holding her close and burying my face in her neck. "Don't," I begged. "Please don't."

My muscles strained, holding her so tight, and I heard her suck in quick breaths. I spun her around, wrapped my arms around her waist, and lifted her up, kissing her deep and hard.

"I can't let you go," I panted. "I want you all the time. I'll be unbearable, Juliet. They won't know what do with me."

Her hands clasped my neck, as she looked into my eyes.

"I like you, Jax." She ran her fingers through my hair above my ear. "I like you a lot. You're important."

I closed my eyes, meeting her forehead. "Say it," I whispered.

Her sweet breath fanned over my lips. "Only ever you."

And I groaned, hating and loving how those words affected me.

In the years I'd wanted her, I'd thought I was good enough. I thought she should thank her lucky stars that I even gave her the time of day.

But now . . . there was an ache in my chest and guilt in my heart. I had no right to her. I'd slept with a lot of women, and she deserved someone good. Someone clean. What if I failed her?

I looked into her eyes, taking the leap. "I need to take you somewhere. Tuesday, after we all leave here, I want to take you into Chicago," I said, kissing her lips softly. "There's something I want you to see. Someplace I go . . . at night."

She nodded, never blinking. "Okay," she said quietly.

My lips were so close to hers, but my eyes never faltered. "I want you," I whispered over the lump in my throat. "More than anything. I think of you first thing in the morning, and last thing at night. You're the most important person in my life, Juliet." No matter what happened, I needed her to remember that. "I'm trying to let you know me, okay?"

She nodded again. "Just as long as it's not more cliff diving, okay?"

A grin spread across my face. "No, it's not that tame."

By the time Tuesday rolled around, I didn't want to leave.

The days were fun. The nights were fun. And the fun was easy.

I realized how nice it was to have a girlfriend, and I enjoyed the little things we'd gotten comfortable with each other enough to do, like the familiar little touches, someone to wrap my arms around at the campfire, and waking up with the person I wanted right next to me in the morning. Someone warm and soft and made just for me. It was consistent and comforting.

And after a lifetime of feeling as if I didn't truly have a home, I finally had something that came naturally.

I'd kissed every inch of her skin, and sucked and bitten anything and everything I could get my hands on. I'd lost count of her different smiles, and my favorite feeling was her teeth on my skin.

She had gotten inside me, but when I slowed down long enough to think, then doubt crept in like a thick fog.

I wouldn't live up to her expectations, she'd start getting demanding, and we'd get ugly.

Fuck. I rubbed my hand over my face, zoning out on the road as I drove. *Fuck the doubt.* I was good enough. I was strong enough. I was powerful enough. And I was worthy enough.

"Are you sure this is how I'm supposed to dress?" Juliet asked from the passenger seat.

I looked over, instantly biting back a smile. She looked the hottest I'd ever seen her, and I couldn't wait to show her what I needed to show her and then get back in the car and get the hell home.

She wore a black-and-white schoolgirl skirt that barely fell below her ass and a gray half-shirt tank top. Her makeup of black eye shadow and red lipstick was thicker than soup, and her severely straight hair fell in a shiny wave down her back. Fallon and Tate had finished the look for her with combat boots with metal buckles.

"You'll blend. Don't worry."

"I look like a slut," she mourned.

"Those are Tate's clothes," I pointed out.

"Which she bought on a whim and never wore," she shot back. "What about your clothes?"

I wore medium-washed jeans and a short-sleeved black V-neck. I don't dress up.

"I'm big, and I'll have a hot goth chick on my arm." I smiled. "They won't cry over my lack of eyeliner, okay?"

She rolled her eyes and looked out the window. "I hate that you're not telling me anything."

"I confided in Madoc once. He almost vomited," I joked but not really. "It's not something I'm going to give you a chance to run from."

She turned her wide eyes on me, probably wondering if now was too late to get scared.

In all fairness, Madoc had been a good friend about it. One night, I'd dragged him to Chicago with me, to the Skull & Feather, because I'd needed to share it with someone.

And for some reason, I didn't trust Jared's reaction. Madoc was unnerved, and I could tell it wasn't something he was ever interested in experiencing again, but he was supportive. He kept the secret and even covered for me when Jared got suspicious about my long nights out in high school.

We parked in the garage across from the club, and I took her hand in mine as we ran across the busy downtown street. The black-top, bright with the glow of streetlights, glistened with the rain that had fallen earlier, and the sounds of car horns and tires kicking up water filled the air.

Juliet kept pace with me as I walked through the club door, the stench of cigarette smoke instantly filling my nostrils, and I handed the bouncer two twenties for our cover. I came here nearly every week, and I knew the guy remembered me, but I never attempted to make friends. I never spoke to anyone, and I never hung out long.

I didn't want these people to know me.

"Five minutes?" I confirmed.

He nodded, knowing what I always came to see. "Five minutes."

I looked to Juliet, who was completely focused on the club scene. Since I came here so often, it was nothing new to me, but from her perspective I was sure it was an interesting sight.

The old club sat on the first floor of a large warehouse, and even though the building itself was massive with sky-high ceilings, the actual club gave off an intimate atmosphere. There were two levels, with the top level in a U shape. Walking around up there, you could stand at the railings on all three sides and peer down into the bottom level where we currently stood. Several high round tables with stools were scattered around the room, along with a long bar that featured mirrors on the back wall, and gothic-looking chandeliers hanging from the ceiling above us.

And everything was black. The walls, the furniture, the equipment, the floors, the ceiling, and even the employee dress code.

But by far the best feature was the theaterlike stage. Intricate old-world design still survived in the carving of the frame surrounding the wide and high platform. With the full-on black, this place felt like a cave hidden away from the rest of the world where hard music gave the finger to the world outside.

"You want a drink?" I asked, putting my hand on her back.

She widened her eyes, curling her lips in a nervous smile. "I think I might need one."

I smiled to myself, leading her over to the bar. I still hadn't figured out why I wanted to bring her here, but she hadn't run away yet, so . . .

She stopped at the bar, turning to look at me as the bartender stepped over.

"You won't get carded," I said, knowing what she was thinking.

"Uh." She held the railing of the bar, tapping her fingers. "Parrot Bay and pineapple juice, please," she ordered, and then immediately looked at me. "And shut up," she scolded.

"I'm not laughing." I laughed. "I told you. I like that you're a girly girl."

And I did. Jared loved Tate's no-nonsense, tomboy demeanor, but that had never been my thing. Juliet reminded me that the world could be pretty and soft.

I paid for her drink and my bottle of water and took her over to one of the high tops facing the stage. Disturbed's "Stupify" beat over the sound system, and I leaned down, placing my forearms on the table and trying to look relaxed.

But while everyone else around us talked and smiled, moved and bobbed their heads to the music, I felt as if my tongue was stuck in my throat. It was like this every time I came here.

Knowing *she* was in here somewhere.

I let the rush of blood heat up my chest, and I tried to keep my legs under me, because I was so nervous. I thought Juliet would be a distraction tonight, but unfortunately I had to pay more attention to my breathing than usual. I looked around the room when I really just wanted to look at her.

Why was I showing her this? Why, when I hadn't even shown Jared?

I clenched the water bottle instead of running my hand through my hair. I'd been better at reminding myself that I no longer had hair, so I learned to stop myself before I ran into the short hairs that I still hadn't gotten used to.

It wasn't bad, actually. I liked the haircut. But as Juliet and I got closer, I realized I was changing more and more. I'd abandoned my routine, changed my style, and Jared and I were constantly fighting. None of which was her fault, but it still proved to me that I was spiraling. Up or down, I wasn't sure.

"Okay." She let out a sigh, sounding frustrated. "I've been patient for three days, and—"

I jerked my head to the stage as the lights—what little there were—began to dim.

"Here," I interrupted, tipping my chin to the band coming out.

She stopped talking and turned her attention to the two guitarists, the bassist, and the drummer strolling out. All four members of Skull Feathers—the name clearly taken from the name of the club or vice versa—took up their instruments as the music stopped and the crowd started cheering and calling out.

"Who . . . ?" Juliet looked to me, confusion written all over her expression.

I held up a finger, asking her to wait.

The drummer pounded twice, sending fire shooting up from the two flamethrowers on each side of the stage, and Juliet laughed, probably out of shock. Her eyes shot to me, lit up with awe.

I smiled and watched her. I'd seen the show before, after all. A hundred times.

The glow from the flames blazed across her face, making her green eyes dance with light. Her mouth was open slightly, and the amazement in her expression was like looking at a child seeing fireworks for the first time. Entranced, she followed every movement with her eyes.

The band started, the heavy vibrations of the drums humming through our bodies, and the crowd went wild. Pounding feet, banging heads, jumping, losing themselves. The band was doing a cover of Rob Zombie's "Dragula," and when the crowd cheered louder, I knew who was onstage, but I didn't look.

I had to see Juliet see this for the first time. If she was grossed out, I'd whisk her away and apologize. If she liked it. . . . Well, I doubted she would. This show wasn't for most.

"Wha . . ." She looked to me, the question in her eyes, but she hurriedly turned back to the stage.

I watched her, knowing what she was seeing.

She was watching a dark-haired woman, midthirties, who wasn't in the band. She didn't play an instrument, she didn't sing, and she didn't dance.

"Oh, my God." Juliet's eyebrows, pinched together, and that was when I saw it.

The realization of what was happening. Her eyes flared, and her head cocked to the side as she watched, completely interested.

And I closed my eyes and smiled, relief flooding me. She wasn't scared.

Turning my body around, I stood up straight and gulped down half the bottle of water, before fixing my eyes on the woman onstage.

Her black corset shaped her waist, giving it a beautiful natural curve. The frilly black ruffled underwear brought everyone else's attention to her behind when she walked across the stage, and the tall black top hat tipped lower in the front, covering eyes I knew were hazel. Her black hair hung in an abundance of curls down her back, and her black midcalf boots and the black pearls around her neck completed her goth-steampunk flair.

Her full lips were red, and her eye shadow was a deep purple, but these didn't distract from the natural beauty she possessed—her high cheekbones, slanted eyes, and olive skin.

She was utterly beautiful, vibrant, and the life of this place. Everything and everyone revolved around her here.

Her head swayed, and her wrists rotated to the music. She smiled, sang along to the hard music, taunting the crowd to scream louder for her.

And behind her, the two stagehands, looking exactly as though they belonged here in their long dreads and black shorts, shirts, and boots, continued to grab the metal hooks hanging from the ceiling.

My eyes flashed to Juliet. Her eyes were full of amazement, and I could tell everything she was feeling just by her expressions.

Narrowed eyes? Confusion. Wide eyes? *Whoa*. Chin up with narrowed eyes? Interested.

Looking back up to the stage, I saw the woman smile at the crowd, holding up her arms and looking like a goddess. I couldn't see her back, but I knew what was about to happen. I tipped my head back, a rush hitting my chest as the cables lifted her into the air.

"Jax?" Juliet said, sounding as though she couldn't believe what she was seeing. "She's hanging. From hooks."

A smile spread over my face, and I leaned down on the table again.

"It's called body suspension. Weird, huh?"

She nodded. "Yeah. But"—she tipped her head back, watching as the woman spun around in the air, her skin stretched where the four hooks held her—"she . . . she kind of looks . . ."

"What?" I pressed, urging her on.

"Like an angel. She kind of looks like a dark angel, doesn't she?"

I glanced back up, remembering my first time seeing what she was seeing. The woman was suspended above the crowd, dark and menacing, but completely stunning in her power. She held the attention, the eyes, and the hearts of everyone in this room.

Nearly everyone.

"I didn't know people did things like this," Juliet said thoughtfully, "but she's really beautiful."

I looked back up, the purple, red, and white feathers in the woman's hat contrasting with all the black in the room. "Her name is Storm Cruz," I told Juliet. "She owns this club."

Juliet's gaze left the woman and turned to me. "You know her?" she asked.

I barely shook my head, looking way. "We've never met."

"But you come here to watch her shows."

"Here and other venues where she performs," I admitted.

Swallowing the lump in my throat, I looked up at the woman's body swinging around and around above us, wishing just once that she'd look down at me.

My voice was a whisper when I spoke. "She's my mother."

Juliet was quiet, but I could tell she was waiting for me to say something. I punched the clutch and shifted into sixth gear, taking a deep breath.

"She was eighteen when she had me," I started. "Despite her drug and alcohol use, I was born healthy. But she left me." I ran my hand through my hair, thinking about me as a baby. Crying in the hospital. Helpless. The state probably wondering what to do with me.

"She abandoned me at the hospital. No birth certificate had been filed, so they didn't know who my father was until he tracked me down a couple of years later." And I wished he never had. "It still took him a while and a paternity test to get ahold of me, but she, on the other hand, never looked back."

"You don't know that, Jax. I'm sure she was messed up at the time," Juliet said, trying to make me feel better.

But I didn't feel bad. Not about losing a mother I never had. Or losing a father I hated. I guess I just wanted to be acknowledged.

"I don't blame her," I allowed. "Who knows what my father did to her, after all? She escaped. Did what she had to do. She's happy, and successful, and living her life on her terms . . ." I trailed off and then added, "And she's clean. Totally on top of her game right now. I was really happy to see her happy."

It was a comfort to know that my mother—or the woman who gave birth to me—was taken care of. Whether she deserved it or not, I would've cared.

"But," I ventured, "she hasn't looked for me. That I do know."

And if she wanted to know me, she would've tried to find me. Hell, my footprint in the system rivaled the president's. The system had my entire life documented, coded, and stored. That's what happens when you grow up in foster care.

"What does Jared say about this?" she asked.

"Jared doesn't know. The only person I ever confided in was Madoc."

I glanced over at her, seeing the confusion in her eyes before she looked away. Madoc was easier to talk to, and when I needed to confide in someone, I considered him the safer bet.

"Jared thinks that everything hurts me," I admitted. "He doesn't want me to worry or struggle or be unhappy. He would take one look at her and think she was bad for me." The outfit, the environment, the suspension . . . "Exactly what he thought about you," I teased her, smirking.

"Me?"

I nodded. "You knew I wanted you in high school. But I never pursued you. You didn't wonder why?"

"You did pursue me," she blurted out, laughing. "You flirted with me all the time."

I let out a condescending chuckle. "Baby, if I pursued you, I would've had you," I threatened, reaching my hand over and running it up her thigh.

"Jared thought I was too wild for K. C. Carter," I explained. "He thought we'd have fun, and then you'd come to your senses and dump me on my ass."

A smile brightened her face, and she unfastened her seat belt, leaning over close to my ear. My eyes drifted closed as she kissed my neck, and I forced them open again to stay focused on the road.

"So he didn't trust me?" she whispered, her breath tickling my skin, making me clench the wheel.

"Are you saying he was wrong?" I taunted.

"I'm saying I'm tired of people telling me who I am." She leaned in close to my face and gave me a disappointing, quick peck on the cheek. "Go to the Black Debs, okay?"

The tattoo shop Jared frequents?

"Why?" I asked.

"Just go."

When we got back to town, I parked along the curb across from the shop, seeing the lights on, but the OPEN sign off.

I turned to tell her, but her car door slammed shut, and she was already rounding the front of the car, carrying her black journal with her.

Shit.

I shook my head, wondering what the hell was going on. She needed a tattoo? Right now?

But I still hurried my ass out of the car.

Jogging across the street, I followed her into the shop and spotted Aura, Jared's artist, munching on half a sandwich as she pored over some sketches.

She looked up and stopped chewing as Juliet strutted right through the half door leading to the back.

"Can you fit me in?" Juliet asked.

Aura peered around her to look at me, probably hoping I'd explain.

We knew each other. I'd come here with Jared, and Aura had been trying to convince me for years to get some ink. *"You'd be hotter with some tattoos, kid,"* she'd said.

Yeah, because that was a reason to get tattoos.

She must've done Juliet's angel wings tattoo as well, because she seemed to know her way around.

Aura held the sandwich close to her lips, finishing her bite. "The sign on the door did say 'Closed,' right?" Her snarky attitude ever present.

Juliet opened her journal and flipped through the pages, tearing one out and handing it to Aura.

"I want this," she indicated. "Here." She rubbed the inside of her wrist where her scar sat. "Please?" she asked, taking off the Gear on her wrist.

I walked over, standing at Aura's side and taking in the sketch Juliet had made. Actually it was text. The thick black letters in an intricate font read *Non Domini*.

"What does that mean?" I looked up at Juliet.

"It's Latin. It means 'no masters.' "

She looked at me, holding my eyes as understanding passed between both of us.

No mothers. No fathers. No gatekeepers. Non domini.

I liked it.

Snatching the paper out of Aura's hand, I sat down in her chair. "Me first."

Juliet's smile spread over her face. "You?" she said, her eyes lighting up. "You're getting a tattoo?"

I arched an eyebrow. "If you're going to make a big deal out of this . . . ," I warned.

She shot out her hands. "No, no. I just don't want you making quick decisions that you'll cry over tomorrow."

"Yeah, well," I explained, "I like it. It speaks to me."

Actually I loved it. It was me, and it was the first thing I didn't mind having as a constant reminder every time I looked in the mirror. First thing that I felt I needed as a constant reminder.

"Okay." She nodded, accepting my answer.

Coming up, Juliet kissed me on the lips and plopped her notebook in my lap. "I'm going to the bathroom. Be back in a minute."

She walked away, locking her hands behind her back to keep her skirt from swinging up as she walked.

I shook with laughter no one heard and relaxed against the chair.

"I like her," Aura said softly, pushing up my T-shirt sleeve and cleaning the skin on my left biceps.

"Glad you approve," I mumbled.

And then I looked down. "Hey, I thought she wanted hers on the inside of her wrist. Why are you cleaning my arm?"

"She wants *hers* on the inside of her wrist. You're getting yours on the biceps."

I rolled my eyes, feeling like Jared's mom was talking to me. "You're a ballbuster. I'm surprised you're still in business."

I heard her snort. "You'll love it, and you'll be back for more."

"Maybe," I agreed, just to shut her up.

I splayed my hand across the cover of Juliet's journal sitting in my lap and fanned the pages, flipping through to see if she had any other tattoo ideas.

Her pen, clipped to the top of the journal, held her place, and I saw a journal entry.

Close it. Close the book.

I was closing it.

I meant to close it.

But I didn't.

Dear K.C.,

I read once that the best thing that can happen to a woman is to get her heart broken. Before that, she has no real sense of herself. No real sense of pain, because only in love does she know what it's like to find the one thing that gives her breath and then to lose it.

After that, she knows she can survive. No matter what relationships come and go, she can count on herself to pull through, and although it hurts, the break is necessary.

I woke up this morning before Jax did, and I started crying. I realized he was my first love—the one that should break my heart—and when he jumped off that cliff, I realized how much it would hurt to lose him.

What if he doesn't love me? What if he breaks my heart? He's not the one I wanted to learn this lesson on.

I never cried over losing Liam. I cried over his treatment, but I picked myself back up almost immediately.

The thought of losing Jax makes my throat tight, and I can't help it. I'm trying to be casual. To act like we're just having fun, because I know that's what he wants, but I don't feel that.

I love him.

I love him so much, and I don't want to, because I don't think he's ready to hear it. Why did my heart have to fall for him so quickly?

I closed my eyes and dropped the book to my lap.

CHAPTER 25

JULIET

Missed u last night.

stared down at the text I'd sent Jax two hours ago when I woke up. The same text I still hadn't gotten a response to yet.

"Should I pick you up after school?" Fallon asked next to me from the driver's seat.

I clutched the phone in my lap. "I don't know," I mumbled, unease twisting my stomach.

Where the hell was he?

After the tattoo sessions last night—during most of which Jax was silent—he'd said he wanted to me to stay with Fallon and Madoc until he'd upped the security on his house and Tate's. When I questioned that Tate was still staying in her house, he'd shot back with "She is Jared's responsibility," and he wasn't taking any chances with me.

Madoc and Fallon's house was off his father's radar, and it was secure, he'd said.

It was bullshit, and I knew it last night.

I would've believed him if he'd looked at me once during his tattoo. If he hadn't spent most of my time in the chair outside on his phone. If he had smiled at me or looked at me the way he always did.

But the warmth was gone, and something was wrong.

And it wasn't his father.

After I'd packed a bag, he drove me to Madoc's, kissed me, and left. I hadn't heard from him since.

Fallon was taking me to school—something that must've been arranged without my knowledge, because I didn't even have to ask.

I refreshed my phone, my head falling a little when I still had no reply.

"Yeah," I sighed, stuffing my phone in my bag, "if you could pick me up at noon, that would be awesome. Thank you."

I couldn't walk all the way to their house, after all. And I wasn't texting Jax to see if I was getting a ride from him.

I forced myself to swallow the huge lump in my throat as I wiped the sweat from my brow.

I didn't need reassurance every two hours that he wanted me.

I didn't need to be by his side every waking moment.

And I didn't do anything wrong.

The last thing I was going to do was overreact. I'd texted. He knew I was thinking of him. And he had a good reason for his distance. At least I hoped.

I was going to enjoy my day.

After the long weekend, I was ready to get back to school. Spending the Fourth of July at the falls would probably be the highlight of my summer, but I'd actually missed the classroom and my students.

My students.

Strange, now that I'd finally reached them to some extent, it was fun being there. I was going to be sad when it was over in a week.

"Here you go, babe." Fallon cruised up to the front of the school. "I'll be here at noon."

"Thanks," I said, unfastening my seat belt. "I'm sorry you have to play chauffeur."

"I have nothing else to do," she said matter-of-factly, smiling at me.

I opened the door, but she grabbed my arm. "Tate and I are going for a run this afternoon in the Mines. I know you're more of a gym person, but you should come. A good run will always show you how out of shape you didn't know you were." She smirked.

"Ohhhh." I smelled her challenge, my eyes widening. "Since you put it that way . . ."

I smiled, climbing out of the car and watching her drive off.

I took a deep breath, the weight of the messenger bag below my hip heavier with a phone that wasn't vibrating. I brought up my wrist, rubbing my thumb over the scar and wincing at the pain I forgot was there.

Looking down, I saw the new tattoo and let out a grateful smile, thankful for the reminder.

Non Domini. No masters.

Clutching the strap of the messenger bag, I entered the building.

"Keep going! Keep going!" Tate barked, swinging her arms back and forth like a machine.

I sucked in air—in and out, in and out—until I thought I was going to die.

Holy shit. This wasn't fun! This wasn't even on the same planet as fun!

But I needed to work off some steam.

I'd seen Jax on the field today, training the incoming lacrosse team, looking sweaty and angry and sexy, but when I'd finished my day, his car was already gone from the parking lot. It was stupid to want to cry over something so silly, but I was in knots.

He was ignoring me.

He could be busy or worried about his father, except he'd found time to come to practice but no time to call or shoot me a text?

Little shit.

I grunted, the anger fueling my muscles.

All three of us, including Fallon, were lined up side by side, doing step-ups as if the devil were chasing us, on the wooden staircase at the Mines of Spain.

My heart pounded like a mammoth beast stomping across my chest, and sweat drenched my stomach, face, and back.

And my ears! My fucking ears were sweating.

"I hate you both," I gasped, jamming up the step with my left, my right, and then back down. Again and again and again and . . .

Fuck!

"Come on," Fallon bellowed. "Faster! It's good for the ass!"

"My ass likes BodyPump!" I roared, my legs shaking more each second. "In an air-conditioned room with music and fans and a smoothie bar nearby!"

"Don't be a pussy!" Fallon's temple dripped with sweat.

"Keep going." Tate held the stopwatch. "Just one more minute!"

"Oh, God," I groaned, gritting my teeth. "Nachos and truffles and ice cream, oh, my. Nachos and truffles and ice cream, oh, my."

"What are you doing?" Tate demanded.

I swallowed through the dryness in my thick mouth. "It's what I say when the going gets tough at the gym," I breathed out. "It's motivation. Nachos and truffles and ice cream, oh, my! Nachos and—"

"Truffles and ice cream, oh, my!" they joined in as we all simultaneously picked up pace. "Nachos and truffles and ice cream, oh, my! Nachos and truffles and ice cream, oh, my! Nachos and—"

"And we're done!" Tate exclaimed, cutting us off and smiling through her exhaustion.

Everyone collapsed, relief washing over our tired bodies as our heads bobbed with each breath.

I was too tired to move. Too tired not to move. My legs bent up and then straightened, uncomfortable. My chest ached with the heavy exertion, and I leaned back on my elbows, finding myself getting nauseated, so I leaned back up again and over my knees, trying to get my heart to calm down.

I was out of shape. *Note to self: Need to do more cardio.*

We all sucked down the rest of our water, and I was glad they'd told me to tuck a hand towel into the back of my shorts. There was sweat everywhere, so I wiped off my stomach—bare in its sports bra—and my face, arms, and legs.

"So, do Jared and Jax have any idea where their father is?" Fallon threw her towel down and grabbed her water again, looking at Tate and then me.

"I'm sure if anyone has any idea it's Jax?" Tate spoke up and then glanced at me.

I shrugged, feeling a little lost. Jax was tough when it came to his father. He didn't tell me much, but I soothed myself with the fact that he and his brother probably didn't tell anyone much of anything.

"You know I've never agreed with my father's business," Fallon started, talking with her hands, "but this is one instance when Jax should've just let him take care of it."

"What do you mean?" I asked.

She pinned me with serious eyes. "My father offered to deal with him. Jax said no."

"Deal with him?" Tate repeated. "As in . . . ?"

"As in," Fallon inched out, "set him up with a new pair of cement shoes and go for a walk at the bottom of Lake Michigan."

My eyes bugged out.

By the way she'd confided, I knew it embarrassed her a little. Now I wasn't sure I ever wanted to meet her father.

"Jesus," Tate mumbled, leaning back on her hands and looking to the ground.

"Well"—I cleared my throat—"I'm glad Jax said no, then."

"Are you?" Fallon looked at me, amused. "Chickens always come home to roost, and your boyfriend is always one step ahead of everyone else." She picked up her towel and threw it over her shoulder, looking at me pointedly. "He doesn't disagree with what my father wants to do, Juliet. He simply wants to do it himself."

I spent the rest of the afternoon doing a great job of distracting myself. I completed my lesson plans for the last week of tutoring and then went swimming in Madoc's pool with him, Fallon, Tate, and Jared. They ordered pizza for dinner, but I excused myself to do laundry.

I needed to leave.

Even though Fallon and Madoc were welcoming, we weren't close. At least not yet. I felt as though I was freeloading, a piece of furniture that kept getting shuffled around.

Shane's parents might welcome me, but I'd feel the same there. I had little money, nowhere to live, and no real options that I liked, but it had to happen.

I needed a job, like yesterday, and then I'd see about finding someone who needed a roommate or had a room to rent. I had enough money to get me started, but I'd need a job to keep me going.

I hadn't felt as though I was floundering when I stayed at Tate's— or Jax's—but now the reality of everything that had happened in the past few weeks brought me to a sudden halt. I'd lost my college tuition, my mother, who even though she was a demon with an updo, was still there to catch me as far as providing the basics, and I'd lost my carefully planned future.

I was starting over.

I wasn't unhappy, but I was scared shitless. No one was taking care of me anymore.

I lugged a wash basket full of clean clothes into Fallon's old room and saw the light blinking on my phone that sat on the bed.

Racing to it, I frowned, seeing a missed call from Shane instead of Jax.

But then I let out a sigh and closed my eyes, mentally kicking myself.

Dialing her back, I didn't even let her say hello. "Dude, I'm sorry I forgot to call you. Shit. Don't be mad, okay?"

She was leaving for California, and we were supposed to spend time together.

"It's okay. It's okay." She laughed. "Really. But I am leaving tomorrow, and I want to see you tonight."

"Okay," I blurted out, thankful she wasn't yelling over my forgetfulness. "Well, I'm stuck at Madoc and Fallon's house with no ride and no license, so you'll have to come and get me."

"Wait . . . you're not at Jax's party?"

My face fell instantly.

Jax's party?

I lowered myself to the bed, my heart slowly creeping up my throat.

"Excuse me?" I breathed out, narrowing my eyes to keep my voice steady.

"Jax is having a party tonight," she stated, her tone serious. "It started an hour ago, and I was just about to head over, but I wanted to call to make sure you were there already."

I shook my head, breathing in and out as slowly as I could manage. "Yeah, yeah." I swallowed the lump in my throat. "I forgot about it," I lied. "Everything is slipping my mind lately. I'll meet you there, okay?"

"But you can't drive!" she yelled, but I hung up.

I jetted out of the room and down the stairs, bypassing mirrors for the first time in my life. After the pool, I'd changed into some cutoff jean shorts and a cute tank top, but my hair still hung wet from my shower, and I had on no makeup.

"Madoc?" I called, grabbing his keys off the counter. "I'm taking your car. I'll be back in a while."

"What!" I heard him yell from the patio where they were all still eating and playing.

But I was out the door before he even made it into the house.

Once on the highway, I cruised like a pro. It was only my third time driving a stick, and while my transitioning from gear to gear was still rough, I held it together damn well.

I wasn't really thinking about the driving. Or the car.

There could be a million and one reasons why Jax had been distant the past twenty-four hours. Reasons I would understand and be mellow about. I was agreeable, after all, and I'd played it his way.

Because I trusted him.

But there was no reason to have a party and not tell me. Nothing had been officially said out loud. Was I his girlfriend? Was I not? Who the fuck cared what we called it? He cyberstalked me, I gave him my body, and he pulled a knife on me! That shit affords me some kind of fucking explanation.

He didn't know I loved him, but he damn well knew I cared. What was his problem?

I pulled into Tate's empty driveway, already seeing the packed street and cliques of people carousing on his lawn.

I turned off the car and let out a tired breath, looking over at his house.

Everything was fine.

I closed my eyes, listening for a minute to Devour the Day's "Good Man" blasting from the house.

Everything was fine. I was overreacting.

He was worried about his father and wanted to get drunk or something, and he didn't want me to see. That was all.

He's still mine. I would keep repeating it to myself until I started to believe it.

I climbed out of the car and didn't break pace as Shane came running up beside me on the front lawn.

"Do you want me to go in first?" she asked, out of breath.

"Why?"

"He's having a party, and he didn't tell his girlfriend." She sounded worried, as if there would be drama.

"I'm not his girlfriend," I whispered.

I'm just his. I rubbed the chill from my naked arms, missing the blanketing warmth of his skin.

We walked into the house through the wide-open door and took in the sight of more people than I had ever seen at a party here before. I let my eyes drift up the stairs, seeing people head up and down and wondering where Jax was in this mess.

Was he wasted? Was he outside with his toys like last time? Was he even here?

Peering into the living room, the heavy smell of smoke hit me, and I saw dancers standing on the wooden coffee table. Two girls— still dressed, thank God.

The room was trashed, though. The partiers had made short work of spreading their Solo cups and beer bottles, spilling their drinks, and moving furniture around. A couple of pictures even hung off balance.

I narrowed my eyes. This party had been going for a while.

Walking into the family room, I scanned for Jax, my stomach twisting tighter when I didn't find him.

A guy swayed past me, stumbling over his feet, and the couple in the corner had lost their inhibitions completely.

Men roared from the kitchen, clothes were coming off, and everyone was wild.

Everyone was wasted.

I tucked my hair behind one ear and pushed through the kitchen, wincing when I noticed two girls in their bras playing some drinking game at the table.

What the hell? Jax didn't let shit like this happen. People respected his house and his belongings, and people kept their clothes on.

I stepped onto the back porch, instantly smiling through my relief.

There he was.

Playing with his toys, of course.

He was smiling, the black pants that I loved hanging low on his waist, and his long, muscular torso looking utterly gorgeous. His face was easy and relaxed, and he combed his hand through his hair, making my stomach flutter. I thought I saw him glance my way, but then someone said something to him, distracting him.

Everything was fine. He didn't even look drunk, either.

He laughed at something a friend said and then tossed his wrench into a box on the table. And then I watched, my smile falling, as he came up behind a girl . . .

. . . pulling her hips into his and burying his mouth into her neck.

What . . .

My breath shook, and I shot my eyes down to the floor, trying to steel my face, but the tears pooled anyway.

No.

I quickly glanced back up, desperately trying to keep the fucking tears away.

What the hell? My heart hammered, flooding my body with a nervous energy, and I fisted my shaking hands over and over again.

His fingers held her waist, and I could see her grinding her ass into him as her blond head fell back against his chest. His hand splayed across her stomach, bare in her half shirt, and his mouth touched her skin.

I clutched the wooden post in front of me, watching as he turned her around and let her put her arms around his neck.

I looked away again, wincing. He wasn't doing this. I knew Jax.

My mother, my father, Liam, no one got me, but Jax got me. We made each other better. He would never do this.

"Oh, my God," Shane whispered beside me, seeing what I saw.

I stood up straight, the ache in my chest making me want to crumble and cry instead.

Walking down the steps, I saw Jax's eyes fix on me almost immediately. His back straightened, and the girl with her hands all over him turned, following his gaze.

"Aren't you supposed to be at Madoc's?" He sounded pissed, dropping into a cushy lounge chair and bringing the girl down into his lap as if I was of no consequence.

"You son of a—," Shane barked, but I shot out my arm, stopping her.

I steeled myself and stood there, looking at him.

Only him.

Into those blue eyes that were mine, at least for a while.

I ignored his hand rubbing her thigh. It didn't hurt.

He was touching someone else, and I didn't want to scream, and my heart didn't bleed a thousand times worse than when I'd lost my father.

I clenched my fists and let the fucking lump sit in my throat.

It didn't hurt.

"Is she your girlfriend?" the blonde asked.

Jax smiled his cocky smile and touched her stomach, his thumb grazing under her shirt. "Well, if she is, I hope she plans to share." He kissed her cheek. "You're too sweet to give up."

She let out a quiet laugh and inched her lips into his face. "You just like me because I let you do anything you want to me."

Jax smiled, letting his head fall back as he looked up at me. "If you want to join in, we can all go up to the room."

Shane immediately hooked my arm from behind to pull me back, but I yanked it free, scowling down at Jax.

I'd always told myself that I deserved good things—that I was worthy—but fuck if I ever believed it. You can't tell yourself anything. Your heart only believes what it feels, and experience is the best teacher.

I reached forward, grabbed the girl's arm, and yanked her off Jax's lap.

"Hey," she whined, but I planted my hands on his armrests and glowered down at him.

His gorgeous face watched me.

"Why?" I demanded.

His eyes narrowed. "Because I can."

I shook my head. "This isn't you. You're not cruel, and you don't want her. Why are you pushing me away?"

"It's just summer fun," he retorted. "Now fuck me or fuck off."

I dug my nails into the chair, searching his eyes for anything soft. Anything warm and mine. Anything I could recognize.

But all I saw was his sick smile.

"I barely see her," I whispered, baring my teeth. "I only see you. Your father didn't make you unclean. The shit you've been through didn't make you dirty. This," I seethed, pointing at him and growling low, "this—right here, right now—is what makes you scum."

I pushed off the chair and backed up, seeing his eyes turn dark and wanting the guy who could barely control himself in the kitchen last week when I'd made him dinner. The guy who was jealous my ex-boyfriend called. The guy who called me his girl.

I wanted him to carry me up to his room and close the door so we could be lost in each other as if the rest of the world didn't exist.

But he just sat there.

I'd fought for Liam and look what that got me. It was someone else's turn to fight for me.

I turned and left, letting the hot tears fall. It fucking hurt. My lips pursed together, trying to stop the flood, but it was no use.

I hated him.

And I loved him.

And tonight he was going to be sleeping with someone else, or maybe he had already last night or today, and I was an idiot. I was a fucking nonstop train wreck.

I grabbed Shane's hand, squeezing it tight as I pushed our way through the crowd and out the front door.

I'd see him again. Probably a lot. And I cried more, realizing that. The tears burned my cheeks, and even though they just kept coming and coming, my sobs were silent. Misery usually was.

"Hey, where you going?"

I stopped, looking up at Tate through blurry eyes.

And Jared.

And, fuck me, Madoc and Fallon, too. I guess everyone decided to chase me down.

I sniffled, clearing my throat. "Home." I tossed Madoc his keys and took a step, but Tate grabbed me again.

"Hey, hey. Stop," she ordered, and I looked away when she held my shoulders. "You're crying. What's wrong?"

I said nothing. I didn't need to talk about it. I'd spent my life around people who taught me nothing, and now I just wanted to be alone for a while. I wanted to be proud of myself.

I'd grown up.

I wrapped my arms around her shoulders and squeezed her tight, my face pinching with the heartache and the tears streaming down.

"I love you," I whispered, and then pulled back and spoke to Jared. "I'm sorry I used you in high school," I said, and looked to Tate, whose eyes were bright with concern. "And I'm so sorry I hurt you. I was wrong, and I will never betray your trust again."

Tate's voice shook. "Juliet . . ."

But I'd already turned and left.

CHAPTER 26

JAXON

I *hate how Gordon walks behind me down the stairs. I want to see him com-*
ing, and I always feel as if he'll push me. I move faster than normal, the
bulge in my pocket giving me courage.

"There's my boy," I hear as I reach the bottom of the stairs.

My stomach shakes at the sound of her voice. Sherilynn, my dad's girl-
friend, is always the first to touch me, but I don't look up. Her frizzy red
hair, blond at the roots, and her smeared red lipstick always look the same.
Her clothes, too small for her body, remind me what she wants with me, and
everything is dirty.

Everything.

If I don't look I can imagine that she's pretty. Her wrinkled skin will be
soft, and I can pretend that her voice, hoarse from too many cigarettes, is
sweet.

I know there are pretty things in the world. Girls at school. My teach-
ers. Things could be clean and sweet and pretty. The moms who pick up my
classmates look as though they smell good.

I've never been hugged by someone who smelled good.

I curl my toes inside my old, cracked, secondhand sneakers, and I close my eyes as her hands go into my hair. My body feels sick, as if it wants to breathe but can't, and the world turns black.

The wet, cold smell of mold, cigarettes, and dirt fills my nostrils, and I want to puke.

"Do you want the other one?" Gordon asks behind me.

The other one?

Sherilynn strokes my face. "Yeah, I think it's time. Go get him."

I snap my head up, opening my eyes. "Who?"

"Your brother, dipshit." Gordon pushes my shoulder. "Time for him to join our fun."

I swing around, pushing Gordon's chest. "No!" I roar, and he darts out, grabbing my hair at the scalp.

"Why, you little shit." His hand flies across my face in a loud smack that echoes in the room. My cheek burns, but I don't stop.

I kick him and swing my arms. "Don't touch him!" I yell, my face hot with anger.

My father had just beat the crap out of him while I was in the freezer, and tonight I was getting us out of here. I had to get him home.

I swing furiously, not even thinking. No!

"Take him!" Gordon yells, and I tense as soon as I feel Sherilynn's fist in my hair, stinging my scalp.

Gordon lets go and his fist slams right into my face. I fall to the floor instantly, my ears ringing and my brain fogging over.

I hear footsteps on the stairs, and I dig out the knife in my pocket. The one I'd grabbed off the counter before they brought me down.

I slash at Sherilynn's leg, and she cries out, letting go of my hair immediately. Gordon stops on the stairs and lunges back down, charging me.

I stumble as I try to stand, my body heavy as I raise my fist and lunge at him. "Leave us alone!" I scream.

And sink the blade right into his neck.

He stops. He looks stunned.

Tears blur my vision, and I start gasping in breath as I watch him without blinking.

He stumbles and paws at the knife still lodged in the side of his neck.

And then he falls.

I back up to the wall, my eyes wide, and I watch him gasp and sputter for breath and the tears dry. I remember Sherilynn is in the room, but it's quiet. She should've screamed. I look over.

She's lying on the floor, a pool of blood next to her thigh.

I slide down the wall and watch them both eventually stop breathing. I don't go for help, and I don't cry.

The early-morning rain set in fast, and I just stared, sitting on the back porch with my arms resting on my knees.

The earbuds still sat in my ears, Hinder's "Better Than Me" poetically fucking with my head as I squeezed the damp piece of paper in my fist.

Holding her words tight. Holding all I had left of her.

I love him, and I don't want to. He's not ready.

I carried the journal page everywhere with me.

It had been four days. Four days and nine hours since she'd talked to me or looked at me or been in the same room with me, and every day that passed my stomach got more and more hollow and my muscles got weaker. I reveled in it. I wanted to suffer. I wanted the pain.

I was miserable without her.

School was the only place where I saw her, but she never looked my way. She sat in her classroom, working with her students and smiling, and then she'd stick in her earbuds and quietly walk home—all the way to Madoc's house. I hadn't seen her once over the weekend, and I hadn't checked on her.

I let my head fall, my stomach groaning with hunger.

I'd cut my run short this morning because I had no fucking energy. No energy because I had no appetite. No appetite because I was scum.

I ran my hand over the top of my head, pushing back the drenched hair and licking the rain from my lips.

"What are you doing?"

I lifted my head at Jared's voice, hooding my tired eyes. "I'm not in the mood."

"Well, we need to talk about our father," he pressed. "Have you been able to find him?"

Everything was tired, including my voice, as I stood up and walked toward him to the house.

"I really don't give a fuck about him right now," I said, exhausted.

"Jesus," he breathed out, grabbing my jaw to look at me, but I jerked out of his grasp. "When was the last time you fucking slept?"

I pushed past him and stepped into the kitchen, going for the refrigerator.

"Answer me," he pressed.

"Just leave me alone, Jared." I spoke calmly, but it was a warning.

He tossed his keys on the table and folded his arms over his wide chest. "I've left you alone for four days, because Tate told me to stay out of your business, but look at you." His eyes turned angry as he gestured at me. "You're pale. Your cheeks are sunken in. What the hell?"

The ache sitting in the middle of my brain spread down my neck, and I couldn't look at him.

"Why did you fucking cheat on her?" he asked me, sounding as if I'd made the dumbest mistake of my life.

I turned around and leaned against the sink. "I didn't." I shifted my eyes away from him. "I just wanted her gone."

The girl at the party was someone I'd hooked up with before, but prior to Juliet, I hadn't been with anyone in over a month. I didn't sleep around, and I hadn't been with anyone since her, either.

He stood there, silent, probably waiting for me to explain further, but gave up.

"I'm not K.C.'s—Juliet's, I mean—biggest fan," he said, taking a step forward, "but she was good to you, Jax. I don't understand this."

"You don't need to," I mumbled. "It's not your business. She just deserves better, is all."

"There is no better. There's nothing wrong with you." He sounded defensive. "She was lucky to have you."

"No." I shook my head. "She wasn't. I'd never be good enough for her. She was falling in love, and I . . ." I swallowed. "I didn't want her hurt worse. It was time to move on."

I crossed my arms over my bare chest, feeling Jared's eyes studying me. He was doing that more and more lately. Taking time to process and react. But when I looked up, I didn't like what I saw in his eyes.

Confusion and disappointment.

"Don't," I warned. "Don't look at me like that."

The corner of his mouth turned up in a condescending smile. "You always act so smooth, Jax, like you've got life figured out and you've got everyone else's number. You don't even have yourself straight." He shook his head at me. "It took me a long time to see it, but you really have no idea what the fuck you're doing, do you, Jax?"

My fists clenched, tucked under my biceps. "Don't," I bit out, shaking my head back at him.

He was wrong. Everything was going to be in order again. Neat. Organized. Clean.

He stepped forward, inching closer and taunting me. "You make money working for Fallon's father, you exchange favors with the cops, and you think you can sit up there in that office of yours playing God with everyone else under your thumb, because when it comes to you"—he darted his head out, getting in my face—"and your life, you need to avoid everything to control anything."

He crowded me, his eyes bearing down. "You can boast your power over everyone else," he continued, "but even you don't buy it. You think about where you came from and everything that happened to you, and you think that you don't deserve to have want you want. You think she'll end up being ashamed of you. Down deep, you think you're shit."

I shot up and scowled down at him.

"At least I cut her loose before it was too late," I growled, locking eyes with him. "Someday Tate will see through you. Ten years from now when you're living in the suburbs in your two-story Colonial with hardwood floors and crown molding, and you're trying to shuffle the kids into the SUV so you're not late for another fucking birthday party . . ." I nodded. "She'll see it."

He narrowed his eyes, taken aback.

I continued. "She'll see it, because you've stopped talking to her, you've stopped touching her, and the Boss has been under a tarp for years, and she can't figure out why you don't smile anymore." I held his eyes. "She didn't see that you took on a career you hated because you wanted to feel worthy of her. Because you knew how much a doctor would make, and you didn't want your wife to be ashamed of you. And she'll notice that over the years, your heart grew colder, the house grew more silent, and she'll cry at night because she sees how the new neighbor flirts with you and how you like it. It's the first thing in a long time that makes you feel alive."

Fear flashed in his eyes, and he watched me, not breathing.

I lowered my voice to a near whisper. "You're dying inside, and you're killing her along with you, and you don't even know it." I paused, seeing the pain in his eyes. "At least I cut Juliet loose," I said.

There was nothing more to say. Nothing he could tell me that I hadn't already called, and I saw the hurt all over his face, because he knew what I said was true.

We were both fucked.

"Jared?"

I shot my eyes up, and Jared jerked his head around, both of us seeing Tate take a slow, single step into the kitchen.

I closed my eyes, letting out a quiet sigh.

Shit.

Tears had welled up in her storm-blue eyes, and Jared and I both knew she'd heard everything.

"Is that true?" she asked, her voice cracking. "Are you unhappy?"

Jared dropped his head, looking away from her as the muscles in his jaw flexed. "Get the fuck out of here," he said through gritted teeth, and I knew he was talking to me. "I'm going to put you through a fucking wall. Get out."

He wasn't lying. And I deserved it.

I grabbed my shirt off the kitchen chair and left the house.

I had no right to judge my brother. Maybe he hated going to school, maybe he hated the military, but maybe Tate was his dream, and for her, he'd put up with anything because she was his happiness.

I'd felt like shit, and I'd wanted him to feel it, too.

When did I start hating everyone?

I drove the quiet streets, still desolate at seven thirty in the morning, as I thought about how screwed up my life had gotten in the past few weeks. The routine that I loved had lost its luster, and I'd be happy if I never looked at a fucking computer again.

Pulling a sharp right, I barreled into the school parking lot with only one thought in mind. To run myself to exhaustion around the track.

But as I pulled into a space, I slammed on the brakes, seeing Liam's Camaro parked next to the janitor's truck.

The janitor opened the school every morning at six thirty. What the hell was Liam doing here?

I threw open the door and climbed out, slipping on my black T-shirt before slamming the door and jamming up the steps.

Heading straight for the stairs, I climbed up to the second floor and headed for the chem lab.

Juliet wouldn't be here this early, but I still needed to make sure. My running shoes squeaked on the marble floor, but I heard his voice before I even reached the room.

"I loved you," he said, sounding pained. "I still love you."

I slowed, coming to a stop outside the door.

"I just never felt like you wanted me. Not really," he continued. "I was an asshole. I know that, but"—he paused, and I could hear his heavy breathing—"baby, I just hate seeing you with him."

I heard a chair scrape on the floor, and Juliet sounded stern. "You cheated on me. Twice," she pointed out, sounding out of patience. "You're cheating on what's her name right now by coming here. I have no doubt that I'm partly to blame for our relationship failing, but you're an incredible piece of work. Don't call me and *don't* try to see me again."

A slight grin lifted my lips.

"Now, just go," Juliet said, sounding exasperated.

"Baby," he breathed out, and I heard shuffling.

"Liam!" she cried. "No!"

I charged in, but I immediately stopped.

Liam was hunched over, holding the side of his face, and Juliet looked down on him, spitting fire with her eyes. She'd hit him.

"Let's pretend," she growled at him, "that we're in a parallel dimension where you have a brain. Nod if you know what's going to happen to you if you ever touch me again."

He scowled up at her, looking utterly humiliated, and then both of their eyes turned to me. Juliet blinked but looked back down at him, putting her hands on her hips, while Liam straightened and rubbed his cheek.

"Why am I even surprised?" he said, sneering, walking for the door. "You let me in your pants so quickly, I guess you didn't make him wait long, either."

I reached out and grabbed his collar, wanting his sleazy ass far away from her. I didn't even want him in her memories.

"Jax!" Juliet commanded, and I held him up to my face.

I looked into Liam's angry but scared blue eyes, and I whispered, "You touch her again, and you won't have to worry about what she'll do to you." And I shoved him out the door, watching him stumble into the hallway.

"Why are you here?" Juliet demanded behind me. "You're no better than him. You can get out, too."

I shook my head, knowing she was right, but I was still cemented to the floor. "No," I replied.

"Jax, what the hell do you want from me?" she yelled.

I turned around and rushed her. "This." And I pulled her warm body against mine and sank my lips into hers, tasting her sweet tongue.

She pushed her fists into my chest and pulled away from my mouth. "Get off me," she ordered. "Why don't you go find that girl you liked so much? She lets you do anything, doesn't she?"

Her angry lips and hot breath called me in, and I grabbed the back of her neck, holding her to me.

"I haven't had any other girls since you," I whispered. "And I don't want anyone else," I breathed against her mouth. "I just want you because it's the only time I know I'm exactly where I want to be, Juliet."

She tore her face away, tears running down her cheeks. "No."

"You feel it, too," I pressed, making her listen. "I don't want you on my arm." I jerked her into me. "And I don't want you to love me. Just come when I call, and get in my bed when I say."

Her lips trembled, and her breath shook as she tried to pry her body away from mine.

"And it'll be only you," I promised, my throat tight. "You're the only one I want."

I covered her mouth with mine, drowning out her whimpers and begging her with my body. My hands gripped her ass, pushing her into the edge of the desk, and I kissed her fast and hard. The salt of her sweat hit my tongue.

I pulled back, seeing her scared eyes looking up at me, but I didn't hesitate. Reaching behind her, I swiped my arm over the desktop, sending all of Penley's shit flying to the floor, and then I hoisted her up, claiming her mouth again.

"Say it," I demanded. I needed to hear the words.

But she simply pulled back and lifted my shirt over my head, throwing it to the floor.

I breathed hard, seeing the heat in her eyes, and tore open the buttons on my shorts as she undid the buttons of her shirt.

My cock sprang free, the pressure of needing her fucking body making me ache. I was swelled and hard, and she was doing this to me.

I bit her bottom lip, ready to fucking eat her as I hooked her under her knees and yanked her down to the end of the desk. Grabbing hold of her thong under her skirt, I ripped it clean from her wet, hot skin.

"Whenever I call. Whenever I fucking say," I ordered.

And I drove inside her.

"Ah," she whimpered, holding my neck.

"Goddamn it," I groaned. "So fucking good."

Leaning over her and grasping the back of her neck, I pumped my hips, sinking into her up to the hilt.

Her pussy tightened around me, holding me strong as I slid back and forth, faster and faster.

The small, hot bursts of her breath quaked against my neck, and I threaded my fingers through her hair, holding her there.

Right there against me—I closed my eyes—where I could feel every shake, moan, and beat of her heart.

And when her nails dug into my arms and she started crying out, I squeezed her body tight, barely noticing that she'd sunk her teeth into the bottom of my neck.

"Harder," I begged, still holding her by her hair and pressing her head into my skin.

She bit harder, her teeth trying to close around my skin, and I absorbed every moan and whimper coming out of her sweet mouth as she tried to keep herself quiet.

"Say it," I demanded. "I need to hear it."

She let her head fall back as she looked up at me and whispered, "Damn, baby, that feels good. I love you inside me."

I narrowed my eyes, hardening my tone. "Say it," I bit out.

"Mmm . . . ," she moaned, closing her eyes. "I'll be your good little slut. I promise."

What the fuck?

What was she doing? Why was she making it dirty?

I pulled out of her, spun her around, and lifted her skirt.

"You know what I want to hear, Juliet," I insisted, sliding back into her again. "Fucking say it!"

She pushed up on her hands, taking what I gave her as I gripped her hip with one hand and wrapped the other around the front of her neck, breathing into her skin. "Yeah, fuck me harder," she begged. "Is that it, baby? Am I good? Am I tight enough for you?"

My eyes burned, and I closed them, feeling my stomach roll. "Don't," I whispered into her neck. "Don't talk like that. It's not you," I said. "You know what I want hear. Three words. Please," I pleaded.

My chest shook, she felt so good, but this wasn't what I wanted. Not like this.

I wanted my Juliet.

Her head fell back softly against my shoulder, and I felt her breath on my skin. "You want to hear it?" she whispered.

A drop of sweat glided down my back, and I kissed her neck, feeling relief. "Yes."

She turned her head, her breath falling over my face, and she murmured, "I love you."

I snapped my eyes open.

"No," I said low, thrusting harder.

"I love you, Jax," she said sadly. "I love you so much."

"Stop it."

"I love you." She dropped her head forward, crying softly. "I love you."

I slowed my hips, coming to a stop as the muscles in my back tensed. I squeezed my eyes shut, a tear hanging at the corner.

"Baby, don't do this," I mourned.

"I love you," she repeated, shaking her head and crying. "Only. Ever. You."

I dropped my head and slowly stepped back, too ashamed to look at her. Why would she love me? I would never hold her above myself. I would never put her first. She deserved a man, not a scared kid in disguise.

I stared at the floor, anguish boiling under the surface of my skin as I blindly fastened my shorts and backed far away from her.

She straightened her back and turned around, her arms hanging limp at her side, but her shoulders squared and her stance strong. She was looking at me, but my eyes shifted, unable to reach her face.

Her pleated white skirt fell to her knees, and her white flats were planted on the floor, everything as still as a statue. Her sleeveless blue blouse hung off her arms in a mess, but her white bra sat against beautiful tanned skin that glistened with sweat.

That was my girl. Mine. And she was waiting for me to do something or say something, to be a man, and I couldn't fucking find the balls to take her back.

I heard her swallow, the room was so silent, and I just stood there as she quietly buttoned up her blouse, tucked it in, and walked out of the room.

I ran my hand through my hair and for the first time in my life, I actually wanted to get drunk. I'd never sought escape like that.

I headed for the door, bending over to swipe up my T-shirt and throw it on as I made my way out of the building.

Home. I'd go home, get obliterated, and check out, because I had no fucking clue what I was going to do without her or what my next move was.

Climbing into the car, I twisted my fist around the steering wheel and slammed the door, thankful that the parking lot was still empty. Very few people ever saw me mad, and I liked it that way. It's hard to anticipate what you don't understand, and I liked to keep myself in check. Most of the time.

I turned the ignition and blasted the stereo, the car vibrating under me. I shifted into reverse and checked the rearview mirror.

And stopped.

I narrowed my eyes, seeing her marks on my neck—her bite marks.

I reached up, running my fingers over the deep abrasions, feeling the dips where her teeth and mouth had been. She hadn't broken the skin, but it was bruised red and purple.

And I wanted to smile.

She'd bitten me.

My gutless, helpless wallflower was wild, after all.

Someday when she'd moved on, and she'd found another guy, I would be able to look at her and remember that she was almost mine.

I would be able to remember that while he slept with her every night, I had had her soft body—sweating and needy—in my arms, looking at me as if I were her angel.

I would remember that she loved me once.

I drove to the Black Debs shop and walked in the door, pulling off my shirt immediately. Sitting down in Aura's empty chair, I waited for her to come over from her desk with her hands on her hips as Jay Gordon's "Slept So Long" played in the background.

"Do you know what an appointment is?" she snarled. "Jared makes appointments."

I leaned forward, my elbows on my knees as I cocked my head, indicating the bite mark. "Tattoo it," I said.

She pushed my head to the left and inspected the mark up close. Standing up, she looked at me as if I were crazy.

"You sure?" she asked, her lip arching up.

I nodded. "I want to remember."

CHAPTER 27

JULIET

I jerked awake, yelping as my body vaulted up and down.

"Good morning, sunshine!" Madoc jumped on the bottom of the bed, sending me flopping. "I hope you're naked!"

I scurried for the covers, bringing them up to my chin. "Madoc!" I screamed, covering my face with the sheet. I was in my pajama shorts and tank top, but still!

"Come on, Tiger," Madoc taunted, still pouncing like a seven-year-old. "Time to stop snoring. Although it was supersexy."

He was joking. I didn't snore. Oh, God. Did I snore?

"Madoc, stop it!" I screamed, freaked-out by the half-naked man—someone else's half-naked man—jumping on my bed.

He wore some Polo lounge pants—I could tell, because there were little polo players all over them. And no shirt. And he shouldn't be in my room. His room. Fallon's old room. My room!

"Fallon!" I called for his wife.

"Madoc!" I heard her shout, probably from their room across the hall. "Leave her alone!"

"What?" He acted innocent but kept jumping. "Two hot chicks under my roof. I have a big bed, and Freud says everyone is bisexual. I say you two take a shower. I watch. Win-win."

I popped my head off the bed, fury burning my face. "Get. Off. The bed!" I bellowed from my gut.

"Whoa!" His eyes went wide, and he laughed as he dropped his whole body to lie beside me. "Is Satan your father or did he just raise you?"

I growled and threw the sheet over my face again. "I hate to complain, what with the free room and all, but . . ."

"Then don't," he said, brushing me off, pulling the sheet down. "Seriously, though. You have to get up. We're having a party."

"Huh?"

"Tate's dad flew in this morning," he started explaining. "His assignment is on break for a couple of weeks. And my dad and Jared's mom will be in town for the weekend. Everyone's kicking back," he sighed, lying back and fixing his hands underneath his head. "We're barbecueing and having a shitload of people over. We need someone to clear away the trash."

I jerked the sheet back over my head.

"I'm kidding." He pulled the sheet away again, grinning. "You know I love to tease you."

I rolled my eyes.

Playing with the hem of the blanket, I swallowed the lump in my throat. "Jax will be here, then?" I asked, not looking at him.

"Jax will be at the Loop," he shot back. "Adam will be here."

Who . . . ? Oh, right. Adam, his preppy friend. The one . . . I kind of ditched . . . when I got "lost" in the fun house. Yeah, class act right here.

Madoc rolled off the bed and walked toward the door, calling behind him, "Get dressed. Preferably in something Fallon can rip off with her teeth!"

"Madoc!" Fallon's screech poured into the room, and I shook my head, burying my laugh in my pillow.

Tutoring had ended yesterday, so this was my first day without anything to do or to plan. I started back at the movie theater tomorrow, reclaiming my first and only job from high school, and as much as I enjoyed the job back then—hey, who doesn't like free movies?—I was having a hard time getting excited. Spending the rest of the summer making minimum wage with kids who still went to high school felt like a significant step backward. But I knew it had to be done. I couldn't live with Madoc and Fallon forever, and not only did I need a job, but I needed two.

My phone started buzzing, and I popped my head up, grabbing it off the charger on the bedside table.

"Hello?" I sat up, not recognizing the number.

"K.C.?" a woman's voice asked. "Hi, honey. It's Meredith Kenney. Your mom's friend."

"Oh, hi, Mrs. Kenney," I greeted, puzzled as to why she was calling me. "How are you?"

"I'm fine. I was just calling to make sure your mom was okay," she explained. "She's missed the last two Rotary meetings, and when I've tried to call, I haven't gotten an answer."

I opened my mouth but then closed it again.

That was weird. My mother was always punctual, and I was sure she'd call if she needed to miss a meeting. Which never happened.

"Uh, well," I stammered, "I don't know. I'm sorry, Ms. Kenney, but I'm visiting with friends right now." Chills spread down my arms as worry set in. "I'll swing by the house, though, okay?"

"I've done that. No answer," she said. "Now I'm worried."

I shook my head, trying to figure out what could be up. I shouldn't be worried about her. Had she called me since I came to get my journals? No, she'd abandoned me, and I shouldn't care about her.

But she was alone. And I was different now.

"I'll check it out and get back to you." I nodded, throwing off the covers and standing up. "Thank you."

"I'll be waiting. Thank you, sweetie." And she hung up.

Grabbing a white summer dress from the closet, I dived into the bathroom, got dressed, and brushed my hair.

Snatching up my purse and fastening the Gear to my wrist, I stumbled into the hallway, trying to put on my sandals. "Madoc?" I called. "Can I borrow your car?"

"No!"

"Thank you," I chirped, jetting down the hallway and then the stairs, grabbing Madoc's keys off the entryway table before slipping out the door.

I had to hand it to Jax about one thing. I was glad he'd taught me to drive a stick. It was the only thing these people drove.

The drive to my house—my mom's house—took about twenty minutes, and even though it was hard not to speed in Madoc's car, I took my time.

I wasn't really worried about her. She always took care of herself.

But the truth was, I never worried about my mom. Her presence was constant, like a lamp or a car, and I hadn't really thought about her having a life unless I was there to see it. What did she do with herself when I was away at college? What did she think about when she was alone?

Who hurt her to make her so vile?

And now, for the first time in her life, she was causing others to worry.

Pulling up outside the house, I slowly climbed out of the car and shoved the keys in my purse. The brick stairs to my front door loomed ahead of me.

I didn't care. This wasn't my responsibility.

But I walked anyway.

Climbing the stairs up my lawn, I took out my key and unlocked the front door, taking in the sight right away of unopened mail spilling over the entryway table and onto the floor.

I studied the heap, letting the door close behind me.

What the hell?

I shifted my eyes left and right, noticing that the rest of the downstairs seemed completely in order.

Clean house, polished floors, everything same as always. Except for the vacuum plugged in and sitting in the middle of the area rug.

Other than that and the mail, everything looked fine. She had to be out of town, and someone was collecting the mail for her.

My shoulders relaxed.

Well, since I was here . . . I still had clothes, some keepsakes from my father, and—if I could handle it—my vintage Nancy Drew collection that I could pack up and still be back in time for Madoc and Fallon's party.

I set my stuff down on the round entryway table and jogged up the stairs. Swinging myself around the banister, I pushed through my bedroom door and jerked to a halt.

I sucked in a breath. "Mother?"

She lay on my bed, wearing her navy silk bathrobe, tucked in the fetal position, and I just stared as her eyes fluttered open.

Why was she in my bed?

She focused on the wall, not seeming to notice me in front of her, but then she blinked and looked up.

The sadness in her bloodshot brown eyes paralyzed me. This wasn't my mother.

Her unkempt hair was stuffed into a messy ponytail, stray hairs falling over her face, and the usual smooth surface of her cheekbones and jaw was now showing visible signs of age and stress.

She'd been crying. A lot.

Her eyes fell, and I watched as her shaky arms pushed her up to a sitting position. She barely had the strength to move.

Her heavy eyes were tired, and I swallowed the fat lump in my throat seeing the misery on her face.

My eyes stung.

"Mother?" I whispered.

And just then her face cracked. She broke into tears and buried her face in her hands, and I watched her, wondering what the hell was going on and if this was real. My heart felt as if it were being torn in two.

Tears blurred my eyes as I scowled at her. This wasn't real. It was an act.

She was hunched over, sobbing into her hands, and I shook my head, unable to believe her. I had no idea how to take this.

Then I saw my bedside table. There was a picture of my father with me.

Me. Juliet. Not K.C.

I was ten years old, and he had snuck me to a carnival without my mother knowing during one of his stints out of the hospital. He'd kept the picture in his hospital room, but I never knew what happened to it after he'd died.

She'd kept it.

And then I saw another picture. Cracked and dull, the photo was clearly old. Picking it up, I looked into the face of a little girl, standing with two adults. It was my mother as a child with her parents. Her father wore a suit as he stood above her mother, who sat on a chair, stiff with her hands resting in her lap. My mother—about thirteen or so—stood to the side, untouched. No one was smiling.

I looked back down at her, seeing her drop her hands to her lap and keep her head down as she fisted her robe and cried.

I blinked, letting my silent tears spill over. I didn't know what to do. I didn't love my mother. I didn't even know her.

But as I looked down at her and saw her broken life and the weight of her mistakes crumbling her composure, I felt the despair she must be feeling. What a horror it must be to realize you've gone too far to go back. And what pain it must be to have a life full of regret and know there are not nearly enough years to undo the damage.

Through all of her faults—the abuse, the neglect, the pain— she'd lost everything, and I was happier without her. I didn't fear her, and I could go right now and not lose anything.

But I didn't go.

I sat down, next to her on the bed, and waited for her to stop crying.

"Hey, you." Tate fell down next to me on the lawn chair where I sat. "Where've you been?"

"To hell and back," I muttered, sipping my wine cooler. "You know, the usual."

After my mother had calmed down, I got her in the shower, put her in clean pajamas, and made her eat a sandwich.

She didn't say a single word the entire time, and after she'd gone to bed—in her own room—I'd stayed until she was asleep.

I'd return tomorrow. And if she finally spoke and said things I didn't like, I would leave. But I had to go back to check on her. I was strong enough.

"So, where's your dad?" I asked Tate, looking her up and down and noticing the relaxed demeanor.

She blew out a breath. "Jet-lagged. Went home a while ago."

I narrowed my eyes, studying her with a slight grin. "Are you drunk, Tate?"

She snorted as if I'd said something funny, and I glanced over and saw Jared, sitting on a chair, staring off as he tipped back a shot of liquor. Aura hovered close to his side, sitting next to him and drawing on his biceps, the one that didn't currently sport a tattoo. Since she did everyone's tattoos, it was nothing to see her here. She'd become close to us all. But it was odd to see Jared drinking and Tate . . .

"You are drunk, aren't you?" I teased, but still felt somewhat concerned.

"I'm not drunk!" Fallon nearly bowled me over as she crashed to my other side. "I'm severely and illegally buzzed with my father standing right over there but definitely not drunk."

She and Tate laughed, and I smiled, peering over through the glass doors to the man she pointed at. Her father, the infamous Ciaran Pierce, who employed Jax, didn't look as intimidating as I thought he would. With light brown hair, grayed but distinguished looking, and wearing a suit coat, shirt open at the collar, and black slacks, he seemed more like a Ralph Lauren ad.

Bringing the bottle back up to my lips, I laughed quietly. "Well, I guess I'm behind then. I'd better catch up."

I hadn't gotten back to Madoc's until an hour ago. After I'd dealt with my mother, the afternoon had been shot, and by the time I'd shown up to the party, the "parents" had retired to the bar area in the basement, letting the young people have the pool.

"I need another drink," I said, standing up. Leaving them together on the chair, I walked to the beer tubs between the brick wall and the pool, both overlooking Madoc's extensive manicured lawn and the wooded area beyond.

The emerald green grass now looked navy blue with the moonlit sky overhead, and I envied that Madoc got to grow up here. No wonder he loved life the way he did. What person wouldn't who was allowed to roam and explore the way he must've been? He was the only one out of all of us who had had two loving parents. Except Tate.

"So, I hear"—a man's voice approached me from behind—"that you're not with that guy anymore?"

I turned, seeing Madoc's friend from the carnival. Adam.

That guy. Yeah. I closed my eyes and spun back around, embarrassed. I hadn't really thought about my five-minute setup with Madoc's friend, but after my disappearance in the fun house and reemergence with a half-naked Jax, I can't imagine what I looked like to this guy.

Easy. *That's what I look like.* I laughed to myself.

I tossed my warm, half-empty wine cooler away in the garbage can and grabbed another. "No," I sighed. "I'm not with him."

He stepped up to my side, taking the bottle out of my hands and twisting off the cap. "Good." He looked at me, full of suggestion as he handed the bottle back.

I turned and leaned on the edge of the half-brick wall.

"And Madoc says you might be staying here in town for college," he said, leaning on the wall next to me. "I'm in Chicago. If I were willing to drive back sometime, would you let me take you out?"

I let out a nervous laugh and looked away. "Believe me, I'm no fun right now."

"Why?"

I chewed the corner of my lip, thinking. Yeah, why?

Because I liked the idea of being alone right now.

Because the thought of another guy touching me made me sick.

Because just then I looked up and saw Jax come through the sliding glass doors, and I stilled, feeling every hair on the back of my neck stand up.

He had just stepped through, his tall frame filling the space as Madoc hooked his neck and hollered over the music.

Both were smiling, and I noticed Jax's friends—a small crowd—trailing him. Everyone had no doubt just finished at the Loop.

The heat outside escalated, making my white sundress stick to my body, and everything felt tight inside me. Watching him happy and talking to friends. Watching him carry on, not knowing I was here and falling apart because he was so close and yet too far away.

"Are you okay?" I heard Adam ask, and I blinked, coming to my senses.

Taking a deep breath, I gave him an apologetic smile. "I'm sorry Madoc tried to set us up and wasted your time." I stood up. "I don't think I'm interested in seeing anyone for a while."

"No relationship, then," he shot out, shrugging. "Purely physical. It'll be tough, but I can do that."

I busted up laughing, shaking my head at him as he smiled.

"See you around, Adam." I tipped my bottle at him and walked away.

I didn't want to see Jax, and my friends were already drunk, so I just made my way back into the kitchen to grab a few things before I headed to my room.

Picking up my purse from the table, I dug out my phone and checked for any missed calls from my mom.

None. Hopefully she was still sleeping. I walked to the fridge for a bottle of water, thinking maybe I should've stayed the night with her. Maybe Madoc would let me take his car again.

"Adam," the deep voice said, startling me. "He must be a good guy if Madoc is friends with him."

I looked up, seeing Jax nod gently as he stood on the other side of the dark gray granite island with his T-shirt tossed over his shoulder.

I braced myself, turning away from his eyes as I slipped my phone back into my purse.

His slow footsteps fell behind me. "He looks like he comes from a good family."

I focused on the cabinets ahead, speaking firmly. "What does someone who comes from a good family look like?"

Did he think he wasn't good enough? Or that his baggage was too heavy? After everything he knew about me, that couldn't be what he was worried about.

I felt him brush against my back, but he didn't put his hands on me. His voice hovered everywhere, though. "Do you want him?" he asked in barely a whisper, and I winced.

Jesus.

"Yeah, I want him." I swallowed the tears. "Five days ago I let you fuck me on a desk while I cried and told you I loved you, but I want him."

Turning around, I locked eyes with him, unable to hide the pain I was feeling. He raised me up and then tore me down, and I knew it showed.

And then I dropped my eyes, noticing them. He'd pulled the T-shirt off his shoulder, and my composure broke. I let my stunned gaze wander over his naked chest, seeing the bite-mark tattoo on his neck and the script over his heart.

These violent delights have violent ends.

"Oh, my God," I whispered, remembering the words from *Romeo and Juliet.*

"*I don't care about anything that much.*" He'd said that when I asked why he didn't have tattoos, and now he had three. He had my bite marks.

I reached up to touch his face, but he pulled away from me, backing up.

His face looked so childlike, confused, and sad as if he didn't know what move to make next. Then his stunning blue eyes blinked, and he finally looked up at me.

"Everything was real," he rasped, his usual stone expression gone. "But he'd be better for you, Juliet. Anyone else would but me."

He backed away and finally turned, walking out the patio doors, while I just stood there staring after him.

My face ached, and everything hurt. Everything, all at the same time. And I brought my hand back to my chest, trying to soothe my heart.

No more.

I set my bottle down and left the room, walking toward the stairs without even one glance back. I was going to bed, and then I was going to rebuild my life.

Closing the door to my room, I felt my phone vibrate, and I shoved my hand into my purse, letting out a heavy sigh. This day needed to end.

Seeing a number I didn't recognize, I answered anyway as I threw off my purse. "Hello?"

"Juliet Carter?"

"Yes?" I plopped down on the bed.

"Hi, this is First National. We're calling to verify recent activity on your account?"

My bank? I sat up, wondering what recent activity they needed to verify. I hadn't purchased more than a Diet Coke with my debit card in over a week.

"Um, okay," I answered, giving her the go-ahead.

"We have a deposit made into your checking account yesterday," she started, "in the amount of fifty thousand dollars . . ."

Fifty what?

". . . and then a transfer out of your account," she continued, "in the amount of twenty-nine thousand five hundred to Arizona State University."

I felt my heart leap in my chest, and I shot off the bed, gritting my teeth. Twenty-nine thousand five hundred was exactly what my out-of-state tuition cost.

She spoke up again. "Do you verify this activity, ma'am?"

I jerked the phone away from my ear and clicked END.

"Motherfucker," I snarled, shoving my feet back into my flip-flops and tossing my phone on the bed.

Running back downstairs, I rushed into the kitchen, seeing Jared sitting alone at the kitchen table, Three Doors Down's "Here Without You" drifting in from outside.

"Where's Jax?" I demanded.

"Just left," he answered, resting his hand on his chin. "Need to borrow my car?"

And he slid his keys across the table, shocking me. No one drove Jared's car.

But he was in a mood, Tate was drunk, and shit was wrong. And I couldn't think about other people's problems right at this moment, so I grabbed them and ran.

"Thanks," I called.

Jamming out the front door, I climbed into Jared's car, turned it on, and released the clutch as I pressed the gas.

And my angry shoulders sank when the car stalled.

New car, new sweet spot. I hate clutches!

Okay, not really. Turning the ignition again, I shifted my feet, feeling for it the way Jax had taught me, and finally took off. Accelerating quickly, I shot into second gear and then third, not stopping as I barreled onto the highway without even checking oncoming traffic.

Pushing in the gas, I shot into fourth and then fifth, barely noticing the trees flying by. Lord help any animal crossing the street, because the only thing lighting up the road were my headlights. There was no way I would be able to stop quickly.

I squinted, seeing the taillights of another car, and immediately recognized Jax's NATIVE license plate.

Speeding up, I damn near climbed on his ass, letting him know loud and clear that I was here, before swerving around him and cutting in front of him on the road. He honked his horn and swerved, probably afraid I would hit him.

But I knew he had to recognize Jared's car.

Jerking the wheel, I skidded to the side of the road, where I pulled to a stop.

I heard the gravel kick up under the tires and saw Jax had come in right behind me.

I pushed my hair behind my ears and turned off the car.

"What the hell are you doing?" I heard him shout from behind me, and I swung the door open, climbed out, and slammed it shut.

"You know what?" I shouted, charging up to him. "I had a clean-cut boyfriend from a good family. His mom made brownies, and his dad played golf with the mayor." I shoved Jax in the chest. "He cheated on me!"

He stared at me wide-eyed as I pushed into his space again.

"And Shane dated the student class president," I pointed out, advancing as he retreated. "He got straight A's, wore cuff links to church, and his pants were always ironed." I shoved Jax again, watching him stumble. "He was gay!" I yelled.

I bared my teeth and kept pushing him. "You know that football jock who's on the cover of this magazine or that?" I jeered, shoving his chest again. "Well, he date-raped a girl in college. Or how about the mom you were jealous you didn't have in the third grade?" I pushed him again. "Yeah, she's on every antidepressant under the sun!"

He just kept backing up, speechless, with shock written all over his face.

"Stop being a fucking moron," I growled, "and break the cycle, asshole!" I pushed him back again. "It's all an illusion, Jax! There's nothing wrong with you, and there's nothing in this world better than you!" I cried, gritting my teeth and feeling the tears pool in my eyes.

"You saved me, and I love you!" Every muscle in my body was hot with fury. "You're the best thing that ever happened to me! The best thing in my life, jerk-off!" Completely worked up, I slapped him on the arm, seeing him wince but take it. "And if you don't want me"—I slapped him again—"then stop taking care of me!" I ordered.

"Take your tuition money," I snarled, shoving him again with all my weight, "and shove it up your ass!"

And I whirled around, marching back to Jared's car as I swiped my hand across the tear on my cheek.

Asshole little shit.

But before I reached the car, Jax hooked my elbow and spun me back around.

"Come here," he growled, and lifted me underneath my arms, holding me above him.

I gasped, looking down at him and seeing the veins bulging on his neck.

He smiled, excitement flashing in his eyes as he stared up at me. "I fucking love you, baby."

My eyes rounded, and I whimpered at the shiver shooting straight from my heart down to my core.

"Huh?" My voice was barely a peep. *Oh, my God.*

He shook his head, surprise and happiness written all over his face. "I do. I love you, Juliet. And you're right, okay?" He nodded. "You're right. I thought I wasn't good enough. I thought you'd wind up being sorry that I was in your life, that I wasn't the man I was supposed to be, and I wouldn't be able to make you proud. But I was wrong. We belong together."

And he brought me down, crushing his lips to mine.

The moan came from the back of my throat, and I wrapped my arms around him, holding him tight.

He kissed the corner of my mouth and hugged me close, whispering against my neck. "I love you, and if you love me," he breathed out, "and I've been good for you, and you're not lying to me about that, then I'm keeping you. I'm fucking keeping you."

"Jax," I cried softly, letting my head fall back as he moved his lips over my cheeks and jawline. "I love you so much. Only ever you."

His arms, still under mine, reached behind me and threaded through my hair, holding my face still. "Don't go to Arizona," he whispered against my mouth. "You belong with me, and I don't want you more than ten feet away. Ever again."

His soft lips melted into mine, playing with me in short, deep kisses.

"Okay," I muttered between kisses, "but you have to stop paying for things."

He backed me into Jared's car, one hand holding my neck, the other skimming down my back to grab my ass. "How are you going to pay for college, huh?"

I kissed him again. "Loans."

"College loans are slavery." He kissed me again, pressing himself between my legs.

My eyelids fluttered, the wave of his heat hitting me hard. "If we don't work out," I gasped, "I'll owe you money. So no."

"And if we do work out"—he hoisted my legs up and around him—"it'll become my debt. So no."

I grinned, eating up his lips fast and hard. "Tomato, to-mah-to."

I fired a trail of kisses across his jaw, fingering his nipple rings through his black T-shirt.

"Shit. You need to stop." He twisted his head, his eyes closed and looking utterly undone. "You're obsessed with those damn things."

"Yep." I lightly bit his neck, close to the bite-mark tattoo. "Oh, and I'm not doing any threesomes with Cameron," I pointed out, laying down a stipulation of my own.

"I know."

I nibbled his neck. "At least not for a while," I clarified.

I felt his chest shake with laughter. "I love you."

"So get me to a bed."

CHAPTER 28

JAXON

"No!" Juliet squealed, running after me into the hallway as I halted in front of my office door, blocking it.

I tipped my chin up, challenging her.

"I want in!" She planted her hands on her hips, a smile tugging at her stern lips.

I shook my head, biting back a laugh.

"I want to see, Jax," she ordered. "Move!"

"There's no porn in there, I promise!" My chest shook as I secured my hands above my head on both sides of the doorframe. "But we can make porn if you want."

Her eyes narrowed, and I let mine scale down her cute little body in my dark gray V-neck T-shirt. It was after midnight, but we hadn't been to sleep yet.

She stood there for a few seconds, eyeing me, and then sighed. "Well, I'll get in there eventually." She brought a hand up to her mouth and faked a yawn. "I'm tired. Coming to bed?"

I smirked, stepping away from the door to follow her, but then I let out a laugh when she spun back around, darted to my side, and tried to get past me again.

"Oh, no, you don't." I caught her, my chest rumbling with laughter as she squirmed in my arms.

"I will get in there!" she shouted, hunching over as she tried to squirm away.

"Of course you will," I whispered in her ear. "I'd like to relive that desk chair. And the window," I added. "Tonight."

She twisted her head around to look at me, and I felt her body relax as she smiled gently at me.

And then her stomach growled.

"Ugh," she sighed, dropping her head back. "Of course."

I let out a quiet laugh. "You need to eat more," I said as I unwrapped my arms and stood up straight.

She glared at me. "I would if you'd stop trying to keep me on a Jax-only diet." She waved her hand. "Go shower. I'll make sandwiches. And popcorn," she added. She must've seen all the different seasonings and bags of popcorn in my pantry.

"Okay." I held up my palms in a hands-off show and backed away to the bathroom, making sure she went down the stairs instead of trying to trick me again. I actually didn't mind her in the office. I just liked playing with her.

And she certainly wouldn't find any porn, so there were no worries there.

I closed the bathroom door and switched on the light, leaning over to grab a towel off the shelf.

A scream pierced the air, and I dropped the towel, my heart stopping.

"Jax!" Juliet shrieked, and I wasted no time.

Yanking the door open, I bolted into the hallway and thundered down the stairs, fear filling my chest as I leaped and landed in the foyer.

Racing for the kitchen, I stumbled, feeling something hit my head, and then I fell to the floor.

I growled, yanking and thrashing at the handcuffs and feeling the sting of broken skin as I pulled against the metal.

"You're dead!" I raged, planting my feet against the bottom step as I sat on the floor and used the leverage to push myself against the strain of the cuffs wrapped around the banister. "You better fucking kill me, because you're dead!"

I gritted my teeth and pulled with every muscle in my body. I curled my wrists and felt sweat glide down my temple as I held my breath and pulled until my body was burning.

Juliet. He had her. My father fucking had her!

My heart thundered in my ears, and all of a sudden I was in the basement again. Powerless. A hostage. Forced.

When I ran downstairs, someone had hit me over the head. I wasn't knocked out, but I was knocked off my feet, and by the time I'd been able to stable myself, I was handcuffed to the banister.

Blood trailed down my arms from where the cuffs cut my wrists, and I kicked the stairs, growling my frustration as I thrashed.

"I'll kill you!"

"You know," my father started as if he hadn't heard me, "between your brother's girl and yours, I can't tell who's got the better piece of ass." He narrowed his dark blond eyebrows, thinking.

"The blonde is more athletic. Nice thighs," he continued, his jeans-clad legs sauntering over to Juliet sitting in a kitchen chair in the middle of the foyer. Another man—a friend of my father's, I assumed—had his hands on her shoulders, keeping her in place.

"But your little brunette here?" He ran a finger up her bare arm, and I clenched my fists, my stomach blazing like a bonfire.

"She's petite but a handful in all the right places." He smiled and turned to me. "My sons sure know how to pick 'em."

I locked eyes with Juliet, seeing the fear on her face that was almost completely covered by her hair. Her cheeks were dry, but I could tell by the way she fingered her scar that she wasn't okay.

My father's blond hair had grayed over the years, but his blue eyes still pierced the darkness. Even though the wrinkles showed a hard life spent abusing his body, he still stood strong and muscular, and it made me sick.

I should've let Ciaran kill him in prison.

I breathed in and out, lowering my voice. "Touching her will be the last mistake you ever make. Don't be stupid," I said to his friend, a heavy-set man about the same age as my father, tall with greasy black hair.

Juliet started crying, and I shot my worried eyes to her.

"Please don't hurt us," she sobbed. "Please, Mr. Trent! Just—just let me leave Jax's house! Please!"

I blinked. Let *me* leave?

And that was when I noticed it. The Gear I'd given her.

She hadn't been holding her wrist and fingering her scar. She'd been holding her wrist, pretending to cower, as she used the fucking phone.

Holy shit. I hadn't seen her dial, and I hadn't heard it ringing—which I would since it was a speakerphone. Thank God she'd been smart enough to mute the sound.

I swallowed down my pride in her, afraid it would give us away.

"Please don't hurt me!" Her shoulders shook as she clasped her hands in front of her chest. "Please! Just let me leave. I won't tell anyone. Please let me leave Jax's house!"

Her head hung low, the long strands of her chocolate hair falling around her and covering the fact that she was talking into her watch.

My father raised a knife, and I . . . *my knife*. I swallowed, realization hitting me. He had my knife. From my pocket.

He slipped it inside the V of my shirt that she was wearing and traced her skin with the blade.

I jerked, fighting the fucking cuffs. "Stop!" I bellowed. "Just let her go, and you can deal with me!"

He turned his head, regarding me. "What do you think I'm doing?"

The knife dipped down under the hem of the shirt sitting at her thighs, and I felt the bile rise in my throat.

No.

He was touching her, and I felt the fire on my face as I growled against the restraints, damn near ripping my goddamn shoulders out of their sockets.

"Fuck!" I kicked and pounded.

Tears blurred my eyes, and I gasped, desperate, because I couldn't get free. *Please not your hands. Don't touch her with your hands. Please.*

I let my head fall back as I threatened, "You shouldn't have come here. It was a mistake."

"No, no." He yanked Juliet up under her arm and dragged her over to me. "Your mistake was in ignoring me." He stared down. "There was a time when you needed me, and I helped. Now I want what's owed to me."

"I owe you nothing!" I shouted.

And then he held the knife up to her throat, and I sucked in a breath.

"Your arrogance is going to get her hurt," he warned, and I saw a tear fall down her frozen face.

"Now we're going upstairs to your little computer room." He dug out a small piece of paper from his pocket and showed me. "And you'll have exactly five minutes to access this account and transfer everything in it into this account." He pointed with his finger. "At minute six, he starts having a lot of fun with her." And he jerked his chin to his friend behind them.

My father was a lot of things, but he definitely didn't make threats he didn't intend to keep. Something Jared and I inherited.

I shifted my eyes to Juliet, seeing that her smart watch was still on and wondering how much time I had. My father wouldn't hurt me—not fatally as long as he could use me—but he'd hurt her. In a moment he'd hurt her without any hesitation from his sick, twisted mind.

And this was what I'd wanted her to be a part of? What if I gave her kids and we ended up getting terrorized by him again? Or what if he took her with him today?

He couldn't be allowed to leave.

Juliet yelped, and I snapped my eyes up, seeing a thin line of blood surface as the knife trailed down her neck.

"Stop!" I yanked at the cuffs, kicking the banister, knowing it wouldn't break. "Fuck! Leave her alone!"

"Are you ready, then? Huh?" He pulled the knife away and bellowed, "Now do you fucking get it, you worthless little bastard?"

At hearing one of the names he was always fond of calling me, I felt my throat ache with tears and then I exhaled. "Fine," I gritted out. "Just stop touching her."

I saw him relax and smile. "There." He nudged Juliet. "He does love you. Now go sit your ass down, and be a good—"

She slammed him across the face, cutting him off.

Oh, no.

With both fists locked together, she knocked him to the side again, making him stumble, and I watched with fear and awe as she snatched my knife out of his hand and ran for the kitchen.

Fuck.

I started yanking at the cuffs again, but the other guy was on her before she got far. He lunged, pushing her down to the floor as they both fell, and she kicked her legs as he tried to catch hold.

"Help!" she screamed, trying to scurry away. "Help! Someone, help!"

"Come back here," the other man growled, ripping her shirt as she thrashed.

"Don't touch her!" I yelled, struggling against my raw wrists, stinging the torn skin even more.

"Stop her!" my father yelled, and grabbed a gun I hadn't seen out of the back of his pants.

But then I heard the other man cry out, and I snapped my eyes over to see him holding his face, a deep red slash marring his face.

Juliet scampered backward as he stumbled away from her, and I watched her come to her feet, holding my knife out and looking at my father.

And her eyes went wide when she saw the gun to my head.

"You're killing him," my father threatened, pressing the nozzle to my temple.

I blinked long and hard, a dozen different scenarios of what to do running through my mind. The cuffs cut into my skin and held me too tight. I hated this. I fucking hated this!

"How can you do this?" Juliet shook her head. "He's your son."

"That's right," my father shot back. "He is. He's my son." And then he looked down to me, baring his smoke-stained teeth with every word. "Your mother didn't want you, so who took care of you? Huh? Who cleaned up your mess in the basement? I built you. I'm all you've got, Jax."

No. I had a family. Jared, Katherine, Madoc. Juliet. I had a family.

"Get away from him." I heard Juliet's voice as I held my father's eyes.

"You know it's true," he pressed, looking at me calmer now. "She'll leave. All bitches do. You won't be good enough. You won't make enough money. She'll find something wrong with you or another guy."

No. She loves me.

"And Jared resents you," my father continued, "because you're smarter. You're stronger. He'll always put himself first when you need him most."

I dropped my eyes, feeling the vein pulse in my neck.

"Jax, look at me!" Juliet urged.

"And Katherine?" he jumped in, laughter coating his tone. "That cunt barely stayed sober enough for her own son. You don't mean a thing to any of these people," he said, sneering. "They have no connection to you. You'll be the first thing they all dump when life gets too hard. You're the *only* one that doesn't belong!"

"Shut up!" Juliet screamed. "Jax! Look at me!"

I shook my head, wanting him gone. Wanting them all gone.

I was good enough. And no matter who left, who forgot about me, or who looked down on me, I wasn't the little shit kid, lonely and crying in my room, anymore.

But then I blinked, coming out of my thoughts. We all straightened, hearing the screech of hot tires skidding to a halt outside.

A flood of headlights shone through the porch windows, washing over us, and I looked over at Juliet and jerked my head to the back door, telling her to get out of here.

But she squared her shoulders, defiant.

My father was fucking desperate, and everyone knew what was outside.

And what was coming. I looked at her, pleading.

I heard more tires, recognizing Tate's and Madoc's engines as if they were my own.

My father shifted, and I quickly glanced at the other man, hunched over next to the couch, still holding his face.

Footsteps pounded on the porch, and my father pressed the gun into my temple as Jared kicked through the door, taking in the sight of me on the floor.

"Get away from him!" he thundered at our father.

And he and Madoc charged in, rushing him and not giving anyone time to think or assess.

My father raised the gun. *Shit!*

"Stay back!" he yelled, but Jared reared back and threw a fist across his face, making him drop the gun.

Tate's dad ran in—closely followed by Tate, who must've gone to get him next door—and he rushed over, guarding the other guy on the floor. My brother backed our father up to the wall, he and Madoc grappling for his arms.

Everyone poured in: Tate and Fallon ran for Juliet, Tate bringing her hand up to the gash on Juliet's neck. Katherine and her husband, Jason, followed, Katherine rushing over to me, tears already streaming down her face.

And Fallon's father, who'd come to the barbecue, stepped in, looking calm as he took in the scene as if it was nothing he hadn't seen before.

"Oh, my God," Katherine cried, looking to Jason. "Get these off him," she pleaded, pulling frantically at the cuffs.

"Jared!" Tate yelled, and I jerked my head to see my brother slamming another fist into our father's gut as Madoc held him.

"Are you okay?" Katherine asked, holding my chin to inspect my face.

I nodded, breathing hard. "Just get the key. Please." I rolled my wrists, desperate to get out of the restraints.

Katherine shot her eyes up. "Jared!" she barked at her son, standing up. "Enough!" And she rushed over to my father, her ex-husband, and dug everything out of his pockets until she found the key.

She unlocked me, and Jason helped me up as Jared grabbed the gun off the floor and pointed it at our father, keeping him against the wall.

I threw the cuffs to the floor and immediately locked eyes with Juliet. Her bloodshot eyes and the worry written all over her face told me everything I needed to know.

She rushed over, letting out a cry as she threw her arms around my neck. I scooped her up, holding on to her as if I needed her to breathe.

Because she filled my heart, and this was it. All I needed or wanted.

My father laughed, breaking the silence. "You know it's true, Jax," he taunted as I closed my eyes, inhaling her scent. "No one wants you but me. I'm your family." He raised his voice. "You're my son!"

"He's *my* son." I heard Katherine's deep, tear-filled voice, and I pulled my head back, staring at her.

She met my eyes, and I saw her tears for me. Her fear and her worry, and in that moment, for the first time in my life, I felt as though it was true. I had a mother.

"And he's my son, too."

I snapped my eyes over, seeing Jason step forward, next to her.

"Hell, mine, too." Ciaran nodded.

I narrowed my eyes, stunned, as I looked at these people.

And then Tate's father stepped forward, nodding once, and my chest swelled.

What the hell?

Jared dropped the gun on the table near the stairs and stepped back, looking at our father. "And he has me."

"And me." Madoc got in my father's face.

"Me, too," Tate called out, and I saw Fallon step forward as well, folding her arms across her chest and scowling at Thomas Trent.

I blinked away the stinging in my eyes, but I couldn't swallow over the lump in my fucking throat.

I couldn't believe it.

I'd never really thought that they didn't love me, or at least like me, but I guess I didn't really believe it until now.

This was my family.

"Jax." Ciaran stepped forward. "Just say the word."

I looked down at Juliet's glittering green eyes, rubbing her chilled arms, and I knew exactly what I wanted. Exactly what I needed to do.

I dug out my phone, making a call as I walked over to stand right in front of my father and look him straight in the eye.

"Hi," I answered when the call picked up. "This is Jaxon Trent. Twelve forty-two Fall Away Lane. We need the police. Two men have broken into my house. No ambulance needed."

I hung up and handed the phone to Jared. "I'm going to bed," I said, and then walked away. "Tell the cops I'll be down in the morning to file my report."

I circled Juliet's waist, scooped her up under her knees, and carried her up the stairs, cradling her in front of me.

Stepping into the bathroom, I kicked the door shut behind us and set her on the counter. I skipped the lights and instead lit the candle sitting on the sink counter.

Her forehead immediately fell against my chest, and I felt her shoulders shaking. "I love you," she whispered.

Clasping the back of her neck, I kissed her hair. "Are you okay?" I asked.

She nodded into my chest, and I pulled her back, tipping her chin up to look at the cut my father had made.

The thin crimson line had stopped bleeding, but guilt weighed me down. "We should go to the hospital," I said, concerned.

She closed her eyes, shaking her head. "I'm fine," she assured me. "I don't want to leave. Just you and me. No one else."

Yeah. I felt it, too.

"Come here." I pulled her off the edge and lifted the shirt over her head, letting the thin, gray fabric pool on the floor.

Hurrying over, I turned on the shower and stripped out of my clothes and then came back to her. She slipped her underwear down her legs, and I hoisted her up, wrapping her legs around my waist.

I carried us into the tub, feeling both of our bodies erupt in chills with the soothing touch of the hot water pouring down over us. Sitting, I kept her straddling me as I lay back and brought her body down against mine, holding her tight. Her cheek rested against my shoulder, and I closed my eyes, indulging in this dark, warm, and cozy cave we'd created.

Yeah, we were escaping. Behind a locked door and under the guise of getting a shower, but we deserved it.

I rubbed her back in circles, remembering how she'd fought tonight. How she'd fought for me.

Other than Jared, no one had ever done that.

I had set out to turn Juliet's world upside down—draw her out—but in the end, it was me who had his world flipped on its side. I'd fought for her, but she'd fought for me, too, and even though I'd been scared to let her in, it was all worth it.

Nothing mattered without her. She nuzzled her lips into my neck, and I tightened my arms around her waist.

"I want to stay here forever," she said, sounding calmer.

I smiled, liking the sound of that.

I kissed her temple. "Forever."

CHAPTER 29

JULIET

We didn't stay in the shower forever. Three days later, we had our bags packed and plane tickets in hand.

"You're not wearing any makeup," Tate observed as I threw my new hiking backpack into Jared's trunk.

I stuffed the bag down, trying to fit it next to Jax's. "I know."

"And you're wearing a baseball hat." She pointed this stuff out as if waiting for an explanation.

I slammed the trunk closed and smiled at her knowingly. "It's not the end of the world, Tate. I still have red toenails."

She crossed her arms, looking uncertain. She was worried about me.

Or she was going to miss me. Either way, it felt good.

After the police had taken Thomas and his friend to jail, Jax and I didn't leave the house for two days. It was the best two days of my life.

We slept, I cooked, we talked, I found out he was ticklish on the inside of his elbows, and there was hardly a time when I could leave the room without him following me.

We were in love.

And Jax decided he wanted time away without distractions.

So he'd gotten online the other night while I was asleep and scheduled a trip. To New Zealand.

I freaked out, and not in a good way.

When I'd woken up, he'd already hit a Bass Pro Shop and gotten us gear. The living room looked like a campsite that had exploded. Backpacks, water bottles with the built-in purifiers, sleeping bags, first aid kit, clothes, and shoes. He'd even picked out my clothes and shoes!

"Chicks take too long to shop, and we don't have time. I like this stuff. You'll wear this."

The only problem was I had a job I was supposed to be starting!

"I called them. You can start in the fall. Everyone loves me, so don't worry."

Huh?

And two round-trip tickets to New Zealand, not to mention the money spent while there? I couldn't let him pay for that!

"Nonrefundable tickets, babe. If we don't use them, they go to waste. And that will piss me off. Don't piss me off."

And after he'd unrolled a sleeping bag and spent the next hour helping me test it out, I finally gave in.

Oh, God, did I give in! I fanned myself with my hand, walking around the car to Tate. Jared was driving us to the airport

"So, when do you get in?" she asked.

"We have a lengthy layover in Hong Kong," I said. "I'll call you from there."

We'd be gone for three weeks, and by the time we got back, the fall semester would be about ready to start. Jax got me into school with him at Clarke, but I'd insisted on taking out loans. And I wasn't sure yet where I was living, but I had a feeling I wouldn't have to worry about it.

When I'd gone to check on my mom—who was at least back to showering and eating—and collect my passport, I'd packed up some more clothes and brought them to Jax's house.

Tate reached out and hugged me. I wrapped my arms around her, enjoying her tight squeeze.

"New Zealand," she mused. "You always wanted to go there. I remember your *National Geographic*s."

I laughed a little, pulled back. "I wanted to hike, actually," I pointed out. "I told him a road trip to Yosemite would be awesome, too, but he . . ."

"Yeah, he's Jax." She nodded. "He has a mind of his own. Good luck with that." But then she shook her head, amazed. "I'm so happy for you."

"I'm scared." I let out a nervous breath. "But I'm crazy about him."

"I know." Her face fell a little, looking thoughtful.

I narrowed my eyes, picking up on the sadness in her voice.

"Tate?" I leaned in. "Are you okay?" I asked quietly. "I mean, you and Jared. The barbecue the other day. Is anything wrong?"

She blinked, looking uncomfortable, but then plastered a grin on her face. "Still worrying about me, huh?" she joked. "Relax. It's not high school. Jared and I are fine."

I was about to press her more, but then I jumped, seeing arms come over my head, snapping a belt right in front of my face.

"Jax!" I laughed, my heart leaping into my throat as he walked for the other side of the car with a self-satisfied smirk on his face.

He's bringing the belt. *Shit.*

"Okay, yeah, don't tell me everything about your trip, okay?" Tate teased. We both hugged again, and she followed me as Jax held the back door open.

"So, you're both registered for your classes, right?" she asked. "Because you're cutting it close when you return."

"All set," Jax answered, but then my smile fell.

Behind Tate, I could see my mom crossing over from the sidewalk.

She looked right as rain in her light pink cotton skirt and sleeveless white blouse. Her hair hung down, though, in loose waves, sprayed to perfection.

My stomach twisted for the first time in days, and I met her in the middle of the quiet street. She'd been agreeable when I was over to the house, but looking at her pressed clothes and perfect face, I didn't know what to expect. I didn't want her embarrassing me or being cruel to Jax.

"Is everything okay?" I asked, guarded.

Her eyes fell, and her breathing turned ragged. "Yes, everything is fine. I just . . ." She reached into the shopping bag she held by the handles and pulled out an envelope.

"The funds from your college account." She handed the envelope to me, her hand shaking. "It's a cashier's check, so keep it safe."

My college money? I swallowed, taking the envelope and for some reason feeling that I wanted to either cry or throw it back in her face.

She narrowed her eyes, still looking down as her lips trembled. "And, um . . ." She licked her lips. "I was at the salon yesterday," she said, reaching nervously into the bag. "I got you this shampoo for sun-damaged hair and sunscreen and some lip balm, and I didn't know if you'd be going out for the evening on your trip, but if you wanted . . . maybe some hair products or, um . . . makeup, I can . . . I can send you—"

"Mother." I touched her arm, leaning in. "This is fine. Thank you," I said, seeing her shoulders relax.

"I'll see you in a few weeks." I took the bag.

She glanced up, straightening her shoulders and face. "Jaxon." She nodded somewhat kindly.

I looked to my side, seeing Jax there.

"Mrs. Carter." His deep voice sounded like a warning as he put his arm around me. I twisted my lips to hide my smile. I doubted Jax would ever call my mom anything other than "Mrs. Carter."

Her timid eyes fell back to mine, and she gave a half smile before turning and walking away. I still didn't know what to think. Maybe she was up to something. Maybe I should stay home and get her to a doctor.

Or maybe I was finally happy, and I just had to go with it.

Jax pulled me in. "Are you ready?" he taunted. "Hostels and roughing it?"

"Are you?" I challenged, smiling up at him. "Do they have Wi-Fi on these multiday hikes and rafting trip you've signed us up for?"

He turned me around, pulling me into his chest. "No showers. No beds."

"And no bikini," I singsonged.

His eyes widened, and I nodded smugly. "Yep. I didn't pack it."

"What if you decide you want it?"

I wiggled my eyebrows. "That's part of the excitement."

He picked me up, staring up into my eyes as he carried us to Jared's car. "You're a wild little thing—you know that?"

I pressed my lips to his forehead, whispering, "Don't worry. You can keep up."

Please turn the page for
a sneak peek at the continuation
of Jared and Tate's story in

Aflame

Available wherever e-books are sold in April 2015.

TATE

blinked awake, the cool summer breeze caressing my face. The early-morning light crept in through my French doors, and I stretched my arms over my head, hearing the buzzing of my phone on the nightstand. The noise that had woken me.

I sat up, ready to check the phone, but I stopped.

Jared sat in my armchair next to the windows. Apparently watching me sleep.

His presence filled the room, drowning out everything as it always did, and I couldn't help the weight on my heart.

He looked different.

His hair was gelled, so unlike the reserved military style he'd adopted, and he was dressed in his jeans and black hoodie, since it was a cool morning.

A sensual thrill shot through me, and I almost smiled. I'd missed this dangerous, foreboding look on him.

Except for the bags under his eyes and the extra muscle, he looked exactly like the guy I had fallen in love with nearly three years ago.

But we were barely talking these days, and I hadn't gone home with him since my father had gotten back into town. Even though I was nearly twenty-one, Dad didn't allow me to have overnight guests, and I'd opted out of going to Jared's.

After what I'd overheard at Jax's, Jared was still holding back, and I was afraid.

My phone buzzed again, and Jared tipped his chin, telling me to check it.

Picking up my phone, I saw a picture from Juliet. I smiled, seeing a happy selfie of her and Jax with a bustling city behind them.

In Auckland, baby! the text read.

I set the phone down, rubbing the sleep from my eye. "They made it," I said softly. "They're in New Zealand."

Jared stayed still, eerily frozen as he watched me, and that was when I noticed the black duffel on the floor.

I clenched the sheet. "Where are you going?"

He hesitated, letting his eyes fall, almost whispering. "I'm leaving for a while, Tate."

My heart continued to beat even as my breathing stopped. "ROTC?" I pressed.

"No." He shook his head and leaned forward on his knees. "I . . ." He hesitated. "Tate, I love you—"

I sucked in a breath and threw off the sheets, causing Madman to jump off the bed as I turned away. "Jax was right," I choked out, my throat suddenly tight.

"Jax is always right," he sighed. "Continuing like this." He shook his head. "I'd make you miserable."

I turned to look at him, so many questions frantically filling my brain. "Jared, if you want to quit ROTC, then quit," I cried. "I don't care. You can study anything. Or nothing. Just—"

"I don't know what I want!" he burst out, interrupting me. "That's the problem, Tate. I need to figure things out."

"Away from me," I finished.

He stood up, running his hands through his hair. "You're not the problem, babe. You're the only thing that I'm sure of." His gentle voice was filled with sadness. "But I need to grow up, and it's not happening here."

"Here, where?" I asked. "Chicago? Shelburne Falls? Or around me?"

He rubbed a frustrated hand down his face as he stared out the window. I'd never felt so far away from him. Not even when we were enemies in high school.

I couldn't lose him. I closed my eyes. *Please.*

"The apartment is paid up for the school year, so you don't have to worry—"

"A year!" I shot out of bed, turning my scared eyes on him. "A fucking year! Are you kidding me?"

"I don't know what I'm doing, okay?" he yelled, holding out his hands. "I don't feel like I fit in at college! I feel like you're moving a hundred miles an hour, and I'm constantly trying to catch up!" He breathed hard, and I shook my head, disbelieving.

How the hell was leaving me going to solve his problem?

He calmed his voice. "You know what you're doing and what you want, Tate, and I'm . . ." He hardened his jaw. "I'm fucking blind. I can't breathe."

I turned away, misery overtaking me as the tears rolled down. "You can't breathe," I mused, hugging myself against the fist wrapped around my heart.

"Baby." He turned me around. "I love you. I love you so goddamn much. I just . . ." He swallowed. "I just need time. Space, to figure out who I am and what I want."

I stared at him, so much pain simmering under my skin. "So, what happens?" I asked. "What happens when you find the life you're looking for?"

"I don't know yet."

I nodded, defiant. "I do. You didn't come in here to tell me you'll be back. That you'll call or we'll text. You came in here to break up with me."

And I pulled away, turning around.

"Baby, come here." He pulled me back, but I came down on his arms, shoving them away.

"Oh, just get out!" I yelled. "You cut off everyone who loves you. You're pathetic. I should be used to this by now," I choked out, hiding my tears.

He walked toward me. "Tate—"

"Just leave!" I bellowed, walking for the door and yanking it open. "I'm sick of the sight of you, Jared," I growled. "Just go."

He shook his head. "No. I need you to understand."

I tipped my chin up. "All I'll ever understand is that you needed to live a life without me in it, so just go and do that."

He struggled for words. "I don't want this. Not like this." I could hear the tears caught in his throat. "I don't want to hurt you. Just sit down, so we can talk. I can't leave you like this," he insisted.

I shook my head at him. "And I won't let you stay." I hardened my voice. "You need to be free? Then go. Get out."

He stood frozen, looking as though he was searching for what to say or do to soothe me, but it was in vain.

I could be a supportive friend, more understanding and comforting, while he went off and tried to find himself, but the ship with the rest of my patience had sailed a long time ago.

I'd waited for him. Time and again I had waited for him while he humiliated and tortured me in high school. I pined for him even as he abandoned me and left me alone and isolated. I loved him even when he'd brought me to tears.

And I was disgusted with myself.

And as I clenched my teeth and Jared turned blurry in my eyes, I stood strong and unforgiving. "Now," I ordered.

His eyes fell, and his shoulders were broken as he stood there, forced to own up to his choice.

And then he picked up his bag. And walked out the door.

I didn't move as I heard the Boss roar to life and speed down the street, my ears hanging on to the last decibel it could catch of him leaving me.

"I'm not waiting for you anymore," I whispered.

Dear Reader,

I know that was difficult, but it had to happen. Jared and Tate will grow on separate paths, as is usually the case in real life, but they will come together again.

Explosively. You can count on that.

And when they do, I'll finally give you that Epilogue I promised.

Thank you for reading and look for the continuation of Jared and Tate's story, *Aflame*, in April 2015.

Penelope Douglas